THE VEIL

V.B. EMANUELE

Copyright © 2019 V.B. Emanuele

All rights reserved. No part of this book may be reproduced or used in any manner without the prior written permission of the copyright owner, except for the use of brief quotations in a book review.

To request permission, contact the author at vbemanuele@gmail.com

The characters and events portrayed in this book are fictitious. Any resemblance to actual persons, living or dead, or actual events is purely coincidental and not intended by the author.

ISBN: 9798633455625 (Paperback)
ISBN: 9781663557490 (Hardcover)

First paperback edition September 2020

Cover Photograph by Nicoletta Emanuele
Cover design by Nicoletta Emanuele
For V.B. Emanuele

Southlake, Texas United States
vbemanuele.com

DEDICATION

For MJC

Rest in Heaven

"Someone's gotta live to tell about it."

And I will…

CONTENTS

	Acknowledgments	i
1	New Beginnings	1
2	Masquerade	20
3	Arrangement	38
4	Call Me Sir	60
5	Conflicted	82
6	The Plan	103
7	Penthouse	127
8	Interviewing	152
9	First Date	173
10	Great Escape	194
11	Exposed	217
12	Secret Revealed	240
13	Conflict	261
14	London Bound	284
15	New Revelation	305
16	Confession	329
17	Shedding Light	352
18	No Safe Word	374
19	Visitors	392

20	Taken	412
21	Emergency	432
22	Forgiveness	451
23	Defiance & Lust	470
24	Mamma	488
25	Austrian Christmas	508
	About The Author	532

ACKNOWLEDGMENTS

Thank you to everyone who played a role in making this happen:

To my editor and proofreaders, thank you for your hard work and late hours that you put into my work.

To Hana, for once again helping me in so many ways, especially with editing. Words cannot express how much I appreciate your friendship and selflessness. Thank you for your hard work and friendship.

To Emily, you and I had a conversation on June 9, 2019 that forever changed me. This was the novel I was working on at the time. Our conversation helped launched me into the writer I am today. Thank you.

To my family, for being willing to share quality time with my writing and readers. You are the greatest support system I have, and I am so thankful for you.

To all my faithful readers who have been waiting for me to publish this as a novel (off WP), thank you so much for your patience and support. I love you guys so much! I hope I continue to make you smile.

1 NEW BEGINNINGS

Isabelle

    Do you ever believe you have your life entirely planned out, only to be met with a different reality? It is nothing like you imagined it would be. It does not mean it turned out bad, but sometimes, an insignificant decision can change our entire world. That is exactly what happened to me when I left my small hometown in Ohio to pursue a life in New York City.

    I never anticipated that my life would end up the way it was today. When I relocated for college, I ended up falling in love with the city. So, I planned a career here. Having been a small town girl, New York City was the place I always dreamed of being. I loved the busy streets, the traffic, the lights, the park nestled among the concrete jungle; I loved almost everything.

    Overall, life was going well for me in so many ways,

but there were changes I longed to make. Soon after I relocated and got settled, I obtained a job at an upscale bar to make ends meet. In New York, that seemed almost impossible. It was no secret the city is a pricey place to live, but I was determined to make it here, doing whatever it took to survive.

As the months passed, I found myself growing tired of the same routine. Work, to school, then back home to my quaint apartment about a mile away from my job was the routine. What I did not expect was that it was all about to change, forever.

Wednesday night came faster than I had hoped. It was normally my night off, but I picked up a shift for another waitress at work. Closing time was approaching quickly. One customer lingered at the bar, perched on a stool as he quietly sipped on his sixth drink. I made myself busy by tidying up and drying glasses as they came out of the dishwasher. Every few moments, I was interrupted as my boss kept finding excuses to walk past me, grabbing my backside. Sometimes he was subtle. Other times, not so much.

His name was Jesse and he stood around five feet ten inches. He was balding but refused to give up what was left of his hair. So, he would comb it over with gel, giving it a greasy appearance. His beer belly hung proudly over his slacks, peeking out from his sweat stained shirt. I never understood how he was allowed to work in a place with high standards when he looked like a used car salesman from the bad part of town.

Regrettably, his perverted remarks and fondling were both an ongoing occurrence here. I did not even know why

I put up with it for so long other than I needed the money. Living in a big city was financially draining for my roommate and me. We even tried moving out of downtown, but the commute took way too long and public transportation was always unpredictable.

If we were late, we were verbally humiliated. So yes, I continued to put up with my brute manager while I searched for another job in my spare time. I remained positive, believing that a greater opportunity was just around the corner.

This particular Wednesday night, just as we were about to close, four men strode in chatting amongst themselves. They were dressed in pricey suits which was not uncommon for our swanky establishment. I glided across the room in their direction, my long, light brown ponytail swinging back and forth in perfect sync with my stride. The men were so distracted with their conversation that they did not bother to acknowledge me as they waited to be seated.

"Excuse me, gentlemen," I cleared my throat, "we're actually closing everything down."

I had their undivided attention at that instant. The most attractive of the men slowly rotated his head to me, his voice trailing off from his sentence. His gaze lingered over my body before it met my blue, almond shaped eyes but he did not smile.

"I see you have someone already sitting at the bar," he glowered as he lifted his chin, gesturing toward the man.

I nodded sheepishly. His commanding tone promptly

intimidated me. A shiver inched up my spine, triggering my skin to respond with goosebumps. I struggled to avert my gaze, but his eyes were extraordinarily authoritative and mysterious. I identified his accent as Italian, which rendered him more fascinating to me. He articulated his words with great concentration. Extremely entranced in him, I inhaled deeply, pulling myself together.

He sighed, rolling his eyes while examining his wrist. "According to my watch, you close in five minutes," he added sharply, "which means by law you have to serve my friends and me."

There was something about the way he said *serve*, that sent a tremor down my spine. He smirked, indicating he knew the effect he had on my body. His statement was essentially correct. We did close in five minutes, but I wanted to leave, so my statement was rather selfish. My boss had been drinking all night, as he often did, so I wanted to get out of work as quickly as possible.

I opened my mouth to speak but immediately snapped it closed when I heard Jesse. Spinning around, my eyes widened as I witnessed him furiously waving his hands back and forth in the air, shouting obscenities in my direction, rapidly marching toward us. I remained professional as he grew closer, but I internally rolled my eyes knowing he would only see the money new customers brought him. This was going to result in a late night for me.

"No no no," he shouted, planting himself between the men and me.

He did not want them to witness his angry face. He

made sure to position his back toward them so he could attempt to frighten me. I winced, half expecting him to hit me. When Jesse was drunk, he was unpredictable.

"You will seat these gentlemen," he grumbled, clenching his jaw. He then spun to the men with a fake smile plastered on his face. "I apologize for her," he chuckled nervously, "I've had issues with her since she started working here."

That was untrue, and he knew it, but it did not stop him from lying to them. I was a fantastic employee and always worked hard. I never complained to anyone other than my roommate, and I was very faithful to my job. Unfortunately, Jesse saw it otherwise.

All four of the men glanced toward me except the most attractive of them. He scowled off into the distance, pursing his lips. It was hard to determine what he was contemplating. A fake smile suddenly washed over my face as I cheerfully leaned around Jesse.

"I will seat you guys," I declared as I gestured toward the dining area. "I apologize."

It was now after closing time, but choosing to comply with my manager, to avoid further embarrassment, I escorted the men to a booth near the back. The most alluring one inspected the bar area then pivoted himself to face me. He pointed to another half round booth nearby, but it faced both the dining area and bar.

"May we sit here instead?" he requested as he lifted his hand to his chin, stroking his black stubble. "I think I'll like this one better."

I nodded willingly, "Of course." *The customer is always right.*

He positioned himself on the back side of the table, so that he was directly facing me. The other men arranged themselves around him. I handed them the drink menus I had swiped from the hostess stand on the way.

"Our kitchen is closed, but I will be happy to make any drink for you," I offered, making eye contact with each of them. "I'll give you a moment to look over everything and will be back in just a second."

I casually strode to the bar where my boss was taking another shot of tequila and chatting loudly with the lonely man on the stool. I cautiously approached them to ask the man if I could call a cab to take him home.

"No, sexy," he shook his head roughly with a smirk, "I'm walking tonight."

I nodded with a smile, preparing to reply but Jesse interrupted.

"Woo!" he slammed his shot glass down on the bar top then threw his fists in the air before he poured himself another drink.

He glistened profusely, sweating now. Alcohol seeped through his pores. His hair appeared as if he had just showered. I busied myself as I wiped the surface of the bar down, beginning my cleaning process. I peeked to see if the gentlemen were still looking over the menu.

The most handsome one was watching me with great intent while smirking. His piercing blue eyes focused keenly on my every move. My cheeks began to heat with embarrassment. The man ran his fingers through his dark hair before his eyes slowly peeled away from me. He focused his attention back to his friends. Moments later, he waved me over with a nod of his head, and that is when I realized I had never turned away from my gaze.

I shook off my feeling, approaching the table. The four of them provided me their full attention as they placed their orders, one by one. Nodding, I repeated the order back before I returned to the bar, making their drinks as quickly as possible. This meant my night was almost over and I could not wait to leave.

I delivered their order to them before performing a final walk through of the dining area, making sure the area was spotless. I started wiping off the table and chairs that were closest to them. As I worked my way to the middle of the room, my belligerent boss marched out from behind the bar, making a beeline for me. I paused, gripping the rag tightly in my palm.

The moment he approached, he leaned forward about an inch away from my face. "I want to see you in my office immediately," he exhaled his alcohol infused breath directly into my nostrils.

I winced at the smell. Knowing my night was about to take an ugly turn, I sighed. Every time he wanted to see me in his office, he would try to touch me. I would always reject, causing him to become irate. Then, the rest of my night would be horrendous since he was insulted that I did not give him the attention he desired. I was not the only employee he did this to, but it did not make it right.

I followed him down the long hallway to his office. He held the door open for me to walk in ahead of him. Just as I nervously stepped through the threshold, he closed the door, locking it behind him. Slowly approaching me, he began choking back watery burps as he gave a predatory smile. I was scared this time, but he shocked me. He did not try to touch me. Instead, he did something I did not see coming.

"Listen to me bitch," he hiccupped while swaying, "how dare you not seat those men?" He chuckled, "Do you know who they are?"

"No," I shook my head, "do you?"

He laughed menacingly, "They are very wealthy businessmen who like to come in on your nights off."

I did not normally work on Wednesdays, so I just let him speak while I remained silent.

"They are some of my best customers," he resumed, "and I will not allow you to be the reason they do not return."

"I'm sorry," I only agreed with him to get out of the office unscathed. "I had no idea," I sighed. "Since it was late and we were about to close, I--."

"I don't give a flying fuck if we had been closed for an hour," he interrupted me, "when those men show up, we open for them!"

"I'm sorry, Jesse," I began to tear up, "I won't let it happen again."

He laughed boisterously, "Oh bitch, I know it won't."

I gasped, covering my mouth to conceal my terror. His tone instilled fear into me. He did not stop there.

"You are fired!" he snapped as he reached toward me, attempting to remove my apron. "Give me your apron and get out of my bar!"

"But--," I tried to reason with him as I wiggled away from him, taking a step backward.

"I said take off your apron," he gurgled on a burp as he struggled to grab for me again.

I finally wrapped my hands around my waist, freeing it from my body. I slid my hand in the pocket to take my tips out, but Jesse grabbed my wrist, snarling.

"Everything in that apron belongs to me too!" he bellowed, turning red with anger as he began to grind his teeth.

"But my tips--," I cried, reaching for my apron.

Holding it behind his back, he shouted as loudly as he could, "Get out of my bar, Isabelle!"

I choked back tears as I hurried to my locker, grabbing my handbag, then headed for the office door. Forgetting he locked it, I attempted to turn the knob, jiggling the handle through my tears. He crept toward me, but I managed to unlock it seconds before he got his hands on me.

It was then that I felt his hand on the back side of my thigh. He began to howl with laughter. I finally got the door open and ran down the hallway, then through the dining room. The man at the bar was long gone and the gentlemen at the table were staring in my direction as I passed them, sprinting out the front door as fast as my legs would carry me.

When I arrived at my apartment, my roommate, Tanya, was sitting on the living room couch eating pizza while watching a movie. She and I met at work months ago, becoming instant best friends. Recently, she had found a better job as an executive personal assistant. She seemed happier since she started working there, and I was happy for her.

I trudged through the living room, dramatically throwing myself backwards into a chair next to the couch she was stretched out on. Running my fingers through my hair as I freed my ponytail, I could feel the stress radiating off my body.

Tanya paused her movie, resting her elbow on the couch arm. She leaned her chin into her palm as I let out a deep sigh.

"Rough night, girl?" she giggled.

I could sense the sincerity in her tone, but the amusement overcame her. We always laughed about Jesse, but we also cried just the same. I did not find her to be insensitive right now, but I was in no mood to laugh. My emotions intensified, and I erupted into tears, spewing all my feelings out at once. I was so upset, unsure how I would pay my portion of the bills now.

"What happened?" Tanya gasped, leaning forward on the edge of the couch. She reached over resting her hand on my knee. "Are you okay?"

"He fired me!" I wailed into my palms.

She withdrew her hand, folding her arms across her chest. "He had no reason to fire you, did he?" she scoffed in disbelief, knowing I was a hard worker.

Rolling my eyes, I choked back my tears, wiping my eyes on my sleeve. "I tried to turn some important men away who came in five minutes before we closed," I sniffled. "I know I shouldn't have, but I just didn't want Jesse touching me and wanted to leave." Taking a deep breath, I calmed myself a little before I concluded, "He kept touching me all night and I wanted to get out of there."

"That ass!" she snapped as she stood.

My eyes followed her as she strode over to the bar that separated our living room from our kitchen. She poured herself some more soda then gestured to it, silently asking me if I wanted any. I shook my head. She returned to the couch, curling a leg under her as she sat. Leaning her elbow on the arm of the couch once again, she listened as I continued.

"I just don't know what to do," I admitted. "I lost about two hundred and fifty dollars in tips tonight."

She took a long, slow sip of her drink then tilted her

head as she stared straight ahead in deep thought. "Do you still have that mask in your closet?"

I was taken aback but I nodded, "Um, weird topic change but yeah," I shrugged, "why?"

"There's a masquerade this Friday night and we should go!" she suggested cheerfully as she leaned forward and took another slice of pizza from the box. She rapidly wiggled her eyebrows up and down at me.

"Are you serious right now?" I blurted, confusion washing over my face. My mouth fell open as I shook my head in disbelief at her lack of concern for what just happened to me. "I just lost my job and you want me to go to some mask party?"

She swallowed her food then grinned. "It's a special kind of party," she hinted with a smirk.

I curled my lip in disgust, leaning forward to grab a slice of pizza. I slowly munched away on it, waiting for more information.

"It's a big annual masquerade ball and it's free," she resumed, "in fact, everything there is free."

Confused where this conversation was heading, I sat silently, uncertain how to react. I knew there was more to it that she was not sharing with me.

"In other words," she rolled her eyes, beaming, "we have to pay for nothing, and we get to just let loose and have some fun." Raising her hands, she gestured to her face, "We just have to wear a dress and our masks, that's all."

Doubtfully, I studied her, expecting the catch, but there was none. After a long pause, I broke the silence, "Can I think about it?" At the moment, I was too upset to decide about a party and I just wanted to go get ready for bed.

"Of course," she nodded, "but I have to RSVP by tomorrow so let me know as soon as you can."

I stood, wordlessly trudging to my room. I got ready for bed and climbed under the blankets, replaying my evening in my head. I tried to sleep, but I could not, tossing and turning all night.

Every time I closed my eyes, I had visions of my boss yelling at me, both in front of the gentlemen then in the privacy of his own office. Memories of every time he grabbed my breasts or bottom, came flooding back to me. Sometimes he claimed it to be an accident and on occasion he just threw his head back, guffawing at his actions.

Could a meaningless masked party really hurt anything? It was in two days which gave me time to put in some applications at businesses. I would then use my Friday night as a break and go have fun with Tanya. I did not bother getting out of bed, but I sent her a text instead.

Fine ugh I'm in.

She replied almost instantly, *I promise you that it will be a memorable night ;)*

If any other friend had texted me that, I would have instantly become suspicious but coming from her, it was normal. I did not even think twice about it.

THE VEIL

The next morning, I woke up, rubbing the sleep from my eyes as I yawned. Stretching, I rolled over, checking my phone. I scrolled through my social media and email before I forced myself to get up.

I strolled into the kitchen, starting the coffee maker. While it was brewing, I opened the refrigerator to get the coffee creamer, but I noticed our fridge was overflowing with food. None of it was generic brand, but instead, it was full of name brand products. Not that there is anything wrong with that, but we usually shopped on a big budget, splitting the bills, which included groceries.

Cautiously, I opened both the freezer and the pantry, seeing it was the same. Arching a brow, I shrugged it off, assuming Tanya got a bonus. I made my way over to the dining table to sit while I waited for my coffee to be finished. It was then, my eyes fell on an envelope next to a little bag. I would recognize that robin egg blue color anywhere.

Not that long ago, we could barely afford things. Now she was buying brand name groceries and shopping at Tiffany's. Just as I was about to stand, she sleepily stalked into the room. Turning to her, I pointed at the bag with my mouth playfully agape.

"Oh," she smiled shyly, "you see that?"

"Heck yes, I see it!" I giggled. "What did you buy at Tiffany's?"

"A necklace, but I didn't buy it," she smirked as her eyes focused on the floor. "It was a gift from my boss."

Crossing my arms, I leaned back in my chair. Raising my eyebrows with curiosity, I questioned, "Your boss bought you a necklace from Tiffany's?"

She blushed, twirling a strand of her hair around her index finger, "I mean, yeah."

"That's all you have to say?" I huffed with a wide grin.

"I don't know," she sighed, blushing, "he's just a really great boss, I guess." Failing to hide her smile, she awkwardly shifted her weight, nervously trailing her fingertips up and down her arm.

"It sure seems that way," I snickered. "I need a boss like yours."

Placing her hands on her hips, she exhaled, "Yeah, I think you do too."

After spending my morning relaxing, I went for a run in the park before filling out applications. I quickly got dressed in a black sports bra with matching shorts and shoes. Standing in front of my apartment building on the busy sidewalk, I plugged my ears with my headphones.

Central Park was located just across the street from our

building, so I jogged across the crosswalk the minute I got the signal. I pressed play on my music app and strapped it to my arm before I began to stretch. The park was crowded this morning with a variety of people, most notably a group of very nice-looking men playing soccer in a nearby, grassy area. Half of them were shirtless. I was not complaining about my view as I made sure I was limber before my run. I might have stretched a little longer today.

I had to run past them when I started my route. I did not think this part through very much. Not that I was a clumsy runner, but if I were going to fall, it would have been in front of guys. I turned my music up, blaring it into my ears at a deafening volume and took off jogging on the park's path. Thanks to my sunglasses, I was able to go enjoy the eye candy, undetected, as I passed by them.

When I got further into my run, I processed what happened to me. I was beginning to think about what I was going to do to pay my bills. I was scared, hurt, and sad. Before tears could escape my eyes, I realized that I had already made my usual three mile circle through the park. I removed my ear buds, turning my music off.

Just as I was crossing the street to go home, I saw a familiar face walking out of the coffee shop next to my building, followed closely by a larger man. I felt sweaty from my run, so I tried to shield my face from him, but it was too late. He stopped, waiting for me as he took a sip of his coffee. He lifted a cigarette to his lips, taking a long drag. I could not avoid him, so I came to a halt in front of him and his friend.

Smirking, he asked, "What happened last night?"

"It's okay," I dropped my head, shyly shuffling my feet. "My boss was a jerk," I shrugged, "and I didn't want to be there anymore anyway."

"Yeah, none of us like that guy," he rolled his eyes, chuckling darkly. "We go there because it's convenient." Inhaling his cigarette deeply, he recounted, "We decided after last night, we will not be returning."

Fidgeting with my fingertips, I gulped, "You don't have to stop going--."

"We heard him yelling at you," he unexpectedly interrupted. "No one deserves to be yelled at like that. I'm sorry."

"I've been trying to figure out how to quit anyway," I casually responded with a shrug.

Tilting his head intriguingly, his gaze focused on me, "I'm sure you'll figure it out." He gently placed his fingertips on my forearm, "I have a good feeling anyway."

I drew in a sharp breath, "Thank you." I anxiously giggled. "I hope so."

He smiled coyly, as he studied me with amusement. I am fairly sure he could tell that he made me nervous. He passed his coffee cup off his friend, then pulled his phone from his pocket.

"I have to take this call," he stated as he examined the screen.

Before I could reply, he held the phone to his ear, whispering, "Great seeing you again."

Speaking to the person on the phone in Italian, he winked at me in passing, rendering me speechless. I watched as he and his friend faded into the crowd of people.

That same night Tanya was out late, so I watched a movie in the living room. During an anticlimactic part of the movie, I pulled out my phone and found myself sucked into the black hole of the suggested posts on my social media. Out of the blue, I came across a post by a woman with a man at her side. The man was the same mysterious Italian man I had met twice.

My curiosity got the best of me as I tapped on the post. The woman was locked in arms with him. The caption read, *With my babe on holiday in London.* The photo was taken in front of the London Eye Ferris Wheel. There was no name, no tag, nothing. I scrolled through her comments, but nothing stood out to me. None mentioned his name, so I was left to wonder.

It was getting late, so I went to bed. Tomorrow was going to be another day full of job searching, then the masquerade ball at night. I was looking forward to it. At some point in my daydreaming about how I would style my hair and who I would dance with, I fell asleep. I was briefly woken up by the front door slamming. Hearing muffled moans, I realized it was Tanya with a guest, and I quickly fell right back to sleep.

2 MASQUERADE

Isabelle

The next morning was a complete blur. I settled myself at the dining table in front of my laptop with my coffee and a notebook, spending the day applying for jobs. I began daydreaming more about my night, as I loved parties or any excuse to dress up. This was not a part of my everyday life, so I was excited when the time came to get ready.

I allowed myself two hours to get ready. Leaning forward in my bathroom mirror, I was applying eyeliner when Tanya suddenly appeared in the open doorway. My eyes caught her reflection, and I smiled.

"Are you looking forward to tonight?" she gushed with excitement.

"Actually, yes," I stopped applying my eyeliner. Smiling, I pivoted to her. "I'm very excited, and I think this is just the kind of night I need."

She nodded, crossing her arms.

I spun back to the mirror. "Who's hosting this party?" I mumbled with my face contorted as I drew on my other eyelid.

She stepped through the doorway into the bathroom, checking her already perfectly applied makeup. "My boss's best friend."

I stopped, turning to face her. "Not to sound rude," I giggled, "but how'd you get invited?"

She laughed, "Want to know a secret?"

I had a feeling I knew what she was about to say. "Uh huh," I muttered while puckering my lips, applying lip gloss.

"I have been sleeping with my boss," she whispered as if we were in a room full of people, but she did not appear embarrassed as she continued. "He is amazing." She gripped her hips, smirking, "I have zero regrets."

I glanced at her as I picked up my makeup setting spray. "And is this the guy I heard you come home with?" I snickered.

"He wasn't planning to come in," she blushed as her eyes fell to the floor, "but we couldn't keep our hands off each other when he dropped me off."

I held my breath, spraying my face. I then peered up at her, seeing that she was making the same face as me. I erupted into laughter.

"Sorry, I always make the same face as you when you do that if I'm in the room," she giggled.

"I'm actually excited for tonight," I shifted the topic as I began to style my hair.

She appeared nervous as her eyes found mine in the mirror's reflection. "I hope you will have an open mind about tonight," she muttered.

I twisted, intriguingly examining her, "What's that supposed to mean?"

She masked her concern with a smile as she veered to walk away. "You'll just have to wait and see," she shouted back toward the bathroom from the hallway.

I rolled my eyes as I finished getting ready.

I finished getting ready in my penthouse suite of the hotel I owned. Making our way to the elevator, my security, friends, and I descended to the swanky, modern lobby. The hotel was bustling with tourists and business travelers, so my bodyguards shielded me as we stepped out.

It was not that I avoided the public per se. However, I was never one to go out of my way to be seen, especially now. Once a year, I would host a masquerade. Why? I did not trust women nor believe in relationships, so this was the easiest way for me to interact without having to be further involved. I would choose one or multiple women, making them mine until I was done with them. The catch? They could never know it was me.

It was important to conceal my identity as I was well-known. My real identity could not be publicized as this activity was considered illegal. Why? I paid these women to sleep with me. They were not professional prostitutes, call girls, escorts, whatever you wish to call them. These women were unsuspecting and beautiful. Some might even say a few of them were innocent; that is, until I was finished with them.

Some were experienced while others unquestionably lacked. I usually got bored with these women very quickly. All of them, regardless of their experience level, were all the same to me. They remained only a toy; nothing more, nothing less. I never pushed them into anything. They wanted it, badly.

We swiftly rounded the corner to a hallway that led to the main ballroom where the event took place. Approximately one hundred guests were already lined up outside on the ballroom patio as they had come in the back entrance of the hotel. I stood in the middle of the dance floor, slowly rotating in a circle, admiring the elegance as I slipped on my mask.

"It looks great," I nodded toward the event planner.

I signaled for one of my staff to let guests in. The moment the doors opened, I was no longer Valentino Greco. No one knew the name of the event host other than a few people. No one needed to know. It was an exclusive time for a dark side of me to emerge the instant the mask was over my eyes.

Isabelle

We arrived in front of a hotel that towered over the buildings around us. I suddenly found myself feeling small and unimportant. I could never afford a room here, but I kept reminding myself that we were only here for a party. Still, I was exceptionally intimidated.

Stepping into the lavish ballroom was a bit more overwhelming than the exterior, but it was absolutely magnificent. Dim lights illuminated the room as faux candles were scattered throughout, creating a sensual atmosphere. There were hired performers moving in sync on the dance floor while acrobats hung from the ceiling twirling and flipping around aerial hoops and silks. Other performers strolled around the grand ballroom, performing smaller tricks for the guests as they applauded.

A gentleman approached us, giving Tanya a kiss while picking her up, then twirling her around. I noticed they both smiled in the middle of their kiss, happy to see one another. Feeling awkward in the presence of a kissing couple, I shifted my weight while waiting for them to finish. I did not know where to redirect my eyes. She withdrew her lips, whispering in his ear. Setting her feet back on the floor, he pulled her into his side, wrapping his arm around her waist.

He extended his hand to me as he bowed. I giggled, resting my palm in his. Kissing the back of my hand, he peered up at me, still in mid-bow.

"It's a pleasure to finally meet you, for real."

Dropping my hand, he stood up straight, once again pulling Tanya against his body. He was charming and polite. I could see why she liked him. Glancing at her, I grinned when I saw how she was gazing at him, happiness radiating off her.

Unsure of what to say to him, I gulped, "I'm Isabelle."

"Oh, I know exactly who you are," he grinned.

I felt there was more to that other than that statement, but I awkwardly smiled in return.

"I'm William," he introduced himself, "but tonight I'm someone else."

Confused, I wrinkled my nose, "Huh?"

Tanya hooked her arm in mine, spinning us both away. "We're going to find the drinks," she called back over her shoulder, a large grin plastered on her face as she drew me to the other side of the room.

A devilish smirk spread across his face as we hurried away, leaving him standing alone. I continued to stare over my shoulder as another man cautiously approached him. They both watched us with great concentration as the corners of the other man's mouth formed a smile. Before I could fully study him, Tanya reached for my chin, turning my face toward hers.

"Now don't be mad at me," she cupped my cheeks in her palms, speaking warily.

This was never a good sign. Over the course of our friendship, I had heard this said to me about five hundred times. It was usually followed with some crazy scheme or plan. Other times it was a decision she had made for me without consulting me first.

"Oh no," I sighed, taking a step back. Folding my arms, I whispered harshly, "what did you do?"

Inhaling deeply, she braced herself, gulping, "Promise me you won't get mad." She winced, anxiously pinning her lower lip between her teeth.

"Promise you?" I hissed. "You know I will not promise someone something if I don't know what to expect."

"Okay," she sighed before continuing, "well this event is kind of a hook up event." She quickly glanced over my shoulder before redirecting her attention back to me.

Perplexed, I turned my head, peeking back at the men again. They were clutching drinks and now deep in conversation with two other men. They all took turns nodding in our direction as if they were discussing us. I would have worried, except one of them was distinctly Tanya's boss.

"What do you mean," I faced her once again, growling, "and you better be blunt with me or I'm out of here!"

"You need money, right?" she shrugged.

I nodded, taking a deep breath.

"Well the men here kind of pay women for sex," she mumbled, unsure how I would take the new information.

"Are you kidding me?!" I snapped way louder than I should have, but I was fuming with anger.

"Shhh," she pressed her finger to my lips.

I huffed, glancing back at the four men, who were looking our way. They were not trying to hide their interest in our discussion but maintained their distance. Tanya placed her hand on my cheek, turning me back to her.

"Belle, trust me."

I averted my gaze to the floor, awkwardly crossing my arms. Suddenly feeling like everyone in the room was silently judging me, I wanted to cry. I took a few deep breaths, keeping myself collected. I lifted my head and scanned the ballroom, looking for any sign of escape.

"I am so angry at you right now," I muttered.

"Belle, stop looking around all paranoid," she declared. "Everyone is here for the same reason."

"I'm not a hooker," I hissed, glaring at her, unsure how she was remaining so calm at the moment.

"Neither am I," she smiled, "but Liam pays me for more than just the work I do for him."

My mouth fell agape in shock, "You get paid to have sex with him?"

She nodded, giggling, "Well, that's not all." Shuffling her feet back and forth, she blushed, "I spend time with him too, and we don't always just have sex."

"So basically, you have a Sugar Daddy then?" Slightly amused, I snickered, but not surprised. She was more liberal than I was when it came to that stuff.

"Well, it goes deeper than that," she murmured, internally battling telling me the entire story. "It was sort of when I needed money after I left the bar and--."

Before she could finish her sentence, we heard a tapping sound come from the speakers. We both spun toward the stage at the back of the room. A beautiful woman was standing behind a microphone, commanding the attention of everyone in the ballroom. The music slowly faded to a dull background noise. A hush slowly dispersed through the crowd.

"Oh no," Tanya mumbled as her eyes sympathetically found mine.

It was then I knew something was wrong. There was something she was not telling me, causing me to grow suspicious. She pulled me to the front of the crowd as her boss and the other three men gathered with us. The lady on stage called out a name. A young woman walked out on stage, standing about five feet away. She beamed with pride as she swayed back and forth, playing with the stitching on her dress.

"Lacey is from Los Angeles and has just moved here," the woman with the microphone started an introduction.

"She is looking for a great time and wanted me to make sure you men know that she is proud of her oral skills."

There were whistles and howls from the crowd as a few of the men around the room grew excited. I am not quite sure my brain was processing what was happening until she continued.

"We will start the bidding at one thousand dollars!"

They were auctioning her off! Men started holding up numbered paddles, but they were not the standard auction paddles. They were shaped like BDSM paddles. Everything was happening so rapidly that my head began to spin.

"Sold!" the woman shouted, pointing toward the back of the room. "Seven Thousand Dollars!"

One by one, fifteen more women went up on stage before one more was called. She was visually flawless by society's standards. One of the men standing next to William started bidding on her. He would not allow anyone else to have her.

"Sold!" the woman called out once again, pointing toward William's friend. "Five hundred thousand Dollars!"

What?! I froze while I momentarily zoned out. The amount of money these men were paying to have sex with these women, baffled me. My mouth hung agape as Tanya looked at me with an apologetic expression on her face. I realized why.

During my state of shock, I had zoned out for an unknown amount of time. She jolted me back to reality when she nudged me toward the stage. I took a few steps forward, almost stumbling. Spinning to face her, I glared in her direction, confused. That was when I heard it.

"Come on up, sweetheart," the lady on stage was speaking to me, "it's okay."

A spotlight fell on me and I froze. Everyone looked on as I was paralyzed. Slowly, I turned toward her with eyes the size of saucers. She nodded, gesturing with her hand toward the stairs on the side of the stage. I reluctantly approached, ascending the steps in disbelief. Sheepishly, I stopped on a piece of tape shaped like a X on the floor. I searched for Tanya, but the lights were so bright, it was hard to see her. I was able to slightly make out that she gave me a nervous thumbs up, then buried her face into William's body as he held her tight.

I felt like I would lose consciousness as the woman started her opening about me. "This is Isabelle. She is twenty-two and originally from a small town in Ohio."

My eyes snapped toward the woman as I listened to her spill my information to the crowd.

She continued without missing a beat, "We've been told that Isabelle is a virgin and is ready to make some man here very lucky."

Embarrassed, I felt heat rise within my cheeks. My eyes widened once again, darting toward Tanya, but she was not watching me. She knew I would be seething with fury over this, yelling at her the moment we were alone at our apartment. How dare she give my very personal guarded secret to a stranger, who turned it around, revealing it to a room full of masked guests.

The bidding started. I felt all the blood drain from my face as I began to panic. The figures climbed. She passed five hundred thousand, and I gulped.

"Oh," she grinned, "I see two men who are incredibly determined to have you, honey."

She glanced over toward me, but I was too mortified to adjust my eyes. I continued to stare at the floor, as the bids continued to pour in. When they reached seven hundred thousand, I knew that I would surely faint. I prayed that I would; anything to be away from here.

Suddenly I heard a loud voice bellow from the crowd, "One million dollars!"

I froze, snapping my eyes up toward the sea of people, searching for who shouted. *Someone just bought me for one million dollars!* Surely this was a joke. How was this possible? I am a human being! How could someone just purchase me like an item on a shelf in a store?

The crowd roared in celebration. These people were applauding that I was now a forced *hooker*. I trudged off the stage, unsure of who bought me. I did not even care. I needed to escape as quickly as my legs would carry me. Spotting a set of large French doors to my side, I took off sprinting from the stage. I scurried over to the patio railing, facing away from the building as tears flowed down my face, under my mask.

Suddenly, a deep voice spoke behind me, "You're supposed to go backstage and check in."

I was startled. Twisting to confront the man, I wiped my tears away from my cheeks. He was one of William's friends, standing over six feet tall with a muscular build.

His dark, slightly wavy hair was professionally styled. A neatly trimmed beard hugged his face. It was too dark to see much more because he wore a mask, obscuring the majority of his face. His pricey, black suit gave him an aura of power and value. After examining as much as I could of him, I relaxed my posture in defeat.

"You don't want to be here, do you?"

I shrugged, "Honestly, not really."

"Rules are rules."

Fidgeting with my fingers, I glowered, "Does it count if I didn't sign up for whatever that was?"

"Yeah, well," he chuckled, averting his gaze, "virgins don't really come to this sort of thing anyway."

"It's not like I had a choice," I peered off into the distance, feeling betrayed by Tanya for the first time in our friendship.

"I'm sure you'll figure it out," he commented in a familiar tone, but my mind was already playing tricks on me, so I shrugged it off.

"I just think things like this are gross," I whispered, not wanting to insult anyone who might be listening. "Why do people come to these things?"

Taking a small step toward me, he casually ran his fingers through his hair as he muttered, "I guess some guys just don't trust women and like their privacy." He slowly slid his hands into his pockets, concluding, "So this is the safest option."

"Safest?" I snorted. "Sleeping with a strange woman who's been God knows where, makes no sense and is certainly not safe."

He took an additional stride toward me, leaning close to my ear. "Then I guess whoever ended up with you will be a very lucky man."

A chill inched over my entire body, my knees feeling fragile at the intense, dominating tone in his husky voice. Every syllable of his words tickled the small hairs on the back of my neck. Just as my legs were about to give way beneath me, an older man stepped outside with a clipboard, approaching me. The gentleman I was talking to, slowly spun around. Sauntering back inside without another word, he gave the other man a nod.

"Ma'am, you are needed as we will require your signature to complete the transaction," his monotone displayed zero emotion.

Transaction. That word repeated in my head. I was a literal transaction. Sluggishly, I trudged inside, following the man as two others closely trailed behind me. We navigated our way through the mingling guests, coming to a door. There was no escaping now as the man led me down a labyrinth of hallways. To say I was now terrified, was an understatement.

I followed him into a large, faintly lit office. Peering around carefully, I examined the interior of the room which was just as daunting as the situation. Dark wood covered the floors, and bookcases lined the walls; all but one. The man rounded the large mahogany desk that sat in front of a large window.

He laid a briefcase on the desk and opened it. Thumbing through several sheets of paper, he pulled out a few, placing them on the desk with a pen laying on top. He closed the briefcase, sliding it out of the way.

Picking up the pen, I started to sign all the documents without reading them. I knew that was a mistake, but I did not care. I was eager to have this done. I signed the last document then laid the pen back down on top of the papers. The man reached out, sliding them toward him.

"Right, well that will be all I need from you," he announced.

Slowly staring around, I realized that I did not know what happened next. "What now?"

He nodded toward the door without a smile. Pivoting, I was faced with the gentleman I spoke to outside. Still in his mask, he leaned in the doorway with his hands tucked into his pockets, unhurriedly trailing his eyes up and down my body.

"Oh my God," I gasped, pressing my fingertips on my lips, "you bought me?"

Lifting his fingers to his chin, he smirked. "Relax, let's go."

He placed his hand on my lower back, causing my legs to lock up. I stood frozen. This was all too real now. A part of me wanted to shout, *ha-ha the joke is over*, but I knew deep inside that this was no joke. I was very aware of what I had just allowed to happen, and it was evident that I would not be able to get out of this one. At this point, I could only pray I made it out of this alive.

Planting my feet firmly on the floor, I folded my arms suspiciously, "Where are we going?"

"Just trust me," he mumbled, gently guiding me out of the room and down the long hallway.

We came to the doorway of a slightly nicer office that boasted a more modern appearance in decor. It was brighter with lots of abstract artwork covering the walls; the complete opposite of the room I had just been in. The other two men remained outside in the hall as he gestured for me to enter before him. He closed the door. We were completely alone.

"Will you require anything for tonight?"

A bewildered expression spread across my face, "Tonight, what?"

Surely, he did not think this was going to happen right now. He walked behind the desk, tapping his fingers on the surface twice. I assumed he wanted the only thing I had in my hands right now, so I gave him the contract. Turning through several pages, he handed it back to me. I scanned over it, my eyes paying close attention to each line.

"Paragraph four," he affirmed, pointing to the small stack of papers in my hand.

My eyes darted to the mentioned paragraph, then my mouth fell open. I dropped the papers to my side and glared at him. His lips pursed attempting to conceal a smirk.

"I have to live with you?" I blurted, throwing my hands out to the side. "Ugh," I huffed under my breath.

"That's what the contract says, doesn't it?" he countered, nodding his head toward the documents.

Rolling my eyes, I folded my arms across my midsection defensively, the papers dangling from my fingertips, "When does this happen?"

"Darling, the minute you signed it." Through the dim lighting and the mask, it was hard to tell, but I was sure he winked.

I teared up, overcome with emotion, "I have to go home with you?"

"Yes," he sighed, "but you will be taking another car." He pressed a button on his smart watch, speaking into it, "She is ready."

Pouring himself a drink from a nearby liquor table, he held it up toward me as an evil grin spread across his face.

"Says who?" I challenged him.

"My lawyer." He took a drink, smiling behind the rim of his glass.

The ride to his house was quiet. Silently, I sat in the back of a Rolls Royce as it left the city, the tall buildings disappearing behind us as we got further away. An exceptionally large man sat in the front passenger seat on his phone the entire time. I did not speak at all. As I peered out the window, a small tear plummeted down my face, dripping off my chin onto my lap.

We were in the car for about an hour and a half before we came to an enormous, black wrought iron gate. The driver pressed a few buttons then scanned a card on a security system. The magnificent gates slowly opened, triggering an exceedingly long path of LED lights to turn on. We slowly traveled down a driveway lined with trees until we came to a clearing.

That is when I saw it; an overpowering Châteauesque-style four-story home. Greyish tan limestone, and a steeply pitched roof, punctuated by many chimneys and covered with dark slate tile, gave the residence a magnificent appeal. Countless windows lined the exterior of the home, undoubtedly providing stunning views in the daytime.

It was the largest building I had ever laid my eyes on in person. Speechless, the mansion intimidated me far more than the ball did.

3 ARRANGEMENT

Isabelle

Quietly, I was escorted to my room by the man who sat in the passenger seat of the car. I was in a state of shock, paying no interest to where I was going in the house. I blindly followed behind him, eyes glued to the floor, watching the pattern on the long hallway rugs. My thoughts were racing, but I was unable to articulate a sentence.

We stopped at a set of double doors at the end of a hallway. Stepping to the side of the door frame, I waited for him to make the next move. I was not going to open strange doors in front of me. For all I knew, they could lead to a room of torture, or worse. Just because this was an enormous, elegant mansion did not mean the owner was not a complete psycho. Who buys sex from a strange woman?

Glancing to me expressionlessly, the tall man placed both hands onto the doorknobs and pushed. I was then faced with an exquisite, marginally Gothic style room with an elevated canopy bed. The room was adorned in variations of red and black throughout. Warily, I stalked to the center of the room, slowly rotating as I took each step. Finally, he spoke.

"Miss, your things will be moved over tomorrow," he informed me with a prominent Italian accent. "For now, you will find all you need in your suite."

I nodded, wordlessly. Even if I wanted to speak, I did not know what to say. What do you say in a situation such as this? *Yippee? Oh my gosh, thank you for this?* No. You say nothing and hope it was all a weird dream.

Never had I imagined that I would be bought for my virginity. I felt used and damaged. Soon, I would have nothing special left about me. It would all be taken from me. It was not that I was waiting until marriage, but I at least wanted the choice of when I gave up my innocence to someone.

My weight shifted back and forth nervously as I ran my fingertips slowly up and down my arms. Rotating, I absorbed my surroundings, sadness rising within me. I fought back any tears that tried to escape as my eyes watered. I opened my mouth to speak, but to no avail, I could not. Silently, I stood in the middle of the room, completely numb.

"You are not to leave this room tonight," he continued with a serious yet approachable tone. "Your bathroom is through those doors and that is your closet over there with clothes that fit you." He gestured at the various doors in the room, "You will find everything is stocked with new things to your liking, and the garments in the drawers are new but have been washed for you."

What did he mean, *to my liking*? This was the first time I had ever been here. How was anything to my liking? Questions rose up within me, but I did not bother to ask. I scuffed toward the closet, running my fingertips over a couch in the center of the room as I passed. Studying my surroundings, I finally gained the courage to speak.

"How is everything already my size?"

Silently, he analyzed me. Turning around, I glared in his direction with folded arms, waiting for his reply. Still, he did not respond, standing like a statue as he glowered at me, mimicking my expression. Rolling my eyes, I faltered over to the windows, peeling back the long, white, sheer curtains, peering outside into the darkness of the estate grounds.

"If you try to escape, you will be severely punished," he called out. "My boss paid a pretty penny for you."

The reality resurfaced again that I was a virgin hooker if

there were such a thing. Sighing, I leaned my forehead on the glass slowly inhaling, then exhaling.

"There are cameras everywhere in the home and on the grounds outside," he warned. "There are also alarms everywhere."

Slowly, I pivoted around to face him with arched eyebrows. His expression hardened as he grimaced in my direction once again. It was almost as if his words carried little to no influence. Still, he was attempting to appear threatening to me. I pursed my lips, growing impatient with the entire procedure.

"And also armed security in various posts on property, inside and out," he conveyed, trying to threaten me a bit more.

I must have had a strange look on my face by this point, because he broke the tough guy act briefly, smiling amiably, "You are safe here, so don't worry." Dropping his arms to his side, he sighed, then gestured to the air in front of him. "My boss means you no harm, and eventually you will come to learn that."

Closing my eyes, I inhaled deeply, accepting whatever fate had to offer me. "Will I see him tonight?"

"No ma'am, he was called into a late meeting," he blustered as he strode toward the door, "but you will meet him in the morning."

Without saying another word, he stepped out of the room, closing the doors together. I was left alone in my thoughts. Creeping around the room, I ran my fingers over the furniture and curtains, processing what was going on.

I could not wrap my head around any of this. It seemed like a joke, a sick joke. Forty-eight hours ago, I was being screamed at then fired by Jesse. Now, I was standing in the middle of a mansion bedroom, in the house of a stranger who bought my virginity for one million dollars. Fear, confusion, anger, and a slight tinge of amusement filled my mind. No one would ever believe this happened even if I managed to escape. These things did not happen in real life.

I suddenly recalled the man mentioning the closet. Temporarily forgetting that I was in a stranger's home, I breezed through the room, wanting to get a closer look at what had been offered to me. There was no way anything would be in my size. How could anyone know this before I even moved into the home. Entering the room, I gasped as my eyes trailed over every inch of the first space in the closet. It was meticulously organized with dresses, tops, pants, and skirts.

Cautiously, I crept closer, noticing the tags were still on every item. Trailing my fingertips through them, I read the sizes, confirming they were all indeed, made to fit my frame. Then, it occurred to me, that maybe this man preferred a certain body type and I was reading too much into this.

An open door across the closet captured my attention. I meandered through it into another section. My mouth fell agape as I took in the sight before me. It was a special room dedicated to shoes, handbags, belts, everything I could ever want to go with the perfect outfit.

I exited the closet in disbelief, sauntering to the dresser. Yanking the drawers open, I discovered a surprise. A strange feeling overwhelmed me as I was greeted with lots of revealing panties, bras, and pajamas. That is when I remembered why I was here. Sighing, I gently closed the drawers and fell onto one of the couches in the middle of the room. Taking a deep breath, I gazed at the ceiling, wondering if this would be the way I perished.

From a visual aspect, this place was remarkable. Anyone in my situation would have enjoyed this if it had not been for a contract promising sex to a stranger. Sitting up, I threw my palms onto my face, groaning. So far, I was unharmed, but I would not let my guard down. This would all be over the minute I gave up my virginity to the man who bought me. I decided that I would relax tonight, as much as one could in this position. The man told me I would not meet his boss tonight, so that gave me a little time to calm myself down.

Entering the bathroom, I trudged to the luxurious clawfoot bathtub in the middle of the room, filling it up with water as hot as my body could stand. Undressing hastily, I stepped into the tub. Sliding my body down the edge, I rested my head against the back, closing my eyes. Now, my body was beginning to relax, but my brain started overthinking everything once again.

What was happening? How did I get into this situation? As relaxed as I was, I wanted to murder my best friend. How dare she practically sell me?! Why did she think that was a great idea? Yes, I needed money. God knows, I needed money badly. I officially had no income now.

I started to reflect on the night, realizing I never looked at how much I would receive for this transaction that I was a part of. Here I was, soaking in a tub that was not mine, having just had my body sold to some strange man. Why did he even want me out of all the women who stood on that stage? The buyer had not revealed himself to me just yet. What if he was the face for the operation? The real guy was possibly disgusting and forty years older than me. For the first time, I stopped myself from having those sorts of thoughts. I would end up driving myself insane.

After a while, I started to prune up so decided to get out and try to sleep. I picked up my soft, oversized towel, drying off. Wrapping it around my body, I moped into the bedroom. Remembering that there were only sexy things to sleep in, I smiled. I did love pretty lingerie, though I had never had the chance to wear it for anyone.

As I rummaged through the drawers, I pulled a few pieces out for inspection, wondering how anyone was supposed to sleep in it. Some of them had so many ties and strings. I snorted as I envisioned myself waking up being strangled by my own lingerie. I hastily shoved it all back in the drawer, slamming it closed before opening the underwear drawer. I dug out a black lace thong from a pile of panties. This was more what I was used to, so I slipped it on then opened a final drawer. There were some small, cute tank tops neatly folded, so I slipped one on. Shuffling to the bed, I fell onto it with my arms and legs out, exhausted from the emotional rollercoaster this night had been. I felt like I could sleep for days.

"He will see you now," a mature female's voice greeted me in a cheerful tone.

For a moment, I forgot where I was as I peeked out from behind my sleepy eyelids. I flinched when I saw a woman standing over my bed, peering down at me as if she had been watching me sleep for hours.

Slowly, I opened my eyes wider when I realized I was not at home. This was not a dream. The woman smiled as she stood, waiting patiently for me to rise. She wore a black and white dress with grey hair twisted into a bun.

She appeared friendly, yet I did not trust anyone at the moment.

I rubbed my eyelids as I yawned. "Morning," I squeaked.

"Good morning, Miss."

Sitting up slowly, I pushed the blankets back while she assisted me. Neatly, she began making my bed as soon as my feet hit the floor. I trudged into the bathroom, still groggy. I had not been awake long enough to panic just yet, but I was certain it would kick in any moment.

She called out to the bathroom, "I must go over the rules with you before you see him."

"Okay just a second," I shouted back to her.

I took a quick shower so I could at the very least, make myself fully presentable. Wrapping myself in a towel, I returned to the bedroom, my nervousness building. While I was in the bathroom, she had laid clothes out for me on the bed. I noticed a strange black lacey piece of fabric next to my outfit.

Getting dressed, I ignored it for the time being. However, once I was ready, I picked it up, inspecting the lacey fabric. I traced the outline of the cloth with my fingers. It was a nearly translucent blindfold with long, black ribbons dangling from either side. I opened my mouth to speak, but no words would leave my lips. *A blindfold*? I asked myself.

"You must wear that whenever you are in the presence of him."

I held the fabric out toward her, muttering, "It goes over my eyes, right?"

She gently took it from my hands as she stepped behind me, reaching around the front of my face. Securely, she placed it against my head, tying it.

"He insists that you wear it," she declared as she walked around to the front of my body, analyzing my appearance.

I could make out her shape and general outlines, but I could not tell what she looked like with this material over my eyes. Bewilderment rose inside me causing so many questions. Once again, I was rendered speechless.

"I know it's confusing, but he does not want you to see him so you will have to wear it," she blurted, stating the rules. "You are to join him for every meal." She sighed, "You will have time to get to know him when you eat together."

"I'm supposed to eat blindfolded?" my uncertainty turned to astonishment. "How am I supposed to get to know him if I wear this?" I groaned, "I'm lucky I can see where I'm going."

"I'm Helen by the way," she introduced herself with sympathy in her voice as she dismissed every concern I had. "If you need anything, please don't hesitate to ask for me." She placed her hand on my arm, "I will always be right down the hall."

"Do you live here?" I inquired.

"Yes," she replied cheerfully, "There is a full-time live-in staff, and a full-time off property staff who come here every day."

I nodded. She took my hand, pulling me into the bathroom where she applied gloss to my lips.

"There," she beamed, "you look perfect."

"Thank you," I giggled, "I think."

Helen was so friendly, that I almost forgot why I was here. She spoke with a soothing tone. I knew she was used to women coming and going before me, so I reminded myself that I was not special to anyone here.

"Come with me, Miss."

She escorted me down a long hallway until we came upon two doors. She pressed a button on the wall. That is when I realized that there was an elevator in the man's home.

DING!

The doors opened.

"I don't remember this from last night," I observed as we stepped inside, the doors closing a few seconds later.

"You took the stairs last night," she noted, "but I didn't think you would want to bother with the stairs, a blindfold and heels this morning."

I snickered, "Good thinking."

DING!

The doors opened again. She hooked her arm in mine, leading me through several corridors until we arrived at a set of large, mahogany, double doors that stood at the end of a small hallway. I could not see much but I could tell they were impressive as was the entire house. I sighed, my nerves cracking. Fighting back my emotions, I gulped.

"What's his name?"

"He will answer what he wants you to know," she alluded as she opened the doors before I had a chance to respond.

Warily stepping into the large room, I inhaled, apprehensive of the unknown before me. Surprised, I jumped when I heard the doors close, the room falling completely silent. I tried to search for any sign of life, but it was hopeless. The lace allowed me to see very minimally.

Moments later, I finally caught a glimpse of movement

behind a grand, wooden desk. Clearing my throat, I awkwardly shifted my weight back and forth between my feet, fidgeting with my fingers. Assuming that I was in the presence of the man who bought me, I remained quiet, allowing him the chance to speak first.

"Walk closer."

I faltered in his direction, obeying, yet uncertain of my immediate future.

"That's good," he snapped, raising his hand, signaling me to stop.

I froze instantly, scared to take another step toward him. Placing a hand on my chest, I inhaled deeply before dropping my hand to my side. Unable to predict what would happen next, I remained silent. I did not know this man or what he was capable of.

"How did you sleep?" he inquired as he leaned back in his chair, causing it to slightly creak.

I closed my eyes, exhaling slowly before I was able to reply. "I slept okay."

"Just okay?" he countered, as if I insulted him. "And here I thought I provided you with everything to make you more than just *okay*."

"I mean," I sighed, "it was extremely comfortable, thank you. I just was taken by surprise by coming here."

Even though I was unsure if I should continue, I took a chance anyway. "I just have so many questions to be honest, but I'm kind of scared."

He slowly rocked forward in his desk chair, propping up on his elbows. I could tell he was observing me thoroughly, studying every movement I made. After a few moments of silence, he stood, taking a few short strides to me. Delicately, he ran his fingers up and down my arm as I continued to stare forward, frozen in fear. Leaning close to my neck, he began to inhale my scent.

"Why are you scared?" he taunted, circling me like a predator moving in on his prey.

"Do you not understand how scary it is to be auctioned off for sex," I choked, barely above a whisper, "especially when you've never done it?"

He sighed deeply as he continued to stalk around me.

I was becoming increasingly terrified. "Human trafficking is horrible," I mumbled, the shakiness in my voice evident.

Instantly, he came to a halt, freezing in front of me. Leaning in close to my face, he growled, "No one is shipping you off to be a sex slave."

I shivered nervously, blinking back tears. A slight aroma of mint and liquor drifted from his breath to my face.

He placed his finger under my chin, lifting my gaze to his. I gulped as I peered into his eyes. He barely circled his thumb on my jaw for a moment before he let go, dropping his hands to his side and backing away. Spinning around, he took a few steps away then turned back to face me.

"No one is trafficking you so I would watch the terms you use around me," he suddenly snapped.

I gasped, hearing his accent suddenly change. He had only a hint of an American accent now. I could not place the origin because he was still masking his speech.

Bracing myself, I decided to push more buttons so I could learn more about the mysterious man. I had to know what was going on, and this may have been the only way. Something was not right. The sharp edge of fight or flight filled me. If nothing else, at least I may have more answers after this.

"Just force me to sleep with you so we can get this over with and I can go home," I provoked, quaking anxiously.

He chuckled humorously, but he was now fuming as he called my bluff. Marching to his desk, he fell back into his chair, sliding forward. I felt his glare, as his mood shifted with great intent to harm me.

"Sit!"

I caught a glimpse of two chairs next to me. Reaching out, I grabbed the arm of the chair on the right, slowly perching on the edge. I steadied myself, not wanting to get too comfortable. I was unsure of how to behave in the presence of him.

"I'm sure you would like to know how much you will be paid for our arrangement." His strange American accent returned.

"I don't even care," I stammered, ready to be alone. "Do whatever you want to me and keep the money because I just want to be alone right now."

"And why is that?" he placed his arms on the desk, locking his fingers together. "All women want my money."

Ignoring his statement, I questioned bluntly, "Why am I blindfolded, Your Majesty?"

Leaning back in his chair, he formed a triangle over his mouth before he dropped his hands to the arm rests.

"Your Majesty?"

I shrugged as I peered around the large room with a hindered view, "You live in a castle, don't you?"

The smirk disappeared as he pursed his lips. Leaning forward, he propped on his elbows.

"I don't want you to see me."

"And why is that?" I challenged. "Are you ugly?"

Throwing his head back he stared at the ceiling. Sighing audibly, he lowered his gaze on me once again. "Absolutely not," he argued, "I am quite charming."

"And how am I supposed to know?"

"You will just have to trust me I guess then, won't you."

"Right now, I don't trust anyone," I noted, relaxing my hands and resting them in my lap.

"Well that's one thing we have in common then," he muttered resentfully. "Listen, I do not want you to know who I am at the moment. My privacy is particularly important to me."

"Fine!" I hoped to be dismissed.

"I'm not going to actually sleep with you right now," he murmured, forming a triangle with his fingertips, lightly tapping his lips.

"Then why am I here?"

"I want to help you," he sighed in frustration, "but it's important to me that my identity remain a secret for now, Isabelle."

A snort involuntarily escaped my mouth, "What are you, some famous celebrity or something?"

"Something like that I guess," he groaned. "I just think it's better for both of us if you don't know who I am."

"I need to get a job," I pleaded. "I cannot stay here."

The minute those words left my mouth, I recalled that I needed to find another job as soon as possible and it was not simply an excuse. Money obviously came easy for him but not me. I sighed, saddened at what had happened.

As my voice began to shake, I stammered, "I recently got fired from a job where I was sexually harassed every shift and as of right now, I can no longer afford my apartment in the city."

His body shot up out of the chair as if someone lit a fire under him. He stomped to where I sat, squatting down in front of me. I scurried to adjust myself in my seat, unsurely placing some distance between the man and me.

"He did what?!" he growled as he clenched his teeth, losing his American accent once again.

"He used to use every opportunity he could to touch me," I whined as my eyes filled with tears.

"He will not be a problem to you again," he abruptly paused, inhaling deeply. "Go to your room and I will have breakfast delivered to you there."

I nodded as we both stood. He slid his phone from his pocket, placing it to his ear.

"I need to make some business calls."

"Uh, can someone show me how to get back to it?" I

mumbled as I awkwardly turned toward the direction of the door before I pivoted back to face him.

He chuckled as he lowered his phone. Placing his mouth to his watch, he began speaking in a language I did not recognize. Taking my hands in his, he sighed while tilting his head a bit as he studied me.

"Before they enter, I want you to know that you are safe here," he assured me. "I will never force you to do anything you are not ready for."

I nodded. He seemed sincere and dare I say, nice.

"In fact," he continued, "I want to know more about you before all this is over."

My mind was beginning to play tricks on me. If I did not know better, I would say that he sounded almost as if he cared about me. I averted my gaze to the floor, unsure how to respond. He slid a second phone out of his other pocket, flipping my hand over so that my palm was exposed. Placing it in my hand, he gently folded my fingertips over it.

"I kind of destroyed your other phone," he admitted, "so here is a new one."

I shifted my weight back and forth. "O-okay," I stuttered softly.

"My number is the only number in the contacts right

now," he sighed, "so call or text me any time."

"But you're in the same house," I snickered.

"Are you planning to walk around the house in a blindfold hoping you run into me?"

"Good point."

"Like I said," he quickly continued, "call me or text me any time you want to chat." He leaned in close to my ear. Placing his hand in the crook of my elbow, he whispered softly, "I'm sure you have a lot of questions."

I gulped at his deep, husky tone just as the doors opened. He swiftly let go, taking a few steps backward.

"That wasn't so bad was it?" Helen called out, interrupting the moment.

Shuffling over to me, she took me by the arm, escorting me out of the room in an instant. I kept glancing backward, but the man's gaze had shifted to the floor. As soon as the office doors were closed behind us, she pulled the blindfold off my eyes.

"Won't he be angry?" I frowned as my eyes darted around the wide hallway.

"No," she gestured for me to walk. "He will be in his office for a while and when he is not present you do not need to wear it."

Valentino

As she exited the room, I sighed, unable to watch her. Picking up a letter opener off my desk, I grumbled, throwing it toward the wall across the room. Rolling my eyes, I angrily slid my phone out of my pocket. I made a phone call to some of my men, informing them I wanted to see them immediately. While I waited, I poured a glass of whiskey.

Slouching in the chair she was in moments ago, I stared ahead blankly sipping my drink. What had I gotten myself into? There is no way that this would ever end peacefully. Suddenly, my office doors swung open as five of my men marched in. I stood, adjusting my suit as I spun around to face them.

"Close the fucking door," I mumbled, grinding my teeth in mental turmoil.

My business partner and best friend, William, stepped ahead of the others. His eyes scanned the room, then fell on the letter opener sticking out of the wall.

"Judging by the knife in the wall," he chuckled, "I'm guessing she told you about Jesse, didn't she?"

Rolling my eyes, I chugged the rest of my whiskey before responding. "Letter opener, not knife," I sighed as I closed my eyes, exhaling, "and yes she did."

"Thought so," he murmured, turning to the rest of the men in the room then back to me.

"I want that mother fucker brought to me immediately," I demanded. I was failing masking my emotions. "Do not harm him as he is mine and I want to watch him suffer," I snapped, slamming my glass down on my desk. "He touched her!"

"She is safe now," William nervously reassured me, "and he did not ever get far with her from what Tanya said."

"Is she here?" I exhaled, rubbing my temples with my fingertips, trying to relieve the stress. "I want to see her if so."

"She is here yes," he confirmed, glancing at the door where one of my security guards was standing. "Would you tell Tanya to come in here please?"

My guard bowed his head and exited the room to retrieve Isabelle's best friend.

4 CALL ME SIR

Valentino

Tanya apprehensively staggered into my office, her eyes darting around the room at my men as if she were in distress. She glanced to William for reassurance, shyly twisting her lips into a small smile. He bowed his head toward her, giving her a small wink as she slowly approached me. Towering over her, I lowered my gaze onto her fearful eyes.

Removing my pistol from my waistband, I laid it on my desk, eliminating the threat from the situation. She anxiously fidgeted with her fingers as she observed my every move. Sauntering to my table of liquor, I poured myself another glass of whiskey as I turned around. With one hand in my pocket and the other holding my drink, I strolled back to my desk. My eyes never left hers. Setting my glass down on my desk, I clasped my hands together, causing her to jump.

Smirking, I strode to my safe with all eyes in the room tracking me. Pushing my index finger on my safe's biometric sensor, I unlocked it and the door popped open. Pulling out a small stack of bills, I then closed it before counting out five thousand dollars for her, returning to my desk. Wrapping a small band around the bills, I tossed the stack in her direction before I sat down, locking eyes on hers once again.

I nodded toward the chair, "Sit."

Glancing at William for approval, she tucked her skirt under her as she slid into the seat then crossed her leg. Lacing her fingers together, she waited for me to speak as William moved behind her, resting his palms on her shoulders.

"You saved her life, you know."

"I would do anything for her," she sighed, "and I agree that auction was the best way to get her here for you." Leaning forward, she pushed the stack of money in my direction. "I appreciate the money, but I cannot take it since I did it for her, not the money."

I do not take no for an answer. Reaching forward, I slid

it back toward her and glowered before sitting back in my chair, crossing my leg. William moved next to her and she stood, uneasily trembling.

"You don't have a choice," I retorted, as I stood, sliding my hands into my pockets.

She promptly reached for it, grabbing it, and shoving it into her bag without further question.

William exhaled, relaxing. "I was so scared that mother fucker was going to keep bidding against you."

Rubbing the back of my neck, I massaged out the tension from my body. "Who was that guy anyway?" I inquired as I searched the faces of my men.

They exchanged glances, shrugging while shaking their heads. I focused my attention on William instead.

"No one knows," he rolled his eyes.

"I would have never him let win anyway," I declared, "and I was prepared to take the bid as high as I needed."

"Or the guns?" My friend, Blaine, chimed in from the side of the room.

My eyes darted toward him quickly. Before I could respond, Tanya interrupted my thought.

"So, she will be okay here then?"

"Of course," I nodded, "but give me some time with her

then you can visit her as much as you want." Biting my bottom lip, I paused. My eyes darted toward the wall as I stared blankly. "I don't want her to get suspicious."

Tanya was a bold woman in general, but she never crossed me in the month I had known her. We met when she began to work for William.

Balling her fists, she rested them on her hips as her eyes trailed down my body and up again. Tilting my head, I waited for her to stop. She jumped, defensively crossing her arms over her midsection when she noticed I was glaring at her.

"Do you need something?"

"You know you'll have to tell her how this all happened right?"

"Excuse me?"

Raising her hand, she pressed her fingertips to her forehead. "She was terrified but now she hates me," she carefully articulated, her eyes finding mine once again, "and she has no idea what's actually going on."

I nodded. "I will tell her in time but right now is not that moment," my jaw stiffened, "and she would never believe me anyway."

"You like her a lot," Tanya grinned widely.

"Liam," I growled, "keep your pet on a leash before I

kill her."

Tanya inhaled sharply, dropping her head as I shot daggers her way. Her gaze fell to the floor as her smile faded into a hint of a lingering smirk. My eyes narrowed on William's. He cleared his throat, nudging her ever so slightly in the side.

"Babe, you have to learn how to speak to him and what is appropriate," he gently scolded.

Tanya buried her face into her palms, apologizing, "Sorry, I'm not used to this lifestyle yet."

Wrapping his arm around her, William pulled her into his body, smiling, "Well you better get used to it, baby, because you're not going anywhere." He planted a soft peck on top of her head. "You're mine," he asserted.

I gave them both a nod. They turned to leave but I called after William. He whispered something to Tanya, and she exited the room before he spun back to me. Taking a few steps toward my desk, he folded his arms waiting for me to speak. I inhaled deeply as I raised my hand to the stubble on my chin, stroking it.

"I want Jesse brought to me tonight," I ordered, tapping on the surface of my desk with my index finger. "Got it?"

He nodded as he reached out to shake my hand before he left. I lifted my hand in the air, signaling for my other men to leave me alone. The minute the door closed I sat, running my fingers through my hair, sighing.

Reaching for my cigarettes, I pulled one out of the pack, lighting it. Taking a long drag, I leaned forward, propping my elbows on my desk. Mindlessly, I slowly twisted my glass back and forth in deep thought.

To say I envied William and Tanya was an understatement. They once had a simple arrangement, but William was growing to love her. It was apparent. The relationship was now confusing, but they understood it, which was all that mattered.

Tanya had applied for a job with William's company after leaving her position at the bar. The minute he interviewed her, he took a liking to her. He would spoil her, taking her to dinners; no masks, no facades, no holding back.

Tanya being a sexual person, was ready to sleep with him the minute he wanted it. She went from being his, what society labels, a Sugar Baby to being someone he could see himself with. He would not admit that verbally yet, but I saw it in the way he treated her. He never treated women with the kind of respect he gave Tanya. There was no doubt they would end up married one day.

Isabelle

I was not a big fan of breakfast in general. Not because I did not like the food, I was just never used to eating breakfast in the morning. However, I was starving. Suddenly, there was a knock at my bedroom door. Was it odd that I was hoping it would be the mysterious man? I peeked at myself in the mirror, smoothing my outfit before I stepped over to the door, opening it. I wanted to get some answers from him. Instead, I was face to face with a chef.

"Good morning, Miss," he greeted me in a French accent, wheeling a silver cart to the center of the room, uncovering multiple platters of food.

"Wow," I blurted, my eyes widening, "um thank you."

There was enough food for at least five people. I would not be able to eat all of it on my own. Sighing as I watched him arrange everything on the tray, my mind began to wonder why there was so much food before me. I swallowed hard, stepping closer to the spread.

"Are you planning to eat with me?"

He chuckled as he arranged the platters food on the coffee table, "No, Miss Isabelle," he glanced toward me then continued his duty, "but the boss didn't know what you would like, so he asked me to make a little of everything."

I slowly approached the table of food, wrinkling my nose, "That's more than a little of everything."

"Just doing as I'm told, Miss," he smiled warmly, "so if you need anything else, please ask."

"Thank you for this," I acknowledged his hard work, studying the food once again.

He still smiled as he headed for the doors, bowing his head politely in my direction before exiting and pulling the doorknobs toward him, leaving me alone once again. Exhaling I turned back to the table. My eyes trailed over the food once again.

Tucking my bottom lip between my teeth, I attempted to hide a small smirk that was forming on my lips. Everything looked mouthwatering, but there was no way I would be able to eat this on my own. How could a man who paid to have sex with me be so kind? He offered me a nice room, food, clothes, anything I needed.

My eyes noticed my new cell phone laying on the nightstand next to the bed. I sighed as I lifted my hand to my lips, barely nibbling on my thumb nail in deep thought. Slowly plodding toward the table, I scooped my phone into my palms and opened my lonely contact on the screen.

Your chef just brought me enough food for a small army, I typed.

My thumb hovered over the *Send* button. I winced as I touched it. Throwing myself onto the bed, I stared at the ceiling, waiting to see if he would reply. I was not sure if I even wanted him to eat with me. I was confused and scared, but he had not killed or raped me. Still, I wanted to be cautious. My phone buzzed. I raised myself into a sitting position, reading his reply.

I did not know what you wanted.

He did not offer to help me eat it, so I decided to push my luck. At this point, I had nothing to lose. I gulped, forming a simple text that may or may not have changed the course of my future.

Do you want to join me? I caught myself smiling as I sent him the question.

I have a meeting soon, but I can do that, I guess, he causally responded. *Blindfold before I enter.*

Okay, I sent the last text then laid my phone back on the table.

Stupid blindfold, I thought as I picked it up, tying it to my head. Why did he not want to be seen by me? He must have been hideous, not wanting me to see his horrendous face. It bothered me immensely. I felt so exposed as I was left to wonder when he would drop the bomb about the sex. Inviting him may have been a terrible idea but I could not help it.

So many thoughts were running through my head. Maybe he did not want to see *me*, he only wanted to have a virgin. I was so lost in my thoughts, that I barely heard the knock on my bedroom door. Glancing in the mirror, I flattened my outfit before he joined me. I stumbled to the couch that faced away from the door, practicing different positions to make myself appear more confident before I invited him in.

"Come in!"

Gradually, the door opened. I turned toward the entrance to see him, or what I assumed to be him. Inching toward where I was sitting, he cleared his throat before taking a seat on the other sofa facing me, crossing his foot over his knee.

He stared at me for a moment, before he snickered, "Can you see okay?"

I crossed my arms, attempted to appear annoyed. "Well I guess we will find out if I stab my cheek with a fork." Involuntarily, I snorted then immediately cupped my hands over my mouth in embarrassment.

He leaned forward picking up a plate. "Here then, I will help you," he offered. "What would you like?"

"Bacon," I blurted, "all the bacon actually, eggs, and

whatever fruit that is."

"It's watermelon, strawberries, cherries, cantaloupe, and grapes," he identified all of it.

I raised my hand to my chin thinking.

"But don't say cherries," he teased, "because that belongs to me and only me."

An uncomfortable screeching laugh escaped my mouth at his dreadful joke. I could not identify the sound, but I was embarrassed.

"Good to see you laughing at least." I could hear the smile in his words.

He handed the plate to me then reached out with a fork. Gently, I took it from him, our fingertips touching in the process. A surge of electricity ran through my body. I swiftly withdrew my hand before shrugging it off.

Eating proved to be humiliating and trickier than I had hoped as I attempted to stab the fruit then eggs. Food plopped back onto the plate as my mouth grasped at air. Huffing, I dropped my hands to my lap. Glancing up, I noticed he was looking in my direction, mouth open and frozen with food perched on top of his fork. He unexpectedly threw his head back roaring with laughter. Laying his plate down on the table, he stood. He slipped around to my side of the coffee table.

"Scoot," he commanded as he lightly tapped my arm.

I slid over as he sat down, taking my plate from me. I could feel my cheeks becoming warm in shame. Swallowing hard, I squeezed my eyes shut as my nose caught the aroma of his cologne.

"I'm sorry Isabelle," he apologized, his laugh trailing off. "I guess I can feed you this once since you are having trouble finding both your food and your mouth."

"It's hard to do this when you can't see very well," I defended myself.

"You do realize that your mouth has not moved from its original place, correct?" he smirked.

"*Ha ha.*"

"Here," he offered as he rested a strawberry to my lips.

Barely opening my mouth, I took a bite of the tip.

"I actually don't mind this at all," he muttered barely above a whisper, observing my lips.

Awkwardly, I sighed, "I feel like a toddler."

"I assure you that you are all woman," he cooed. "Bite," he commanded as he gently placed a piece of watermelon on my lips.

I took a small bite. Unfortunately, a little juice ran down my chin.

"May I have a napkin please?" I requested as I cupped my palm under my jaw.

He set the plate down, then held my cheeks in his palms, gently tilting my head. Slowly, he trailed his tongue up my neck tasting the fruit that was still traveling downward. I froze. My breathing became unsteady as my back naturally arched. He continued until he reached the corner of my mouth. Slowly, he withdrew his hand, placing it on my knee. Sliding his other hand into my hair, he lightly entangled his fingers around my long strands, pulling my head back.

I closed my eyes, awaiting his next move as I silently gulped. I could have told him to stop but did not. A combination of his scent with the moment, impaired my judgement. Regrettably, I was not even thinking about the contract right now. His tongue felt tantalizing on my soft skin, and I was mesmerized.

I was very inexperienced, only having ever kissed one guy. That was an exceedingly long time ago. Needless to say, right now I was about to already explode at his touch. I sensed he was hesitant, unsure what he was going to do next as his lips moved to my ear.

"Tell me to stop."

Opening my mouth to speak, I found myself rendered mute under his spell. Swallowing hard, I closed my eyes, giving in to his touch.

"Do you want me to stop?"

Still, I could not form words to reply. I remained a statue as he slowly inched his hand up my thigh, coming to a stop just before the hem of my panties. His breath grew shallow as his jaw pressed against my cheek. My body began to quiver, ready for him to take me right here, right now. I would have done anything for this stranger at that moment. I had never been this way. Just as his mouth trailed to the front of my neck, I gulped. He froze.

"You are not ready for me yet," he muttered as his lips barely grazed my skin.

Valentino

God, why did she have to be so pure, so innocent? Why could I not I just use her like I did the others? She was perfect. She was exactly what I had been needing in my life. I was so tired of screwing whores, I wanted her instead. I was so happy to have her in my home but hated it at the same time. A stupid contract and an enormous fabrication is why she was here. It was a contract I did not care about right now. Keeping my hands off her would be impossible. She was trusting me not to hurt her. Suddenly she spoke, breaking my train of thought.

"Am I at least allowed to know your name and age?"

I let go of her, dropping my hands to my side. It seemed almost as if she feared the reaction she would get. I was still physically close to her, trying to hold myself back from ripping her clothes off and taking her right there on the couch. I deeply inhaled memorizing her scent. I wanted to taste her skin, but I was holding true to my word, resisting her, for now.

"I am old enough," I sighed, "and my name is something you will possibly learn one day."

She did not back down. Her constant persistence was going to get us both in trouble, mainly me. I knew that it was only a matter of time before I could not control myself any longer.

"Well, I would like to know what I should call you," she gulped, bracing herself for my reply.

I paused my naughty thoughts, changing direction. Was I going to spare her from my world or was I going to break every rule that had been set in place for this? The reality was that she was now living with me until further notice. Since I knew the inevitable, I decided to take a risk. It was a risk I would either soon regret, or it would be the beginning of something more.

"You can call me, Sir."

"Um," she swallowed hard, barely able to

communicate, "okay, Sir, it is then."

That was all it took. I reached for her, running my fingers through her hair once again. I gripped tightly, slightly bending her neck backward. Leaning further, I observed myself on the brink of caressing her neckline. I could no longer resist the urge. Just as my lips pressed against her nape, my phone rang. As I rapidly withdrew from her, she let out a forced sigh. I glanced at my phone to see it was William. I swiped the screen, answering.

You have news for me? I sharply asked.

He muttered, *They have him and are heading to the house.*

Have them meet me in the tunnel, I commanded. *And, what's their ETA?*

Okay, and approximately three hours, he quickly stated before he hung up without further conversation.

Smiling, I placed my right hand on Isabelle's hip. Her mouth was agape in shock at the moment we had shared seconds ago. I had to leave, and she needed to be able to eat in peace.

"I will leave you to finish eating without obstacles," I chuckled.

Dropping her gaze to her lap, she nodded, her chest heaving slightly. I could not tell if she was disappointed or relieved. Moving my hand to her thigh, I rested my palm on her soft skin.

"Unfortunately, I have somewhere I need to be soon, and I have to change clothes."

She nodded once again but did not speak.

"Would you like to have dinner with me tomorrow night?" I asked as I slid my hand a little further up her leg. "We will still have breakfast and lunch together too," I reassured, "but, dinner will be a bit more special."

She smiled faintly, as if she were trying to appear agreeable, but I sensed that was not the case. Something was bothering her. A part of me felt uncomfortable seeing her so distraught. Unable to tell her what was really going on was killing me, but I had to remain smart about this to protect her.

"Sure."

I leaned forward, pressing my lips against her cheek before I stood to my feet, leaving the room briskly. I did not wait around to see her reaction.

I stood in the middle of my closet, replaying the

moment with Isabelle in my head. I could not believe how close I had come to breaking, causing me to give in to her. Just as I was getting lost in my thoughts, my phone vibrated. Sliding it out of my pocket, I opened my text messages.

We are in the northeast tunnel with Jesse.

Inhaling deeply, I slid my phone into my pocket then pulled my shirt off before I grabbed my gun off a nearby table, placing it in my waistband. I gave myself one last glance in the mirror as I made my way to the elevator in the hall, taking it to the labyrinth of tunnels beneath the mansion that I used in case I needed to ever escape. I had them constructed for safety reasons.

Just as the doors opened, a dark hallway began to illuminate with a trail of lights as I moved out of the elevator. I stomped indignantly to where my men held Jesse captive. Clenching my fists in rage, I felt the pressure tinge my knuckles white.

"Heyyy Mr. Greco," Jesse smiled.

Ignoring him, I turned to William, "That was faster than I thought it would be."

He smirked.

Blaine chimed in, "He was easy to find."

"What are you guys up to?" Jesse breamed.

It was taking everything in me not to pull my gun out, ending him instantaneously, but I craved for him to suffer. Pacing before him, I took a few deep breaths gathering my thoughts before I came to a stop in front of his unsuspecting face.

"You clearly don't know why I have invited you here."

"Probably to play poker or something?" He crossed his arms as he shrugged. "You guys are in my bar all the time and sometimes play it."

I lifted my hand to my chin, glancing at William. "Actually," I corrected, my eyes trailed back to Jesse, "you have been sexually harassing your employees and I'm not really okay with that."

Quickly averting his eyes, he glanced away, scoffing. I pulled a cigarette out of my pocket, lighting it before securing it between my lips.

"But you see," I removed it from my mouth wagging it at him, "there is one woman in particular I'm rather outraged about." I returned it to my lips, inhaling deeply before blowing smoke in his face.

"I think you have me confused with someone else," he coughed, choking on the cloud. "You come into my bar all the time." Innocently, he queried, "Have you ever once seen me do anything inappropriate?"

"Listen up shitbag!" I pointed toward his face before

dropping my cigarette onto the cement floor. "I'm not stupid," I growled, closing my eyes while taking a few breaths to calm myself down. "I know what you do behind the public's back!"

His face contorted into confusion until I continued.

"You planned to sell both Tanya and Isabelle to the human trafficking ring, Stella!" I barked. "However, that will never happen as they're both safe from you now!"

He held his hands out in front of him waving them back and forth, "I was never going to sell Tanya," he poorly defended, "but, virgins are worth a lot of money and it was an opportunity I could not pass up."

Without further questioning, I drew my fist back then connected it to his mouth as hard as I could. Blood spewed from his lips as several teeth ejected from his smile, through into the air. His limp body crumbled to the concrete floor beneath him, cracking his head. I stood over his body, spitting harshly onto his cheek.

"Stand up mother fucker!"

He did not move a muscle. I never took my eyes off him.

"What's wrong?" I chuckled, "you don't have anything to say to me now?"

He began to roll back and forth, holding his jaw. "What

the fuck is wrong with you?"

"What's wrong with me?" I scoffed as I squatted down, bending over into his face, "You are!"

"What I do is my business," he spat as he stumbled to his feet.

I drew my fist back, jabbing him in the face once again. This time, instead of crumbling to the floor, he became stiff, falling backwards. His head bounced off the cement floor with several loud cracks. Blood began to pool under his limp body. Blaine handed me a small towel. I wiped my hands off before shoving it back into his arms.

"Lock him up," I commanded. "I will come visit him later."

I left them to do their job as I went to shower immediately.

Isabelle

It was nighttime and I could not sleep. I started to

wonder about the house. What did it actually look like? I could walk around but was unsure if *Sir* would be awake. So, I decided to be safe, playing by whatever rules he had. Not wanting to get into trouble, I made sure that I had the lace blindfold close by. I opened the dresser drawer looking for some proper pajamas. That is when I realized he was obsessed with both black and lace. I pulled out the most non-revealing outfit I could find in case I ran into him.

I secured the fabric over my eyes before I double checked it in the mirror. When I walked out of my bedroom, I was faced with a long, dark hallway that I had to maneuver with obscured vision. I could not properly eat. How was I going to walk alone around a house I had yet to explore?

Roughly ten minutes later, I found myself being drawn to a dimly lit room. I stepped through a large archway, peering into a room that appeared to be the kitchen. It was a lot smaller than I imagined for the size of the house. I slowly crept further in, unaware of my surroundings.

I heard the sound of a throat clearing from across the room. Jumping, I spun my body toward the sound. That is when I saw the silhouette of him standing before me, leaning on a bar while sipping a drink.

5 CONFLICTED

Isabelle

He propped on his elbow, sipping a drink. Peering down at the glass, he swirled the liquid around. From my point of view, he seemed to be in deep thought, mesmerized by the movement of the ice cubes in his glass. Without glancing up, he gulped the rest of it, before placing the cup on the bar then crossing his arms over his chest.

"What are you doing awake, Isabelle?"

I was not expecting to see him, even though I prepared myself for it. I had not planned a speech in case we bumped into one another. Appearing weak under his watchful eyes, I swallowed my fear as I attempted to mask it with a sense of confidence.

"I couldn't sleep," I mumbled, my eyes focusing on the floor. "I figured I would explore."

"And what were you hoping to find?" he mused as he reached for a nearby liquor bottle, refilling his glass.

"I thought I would start with the kitchen," I smiled, thinking I had found my way there.

He chuckled, "Well, this is not the kitchen."

"O-oh," I stuttered, "well it looks like it."

"This is the butler's pantry," he smirked. "Are you hungry?"

He set his glass on the surface before slowly approaching me. Circling me once unhurriedly, he trailed his fingers around my midsection. Coming to a stop in front of me, he placed both of his hands on my forearms. This strange man managed to awaken every sense inside my body. My nose suddenly identified the aroma of his cologne mixed with his aftershave, causing me to become weak.

To answer his question, I was hungry, but not for food any longer. I did not understand what was happening to me. I could not clearly see him, but every time he touched me, I lost control of my thoughts. Now, I was feeling a sense of peace being in his presence. I was not frightened by him, but I was scared of what was happening to me.

Dare I speak up? Dare I be brave enough to say that? I would risk him laughing at me, or possibly angering him. Maybe he loved the cat and mouse game. I am sure it made him feel powerful, in control, and feared by all women. Here I was, a virgin, but this man, Sir, awakened something hidden down in the depths of my body; a craving I could not identify.

I wondered if he knew the effect that he was having on me. I am sure he had that same influence on all women. How could he not? I started to daydream about what he might actually look like. I squinted, trying to make out more than just the general shapes and colors exhibited on him. I desired to see details. He broke me out of my trance when he withdrew his hands from my arms.

"I'm not sure your silence answers my question."

"What question?" I snapped.

He smirked, rubbing his palms slowly up and down my arms, "Are you hungry, Isabelle?"

"Oh that," I stammered, once again mesmerized by his touch. "Yes, I am a little."

"Come on then," he commanded as he took my hand in his, "I'll take you to the kitchen."

He guided me through a doorway, down a small

hallway, and into a larger room. Pulling a stool back away from the kitchen island, he assisted me as I perched on top of it. I shivered as his fingertips grazed my thighs. Leaning forward, he pressed his lips next to my ear.

"You should maybe learn your way around soon," he whispered.

Without waiting for a reply, he strode around to the other side of the island. I sighed, running my palms up and down my forearms, trying to rid my body of the goosebumps. I was finally able to tame them. Attempting to prop my elbows on the countertop, I bumped one of them, cracking it against the side of the island. I fumbled for a moment, before I finally settled.

"I really wish I could take this off," I mumbled.

"Hmm," he mused as he pulled a pot out of a cabinet.

"I feel like I'm playing pin the tail on the donkey with everything I try to do," I whined, rubbing my elbow.

He set the pan on the gas burner, laughing. Turning around, he leaned on the island across from me with his palms gripping the edge. "You're not supposed to be cute," he teased.

Confused, I folded my arms over my chest, "What do you mean by that?"

"You just make it hard to focus on things," his tone

sounded almost apologetic.

Reality hit me and I dropped my face into my hands, groaning, "Did you have to remind me?"

Valentino

Within an instant, I turned back to the stove, taking a deep breath. I straightened the pan then strode to the refrigerator. Staring into it, I waited for an idea to come to me, but it did not. I knew how to cook, despite what some people assumed about a wealthy, Italian bachelor. Cooking was something that was expected in my home growing up. However, everything I knew how to make would take a lot of preparation. It was late and making anything I knew how to make was not an option at the moment. I spun to her, searching for ideas, any idea. I hoped for an answer.

"What would you like me to make you?"

Shrugging, she mumbled under her breath, "I don't know."

Something was wrong. I was not sure if I had done something or if she truly did not know what she wanted to eat. It seemed as if her gaze became a blank stare. That is when I knew something was definitely not right with her. After a few moments, I opened my mouth to reply, but before I could, she did instead.

"Actually, I think I just want to go to bed," she sighed.

Confused, I nodded, realizing the gravity of our current situation had resurfaced. I could tell from the expression on her masked face that the arrangement was all beginning to settle into her mind. I had seen that look before. I nodded, quickly remembering that she could not clearly see me. Sauntering to her, I ran my fingertips on the surface of the island before I reached her. Resting my hand on top of hers, I attempted to comfort her, but she did not smile. She remained still, staring into an abyss.

"I will take you back to your room."

She was silent as I took her hand in mine, guiding her back to her own bedroom. She was tense. I heard a sniffle from her a few times and hoped she was not crying. The thought of her sobbing bothered me. I knew the situation was not ideal to her. I was torn. The idea of being with her made me crazy, but things were complicated.

Having a masked woman in my home was no strange occurrence for me. Nevertheless, they never lived with me. They were brought to me when I wanted them. They arrived at my mansion blindfolded; completely. There was no lace or light to shine through the fabric. The women were used for my enjoyment then thrown out when I got bored with them. They never knew who I was, but I also never bothered to know them. The women were clean and beautiful which was all I cared about.

They were ordered not to speak to me unless spoken to, with one exception. They were only allowed to communicate with me during sex. My bedroom? No. I had a room that I took them to. The only woman who would ever be worthy of my bedroom, is the one I want more with than just a physical relationship. At this point in my life, I was not sure I would ever want that, considering the mental battle taking place in my mind right now.

When we entered Isabelle's room, she pulled away from my touch, slowly trudging into her bathroom. I did not know what to say as I stood just inside the doorway of her room. It was clear she did not want to have any communication with me at the moment.

"Goodnight, Isabelle."

She ignored me, closing the bathroom door. Sighing, I stepped backwards into the hallway, closing her doors. Leaning against the wall, I exhaled, sliding my hands into my pockets as I stared at the ceiling.

What had I gotten myself into? How was I supposed to protect her when I wanted to touch her this badly? I barely knew this girl, right? Wrong. There was something much deeper only my top three guys knew about. Tanya did not even know yet.

I did not give a damn about Isabelle's precious virginity. Yes, it was attractive to me that she was not a whore like all the others, but that was not why she was in my home. I wish it had not been this way; the lies, the masks, the fake American accent, everything. To say that I was frustrated was an understatement. She did not deserve to live a life under a veil. I made a promise though, so I would need to keep it.

Trudging into my bathroom, I turned the water on, almost as hot as it could go. I slipped my clothes off, sinking down into the tub, hoping it would instantly relax me and wash away my stress. I ran my fingers through my hair then splashed my face trying to rid myself of the nightmare I was now trapped in. What did I agree to? Laying my head back, I closed my eyes recalling the moment the agreement was made. It was a year ago. I was in Spain on a business trip.

I was sitting in a coffee shop, minding my own business when a slightly older gentleman approached me. At first, I did not look up to see who it was until he spoke.

"Mr. Greco?" he asked.

I slowly peeled my eyes away from my newspaper, peering up at the man. "Can I help you?" I inquired, tilting my head.

Moments later, I realized who was standing before me as he removed his sunglasses for a moment. The man was Felipe Ayala, one of Europe's most feared drug lords and weapons experts. In fact, I had bought some of my firearms from his family in the past, but our dealings never drifted beyond that. I was shocked that he bothered to approach me. I was even more shocked that he appeared nervous. Last I knew of him, Felipe was not nervous about anything. He thrived on intimidating people.

"Can I speak to you for a moment in private?" he hissed, his eyes darting around the room as if he suspected he was being followed.

I was skeptical, but I did not want to alarm him. I also would not play whatever game he was about to initiate. He was known for toying with his prey.

"You may speak here," I mumbled, lighting a cigarette.

He sat down on the couch next to me then leaned forward, propping his elbows on his knees as he spoke. "Mr. Greco, my name is Felipe," he sneered.

Who did not know who he was? Everyone did! He continued in a tense whisper while he glanced around. I nodded, acknowledging but was annoyed that he acted as if I had no clue who he was.

"I have people after me and I need to see to it that should something happen to me, my daughter is looked after," he blurted rapidly under his breath.

I took a drag of my cigarette, using a moment to process his request. I smirked, "And I look like a fucking babysitter to you?"

I did not allow him to intimidate me which took him by surprise. He appeared to be rewinding the words in his head with a serious expression before the corners of his lips curled up into an evil grin. He folded his hands together, locking his fingers as he glared into my eyes with authority.

"Let me start over as we are not on the same page," he declared. "My name is Felipe Ayala."

I sarcastically contorted my face into disbelief, my mouth gaping open. "The Felipe Ayala?" I smirked, glancing away as I took another drag of my cigarette.

He squinted as he pulled a cigar from his jacket pocket, lighting it. "Mr. Greco, there is no need to be an asshole." Taking a long puff of his smoke, he scolded, "We are not enemies, but I need your help because you're the only one who can actually assist me."

I pointed my cigarette at him, grinning as I wagged it in his direction. "I think you have me confused with someone else."

I stood to walk away, but he reached up, grabbing my wrist. My gaze snapped to his chubby fingers tightly wrapped around my arm. Rolling my eyes, I jerked away from him as I leaned over, snuffing my cigarette out in the ashtray on the table.

"Please, sit," he ordered in a menacing tone.

Normally, I became enraged when someone like him touched me, but I chose not to make a scene. I sat down, tucking my bottom lip between my teeth as I leaned back, resting my arm on the back of the couch. He pulled a black folder out of his bag, dropping it in on the table before me. I proceeded to open it, flipping through the pages while scanning over the information I was given. I closed it, trying to hand it over to him, but he crossed his arms over his chest.

"Why do I need to watch your daughter," I interrogated, "and why is someone after you?"

He slightly raised his hands, gesturing for me to keep the folder. "Turn to page ten," he instructed.

I thumbed through the pages until I came to one with photos in a plastic pocket. I angled my head as my eyes fell on a photo of a young woman with light brown hair and sapphire blue eyes. Her sun kissed skin was flawless, and a radiant smile caught my attention immediately.

"What's this?" I asked, exhaling.

"That's my daughter, Isabelle," he gushed proudly, shifting in his seat.

I looked through the photos one by one, making mental notes of how stunning she was. Now, I was more curious about why he was asking me of all people. I was a well-established businessman, but I was in no way a good guy. The last place she needed to be, was under my watch and protection. She was trouble. I could sense it. Or maybe it was I who was trouble. Either way, this was a terrible idea.

"Why you?" he chuckled as if he read my mind.

Still eyeing at her photos, I became intrigued by one in

particular that was a close up of her lips. "Yeah, why me?" I sighed, raising my eyes to his.

"I know who you are," he leaned forward, moving closer to me on the couch. "I know what you do, and I know what you do when no one is looking," he insinuated with a smirk. "You are the only one strong enough to keep her safe, Valentino."

Growing impatient, I became irritable with him, but I let him speak. I slipped another cigarette out of its pack, lighting it. Taking long, slow drags, I glanced down at her face once again then gently closed the folder, sliding it away from my body to the middle of the table.

"I know you will not let anything happen to her," he concluded.

Shaking my head, I roared with laughter, "You don't know me at all."

"Yeah, but I have a lot of people after me," he added. "They're evil people, and they will be after her next." He sighed, raising his hand to his forehead, "I just want her to be kept safe for the time being."

I nodded, rolling my eyes.

"I am not asking for anything more or anything less," he shifted his weight on the couch then picked up a briefcase. "I will give you fifteen million dollars in cash to watch her."

I smirked, "Twenty, and I want the remaining five by

tonight," I sneered as I grabbed the briefcase out of his hands, placing it next to my leg on the floor.

"Done," he confirmed as he held out his hand to shake mine.

After we exchanged a handshake, he stood to his feet, peering down at me in a menacing manner. I ignored him, staring ahead while puffing on my cigarette. He cleared his throat, but I did not turn to face him.

"There is one more condition," he murmured.

I smirked, slowly lifting my gaze to his, but did not speak. Instead, I waited for him to continue, but he glared down at me. I was not sure if he was using the silent treatment as a power tactic, but it was not working. I rolled my eyes, looking out the window.

"You are a very handsome man," he observed. "She is not to know you are protecting her because she is naive and you're so...you."

Wrinkling my nose, I snapped my head up and I snorted, "You're kidding right?"

"She is very innocent," he glowered, "and should never be caught up in your messed-up life."

At least we agreed on something. I did not want anyone involved in my life on any level. I did not respond verbally but only nodded that I understood before he walked away.

Three weeks later, my men and I were practically stalking

Isabelle. I wanted to watch her from a distance. Then, when people started to close in on her, her boss started with his nonsense. I knew it was time to move her into my home so I could watch her closely. The only thing was, that I could not just kidnap her. The masquerade ball came at a perfect time for me to make my move and execute my plan with the help of a few others.

During the time I was watching her, I started to take a liking to her, but I was definitely fighting it. Not only were we guarding her, we were watching her boss. The human trafficking ring called Stella, was run by some of her father's associates or rivals. We had not figured that out yet.

If you met Isabelle, you would never in a million years think she came from a family like that, but the reality is, little innocent Isabelle, was the daughter of one of the world's most dangerous men. He was wanted by many other gangs, the CIA, FBI, and God knows who else. At this point, I had pretty much agreed to put a target on my back.

I stood up in the bathtub, drying myself off then marched to my closet, getting ready for bed. As I was getting dressed, I realized that she had no idea what her father did. She was essentially broke while he was sitting on millions of dollars. She was just trying to earn an honest living.

It was hard to fight back the urge to like her. I had

originally wanted no part of her life but all that time watching her, I grew to want her so much that I could tell you so many things if I were asked. I felt like I knew her inside and out by now.

    Picking my phone up off a nearby table, I unlocked the screen, dialing my assistant.

    Hello Mr. Greco, she promptly answered.

    I will be out of the office for a few days and working from home. I had a personal matter come up, I informed her.

    Not waiting for a reply, I hung up my phone then walked into my bedroom, collapsing onto my bed.

Isabelle

    I woke up the next morning and reached over to my nightstand. There was a note resting under my phone. Rubbing the sleep out of my eyes, I picked it up and read it:

> *Meet me for breakfast on the back patio. Your outfit is already waiting for you on the sofa.*
>
> *Love, V*

So, his name starts with a V, I thought. I would have to remember to ask him about that later. I strode over to the couch discovering an airy, white sundress with matching sandals laid out across the arm for me. Of course, there was the veil next to it. He did not even think to give me a white one that matched?

Giggling at the thought, I waltzed into the bathroom to style my hair and apply makeup before putting on the dress and veil. I was unsure why I bothered applying my eye makeup, but I knew I would not feel complete unless I did. Navigating through the house, I stumbled a few times over various pieces of furniture before a staff member came to my rescue. She discovered me aimlessly wandering around downstairs and kindly asked me if she could assist me. I was pleased when she guided me to the back patio.

The man, V, was seated at a round bistro table, dressed in a navy blue suit, or, so I thought. I was able to see a little more outside as the sunlight brightened him a bit better. He peeked up to face me as he stirred, from what smelled like, a cup of coffee.

"Isabelle, please sit," he grinned, motioning toward the table with his free hand.

A man appeared out of nowhere, pulling my chair out from the table for me. Nodding, I silently thanked him as I sat down. He immediately placed a napkin in my lap and I instantly folded my hands over it, nervously locking my fingers together in my lap. A woman then arrived, pouring coffee and orange juice into the glasses before me.

"Are you going to be able to drink those or should I sit closer and help you?" V teased.

I giggled, "Hush."

He lifted his hand into the air. Promptly, his staff disappeared out of view, leaving us alone. He tilted his head, studying me as I awkwardly shifted my weight in the chair. I had great table manners in general, but when you are blindfolded before a man who paid one million dollars for you, manners are the least of your concerns.

"Breakfast shouldn't be long."

I nodded.

He took a sip of his coffee then folded the newspaper, placing it to the side of the table out of the way. "How did you sleep?"

Lifting my glass of orange juice, I placed it to my mouth speaking with the rim to my lips, "I slept fine but I'm still feeling weird about being here."

I quickly realized I probably should not have said that when he became incredibly still and silent. If it were not for the birds chirping, I would have been able to hear a pin drop. I swiftly lowered my eyes, slowly sipping my juice once again.

"You're unhappy here," he mumbled. "Have I not been nice enough to you?"

"It's not about that," I sighed.

I tried to find words that would not further insult him because the truth was, he had been nice. He did not try to force me into anything like I expected. Weighing my words carefully, I debated if I should digress or continue. I felt him glaring at me, causing me to feel intimidated.

"I just hate wearing this thing," I admitted. "I know that's not what you want to hear, and yes, you have been nice to me." Fidgeting with my fingers in my lap beneath the table, I prudently chose my words as I continued. "I just feel so lonely because I have no friends or family here and I have to walk around in this thing."

Gesturing to my black, lace veil, I lowered my head in shame. He cleared his throat, altering his position in his seat. He appeared to be tense based on his demeanor, but he did not snap at me or yell. Instead, he audibly exhaled as I felt tears welling up in my eyes.

"I'm sorry," I apologized, sniffling. "I don't want to ruin breakfast, but I just didn't want to lie to you."

"Then don't," he glowered. "It's here now."

He turned his attention to the staff, lifting his hand to signal his approval for approaching the table with our food. Pursing his lips, he nodded to them as they placed our food in front of us. I did not need full vision to realize that he was bothered. As we made small talk, he informed me that he was taking a few days off to spend time with me. He was not rude or short, but I could tell he was trying to find the right words to say so that did not sound brute.

When we finished eating, he stood, sauntering to my side of the table. Taking my hand in his, he softly pressed his lips to my skin before he smiled. He gently tugged on my hand, helping me to my feet. Tilting my head, I tried to guess what game he was now playing with me as I tried my best to peer into his eyes.

"Isabelle, take a walk with me," he exhorted with a serious tone.

Silently, we strolled the estate gardens, following along a stone path. He placed his hand on my lower back, guiding me as the paths crossed and broke off into different routes. A strong aroma of flowers filled the air, the breeze swaying around us, caused me to deeply inhale the delightful scent. I stumbled on a water hose stretched across the stones, but he reached out, grabbing my arm before I fell to the ground. We shared a laugh as I smoothed my dress, fighting back embarrassment.

"Just a little farther," he reassured me.

A few moments later, we came to a stop in an open area near a fountain. He placed his body behind mine, curling his fingertips on my hips, gently pulling me back into him. A shiver inched up my spine the minute he caressed me. A small gust of cool wind blew against us, causing me to let out a small gasp.

"Don't move," he warned, leaning forward as he whispered into my ear.

I felt his hands leave my hips, and he trailed his fingertips up my sides over my shoulders. He came to a stop on the back of my head. Suddenly, I felt my veil become loose as he untied it and delicately pulled it away from my face.

Audibly, I sighed in awe as I was faced with a breathtaking, colorful view of the gardens surrounding us, with his mansion in the background. I found myself beaming, forgetting why I was here. The garden boasted a variety of bushes and every sort of flower imaginable that I could see, for what seemed like miles.

   Tucking my bottom lip between my teeth, I contemplated turning around, exposing his true identity. As if he could read my mind, he slowly snaked his hands around my waist, locking his fingers in front of my stomach.

6 THE PLAN

Isabelle

He asked as he wrapped his hands around my waist, "What do you think?"

I was speechless. Never in my life had I ever been faced with something so incredible. An entirely new world had been opened before my eyes. Peering around the grounds of the mansion, I absorbed every small detail that I could. Inhaling deeply, I closed my eyes. It was then I caught the scent of his cologne once again. I was in sensory overload, rendering me speechless with a carnal desire.

"Thank you," I muttered, unable to say much more for fear of humiliation.

Trailing his fingertips softly up and down my arms, he leaned forward, pressing his lips next to my ear.

"Mmhmm, I felt like this might help you adjust a bit more."

"I don't know what to say," I choked. "I'm kind of speechless, I'm sorry."

"I will make a deal with you," he conveyed, holding the veil out in front of me.

Curiously, I tilted my head, staring straight ahead, not daring to turn around.

"If you promise to only remove this when you are outside or I am not home," he reasoned, "I will let you have a little more freedom here than normal."

A tear rolled down my cheek when he said the word, *Freedom*. I began to repeat the word in my head, sighing as it began to set it. It was hard to swallow, but I had to face it. As much as I did not want to admit it, I was unquestionably a prisoner to a man who paid for my body but did not use it.

"What good is a new suit if you purchase it and never wear it?" I challenged him without turning to face him or realizing what had just slipped from my lips.

At this point, I was unsure that I even wanted to see his real face. It is like meeting someone online. You never know what will happen when you are finally face to face with that person. I was undoubtedly in the same position.

What if I saw him and he was nothing like I imagined by his silhouette and scent? What if the man taking my virginity was hideous, causing me to cringe and recoil at his touch? What if the man behind me was in fact sent from heaven and I instantly fell in love with his flawless face?

Before I could think more about it, he gently took my veil from me, placing it back around my head then tying it. He exhaled softly, as if he could read my mind. Caressing my arms, he slowly turned me to face him, but still, I could not focus very well on his appearance.

"What are you saying Isabelle?"

I sighed, "I guess what I mean is--."

Pausing, I leaned my head a bit, trying to squint. It was useless to try to make out his face. I was only able to see basic shapes. I could tell his lips were curled into a slight smile, but he remained silent as if he did not want me to know.

"Why keep me if you don't intend to use me?" I finally continued.

He lightly trailed his fingers across my shoulder, tenderly pulling my dress strap down my arm.

"Is that what you want?"

I inhaled sharply at his question, unable to move an

inch as I gulped.

"You want me to use you like I did the others?" he persisted, taunting me.

Rocking on my heels, I slowly licked my lips, feeling my cheeks warm. "That's not what I mean," I squeaked.

Pulling me into his body, he leaned his head forward, resting his mouth on the nape of my neck. I closed my eyes tightly, failing any attempt to control my breathing. He was playing with me and he knew it. Pursing his lips, he gently placed a kiss on my sensitive skin.

"Then what exactly are you saying?" he whispered.

"I'm not entirely sure to be honest," I admitted in a small mumble before declaring confidently, "but I will work off every penny that you paid for me."

He guffawed, sliding the strap to my dress back up on top of my shoulder. Turning away from me, he placed his hands in his pockets as he looked out at his estate grounds. He appeared in deep thought. Suddenly, he spun back to me, running his hand across his brow in frustration. I rested my fists on my hips, waiting for him to break the silence.

"Do you know how many lifetimes you'd have to work to pay me back for that?" he mused.

Averting my eyes, I folded my arms across my stomach,

attempting to suppress the nervousness. "I'm willing to try, Sir."

Taking two rapid strides over to me, he closed the gap between our bodies. Leaning near my lips he hissed, "I changed my mind. Do not call me that anymore unless you want me to fuck you."

He had transformed from an ostensibly gentle man to authoritative in an instant. I lifted my head up toward the sky, closing my eyes. My breathing pattern began to shift, becoming shallower while my face became hot as my entire body started to tingle at his words.

He held both of my arms in his palms, slowly running his fingertips up to the straps on my dress. Hooking his finger under both simultaneously, a breath escaped his lips. He began to slide them off the edges of my shoulders while leaning forward closer to my lips.

"Isabelle," he muttered.

"Hmm?" I hummed in a trance.

Suddenly he pulled away, sliding his hands into his pockets as he took a few steps back. I yearned for him to close the gap between our bodies. Now, I was confused if I was scared to be here or beginning to lose whatever game he was playing.

"We should go inside," he urged as he peered over my shoulder at someone.

"Actually," I interjected, "I would like to stay out here for a moment if you don't mind." I wanted time alone.

"Sure," he nodded agreeably. "When you're ready just come back inside, but I will leave someone to help you, should you require assistance."

"Okay," I mumbled, averting my eyes to several other blurry figures nearby.

"What's wrong?" he inquired as he brought his hand to his chin in thought.

"Can you please have your security detail go inside as well?" I requested as nicely as my tone would allow.

"I'm sorry I cannot do that," he declined, "but I will have them hang back a little more."

I nodded, sighing, "Fine."

I watched as he walked away, joining two of the four men. They disappeared as they rounded a corner in the distance, and I finally felt like I could breathe. I untied my veil, tossing it on the ground then crumbled next to it. Uncertainty washed over me as I placed my hand on my chest, discovering my rapid heartbeat. Lying back in the grass next to the path, I looked toward the sky, processing the occurrences this morning.

He had flirted with me, but he also stopped himself before he took it to the point of no return. Why had he not tried to sleep with me? Why was he acting strange with me? It was not that I wanted him to, but he had turned my brain to mush moments ago with his scent, his words, and his touch.

I sorted some things in my mind as I closed my eyes, soaking in the rays of sunlight. It was clear that this mysterious man had some form of power over me. I did not mean some silly contract. Could it be that he was beginning to have a hold on me? Why did I feel somewhat connected to him? Was he possibly someone I knew?

Rising to my feet, I began to sway in the breeze, humming my favorite song as a small gust of wind blew passed me. For a moment I actually felt free. I twirled around slowly, absorbing every part of the garden. This place was purely magnificent which made me wish even more that I were here under other circumstances.

Valentino

I strode into my house, sprinting up the stairs. The moment I entered my bedroom, I immediately closed the doors behind me then tossed my jacket onto the bed. I paced my room, running my fingers through my hair in frustration before my eyes focused on the window. It overlooked the garden where I had left her, so I automatically gravitated to it.

Leaning on the wall by the window, I watched as she lied down in the grass. I observed her, wondering what was on her mind. She looked so peaceful without her covering on. Just as I began to lose myself in my own tormenting thoughts, she stood. Turning circles, she watched the sky. I enjoyed seeing her this way.

I felt like a jerk for having to keep her eyes constantly concealed, but I could not risk the price she would pay if she saw me. I was not worried about myself. I was only worried about her. She seemed so carefree out there, dancing while enjoying her time alone in the fresh air. Just as I found myself becoming entranced in her movements, there was a knock on the bedroom door. I was pulled away from the spell she had placed on me.

"Come in!"

William casually strolled in, then leaned on the wall next to me. "What are you loo--," he asked, his sentence falling short as his eyes discovered her. He chuckled, "Oh."

I glanced at him swiftly turning my attention back to her, "Tell me something, please."

He covered his mouth with his hand to hide a smile. "What's that?"

I snapped my head toward him, glaring, before marching toward the middle of my room. I paced, trying to talk myself out of what was clearly happening. I turned back to face William, realizing that he was laughing at me again.

"What if I just let her walk around with nothing?" I called out, walking into my closet to change.

He yelled in return, "I mean, isn't that what they've all done before her?"

I poked my head out of the closet door, peering into the bedroom at him. "What do you mean?" I asked before disappearing into the closet once again.

I rapidly changed then walked out while fastening my jeans. I fell lazily into a chair across from my bed. He sat on the middle of my bed, leaning back, propping on his elbows.

"The girls before her," he snorted. "They walked around naked."

"In one room," I corrected, "not around the house." Sighing, I processed what he had meant, before continuing, "They were not naked," I reminded. "They never ever stayed over. They--."

"Yes yes," he interrupted, "Wore the infamous Valentino Greco blindfold." He drew an arch shape in the air with his hands.

"Liam," I groaned, "I don't trust myself with her." I buried my head in my hand, confessing to him.

"You made her father a promise," he recalled, "You're the one who promised to keep her safe."

"For money!" I argued sharply.

He stood up crossing his arms over his chest. "Bullshit Val!" he barked. "You took one look at her and jumped at the opportunity to be anywhere near her that you could."

Without saying a word, I held out my hand. Reading my mind, he placed a cigarette and lighter in it. We had been friends for a long time. He could practically read my thoughts at all times. I lit it then tossed the lighter back to him. He caught it then slid it into his pocket.

"For months and months, we have followed one woman," he continued. "One woman you refuse to get to know because you're scared."

"I'm not scared of him," I snapped before taking a long drag of my cigarette.

"Who said anything about him?" he smirked. "Her."

I strode to the window again leaning on the side of the frame, watching her walk through the rows of flowers, sniffing them as I continued to smoke. She was captivating. It was hard to admit to anyone how badly I wanted Isabelle, but inside my head, I knew how much I craved for her to be mine.

"None of us are stupid, Valentino," he laughed. "We've seen the way you look at her. Somewhere in the time we were all watching her, you started to like her."

I silently listened, smoking my cigarette.

"You know everything about her," he stated the obvious. "It became less of a job and more of an attraction," he concluded with a snicker, "or, maybe and addiction."

I sighed, knowing he was right I was not about to deny it to my best friend. He knew me better than anyone on this earth and was probably the only one. He was also the only one that I allowed to speak to me the way he did. If anyone else had spoken to me like that, they would have been laying in a pool of blood beneath my feet.

"She's seen me," I grumbled. "At the bar, then when she returned from the park after a jog, she saw me," I sighed, "the real me."

"What do you mean?" he exhaled.

Lifting my hand to my chin, I studied her every move outside once again. "She's heard this accent." I was speaking in my native Italian accent as I did when no guests were in the home.

"Go talk to her," he suggested, leaving me with those

words as he exited, closing the doors on his way out.

"Fucking shit," I mumbled to myself, running my fingers through my hair in frustration.

I promised I would not allow her to know who I was. She was safer this way anyway, but I decided to show her who I was without her seeing me. It would be tricky to pull off, but I was willing to try. I needed some assistance from some of my staff, so I lifted my watch to my mouth.

Joseph, please bring Miss Ayala to my office in thirty minutes, I ordered.

I had an idea. Making a few phone calls before stepping into my closet, I made several arrangements, hoping they would all follow through. I grabbed a shirt off a hanger, sliding it over my head as I walked out of my room. Rehearsing my speech in my mind, I made my way downstairs.

I sat in a Bergère chair in the corner of my office waiting for Isabelle to join me. Tugging on my earlobe, I pondered how this would ever work, but I knew it had to be done. I lost myself in different scenarios when she was escorted in.

She slowly meandered into the room, searching for any sign of movement. I chuckled to myself watching her try to locate me. Once the doors were closed and we were alone, I cleared my throat, indicating my whereabouts. She snapped her head toward me, mildly blushing with pursed lips.

"Sit," I gestured to the chair across from me.

She instantly took a seat, crossing her ankles as she placed her hands in her lap. "Yes Sir?" she asked.

I paused, tucking my bottom lip between my teeth at the sound of her calling me Sir. It never affected me before, but the tone in her voice mixed with her accent, almost sent me over the edge. I slowly exhaled, trying to settle myself before I continued, proposing a deal I hoped did not backfire.

"I want to make a deal with you," I announced.

"More contracts?" she snorted then instantaneously clasped her hands over her mouth in mortification.

"No more contracts," I snickered, "but this will require us to learn to trust each other."

She folded her arms across her midsection, smiling, "I'm listening."

"I will set you free," I murmured, "however, there will be rules."

I paused, giving her time to process my words, but she blankly stared ahead at me, giving me no indication that she understood me. I shifted my weight in the chair, hoping my movement would trigger her to respond in any way.

Rolling her bottom lip through her teeth, she finally

confirmed, "So, a catch?"

"Yes, the rules are that you will have to have twenty-four-hour security with you," I explained. "You cannot leave your apartment unless it's approved first. You will have to text or call me and check in three times a day." I took a deep breath before continuing, "You may not give anyone what belongs to me, per our contract. You will have to return to me on the weekends to spend time with me. If you can follow these rules, I will let you go."

"And what about the money you paid for me?" she challenged.

"Don't worry about it" I dismissed, waving my hand at her.

She tilted her head to show me her eyes were calling my bluff, but she remained silent.

"Isabelle," I sighed, running my fingers through my hair, "I believe you will come back to me, so I'm not worried about it."

She giggled, "What makes you so confident about this?"

"Call it intuition I guess," I muttered, licking my bottom lip.

She sat back in her chair, peering around the room as if she were searching for something, but suddenly fixated her gaze on mine. It almost felt for a moment as if she discovered something. Rolling my eyes, I shifted in my seat, lacing my fingers together as I waited for her to reply.

"You're wrong you know," she desperately tried to convince me she would not return.

I smirked, leaning my elbow on the arm rest.

She leaned forward, placing her hands on her hips. "I won't come back to you," she snapped. "I might even decide to run away."

I shook my head, chuckling at her. She reminded me of an angry juvenile corn snake; small and adorable warning strikes, wanting to appear tough, meanwhile inflicting no damage. She sighed, shaking her head. She stood to her feet, taking a few steps away from the chair. I casually stood as well, sliding my hands into my pockets.

"I'll have Joseph take you home tomorrow," I asserted.

Walking toward the exit, I could see that she was in deep thought, possibly questioning my motives. Such a big deal was made about the contract, that I was sure she was wondering her fate at this point. Just as she got to the door, she whipped around, placing her hands on her hips.

"Wait! I don't even have a home to go back to do I?" she hissed. "That is your plan to keep me here isn't it?"

"I made some calls," I chuckled.

She slanted her head, unsure if I was finished speaking. I was going to leave it and say no more, but I did not want to play a game with her at the moment. I knew that soon enough, I would be playing the ultimate game with her, so I decided to spare her for the time being.

"What do you mean?" she questioned me, dropping her hands to her side while awkwardly stroking her forearm.

"You have a new home," I affirmed. "Your furniture will be delivered tomorrow afternoon."

Folding her arms over her chest, she pursed her lips, staring at me through her black lace. I pressed a button on my watch. Instantly, one of my bodyguards entered the room. Smirking, I waved my hand, dismissing her, motioning for her to be taken from my office. Not another word was said from either of us, as she was quietly escorted back to her room.

Let the game begin.

Isabelle

As I hiked to my room, I thought about what he said. His offer sounded way too good to be true. Falling back onto my bed, I realized I may be in disbelief. Was he truly going to set me free? Something about this seemed very bizarre to me. The man just paid an outstanding amount of money for my virginity, yet he was not even going to bother taking it before he let me go.

Why was I so worried about it anyway? Free was what I wanted, yes? He did show me kindness while I was here, but I did not want to live my entire life under these conditions. I realized that I was only going to be half free. He did not tear up our contract, so I was still technically bound to him. I spent the rest of my day reading until it was time for dinner.

I decided to make the most of dinner, dressing in a formal, silver, floor length strapless gown with a thigh length split on the right side. I paired it with stilettos and nice jewelry he had stocked in my room. Was I thinking about taunting him? Something seemed very strange to me causing me to want to know more. Maybe breaking down walls was what I needed to do. At the very least, my outfit could pose as a distraction causing him to let his guard down.

I stalked down the long hallway to the elevator. I placed the veil on my eyes, a smile spreading across my face just as the doors to the bottom floor opened. I made my way to the kitchen but was stopped by a man before I arrived.

"This way, Miss," the butler commented, gesturing in the other direction.

Taking my arm gently in his fingertips, he guided me to a large dining room where Sir was waiting for me to arrive. Nodding their heads in exchange, the butler quickly disappeared, leaving me alone in the room with the, *still* strange man. I gulped.

Peering around the room, I noticed that it was dimly lit with an array of lighted candles and flower centerpieces on the table. The lengthy table sat maybe twelve people and stretched out across a long rug. Sizeable canvas artwork donned the walls throughout the room, giving it a royal appearance.

My eyes trailed over the room once more, then found the man. He stood behind my chair, holding it out for me, resting his hand on the top. I took a few steps toward him as he reached out, taking my hand in his.

"Are you ready?" he grinned.

"What?" I choked, withdrawing my hand.

He chuckled, "For dinner, Isabelle."

"Oh," I sighed, "yes, I am starving actually."

"Me too," he muttered.

I could tell his gaze was raking over my body. For once, I was relaxed with his eyes on me. Normally something would happen to make me tense up but at this very moment, knowing I would be somewhat free tomorrow, I was happy. Once he settled my chair under the table, he placed a napkin in my lap then took a seat next to me. Tilting my head ever so slightly, I watched him get comfortable as he never took his eyes off me.

"Why are you sitting next to me?"

"I'm sorry?" he questioned.

"Usually when you see a table this long," I explained, "the people sit at opposite ends."

Smirking, he lifted his hand, signaling for his staff to approach from the edges of the room. They had been so still before that I did not notice them until now.

"You watch too many movies," he teased as one of his staff poured us both glasses of red wine.

The moment they left the room, the atmosphere changed. Leaning back in his seat, he propped his elbow on the arm rest, studying me. He seemed more relaxed as well. I silently attempted to control my breathing but started to become nervous. Smirking, he leaned forward, lifting his wine glass into the air and gesturing to me. I reciprocated, holding mine in front of me.

"From lust, to trust, and then to us," he smiled, lightly

tapping his glass on mine.

What a strange toast that was. Surely, I was reading into it. But when there's wine, I would probably drink no matter what the toast is about. Just as I opened my mouth to speak, the staff delivered the food to the table, arranging it in front of us.

They took their posts near the doors, but the man had another plan. Raising his hand once again, he signaled for them to exit the room, leaving us to dine in privacy. I studied the setting in front of me, trying to get familiar with the food and utensils before I attempted to put anything close to my face.

He initiated general conversation with me throughout the meal, but nothing was discussed further about the earlier encounter. I tried to remain agreeable throughout, becoming slightly nervous when my nose caught the scent of his cologne traveling through the air. When we were finished, he placed his hand on top of mine, silently assisting me out of my chair.

Taking my hand in his, he led me through the house to a bedroom. Closing the door behind us, he pulled me into his body, snaking his arms around my waist. I was having trouble standing the minute he touched me, feeling like I would lose my balance and faint any second. It was in that moment, that I knew I would fail miserably when it finally came time to give myself to him.

He tilted forward, resting his lips next to my ear, whispering, "I wish I could have you now."

Swallowing hard, I attempted to hide my emotions as his words penetrated the depths of my soul. I found myself unable to rid my fixation on the way he smelled, spoke, and touched me. Before I could gain confidence to back away, he cupped my face in his hands, pressing lips to mine. His kiss was small and soft, but effective on my body. Without warning he peeled himself away, his breathing shallow.

Slightly protesting, I nervously exhaled, "You're just going to stop?"

He trailed his fingers over my shoulder, brushing the hair off my neck. "I want you to want it, without me taking it," he murmured.

I sighed, averting my eyes to the floor.

"I believe you'll be ready sooner than you think," he smirked as he took my hand, guiding me back to my bedroom.

I took a long, hot bath, but as I soaked, all I could think about was him. I did not realize it, but I had started to quietly massage the inside of my thighs with my eyes closed. I imagined his lips as I moved my other hand up to my smooth slit. Running my middle finger up the soft middle, I found my button. I massaged my sweet spot until I erupted intensely. Moaning incredibly loud, I hoped he was unable to hear me. I laid in the water for a while to regain my sanity before I went to bed.

Morning came too soon. I was convincing myself this was a good thing. No more lace veil. Sir had slipped out of the house early for work today, so I did not get to tell him goodbye before we left for the city. I was informed though, that I would see him again Friday. Remembering that I still had his number in my phone, I sat in the back seat, hovering my finger over his number. Pressing the *Power* button, I slid the phone into my bag and folded my hands over it. He made sure that I knew I could still call and text him any time I wanted, aside from my check in times.

Before I had time to think much more, time had passed, and we had arrived at my new apartment. It was in the same building as my old apartment, but on the highest floor. He had moved me into the penthouse.

I stood frozen in the living room, peering around at the size. I was soaking it all in, unsure what to think right now. I had two security guards in my residence, one of who was in charge. None of my furniture had arrived yet, so I slipped on my running clothes. I walked into the living room, looking at the men as they curiously watched me.

"Do you guys have any running attire?"

Joseph, my lead bodyguard, nodded without speaking.

"Good," I beamed. "I would like to go running."

"Excuse me, Miss?" he cleared his throat.

"Get changed, please," I suggested playfully.

I truly did want to go running, but knew I was not allowed to go alone so my only option was making them go. After everyone was ready, we headed out of the building, stopping. I glanced around, remembering the last time I was here then rolled my eyes. My life had drastically changed.

I took my phone out of my pocket, pulling up my favorite fitness playlist. As I placed my wireless speakers in my ear, I found myself scrolling over to my messages. Nothing. Should I text him just to say hi? I thumbed over his name, sighing while deciding to check in.

Good morning Sir ;)

I slid my phone back in my pocket then my security detail and I went through the park. We ran, we jogged, and we walked four miles. It felt like it had been a while since I went running. The freedom I had felt great, so I decided to extend it for just today.

We stopped to take a breath when we were finished. Joseph passed me a water bottle. I thanked both of the bodyguards for being good sports and running with me.

Neither of them seemed out of breath whatsoever, but I had been slacking in my routine lately.

We strode to the street, getting ready to cross. I looked down, noticing my shoe was untied. I watched my feet all the way across the crosswalk, being careful not to fall. When we got to the other side, I bumped into someone.

"Oh, I'm so sor--," I began to apologize but my sentence fell short.

The man I bumped in to smiled. With the unforgettable Italian accent, he greeted me cheerfully, "Good morning to you!"

7 PENTHOUSE

Valentino

She blushed, "Good morning."

Isabelle was utterly breathtaking. It was so refreshing to see her eyes once again. They were part of the reason I took such a liking to her when I saw her photo for the first time. Though she had no idea who I was, I had to admit that it was fun to see both sides of her.

"Sorry I wasn't watching where I was going," I apologized, smiling.

Glancing down at my phone. It was then, I realized that I was in the middle of replying to her text when we ran into one another. I quickly slid my phone in my jacket pocket, but I pressed *Send* first, ensuring that she would get the text while speaking to me.

"How have you been?" I inquired, crossing my arms over my chest.

"You wouldn't believe me if I told you."

"Try me."

She shook her head, grinning widely, "Nah, I think I am going to have to back out of this one."

I chuckled musingly, "Fair enough."

I peered over her shoulder and saw her security guys looking like they just ran an entire marathon. They were disgruntled, glaring in our direction, knowing I could see they were miserable. Joseph was my Head of Security, but he hated running almost more than anything. To see him like this was quite humorous. I attempted to hold in my laughter, but it was no use.

I gestured to them, snickering, "It seems you have a fan club today."

She did not bother to turn around. Instead she glanced at the ground then met my gaze. "Yeahhh."

"That's part of the thing I wouldn't believe isn't it?"

She nodded, tucking her bottom lip between her teeth.

"Well, I should get to the office."

"Yeah, that's okay," she agreed, gesturing to her building, "I moved into a new apartment and my stuff will be here in a little while so I should get back up."

"You moved in the same building?"

I was testing her now to see how much she would reveal.

She nodded, "Yep, just another place."

I took my coffee cup from my bodyguard's hand, taking a sip. I held my cup in the air, giving a secret signal to the bodyguard behind Isabelle. Joseph slightly nodded, but the other did not move a muscle. Isabelle gazed at me with a smile, almost as if she were bashful.

"Buona giornata," I smirked as I spun to walk away.

"You too to whatever you said!" she called after me while I disappeared into the bustling morning crowd on the sidewalk.

I laughed as my back was turned. Refusing to glance back at her, we continued to my office, but I know she was still trying to see me. Joseph sent me a quick text letting me know, causing me to grin. My plan might work after all.

∞

When I got to my office, I sat in meeting after meeting. My mind would not stop wandering to her. I would speak up when I needed to, but my executive team was running the meetings today. It was all numbers, budgets, and a boring, seemingly endless Power Point presentation. I was paying close attention, but I also continued glimpsing at my phone to see if she would text me again. To my surprise, she did not.

I walked to my office after my last meeting and leaned on the window. Looking out over the city, I watched in envy as all the people below probably lived normal lives, never worrying about situations like mine. What had I gotten myself in to? Now living a double life, I felt as though I could be a secret agent or spy. However, I felt like I had actually become one.

Just then, my phone vibrated on my desk. I snapped out of my thoughts, sauntering over to it, hoping that it would be her. I scooped it off the surface of the desk, reading:

Miss me yet? lol

I chuckled, typing out my reply, *Of course, I do. What are you doing right now?*

Waiting for my furniture to get here but they called and said it would be an hour later than expected :/

Thank you btw, I appreciate this so much.

I sighed, hovering my thumbs over my phone, debating how to respond. I sent two more texts to her in response.

You're welcome, Isabelle.

How does it feel to be free?

She fired back quickly, *Is anyone ever really free? But it is nice not to trip over everything ;)*

My eyes became enlarged as I thought maybe she had figured out that it was me all along. Why else would she send me that last sentence? I mildly panicked, then decided to see for myself if she knew who I was.

I picked up my other phone and called Joseph. He assured me that she knew nothing, causing me to feel a bit better. Still, I wanted to see her again. I told him to take her out for coffee while I headed out of my office.

As I passed my assistant, she called out to me, "Mr. Greco, you ha--."

"Not now Samantha."

Once out of the building, with my security trailing closely behind, I made my way to the coffee shop outside her apartment. Planting myself in a chair with a newspaper, I waited for her to arrive while I looked as inconspicuous as possible. I did not know why I chose a newspaper in this day and age, but I actually enjoyed reading them, and often did.

Studying the paper, I pretended to read so that I would look casual when she strolled up. Before I could get too settled, I saw footsteps stop next to me. My eyes trailed up her body, stopping on her gaze. She peered down at me with her hands gripping her hips in a feisty posture.

"Are you addicted to coffee or something?" She averted her eyes nervously before bringing them back to mine.

"Coffee is good, but it's not what I'm addicted to, no." I winked coyly.

She blushed, shifting her weight as she was unsure how to respond.

"Out for another run?" I teased.

She shook her head slightly, gesturing to the coffee shop smiling, "I'm actually getting some coffee too."

"I see."

"I'm Isabelle by the way," she beamed, before she averted her eyes to the ground, mumbling, "I'm not sure if you knew that."

I snorted before sarcastically mentioning, "I might have heard your boss angrily yell it a few times."

I clenched my fists, thinking about him. He was currently my biggest concern. The way he had been treating Isabelle and Tanya infuriated me to the core. I should have killed him. It would only be a matter of time before that day came. Before I could get too deep in thought, Isabelle spoke.

"Any good news today?" she smiled, pointing to the paper.

I glanced down to see I had carelessly opened it to the obituary section. I snickered, "No, no." Closing it quickly, I slid it to the side of the table. "Sit," I grinned, gesturing across the table.

She inhaled sharply, freezing in place. "What did you just say?" she whispered.

Fuck, I thought. Instantly, I changed my tone, realizing my command was a bit too similar to *Sir's*. I took an inconspicuous breath. Leaning on my left elbow, I covered my mouth with my index finger.

"I mean, would you like to join me for coffee?" I corrected my manners, standing up then pulling her chair out for her.

She tilted her head as she sat, almost as if she had busted me. "Yes," she smirked, dragging out the *S*.

Just as she sat down, a waitress approached us. "Hello, Mr. Greco," she greeted me directly but warmly smiled back and forth between us.

"Hello, we might need a moment to look over the menu," I informed her, glancing at Isabelle who was staring intently at me.

Her gaze slowly peeled away from me as she peered up

at the waitress. "Actually, I'll have just a coffee please with cream and four sugars on the side," she smiled handing her the menu.

"I will have a black coffee please."

The waitress nodded then turned to walk away with the same warm smile on her face. Isabelle's gaze returned to mine. She leaned forward propping up on her elbow, smiling. She began to nervously, twirl a strand of her hair around her index finger.

"I actually haven't been able to safely drink coffee for about a week now."

I arched a brow, trying to hold in my laughter. I started remembering what it was like to sit with her while she ate and drank at the mansion. "Why is that?"

She withdrew her hand from the table, placing it in her lap. Turning around, she checked on her bodyguards, seeing that they were standing off to the side.

"It's a long story actually," she muttered. She then craned her neck, looking over my shoulder at the men behind me, also standing nearby. "You have security?"

Not wanting to make a big deal of it, I nodded my head toward her security as well, "Yet, it seems you do too."

"I didn't ask for them," she defended. "But that one right there," she nodded her head toward Joseph, "he's pretty cool."

I glanced over to see Joseph quickly turn away, tightening his lips, resisting the urge to smile.

"Will you excuse me for a moment?" she shyly smiled. "I need to use the Ladies' Room."

I nodded as I stood, helping her out of her chair.

She sauntered away with her other security guard, Tate, following closely behind her. The moment they were out of sight, I lifted my hand, motioning for Joseph. He approached cautiously, glancing back toward the doorway of the café before he stopped in front of me. I sat down, crossing my arms, looking up at him.

"I think I may have fucked up," I sighed.

He smirked, nodding.

"I need you to take this phone," I directed, handing him my phone, "and send her a preloaded text." I rolled my eyes as I thought of a subtle gesture. "All you have to do is hit enter when I cough," I coughed, demonstrating my signal.

He nodded again.

"Before I leave, give it back to me," I commanded. "If she texts you back, you may give a short reply but make it sound like me."

He smiled smugly but said nothing as he held the phone in front of his torso.

"What?" I cocked my head, arching a brow.

"Didn't you hear?" he asked, shrugging. "I'm *pretty cool*. I got this."

I shoved the phone into his body, huffing, "Just go!"

He snorted as he proudly spun, returning to his previous post. Sliding the phone in his pocket, he dropped his hands in front of his body, grasping one of his hands with the other. I placed my other identical phone on the table just as Isabelle returned moments later. I stood, pulling her chair out for her, as the server returned with our coffee. I took a seat, smiling at the waitress before she disappeared once again.

I sat back. "Have you had any luck with jobs?" I inquired then took a sip of my drink.

She shook her head with the rim of the mug to her lips. "I haven't looked," she smiled as she took a drink, then placed her cup on the saucer in front of her.

"Oh?" I took another sip of my coffee.

She shifted in her seat. "I've been a little busy lately."

I lightly coughed, making it appear as if I were clearing my throat.

Just as she was about to finish her thought, her phone vibrated next to her saucer. She peeked down, slowly picking it up while unlocking it simultaneously. Her facial expression switched from pleasant to seemingly disheartened as she glanced at me before tapping on her phone rapidly with her thumbs. After a moment, she exhaled, laying the phone back on the table.

"As I said," she sighed, "I've been a little busy lately."

"Well are you too busy to see me again?" I grinned wickedly.

Her phone vibrated again. As she turned her attention to her phone once again, I peeked up to see Joseph slightly nodding at me. I pursed my lips, casually stroking my chin as I watched Isabelle reading her screen. Her eyes slowly met mine as she placed her phone in her bag. She then focused her attention on my phone. She stared at it momentarily until I interrupted her thought.

"Everything okay?"

Her head snapped up, her gaze meeting mine. "Yeah," she muttered as if she were unsure. "Yeah, it is, but I just realized I should get back to my apartment because I have to let the movers in."

"Oh," I sighed, "o-okay sure."

She took another sip of her coffee then picked her bag off the ground.

"No," I contested, "I got it."

She grinned, nodding as she stood to her feet, "Thank you."

I immediately stood as well, crossing my arms. "Would you like to have dinner with me tomorrow night?" I offered, hoping that she would take the bait.

"You want me to go to dinner with you?" she tilted her head as if my question took her by surprise.

"Unless you're too good for me," I shrugged, teasing.

Placing her hands on her hips, she giggled, "Oh Mister, I think you have it all wrong."

"Enlighten me then," I challenged her as I sat down, leaning back as I crossed my arms and winked at her.

"Listen Mr--," she blurted, then paused for a moment in thought. "What's your name?" she continued. "Probably Romeo or Casanova or something like that." She giggled, "Am I close?"

"My name is Valentino," I murmured before taking a sip of my coffee.

"Of course, it is!" she snorted, looking away.

I gently set my mug back down then propped my elbows on the surface of the table, clasping my hands together, studying her. She took notice of my mannerisms, then folded her arms over her stomach. She began to shake her head.

"You have this fancy suit, a sexy name," she began, gesturing toward me.

I smiled behind my hands, amused at her visible frustration.

"You probably live in some fancy penthouse apartment and drive a Porsche," she confidently slid the strap of her bag onto her shoulder then crossed her arms, challenging me with a knowing smirk. "Am I right about any of that?"

I sat back, resting my elbows on the arms of the chair, watching her. My silence and amusement only fueling her.

"I knew it!" she exclaimed. "I freaking knew it."

"A house," I slowly trailed a lust filled stare from her ankles to her eyes.

"What?" she hissed as she sat back down.

"I live in a house," I reiterated, "and I actually prefer old classic cars over a Porsche any day." I picked up my phone, checking the time.

"Yes," she blurted suddenly.

"Yes what?" I coyly arched a brow.

Isabelle

"Yes, I'll have dinner with you tomorrow night."

He nodded, grinning widely as he finished off his coffee.

"There may be one obstacle," I sighed, pinching my forehead, "but I'll see what I can do."

He reached over, lifting his phone, unlocked it then held it out toward me. I gently and suspiciously took it from his hand, unsure what to do with it.

"Put your number in it," he ordered.

"Geez, you could say please, you know," I scolded.

I hated being told what to do but I looked down and typed in my information, before pressing *Save*. He was leaning forward with his arms folded in front of him. Reaching out for his phone, he abruptly took it from my hands the moment I was finished.

"I'll be in touch."

He walked over to my security guys. I stood, turning to face them, observing intensely as they shared a private conversation. Valentino shook hands with both of them, which I thought was odd. Maybe it was just some formal Italian gesture, or maybe he was convincing them he was not a serial killer.

He did not speak another word to me as he left, but he did turn to me, winking before he and his own bodyguards disappeared into the crowd. Suddenly reality hit me that I was going on a probable date with another guy. I began to panic, unsure how the man I only knew as *Sir*, would have felt about my date with someone else.

I spun to Joseph, asking, "Am I going to get in trouble for this?"

He placed his sunglasses on his face, vaguely smiling, "Honestly, I couldn't tell you even if I wanted to." Smirking he paused for a moment, lifting his chin. "I really don't know how the boss will respond to this one."

About an hour later, the penthouse house was buzzing with lots of activity as an entire team of movers showed up with new furniture. I stood idly by the bar, watching with wide eyes as they carried and arranged everything with precision. It almost appeared as if they had been in the apartment before. They walked about, not bothering to ask where things went or where my room was. They already had it down to a science. Within four hours, my new home was livable.

The moment they left, I stepped to the kitchen to get a bottle of water then went to my room, but I heard voices entering the penthouse. I quickly returned to the living room, where I was greeted with several new faces. They were all dressed professionally and had ear communication pieces.

Joseph introduced them, "Miss Ayala, this is your new home security team, John, Michael, Caleb, and Barbara."

I smiled, greeting them all at once.

The one he introduced as Caleb cleared his throat. "If you need anything, we will be posted around the home, but we will stay out of your way unless you need us."

I nodded as they all smiled and dispersed through the apartment.

"Joseph, this is too much," I mumbled, watching them. "I don't even know what to say."

"And what exactly did you expect?" he smirked, peering down at me.

Joseph had to be at least six feet two inches in height. His hair was golden walnut brown and his eyes were an incredibly unique shade of hazel. His clean shaven face gave him a youthful appearance, but he was attractive as well as masculine.

I looked around, finally absorbing my surroundings.

The décor Sir chose was modern, yet cozy in a way. I remembered seeing one of the designers, who came with the movers, stocking the wine fridge.

Grinning, I immediately marched into the kitchen. Tossing my handbag on the island, I opened the fridge, pulling out a bottle of Pinot Grigio. I grabbed a wine key and glass before I perched on a barstool at the kitchen island. Opening the bottle with ease, I poured myself a full glass of wine then gestured to Joseph who silently declined.

I shrugged as I began to enjoy the chilled, fruity, floral flavor of my beverage. Closing my eyes, I inhaled the aroma before the sound of my phone vibrating in my bag startled me. I dug it out, unlocking it. Scrolling over to my texts, I saw one from Valentino.

Looking forward to our date. Pick you up at 6pm? -V

The thought never occurred to me that it might be a formal date! Oh my God! My mouth dropped open, remembering the mansion and Sir. It was still awkward referring to him as that, but I had yet to learn his name. I had not contacted him yet. I suddenly felt so naive.

Why did I think it would be okay to go to dinner with another man that I could never have a future with? I would be wasting his time. I had made a promise to Sir regardless of the contract. He trusted me. I knew he would find out. Sighing, I decided to text him, asking for permission even though I knew it was not sleeping with anyone. It was just dinner, right? Yet, I still felt guilty.

Hi, I'm sure you're going to be upset but I was asked out on a date tomorrow night :/

Moments later he replied, *And what did you say?*

Nothing yet. I wanted to text you first :)

I sighed, unsure how he would respond.

As long as you do not give him what is mine, I don't see the problem.

I could not tell from the text if he was mad.

I didn't plan on it but like no physical stuff, right?

Didn't you read the contract thoroughly?

Okay okay, got it. It's just dinner. He's way too good for me anyway, lol

Five minutes of silence came and went. Finally, he replied, *One day you'll see your worth. Have fun on your date and behave.*

I then scrolled over to Valentino's text, responding to him:

That's perfect. See you then :)

Valentino

I finished up a couple of hours of work and it was time to go home. Ever since I got back from having coffee with Isabelle, I had been sitting in my office at my desk, both of my phones in front of me. I stood, smiling while sliding both of them into my jacket pocket. As I headed to the elevator, I waved at the receptionist. The moment the doors opened, Tanya came barreling out pointing at me.

"We need to talk!" she declared sternly, poking me in the chest.

My security team made an attempt to step between us, but I put my hand in the air. "Let her speak."

Tanya crossed her arms, huffing, "I'm so upset with you right now!"

"We will be in my office for a little while," I glanced at my team, informing them. "Please wait out here."

Gripping Tanya's forearm, I firmly escorted her to my office, slamming the door the instant we stepped in. She became a statue the moment she realized we were completely alone. She gulped, unsure what to do.

"What did she tell you?" I interrogated.

I veered around her, perching on the edge of my desk, crossing my arm disapprovingly. Tanya rested her hand on her chest, inhaling deeply with her eyes closed. I cocked my head as she slowly opened her eyes, focusing on me.

"What the fuck are you talking about?" she sighed.

Confused I blurted, "Wait, what are *you* talking about?"

"I haven't spoken to her," she muttered, averting her gaze to the floor. "I betrayed her, or so she thinks."

"No, you actually helped save her," I sighed.

She lifted her head, looking at me as she nervously shuffled her feet.

"Tanya, you were asked to help because someone is after her," I admitted. "I was asked to protect her, and the masquerade was the only way. Though you didn't exactly know why you were getting her there, you knew what I wanted you to know."

"What?" she hissed.

"Liam and I told you all that we could," I apologized. "Any more information would have also put you in danger."

She folded her arms over her chest, glaring at me.

"Her being sold to me was the only way that I could get

close enough to her without raising suspicion," I continued. "The contract is a facade to keep her safe. I would never take her body and make it mine without her asking me to."

"Well I got blamed for it!" she blustered. "She thinks I tricked her."

Tanya and I had something in common and that was that we both cared for Isabelle and her well-being, so I understand why Tanya was upset. She had possibly just lost her best friend because of me.

She flinched, grabbing her stomach, before she sprinted into my office bathroom, slamming the door. I cleared my throat, standing. I stepped over to the minifridge, grabbing her a bottle of water. Waiting by the door, she came out a few moments after the water turned off. I held the bottle out for her. Hesitantly, she took it and drank a little before she noticed me staring at her intensely. I knew she needed her friend.

"How far along?" I murmured.

A tear rolled down her cheek as she attempted to avoid eye contact. "What?" she sighed.

"Does Liam know?"

She shook her head as I pulled a tissue out of a box, handing it to her. She gently took it from my fingers, wiping her tears. I paced my office, uncomfortable around crying women.

"Not yet. I'm scared he'll walk away from me," she sobbed.

Tanya only needed Isabelle right now. I had taken her friend from her for the time being so unfortunately, I was faced with the task of replacing her at the moment. I sauntered over to Tanya, wrapping her in my arms thinking a hug may help, even if a little. William was my closest friend, so this baby would more than likely be my godchild.

"He's not going to walk away from you," I reassured her, awkwardly patting her on the head.

With her face buried in my chest she sniffled, "I hope you're right."

I gently peeled her away from me with both hands on her arms. "He's crazy about you, trust me," I affirmed.

She took a few steps back from me, postulating, "Just like you're crazy about my best friend."

I shook my head, biting my bottom lip for a moment. "I'm not doing this with you," I scoffed.

She rolled her eyes, smirking.

"Shit is so fucked up right now," I confessed, "and I need time to figure everything out."

She nodded as she walked to the door but turned around when she touched the doorknob. "Please don't destroy her," she sniffled, fighting back tears again. "She already hates me and though the situation is so messed up right now, you're all she has." She paused, looking down as she rubbed her stomach in a circle. "I'm going to tell him soon but give me a few days."

"Fine," I mumbled.

Without saying another word, she exited, closing the door behind her. I gave her time to leave the building so I would not be faced with awkward silence in the elevator. Once I knew she was gone, my bodyguards and I headed down to the parking garage where my driver stood waiting to take us to my house.

That night, I could not get her off my mind, so I spent the night tossing and turning in my bed. It was so strange not having her under the same roof as me now. I was worried about her safety even though she had top notch security features and staff at the penthouse. Rolling over, I grabbed my phone off the nightstand, dialing her number then placed the phone to my ear.

Well hello there, Sir, she playfully greeted me.

I warned you about calling me that, I groaned.

She giggled quietly.

Are you in bed?

She sighed, *I am, but I can't go to sleep.*

Me either, I confessed. *Admit that you miss me Isabelle.*

She snickered, *And where will that get me?*

You'd be very surprised to learn the answer to that, sweetheart.

She ignored my comment, *I know this is going to sound weird, but I started to enjoy your company.*

I know the feeling, I muttered, *I also miss you tripping and me catching you.*

I could sense her blush through the phone. We talked a few more minutes about nothing important before she told me she was starting to close her eyes.

I should try to sleep but I'll check in as soon as I wake up, I heard the smile in her voice.

Talk to you then, I confirmed and got ready to end the call.

Sir? she whispered.

Yes? I smirked.

She paused for several seconds. *Nothing, I'll talk to you tomorrow.* She hung up before I could speak.

Scrolling to my gallery, I zoomed in on her photo; the same one that captivated me from the moment I saw it. That photo caused me to agree to watch her and keep her safe. It was the reason I was currently a disaster, living a double life with her.

What the hell was she doing to me? I wanted her so badly, I ached for her. This feeling was so foreign to me. Fuck!

8 INTERVIEWING

Valentino

It was the middle of the night. I had found myself standing in the middle of my closet, naked. Quickly grabbing a pair of black sweatpants and a grey hoodie, I hurriedly got dressed though I was unsure why. I sped out of my closet in a panic, marching to one of the windows in my bedroom. It was pouring rain outside. The water pinged angrily against the glass. The darkness of outside mixed with the glare of the exterior lighting, made it hard to see much. To be honest, I was not quite sure what I was looking for at the time.

Then, my eye caught something in the garden. I squinted, trying to get a better look. What the hell? There she was, in a white dress, twirling while staring up at the sky as the rain saturated her to the core.

I sprinted to my closet, putting on a pair of my sneakers then ran through the house as fast as I could. Finally, I made it out to the garden, but I did not feel as if I had been moving quickly enough. She stopped, slowly turning at an abnormal speed to face me. Gazing into my eyes, she seemed unaffected as the rain rolled down her face. She was not wearing her blindfold, nor was she wearing a bra. I could see her perfectly erect, rosy nipples through her dress as the lights from the house and moonlight illuminated her.

"*I couldn't sleep,*" *she flirted with a devilish grin.*

I gradually crept toward her. "*So, you came here?*"

Water began to drip off the ends of my hair and into my eyes. I wiped my face, running my fingers through my hair. Her eyes widened; her smile faded.

"*You're him,*" *she asserted.* "*You're Sir and Valentino.*"

I did not know how to respond, so I remained still, letting her decide what happened next. She shocked me when she started to seductively sway her hips to the song in her head. I glanced around in a mild panic, looking for any sign of security, but we were alone. Her movements called my eyes back to her. Lightning flashed across the sky. She paid no attention to it as she moved her body, slowly lowering the straps on her dress.

A loud crash of thunder echoed through the night, followed by another magnificent spider web of lightning dancing across the sky, lighting up the entire garden. She was not startled. She acted as if she did not even notice it.

"Isabelle, you need to come inside," I called out to her. It's dangerous out here."

Rain started to tap madly on her face, so I stepped forward, grabbing her. She took my hand just as I pulled her into my body with force. Throwing her over my shoulder, I carried her through the garden and into the house as fast as my legs would carry us. I jogged to my bedroom, thankful none of the staff saw the events that were happening. I was simply happy to get us both out of the cold rain, that was beginning to cause us both to shiver.

I gently placed her on the bed, instinctively pushing her legs apart, crawling up between them as she lay, panting. Her transparent dress gave me a better view of her chest rising and falling as she anticipated my next move. Slowly, I slid her dress up, completely exposing her. It was then that I discovered Isabelle was not wearing any panties.

Burying my face in her ready mound, I teased her with my tongue. She writhed beneath me, moaning my real name. Another loud crash of thunder shook the mansion as I slid a finger into her tight sheath. She cried out once again as lightning lit up the room. I nibbled her button, massaging her insides in a perfect rhythm. She trembled, grabbing my head, pulling me tightly against her core. Another loud crash of thunder shook the world around us.

My eyes shot open as my body was jolted awake. Breathlessly, I lied under my blankets staring at the ceiling. Running my fingers through my hair, I panted, discovering that I was only sweaty and there was no rain. Blinking my eyes a few times, I reminded myself that it was just a dream. Oh, how I wished it were real.

My phone rested on my chest. I picked it up, seeing her stunning photo where I left it. I had dozed off at some point while studying her once again. Her mesmerizing eyes begged me to make her mine, to hold her, to fuck her.

Taking hold of my already rock-hard shaft, I slowly ran my thumb across the tip, followed by my other fingertips, sliding them across my leaking head. Running my hand down the length of my thick shaft, I inhaled a sharp breath. The sensation intensified as I squeezed harder, applying more pressure. Reaching further down I massaged by balls before returning to the base of my rod, gradually but steadily pulling up. Staring directly into her eyes, my gaze made its way to her plump and glossy, red lips. I craved biting them while pulling her bottom lip into my mouth by my teeth, sucking it as I fucked her hard and deep, endlessly for hours. Just as I erupted in bliss, my phone rang. What the hell?! It was 3:30 a.m.!

What?! I answered on speaker.

Boss, we have an issue with the prisoner.

Fuck. Okay be right there.

Marching angrily into the bathroom, I cleaned myself before slipping on a pair of black ripped jeans and sneakers. I grabbed my gun, placing it in my waistband then stomped to the elevator, taking it to the tunnels under my estate. Making my way down the long hallway at lightning speed, I went to confront Isabelle's former boss.

He was secured with handcuffs to the pipes as my men left him. I came to a stop in front of him, crossing my arms and glowering down at his battered body. William rolled his eyes as he nudged him with his shoe.

"What's the issue?" I questioned.

"After he finished eating," Blaine scoffed, "he started to yell some nonsense about the guy bidding against you at the ball."

He stepped toward Jesse as William took a step back. Blaine picked his foot off the ground then forced it forward, connecting his boot to Jesse's rib cage.

Blaine turned to me, sneering, "I had to tape his mouth shut because he was pissing me off."

I nodded, scowling down at Jesse as he arched his back against the pipe in pain, moving his body from side to side, his eyes watering as he tried to shout.

"Full disclosure," Blaine continued, "he spit in my face before that and I punched him too."

Smirking, I removed my gun from my waistband as I squatted down in front of Jesse, resting my elbows on my knees. He refused to make any sort of eye contact with me as he stared at the floor, squirming. I placed the muzzle of my gun under his chin, slowly lifting his face, forcing him to look at me so I could investigate his eyes.

"I'm going to remove the tape," I growled in a low tone. "If you raise your voice at me, I will kill you."

He squirmed.

"If you spit on me, I will kill you," I calmly muttered.

He twisted his body, thrashing from side to side, attempting to break free from his restraints.

"If you do not answer my every question," I retorted, "I will kill you."

He stopped struggling, panting as his gaze finally met mine.

"Are we clear, Jesse?"

He nodded calmly, sweat beading across his brow. I ripped the tape off his face in one quick motion, taking some of his facial hair with it. He yelled in agony as I stood up, tossing the tape on the floor.

"Now, tell me what you told him," I nudged his leg with my foot.

I dispassionately paced back and forth before him, rolling my eyes in anger, trying to hold myself back from killing him before I got any information from him.

"I'm not telling you shit!" Jesse bellowed as loudly as his lungs would allow him.

I smirked, shaking my head in disbelief. He wanted to push my buttons. He sat silently for a few moments, thinking about what he could say that would really mess with my head. Suddenly he guffawed, dragging the sound out as his laugh came to an abrupt halt. I stopped, turning to look down on him with my arms crossed over my chest. He narrowed his eyes at my glare.

"I should have raped her in my office that night!"

I cocked my head and starting laughing. I held my gun to the side for Blaine. He took it from me as my largest bodyguard, Dante, marched over to Jesse, bending down. He unlocked the handcuffs. He assisted him to his feet then took a step back, crossing his arms over his chest, glaring at Jesse.

"You already broke two of the rules," I sluggishly licked my bottom lip. "However, it is very unfortunate for you that I will not kill you just yet."

I clenched my fists, staring down at my knuckles, then turned my attention to Jesse. "I am going to make you suffer," I promised.

"Over some stupid bitch?"

In that moment, I could have taken a superhero down. Every bit of rage and anger I had built up inside me came pouring out. Grabbing him by the shirt, I pushed his body back into the wall, causing his head to smack against the cement, splitting it open. I delivered a jab to his temple, triggering him to crumble to the floor before I hovered over his body, kicking him several times.

He cried out in pain, but I did not care. I wanted him to know that Isabelle was not someone he should have sexually and verbally harassed. I wanted him to pay for his mistakes. Straddling his stomach, I unleashed most of my strength on his face. When blood began to pool on the floor under his head, I stood. I wiggled my fingers, inspecting my bloody knuckles, while making sure that I had not caused lasting damage to myself.

"See to it that he gets medical attention down here but no pain meds," I ordered.

Blaine arched a brow, sighing as he held out my pistol and a clean hand towel. "Are you seriously not going to kill him yet?"

I grabbed the towel, wiping my hands off before taking my gun. "I'm nowhere near done with him," I sneered. "I'm going to need that information from him soon."

He nodded, as I dropped the towel to the floor. Without another word, I spun to leave them to clean up the mess I had just made. Whatever Jesse knew had to be of use to me. He was not the type of guy to just fire off useless information, but I knew he wanted me to suffer.

I had no time for any games right now. Keeping Isabelle safe and continuing to keep my promise to her father, was my focus right now.

I arrived in my bedroom, immediately marching to my bathroom. Turning on the hot water in the shower, I stepped in to clean myself and think. The soothing water cascaded down my body as I washed then rested my forehead against the wall reflecting back on the timeline of events.

My mind shifted to Isabelle, daydreaming about her in the shower with me. I sighed, grabbing my shaft, and stroking several times before frustration overtook my mind once again. I groaned in anger as I finished rinsing my body then went to bed. Work would come early.

Isabelle

This morning, as I opened my eyes, I instantly became startled. Jolting my body into a sitting position, I held the blankets tightly around my chest. I sighed as I recalled relocating to the penthouse yesterday. I was in a completely new bedroom, in a totally new environment with an entirely new life, or so it seemed.

I rolled over, glancing at my phone. Picking it up, I texted Sir as promised.

Good morning, this is my a.m. check in. Have a great day! :)

I put my phone back down then went to shower. Deciding to skip my run today, I thought I would just hang out around my new apartment. As I was brushing my teeth, I heard my phone ring, so I quickly skipped into my bedroom, picking it up without seeing who it was.

Hello? I answered.

Hello Miss Ayala, this is Samantha from VCG International. I have your application and resume in front of me. I was calling to see if you would like to come in for an interview today, she quickly blurted all at once.

I'm sorry. How did you get this number? I queried. *I don't mean to come off rude, but this is a brand-new phone and number.*

It's the only number we have for you, she announced.

Okay, yes ma'am. Sure, I would love the interview, I beamed.

Does 4:00 p.m. work for you? she requested.

Yes, absolutely thank you! I danced in place. *See you then.*

Of course, Ms. Ayala. I will send you over the address in your email.

I hung up. What was that? How did she know my name? I did fill out some applications, but none of them had my current phone number on them. I sighed. I quickly threw on some comfortable clothes then ran downstairs.

The aroma of bacon and coffee filled the air, reminding me of my early childhood. My mother would always cook a large breakfast on the weekend. I smiled, reminiscing as I cautiously approached the kitchen. I assumed maybe Joseph had felt inspired, but I gasped when I stepped through the archway to see the back of a man at the stove. The man turned around with a pan in his hand and memories flooded back, to when Sir and I were in the kitchen late at night, not that long ago.

"I will be your personal chef," the stranger greeted me with a grin.

I took a deep breath, sighing in relief when I realized it was not the same voice from the house. He was definitely the same shape from what I could tell, but it was unquestionably not him. I waltzed to a bar stool at the island and perched on the seat.

"Hi," I smiled, "I'm Isabelle."

He stepped over to a pitcher, pouring a glass of orange juice then placed it on a cocktail napkin in front of me. "I'm Michelangelo."

"Oh, my favorite turtle," I blurted awkwardly.

I took a sip of my orange juice, but immediately placed my lips back onto the rim of the glass, letting it dribble back. I silently gagged, wincing as I wiped any residue off my lips with my thumb. Michelangelo looked on with wide eyes at my rude display.

"But it is fresh squeezed!" he defended.

"It's probably great," I nodded, still trying to rid myself of the taste. "I'm sorry but I just brushed my teeth."

He smirked, turning back to the stove. I rolled my eyes at my terribly rude reaction, but there was no hiding it. Orange juice and toothpaste were never a great combination.

"Donatello," he murmured with his back still turned toward me.

"Huh?" I tilted my head, confused.

Picking up a towel off the counter, he wiped his hands before he threw it over his shoulder. Turning to me with the pan in his hand, he served me some scrambled eggs. He then spun back around to get a skillet. He laid three strips of bacon on my plate before I held my hand up, indicating that was enough.

"Donatello is the best turtle," he countered with a cheeky smile.

I giggled, "Oh."

"I will make you some coffee," he called out as he laid the pan on the stove then sauntered to the coffee maker.

I pulled my phone out of my pocket, scrolling through the screens. I downloaded Instagram then logged in. While scrolling through my feed seeing what I had missed, I got nosy. Clicking Tanya's profile, I noticed she had not posted anything since the event.

At some point during that night, she had taken a photo of herself with her boyfriend, William. Sir was in the background, but with his mask, and his arm covering the lower half of his face, it was impossible to identify him.

Sighing, I laid my phone on the counter. I bit off a piece of bacon as I hovered my clean fingers over the button to unfollow her. Did I want to do it? I did but I also did not. I felt so betrayed by her even though nothing terrible happened to me, yet. Deciding not to make any speedy decisions for now, I just exited from my account then viewed my text inbox.

Sir said I would need to get permission to leave my apartment so I thought I should maybe inform him of the job interview this afternoon. I could not stay locked up in here like a prisoner. I am sure he would understand that I did need to work. He was taking care of me in so many ways, but I felt that it would be best to contribute as much as possible. This lifestyle was too lavish for me; well, at least it seemed that way at the moment.

I decided to call him instead of text. He picked up almost immediately.

Isabelle, hello! Sorry I haven't texted you back. I have been so busy at work, he answered, immediately explaining himself.

It's okay, I giggled. *Hey, I have a job interview today and I was wondering if I could please go*?

I'm not sure I'm okay with that, he sighed. *It's just an interview*?

Yes yes, just an interview, I quickly reassured him.

Okay that's fine, he agreed. *Take security with you and good luck, although I doubt you need it.*

Okay, I beamed. *Thank you so much.*

He chuckled mildly, *I must go but call me later and tell me about it.*

Yes, Sir, I emphasized the word Sir in a flirty way.

Isabelle, he seductively growled.

I snickered into the phone before hanging up on him, refusing to let him get another word in. As I stood, my email notification popped up on my phone. I opened it, seeing that I had the promised text from the woman who called me earlier.

Ms. Ayala,

I am confirming your interview today. We will see you at 4:00 p.m. at 377 Lexington Ave.

Samantha Thompson

Executive Assistant

VCG International

I smiled as I grabbed the last piece of bacon off my plate. Before I could tidy up my breakfast area, Michelangelo took my plate from the island with a smile. He walked to the sink with it before I could protest.

"Thank you," I murmured.

He nodded, "Of course, Miss."

I did not think that I would ever get used to being called Miss. It was strange to be addressed so formally, but still, I gave him a final smile before prancing out of the kitchen, finishing off my slice of bacon.

As I made my way back up to my room, I realized how badly I wished I could call Tanya, telling her the good news about a possible job. Once the shock wore off, I finally realized where exactly it was that I was interviewing. I had heard of the company so naturally, I got excited.

I had hope that my life was going to really start looking up soon. I half danced up the stairs to my bedroom, waltzing into my closet to pick out the perfect outfit. Wanting to impress my potential new boss, I chose a chic business-casual pants suit. Taking a final glimpse at myself in the mirror before I left, I smoothed out my attire then leaned forward, making sure my hair and makeup was nothing short of perfection.

Peeking down at my watch, I realized it was time to go. I noted earlier that the address was not that far away, so I chose to walk. My bodyguards and I traversed down the sidewalk toward VCG International. I had grown used to their company already and Joseph was quite easy to get along with.

Before long, we arrived at the front of the building and crossed the street. I slowly trailed my eyes up the side of the skyscraper, taking a deep breath. Intimidation set in, and I began to quake in my stilettos. Joseph planted himself next to me, crossing his arms. I turned to him with wide eyes.

"You're going to do great, Miss," he confidently reassured.

I smiled, nodding. Because of my nerves, I was rendered speechless.

I would nail this interview. I had to. It was a chance for me to start over. As I took a step toward the entrance, my phone vibrated, causing me to jump. I dug it out of my handbag reading simple text from Sir.

Good luck on your interview.

I blushed as I replied, *Thank you xoxo*

Xo, was all he sent back, which was shocking to me since he did not come off as the *Xo* type.

I grinned, placing my phone back in my bag. As I stepped closer to the entrance, a man in suit and nametag opened the door for me. I thanked him but quickly noticed that my security was no longer following me.

I turned to Joseph, hissing, "Aren't you coming?"

He shook his head, smirking, "This is as far as we go today."

Confused, I shrugged but did not want to be late. "Oh, okay then," I agreed, "I shouldn't be too long."

He smiled, bowing his head as I disappeared inside the building.

Valentino

I smirked to myself knowing she would be interviewing with me. Glancing at my phone, I took note that she would be arriving any moment. I stood, striding to the full length mirror in the corner of my office, adjusting my tie. Lifting my chin, I admired myself as I thought about the dangerous game that I was now playing with her.

The truth was, she honestly did apply with my company through a staffing agency after losing her job at the bar. The moment I saw her application, I intercepted it, changing her phone number to the one I gave to her. I needed my assistant to have the correct contact information when she reached out to her about the position. I wondered what she would say when she saw me…again. After all, we had a date in two hours.

Samantha, my assistant, called into my office, *Mr. Greco, your 4:00 p.m. is here.*

Send her in, Samantha, I ordered in the most professional tone I could muster.

I returned to my desk seat because I got a notification popup from William. It was a video of Jesse talking but the volume was muted. I could not watch it right now, so I rapidly closed my laptop just as the door opened. Isabelle gasped, standing just inside the threshold, still as a statue.

I stood, making my way around my desk, greeting her, "Hello again."

Her eyes widened and she swallowed hard. Staring at me, she began to tilt her head ever so slightly.

I crossed my arms. "Isabelle," I belted, trying to snap her out of her state of shock.

Her head jerked as she shifted her weight, straightening her posture. Barely above a whisper, she choked, "You're *the* Valentino Greco."

I nodded, sliding my hands into my pockets as my lip began to smirk.

"Oh my God!" she exclaimed loudly. "I'm so sorry," she apologized, "I must live under a rock!"

I arched a brow. I am sure the amusement was visible on my face as I watched her squirm.

"I-I have heard of you," she stuttered. "I have seen you, obviously," she declared, "but I never put the puzzle pieces together." She began to shiver a bit.

"Relax," I insisted. "This is a job interview," I reminded her. "You don't want to spoil my opinion of you, do you?"

Mortification washed over her face as she turned a bright shade of pink, immediately sitting in the chair facing my desk.

I laughed, holding my hands up in surrender, "I'm joking."

I lurched to the back of my desk and sat down, rolling my chair underneath as I rocked back. "I think it's safe to say that you've already made a big impression on me."

She shifted in her seat, starting to blush once again as she watched her lap.

"Isabelle."

Her gaze met mine as she composed herself.

"Shall we continue the interview?"

"Yes," she rasped, clearing her throat.

"Very well then," I confirmed. "Tell me why you applied for a job with my company." I looked her in the eyes, waiting for a reply but she blankly stared at me.

Isabelle

I saw him speaking but I could not hear a word he was saying. I went blank. You know the feeling you get right before you pass out when you start to get tunnel vision? Then you lose your hearing? That is what was happening to me and suddenly…

Nothing. It went black.

"Isabelle?" I heard the muffled sound of my name.

I began to blink my eyes, but everything around was blurry. I moved my head back and forth but could not focus on anything. What happened? A figure started to appear over me. I felt like I had been kicked in the head by a horse. It felt like several minutes passed before I saw his face start to come into focus.

Oh no. Abort! Abort! This is not a drill. I passed out during my job interview!

9 FIRST DATE

Isabelle

Wishing the floor would sink in, swallowing me whole, I wanted to be anywhere other than right here. Why did I let this happen? I laid there for what seemed like an eternity contemplating playing dead for the next ten years. I could also sprint out of his office and never look back. Or there was option three, just sitting up fast, saying *Gotcha* and wink at him as if I played a big joke on him.

Instead, I took a few deep breaths, praying he would not laugh at me until I died of embarrassment. I felt my cheeks heating, knowing I was probably flushed as I averted my gaze to the floor. My entire body then became hot. I knew I would never recover from this level of mental anguish. The reality of fainting in front of a gorgeous man that I had a date with, hit me. He also turned out to be the owner of the company I was interviewing with. It was nothing short of mortifying.

Sitting on the floor next to me, he handed me a bottle of water, untwisting the cap as he handed it to me. I sat up slowly, attempting not to make any sudden movements. Still a bit dizzy, I braced myself before I focused my vision on the bottle. Taking a sip, I wondered how long I had been unconscious.

"Um, h-how long was I out?"

A look of concern spread across his face. He furrowed his brow, sighing. "Four days."

I choked on the water then gasped, "What?!"

Throwing his head back, he roared with laughter. "I am just joking, bella."

"Bella?" I mused.

He smirked, "It's *beautiful* in Italian, but is sometimes used as expressions. I'll teach you one day."

Abashed, my cheeks felt hot once again.

He tenderly patted my thigh as he stood. Holding his hand out to assist me, I took hold of it. He pulled me up to my feet, but I lost my footing. My unbalanced body leaned into him causing him to wrap his arms around me. We were both frozen, gazing into each other's eyes for what seemed like an eternity. He cleared his throat, inhaling deeply.

"We should maybe postpone this interview," he contested, peeling himself away. Rapidly, he lurched to his desk. He smoothed his suit before he sat, opening his laptop, inspecting it. I shamefully sat back in the chair that I just fell out of.

Taking a deep breath, he rolled his eyes at whatever he discovered on the screen. "One moment."

Intensely, he glared at his computer, slowly tapping his fingers on his desk. I nodded as I glanced down at my watch to see just how long I was really passed out. Maybe ten minutes which is not as bad as I thought. Much better than four days. I snickered to myself, but it did not mean that I had healed from my humiliation.

Picking up his cell phone, he pressed a button before placing it to his ear. He paused momentarily before speaking Italian. My heart fluttered as I closed my eyes trying not to pass out again. *Breathe Isabelle*. I found his accent incredibly attractive. Maybe too attractive. When I finally opened my eyes, he was smirking at me as he listened to whoever was on the other end of the call. I averted my gaze to my lap, fidgeting with my fingers inelegantly, waiting for him to finish his call.

"Isabelle," he whispered, still on his call.

I slowly met his gaze. Removing the phone from his ear for a moment, he asked, "Do you want to get out of here a little early?"

I silently nodded as we both stood. He grabbed his keys and briefcase off his desk. Resting his hand on my lower back, he guided me to the office door. As we stepped out, he closed it, locking it in the process. He strode over to his assistant's desk, propping on the elevated surface. I stood back a little out of the way as not to cause another problem while he finished his call.

Turning to me, he held his arm out to the side, murmuring. "Come here."

I stepped over, planting myself next to him. He reached around my waist, resting his fingertips on my hip, glancing at me before turning his attention to his assistant.

"Samantha you and Isabelle met already."

She smiled, staring at me, but her eyes no longer appeared warm and welcoming. They were so cold and piercing, appearing as though they could cut a metal door in half. She quickly shot a glare toward his fingertips on my side, gripping the edge of her desk until her knuckles turned white. Slowly, she grinned as her gaze tore away from my body to his eyes.

"Yes, we have," she pursed her lips.

Crossing his arms, he took a more professional stance, clearing his throat and standing straight. "Good."

She turned her attention back toward me, glaring with a smirk, judging my appearance. I pretended as if I did not notice, focusing my attention on Valentino while politely nodding. For a moment it was as if he narrowed his eyes at me, studying me before he focused his interest on her once again.

"Samantha, follow me for a moment please." He smiled toward me. "This will only take a minute."

I nodded then averted my eyes for a second before watching them walk through the lobby and disappear into another room. Just before he closed the door behind them, she evilly grinned in my direction, winking as if to rub their private meeting in my face.

She was visibly flawless, so it was no surprise to me that a man of his status would want to be with a woman such as her, even if for a moment. Maybe there was something I was not aware of. Why would he take me out if they were an item of any sort? Maybe he was just a player.

I was not going to dwell on that. We just met and he was about to take me to dinner. I just passed out in his office during a job interview, so if he had sex with her right now and canceled our date, I totally deserved it. I heard noises coming from the room as if things could not be more uncomfortable for me. I awkwardly shifted my weight, stroking my forearm, wondering if I should cut my losses and run out of the building.

The door flew open and she stomped toward her desk, grabbing her handbag. Her eyes focused on mine and she marched to where I stood. Crossing my arms, I waited for her to speak, pretending to carry confidence but truthfully, I had no idea what to expect from her. She gritted her teeth as she pursed her lips.

"You bitch!"

My eyes widened, but I did not move, holding my ground.

"You think you're the first girl to come through here for him?!" she snapped. "No! And you definitely won't be the last, you whore!"

One of the security guards sprinted toward her, grabbing her wrist just as she was about to slap me. He and another man I had not seen before, pulled her down a long hall into another room. Valentino emerged from the room he had been in, looking rather flustered. I did not know whether to ask what was going on or just let it go. I chose to let it go. We had only just met, and his life was not my business.

He watched me as if he were waiting for me to interrogate him, but I said nothing, only smiling ever so slightly. I did not dare speak about what just happened. It felt awkward to bring it up.

"After you, bella," he offered, gesturing toward the elevator.

Nodding, I smiled as we walked toward the doors, stepping in with two men. I did not speak but Valentino kept glancing my way. He seemed a bit nervous, but I assumed it was because of what had just happened upstairs. The descending elevator seemed to take an eternity. He loosened his tie, pulling his phone out of his pocket, texting.

DING!

The doors opened. We stepped into the lobby then walked outside to a waiting limo by the curb. Valentino stopped, whispering something into Joseph's ear while slyly slipping a piece of paper into his palm with a handshake. Confused why he was speaking with one of my bodyguards, I chewed the inside of my cheek as I started to think.

Before I became too absorbed in my thoughts, Valentino swiveled around walking toward me with a grin spread across his face, holding his hand out. I tilted my head. He rolled his eyes, smirking.

"Come on."

Before sliding in, I spun to Joseph.

"We will be in the car behind you," he assured, pointing to the car parked behind the limo. "It's okay."

I gave Joseph a puzzled look then slowly turned back to Valentino. He wrapped his fingertips around the back of my hand as he helped me into the limo like a gentleman, before sitting next to me. The driver closed the door and we were off to dinner, or so I thought. I glanced over and Valentino's elbow was propped on the window and he played with his lip while staring outside.

"Where are we going to go eat?"

Facing me, he smiled an unforgettable grin, "I have a plan." He picked up his phone and began to text.

Uh, okay? And? He was so mysterious. I sat quietly, at a loss for words. If this was his idea of a dramatic pause, then he just got the world record. He peeked at me, chuckling in a deep voice.

"Oh, were you wanting more details?"

"I'm dressed in interview clothes," I noted, gesturing to my outfit, "not dinner clothes."

The corner of his lips hinted a hidden smile. "Would you be more comfortable if I let you go home and change first?" he offered.

Tucking my bottom lip between my teeth, I squinted, scared to say *yes*. His gaze targeted my lips. He slowly peeled away, focusing his attention on my eyes. Picking up the phone in the car, he told his driver to stop by my apartment.

The driver circled the block, arriving in front of my building. As we stepped out of the car, I turned to Joseph who had gotten out of the car behind us, striding to where we stood. He pulled a cigarette out of his front jacket pocket, lighting it then taking a long drag. Comfortably, he leaned against the limo. It was clear that he had no intent to follow us into the building.

My eyes widened. Placing my hands on my hips, I hissed, "Are you not coming up?"

"Oh right, sorry," he muttered, snuffing out his cigarette in the ashtray outside the building.

I was so unsure why he seemed so relaxed around Valentino. To say that it was odd would have been an understatement. I would have to remember to speak to him about it later. We waltzed through the door as the doorman held it open.

"Mr. Greco," he greeted Valentino, who only nodded.

Valentino

We stepped off the elevator into the large foyer of Isabelle's apartment. I finally got to see what my design team and movers had done with the penthouse. Magnificent, was the only way to describe it. Their skill set, along with design ideas matched the appearance I wanted it to have. Isabelle quickly glided upstairs to change. A few moments after she disappeared, one of my phones vibrated in my pocket. I pulled it out, reading texts from her.

Hey just wanted to check in with you.

He's here at my apartment but I am behaving. ;)

I swear.

I snickered to myself then smiled as I began to conjure up a sarcastic text but decided it was best not to be a jerk. Instead I was nice.

I miss you, just a few more days until I can see you. Xo

I smiled once more before sliding the phone back into my pocket, just in time to see her emerge from upstairs. My mouth fell open in awe as I stood up from the couch, absorbing in the breathtaking view of the most extraordinary woman. I was speechless.

As she slowly descended from the staircase, it took everything in me not to grab her, making love to her on the sofa. I was ready to blow my cover and just tell her everything in hopes that she would be with me.

The sad reality was that I could never be with this woman. I never played by the rules, but this was a contract between her father and me. If I messed up, her life would be in grave danger. I was already playing an extremely dangerous game that could very well result in her heart being broken. I could not think of a scenario in which Isabelle and I could ever be together, but I felt myself wanting it more every day.

In this version of me, I was candidly me; well, as true as I could be. I only allowed the public to experience but so much of me. The other version of myself was the version I kept hidden from the public; the dangerous one. That was the one where you should always sleep with one eye open if I was angry with you.

In both versions, I could never see us being together. It did not matter if it was the contract she and I had or the one I made with her father. I could never fully open up to her or be myself with her. I did not know what the hell I was thinking. Now I was stuck, possibly losing at my own game. I had to walk away, or I had to do this one hundred percent. Tonight, a decision would be made.

We returned to the car. I texted a few people making sure everything for the night was ready to go. I placed my arm around her, pulling her close. She instinctively slid over, leaning against my side. She tilted her face, peering up at me.

"Are you still not going to tell me where we're going?"

I bit my bottom lip while smiling, shaking my head. I stared out the window to keep from breaking my composure. She was slowly penetrating my soul. I was not sure I liked it as I felt like a prisoner in my own mind. Taking her hand in mine, I held on to her.

She looked down at my knuckles, gasping, "What happened?"

"A little boxing incident," I growled, before smiling.

She glared at me with a crooked smile that told me she knew I was full of shit, but she did not push for answers. The car came to a stop just by the Hudson River on a private pier. She sat up straighter, searching around with a perplexed expression. The driver opened my door and I stepped out, reaching my hand back into the car for Isabelle.

"Come with me," I instructed.

Taking my hand with a half-smile, she exited the car. We strolled down the short pier, hand in hand, boarding my yacht. She glanced around suspiciously before turning to me with wide eyes, letting go of my grip.

"You're not going to kill me, are you?" she gulped nervously.

I smirked without saying a word. Taking her hand in mine once again, I helped her onto the yacht, guiding her to the other side by a railing. I twirled her so that she was facing toward the water then snaked my arms around her waist as I pulled her against my body.

Without turning toward me, she joked, "This is where you push me over isn't it?"

"Who's going to stop me?" I whispered in her ear, teasing her.

She spun to face me, causing my arms to fall to my side.

"Actually, I know someone," she scoffed, crossing her arms playfully.

I raised my eyebrows, mocking her, "Oh, is that so?"

Nodding with a teasing smirk, she turned back toward the water. She started to trace my watch with her fingertips, inspecting it. I froze for a moment, wondering if she would somehow recognize it.

"What kind of watch is this?" she pondered. "I have never seen anything like it."

"It's a modified smart watch," I informed, "I use it sometimes to communicate with my security team."

Suddenly, her body tensed up as she swallowed hard.

"Are you okay, bella?" I muttered, gently stroking her arms up and down with my fingertips.

"Yeah."

I twisted her body to face me, searching her eyes for thoughts, or many answers. Her breath was slightly shallow as she gazed directly at me. Her lips parted to speak.

"Sir, dinner is served," one of my security guards interrupted.

She audibly gasped, covering her lips with one of her palms, but I ignored the gesture. Had she figured me out? I held out my hand offering it to hers.

"Are you ready?"

A slow smile crept on her face as she nodded. I took her hand, placing her body in front of mine while resting my hand gently on the small of her back, guiding her to the table on the deck. I pulled her chair out for her then sat down next to her after she was settled.

Our server placed napkins in our laps as Isabelle continued to stare at me. Starting to sense the wheels spinning in her head, I felt that I better address her. I was curious to know what she was thinking, even if she had this all figured out.

"What's on your mind?"

She glanced down at her lap, letting out a small laugh then peered back at me. "Honestly," she exhaled, "I don't even know right now."

"Fair enough."

Boss, I think she knows, Joseph's voice rang out in the small earpiece I wore.

I chuckled quietly out of nowhere, rolling my eyes as the server placed salads in front of us.

"Something I should know?" Isabelle queried with a slight grin.

I shook my head, pointing to my ear, smiling, "Just some of the guys think you look stunning tonight, that's all."

She giggled, gently elbowing me. Picking up her fork, she stabbed into her salad.

Leaning over closer to her, I whispered in her ear, "Understatement in my opinion. I would love to take you right here."

Losing control of her fork, it made a clanking sound as it fell onto the deck. She gulped as I leaned away from her, propping my elbow on the table. I mockingly grinned.

"I'm sorry bella," I taunted, "did I fluster you?"

She grabbed my fork, stabbing it into her salad as she peered at me smirking.

"You have a second fork you know," I pointed out. "You didn't have to steal mine."

"That's the dinner fork," she expressed confidently.

The woman knows her forks, Joseph chimed in through the earpiece.

I chose to ignore him. Joseph loved to push buttons, sometimes too much at the worst time. The server instantly delivered another to me when I signaled her.

By the time we were on the entrees, I decided to push my boundaries with Isabelle. Placing my hand on her bare thigh at the hem of her dress, I lightly gripped her leg, rubbing her soft skin in circles with my thumb. I was testing the waters, wanting to see if it would gain a negative reaction. She was mildly startled but did not shove my hand away. Her leg began to form goosebumps while I grinned at the effect I had on her.

Unable to resist her any longer, I slowly glided my hand up her leg, but suddenly felt her hand on top of mine, stopping me.

"Please don't do that," she whispered.

I froze, not wanting to upset her. "I apologize, I--."

"I made a promise to someone," she interrupted shyly, "and I need to keep it."

Fuck! I knew she was talking about me, well the other version of me. I never thought that I would be a challenge to myself. I glanced away, biting my bottom lip, torn between amusement and defeat. A part of me wanted to pull the other phone out of my pocket, texting her, *Let him touch you it's okay*. The other part of me just laughed at the unfortunate situation I had placed myself in with this woman. I had to play dumb, which would be hard.

"If I had known you had a boyfriend," I indicated, "I would not have asked you to dinner." I felt like a jerk, but I had to keep up the appearance at this point.

She wiped her lips with a napkin, turning her body toward me. "It's not like that but I cannot explain it," she conveyed.

Pressing for more info to see what she would say, I propped my elbow on the table, peering into her eyes, challenging her secrecy. I reached over with my other hand, hooking a long strand of her hair behind her ear. She leaned into my touch, but quickly pulled away.

"Try," I urged, "I am a great listener."

She shook her head, trying to find her words. "I can't." she fretted, "Trust me, the situation is so weird."

I nodded, deciding to leave it be, not attempting to reach up her skirt again. She smiled sweetly at me, but her eyes told a different story. She did want me. She was fighting it. Seeing this sign, I chose a gentler approach.

"Okay, I respect that," I cooed as I twirled a strand of her hair around my index finger.

Again, she leaned into my touch, closing her eyes, enjoying the moment. I slid my hand around to the back of her neck, rubbing my thumb lightly on her aroused skin. She almost moaned, but she opened her eyes, gazing into mine as her breathing began to get shallower.

"What are the rules about kissing you then?"

She tilted her head, her eyes filled with lust and desire. "That's a grey area," she gulped.

Leaning closer to her face, I pursed my lips. Her eyelids fluttered as she readied herself, anticipating my next move. My fingers slid into her hair, entangling into her strands as I lightly gripped. Fuck my other identity right now. Fuck whatever rules I had for her. I did not care what she did, as long as it was with me, either version of me. I pressed my lips into hers, parting her mouth with my tongue as we engaged in a passionate kiss. She reached up to my face, cupping my scruffy jaw.

Isabelle

Internally I was craving this man. I felt as if my body was going to explode any moment. Something about him was too familiar but I knew better. Things like this did not just happen in real life. I wanted to pull away from the kiss so badly, but I was so caught up in the way his tongue romantically danced with mine. Turning away his touch was hard enough but his kiss made me feel the electricity between us. I was a virgin, but I was full of naughty desires.

I needed to stop this before it became something that got me in trouble. The fact remained that Sir had also captured my attention. I made him a promise, and as much as I wanted Valentino right now, I needed to keep my word to Sir.

Maybe I only wanted Valentino because he was so mysterious. I was never one to break promises. Something was going on. A strange sensation rose up inside me. It was a gut feeling of some sort, but I did not know what just yet. Finally, I got up the strength to pull away from his tantalizing lips.

"I'm sorry," I apologized, glancing down into my lap.

He moved his free hand to mine. Interlocking his fingers with mine, he loosened his grip ever so slightly on my hair. "Is everything okay?" He sounded concerned as he slowly circled my neck with his thumb.

I nodded, feeling heat rise within me.

He stood with my hand still attached to his. My eyes followed his movements. He gazed down seductively at me, "Walk with me."

I jerked my hand back, gasping at his words. He also yanked back as if I had shocked him. His eyes widened as I sat staring up at him.

"Something I should be aware of?" he responded as he studied my face with a smirk of confusion.

I shook my head slowly. My mind was playing tricks on me. I stood, then we strolled hand in hand over to the railing of his yacht once again. He positioned himself behind me, resting his chin on my shoulder. I smiled, as my mind wandered, while enjoying him caressing me.

"I didn't want us to miss the sunset," he whispered in a remarkably familiar tone.

I took a deep breath, smiling. The puzzle in my brain

was beginning to form a picture, but I was not sure if it was accurate or I just wanted it to be that way. Questions in my mind were awakened, but I was terrified of asking him the one thing that I wanted to know.

10 GREAT ESCAPE

Isabelle

The ride home after our date was interesting to say the least. The wheels in my head continued to spin as Valentino and I had kissed the entire way back to my apartment. It did not feel as though we were strangers. I felt a connection to him, but I could not understand how it was possible. Other than the bar, bumping into him, and the interview, I felt something bigger was happening. I could not quite figure it out yet.

So much had happened recently. At this point, I was just trying to figure out how I would survive this world. I was still angry about the auction, but I was also trying not to focus on that part of my arrangement since I had not been forced to do anything. Sir had been nothing short of respectful, causing me to enjoy his company.

However, at the moment, I was turned on by another man, craving for him to hold me tighter. The passion between us was organic. I wanted to be ravished but a part of me felt guilty for feeling this way.

The limo pulled up in front of my apartment building, and the driver opened my door. I peeled myself away from him, but as I began to step out of the car, Valentino grabbed my arm, pulling me back into the seat. I nearly fell on top of him.

"Close the door for a moment," he ordered the driver.

The moment the door closed, he pulled me on top of him, arranging my legs on each side of his thighs. Straddling his lap was not how I envisioned the night going, but I was not protesting. He ran his fingers through my hair, scanning my eyes while searching for words. He slowly tucked his bottom lip between his teeth, gently biting down.

I could tell he was the one with a lot on his mind now. He seemed to want to tell me. His breathing became shallow as I felt the hardness of his erection growing beneath my already aroused womanhood.

"Isabelle," he whispered in his seductive Italian accent as his eyes glazed over in lust.

I found it difficult to speak. "Hmm."

He silently continued to search my eyes for whatever he was hoping to find. Before another word was spoken, he finally pulled me in to his lips for another kiss but this time it was a soft and sensual peck on the corner. He pulled away, slowly opening his eyes.

"I had an amazing time with you tonight," he assured. "I hope you will let me take you out again soon."

I nodded, beaming, "Thank you for taking me out even after I fainted in your office."

He chuckled, appearing cocky. "It's not the first time trust me," he winked as he pulled me in to his body, mischievously kissing my neck. "Come on, I'll walk you up."

I placed my hand on his chest. "Um no sir, I'm fine," I playfully retorted. "I can walk myself."

His mouth fell open as he grabbed his chest on top of his heart. "Ohhh, you're throwing me out on the street," he joked.

I giggled, "No, I'm leaving you in your very expensive limo."

"But, alone."

I grinned at him then climbed off his lap. I tapped on the window and the driver opened the door. Stepping outside of the car, I spun to Valentino, bending down, seeing that he was in a staring contest with my backside.

I brought his attention to my eyes with a gesture. "Goodnight, Mr. Greco."

A malicious grin spread across his face. "You can call me Sir," he winked.

Just as my mouth fell agape, the driver closed the door then strode to the front of the car. I could not move. Suddenly, a body popped out of the moon roof. Valentino leaned his elbows on the roof of the car, appearing authoritative.

"See you Monday?"

Arching a brow, I placed my hands on my hips. "What's Monday?"

He smiled, descending back into the car then popped back up again, throwing me a pair of keys with a keycard. I am proud to say, my flustered self, managed to catch them. Holding them up, I inspected them, noting the company logo on the key card.

"What's this?"

"I might have fired Samantha and gave you her job."

My mouth fell agape once again. I did not know what to say, so I stood on the sidewalk speechless at his gesture. Either he had seen how she acted toward me or he had planned on firing her anyway.

"Isabelle," he snickered.

I snapped my mouth closed, peering up at him.

"Are you going to faint again? Do I need to call an ambulance for you this time?"

I shoved the keys into my handbag, rolling my eyes at him while smiling. He tapped the top of the limo and it started to drive away. He turned back to me winking, before he disappeared into the car. I happily danced in place before realizing Joseph was standing behind me when he cleared his throat.

"Joseph," I gasped, spinning to face him. "How long have you been watching me act stupid?"

"The entire time, Miss," he claimed before tucking both of his lips between his teeth attempting to mask his amusement.

Shaking my head, I sped past him highly embarrassed, but he quickly followed, keeping my pace. He did not dare laugh as we marched through the building doors into the lobby, waiting for the elevator. Not a word was spoken while I shifted my weight. I watched the numbers change.

Joseph slid his phone out of his pocket, intently staring down at the screen. He glanced up, checking the lobby doors every few seconds.

We stepped into the elevator and he pulled out his card, swiping it into the access panel. As we ascended, he suddenly got a profoundly serious look on his face. I titled my head, wondering what was on his mind, but then I heard a muffled voice coming from his ear.

Yes, I am, he replied.

Moments later he responded once again, *Okay.*

Right now? he groaned, but this time into his watch.

I was puzzled but I did not say anything. Instead, I watched the floor. Tuning out his words, I continued thinking about the *Sir* comment that Valentino made earlier. It felt odd to me that he would say that.

We are in the elevator, but we will prepare to leave immediately, Joseph replied to the person on the other end of his earpiece once again.

"Miss Ayala," he cleared his throat. "We have to take you to the estate tonight," he calmly muttered.

"What?!" I choked. "It's not the weekend!"

Maybe word somehow got back to Sir about my night and he was livid. I should have been worried about breaking the contract he and I had together. However, I was more concerned about the fact I might have disappointed him in some way. I sighed, feeling like I betrayed him. Joseph did not speak. He stared ahead at the doors, ignoring my statement.

"Is everything okay?" I continued to question him, "What happened?"

The elevator slowed down, coming to a stop. I stepped out into my apartment, but Joseph planted himself in front of me. He began to point his gun in various places around the penthouse, scanning our surroundings. My eyes widened, noting this new approach to entry.

Placing his watch to his lips this time, he announced, "All clear."

"Joseph what's going on?" I hissed.

Without saying a word, he grabbed my hand, practically dragging me upstairs to my bedroom.

"What are you doing to me?" I pleaded, anxiety building within me.

As we entered my bedroom, he dropped his gun to his side, glaring at me with his hand on my arm. I gulped, now terrified that something terrible was about to happen to me. Joseph's grip tightened on my arm, causing my eyes to water. He did not hurt me, but his normal friendly mood had become alarming. He focused his eyes carefully on mine, commanding my undivided attention.

"You have exactly ninety seconds to pack whatever you need," he blustered as he began to look at his watch.

I froze, my eyes darting around the room.

"Eighty," he blurted, never looking up from his wrist.

"Okay okay," I panicked, sprinting into my closet. "Oh my God."

"Seventy," he called out aggressively from my room, his voice carrying through the large suite.

I continued to throw anything and everything into my bag, that I thought I might need. I was only paying minimal attention since I was flustered, confused, and alarmed. Jogging into my bathroom, I repeated the action, shoving all my toiletries and make-up into a smaller bag.

"Forty!" he yelled.

I dashed back into my closet mentally counting everything that I had, trying to make sure that I did not miss anything that I may need in any situation. Circling the room, I grabbed a few more things, panting. Zipping up my bags, I closed my eyes, taking the deepest breath that I could muster.

"We have to go right now!" he loudly warned, emphasizing the word, *go*.

Scooping my bags off the floor, I emerged from the closet, announcing, "Okay, ready."

He placed his watch up to his mouth. "Roof access," he conversed, "We are on our way up."

Leading me to the end of my upstairs hallway, he held his watch up to the dead-end wall, or so that is what it appeared to be. I became astonished as the wall made a small popping sound, sliding out and to the side. A long corridor with silver, metal walls was revealed while blue tinted lights lit up, illuminating the path. At the end of the hallway was a tall, spiral staircase leading to a door.

"Secure access doors," Joseph ordered.

The door behind us slammed closed, causing me to jump.

He promptly reached out, taking my bags from my hands then planted himself in front of me. We climbed the staircase as quickly as we could. He opened the door at the top of the stairs, revealing a helicopter in the middle of a landing pad.

Several men stood waiting nearby with guns drawn, pacing the roof. My eyes nervously darted around, wondering what was happening. If I ran, I would be killed.

Joseph seemed so nice. Why was he doing this? Was I being kidnapped?!

The door on the side of the helicopter opened and he helped me climb in. Oh god, I *was* being kidnapped! Why would Joseph do this to me? I felt lightheaded as the air around me became thick. Tunnel vision set it. Uh oh, I tried to swallow but my throat felt as if I had eaten an entire sleeve of crackers without water. I was going to pass out again.

Joseph secured me into the seat then closed the door, getting situated across from me. The other armed men jumped into the helicopter as well and that is when I noticed they were my security from the apartment, not random people. Joseph gave a signal to the pilot then we took off, high above the city. My eyes began to tear up, uncertain of my future.

Just as we got away from the building, the access door to the roof opened. Four armed men emerged from where Joseph and I had just been. They were holding, what appeared to be, pistols and assault rifles. I was not being kidnapped. I was being saved.

Still peering out the window with wide eyes, I gasped, "Who are those guys?" I turned to him, repeating frantically, "Joseph, who are those guys back there?"

"You do not need to worry about them," he leaned forward, patting me on the knee, smiling. "We will arrive to our destination in fifty-two minutes"

I nodded, sighing, still attempting to catch my breath.

"Relax please," he encouraged.

Concerned, I could not quite relax yet. I was still shaken up about the event that just occurred on the roof. Still, I had no idea what had actually just happened or why anyone would be after one of them, or me. Perhaps it was a case of mistaken identity? I had no clue.

"Will you please tell me where we are going?" I pleaded.

"The estate of course," he confessed as he glanced toward the other guys, rolling his eyes. "You will be very safe there."

I sighed, relaxing a bit.

"By the way, we're not kidnapping you," he smirked.

"Wha--"

"Sometimes you think," he interrupted then paused, "*verbally.*"

I huffed, slumping in my seat, but was restricted by my seatbelt. Joseph chuckled deliberately. The others all exchanged a knowing glance as I pulled out my phone. I started to use my time to think about the massive puzzle that was locked inside my brain.

I had my ear buds with me, so I placed them into my ears, listening to my favorite playlist on full volume. Staring out the window, I watched as the city got further away. Closing my eyes, I laid my head back, trying to relax as much as possible while listening to one of my favorite songs.

Joseph tapped me on my knee again, causing me to pull my earbuds out in a hurry. I jerked my body, stiffing up in my seat, realizing that I had dozed off. I exhaled, peering outside the window. Not more than a couple of hours ago, I was on the greatest date of my life and now I was back to the one place that I actually learned to enjoy being, other than the obvious.

"We're here," Joseph muttered.

Instantly, I became nervous, watching the monstrous, elegant mansion grow larger as we flew over the garden. Just as I was thinking how I hoped I did not get in trouble, Joseph handed me a black, lace veil.

"Of course," I sighed, shaking my head.

Pursing his lips, he shrugged, "I know, but rules are rules."

For some reason, I was not bothered by the veil any longer. I had a sense of peace within me. A grin swept over my face as I thought about the possibility of seeing Sir which caused me to nervously twirl my hair around my finger. The helicopter landed on the rooftop. Shortly after the blades decelerated to a slow rotation, the pilot helped me down and onto the roof. I was escorted into an elevator attached to the house.

"Wait, we passed my floor."

"Yes, Miss," Joseph declared with amusement in his tone as his back was turned toward me. "He would like to see you in his office."

"Are you smiling?" I teased, glaring at him. I could only see the outline of the back of his head.

"I am not," he lied.

The elevator came to a stop and the doors opened. We stepped out into the all too familiar hallway that led to the office. A trace of leather with rich earthy wood scents filled the air. The other security detail and pilot scattered. Joseph and I turned the corner and came to a stop outside the doors.

I shook off the suspicion, smoothing my dress, hoping he would not smell any lingering scent of Valentino on me. Nervously, I exhaled, trying to wave the feeling that I may be in trouble. I also wondered why the men with guns were in my penthouse and what would happen now. Could I ever return?

Joseph interrupted my thoughts, whispering, "Ready?"

Before I could respond, he opened the doors, leaving me no choice but to falter into the room. I almost fell as I veered too much to the right, forgetting that there was a statue just inside the door on a pedestal. It almost fell over, but I caught it, balancing it back in place. Spinning around to face the desk, I paused, trying to allow my eyes to adjust.

"Boss, I will need to speak with you tonight before you sleep." Joseph called out from the doorway. "It's important."

"It can wait!" Sir snapped at him.

Joseph closed the doors just as I saw movement at Sir's desk. I pivoted to face him. He sat perched on the edge at the front, holding something in his hands, but I could not see what it was.

"Come to me Isabelle," he commanded in a low, husky tone.

I slowly crept toward him, sitting in the chair facing his desk.

"Did I tell you that you could sit down?" he growled under his breath.

Confused, I stood. Shifting my weight back and forth, I tried to mask my fear with confidence. I became frightened, thinking he was about to scream at me for making out with Valentino. How did he know? Did Joseph rat me out? I felt terrible.

"You seem a little bothered right now."

"I-I'm not bothered," I stammered, altering my stance again.

He flicked his right wrist quickly. *SNAP!* A sharp pain followed by an intense surge of pleasure spread though my most sensitive area. I realized the object he was holding was a black, leather belt. He had just slapped the top of my slit through my dress and panties, but it felt as if I were naked.

"Ouch!" I gasped in shock.

He stood, slowly circling me as if he were hunting his prey. He came to a stop in front of me. Flicking his wrist again, his belt repeated its action, only this time it was significantly more extreme.

"You know Isabelle," he chuckled wickedly, pacing back and forth before me, the belt almost dragging the floor. "Anyone can pick up a belt, but if you can't fuck her mind, you'll never fully dominate her body."

Feelings of both soreness and euphoria spread throughout my body as I gulped. My entire core began to tremble, causing a remarkably familiar feeling in the junction of my thighs.

He leaned close to my nape, inhaling deeply. "You smell like him," he muttered.

I drew in a rapid inadvertent breath. Without even thinking, I snapped, "You do too actually." It was true.

He jerked away from me very swiftly. "Isabelle I'm not playing games with you," he scoffed, frustrated. "Did you let him touch you?"

He wrapped his belt around his hand, gripping it tightly. His eyes following my every move. I turned to him, reaching for my veil. With a quick movement, he jerked his head back, bracing himself.

"Got you!" I playfully winked, teasing him, but dropped my hands to my side after realizing my *wink* was useless.

Taking a deep breath, he instantly closed the gap between us, cupping my face while pulling me to his lips.

His tongue intruded my mouth, dancing and swirling around as he dominated the kiss, controlling each movement. Moaning, I peeled myself away, placing both of my hands on his chest.

"Sir--," I whispered.

"What did I tell you about calling me that?" he interjected nearly in a deep growl.

"I kissed him for half the night but that's all," I admitted shamefully, even though I enjoyed it.

"I don't fucking care," he conceded as he collided his lips with mine.

I practically collapsed in his embrace, melting into his kiss. Moments later, he peeled himself away. He trailed his tongue from my neck to my shoulder. The craving I had was building within me all night and came crashing down on me at once.

Hooking his fingers under the straps of my dress, he slid the top down, exposing my black lace bra. It was one he had bought and stocked in my room. My breath became thin, my throat became dry. I gulped as his hands cupped my breasts. He circled his thumbs around my nipples through the fabric. I closed my eyes, enjoying his touch.

"Bella, I want to take you to my bed," he muttered.

Instantly, I froze. Bella? Surely my mind was playing mean tricks on me. This was what happened when you felt guilt. I was hearing things. Valentino was the only one who called me *bella*. There is no way in hell this could be...

"Tell me to stop, please," he exhaled with desperation in his tone, interrupting my thoughts. "I'm not sure I will be able to stop on my own."

"Sir--," I voiced softly.

He stopped massaging my breasts but did not move his hands. I could tell that he was deeply glaring into my eyes, though with the threading, I still could not see more than subtle features. I squinted, trying to get a better look at him, but to no avail, I was unable to see if my suspicions were accurate.

My sex was soaking through my panties. I desired to be controlled. Silently, he waited for me to finish my thought as he leaned closer to my mouth, awaiting my permission. My panting turned into a silent gulp as I prepared myself for the moment that he had paid for. Was it even about the money any longer? I no longer cared.

"I'm ready."

Briefly, I felt his lips curl into a smile as he grabbed me, tossing me over his shoulder in one smooth, flawless motion. He threw the double doors to his office open then marched down the corridor to the elevator. Gently, he placed me down before he grabbed my face again, crashing his lips into mine with such force that it pushed me into the wall behind me.

His hands explored every inch of my upper body while his mouth moved to my neck. I gasped as he pinched my erect nipples while dropping to his knees, pulling my dress up. Leaning into the junction of my thighs, he began kissing the outside of my soaked panties. I inhaled sharply as he nibbled, my legs growing shaky.

He stood as the elevator came to a stop. Picking me up bridal style, we exited then entered what I assumed to be his bedroom. He closed the door, making sure to lock it. Taking my hand in his, he guided me to the middle of the room. He took his time unzipping my dress, causing it to fall to the floor. I reached for his chest, but he understood my signal, and removed his own shirt.

Immediately, he picked me up, forcing me to wrap my legs around his muscular body. He carried me over to the bed, gently setting me down. Bending over, he inhaled my scent as my body instinctively reclined back. Every part of me trembled at both his touch and the cool air of the room.

"I am not a good man, bella," he seductively growled.

Inhaling sharply at him repeating that nickname, I froze. It was as if Valentino was scolding me for being with another man. But, the man pleasing me at that moment, had also captured my attention. I was his to take.

Gently, he ran his palms up and down my thighs. "I have a very fucking dark side to me," he warned before lightly kissing my inner thigh. "I like to play very naughty games."

He nipped the inside of my other thigh with his teeth, causing a pinching sensation. I squirmed as a moan flowed from my lips. Unable to focus any longer, I let my mind relax as he took further control.

Covering my sex with his mouth he murmured, "This is your first time so I will play fair."

He spread my essence beneath the fabric, locating my button. Taking it between his teeth, he gently bit, causing us both to moan in unison. The sensation of the humming and his warm breath almost sent me over the edge. I had never been affected this way before. Every sense in my body was awakening under his touch.

Backing away, he crawled up my body to my mouth. Slipping my panties to the side, he began to gently stroke his index finger up and down my slit. My bottom lip found its way between his teeth. He smiled against my skin before firmly and forcefully kissing me as he plunged not one, but two fingers deep into my core.

I squirmed under his body and moaned into his mouth.

He pulled back and his mouth found my neck, "God you are so fucking tight and wet," he whispered against my neck. I was unraveling in every sense. He pulled his fingers out and stuck them into my mouth, "Taste yourself."

I obeyed and moaned, "Yes, Sir." I swirled my tongue around his fingers and he suddenly yanked them out before shoving them back inside my core as his tongue assaulted mine.

"Amo il tuo sapore," he growled between kisses.

Valentino

And that is when we both froze. I dropped my head onto her chest, burying my face in defeat. The game was over, I lost. The end.

"Cazzo!" I blurted with a muffle into the area between her breasts.

I was screwed. She had not moved or spoken but her breathing was labored, and I knew it was more than just her arousal at that point. I could feel her rapid pulse as my fingers were frozen deep inside her tight, throbbing core.

Internally, I battled myself on how I should go about handling this. That is when I did something that would change everything between us from that night forward. Gradually, I lifted my head, only to be met with her faultless, bright, blue eyes already staring into mine. Her mouth was agape as she gripped her lace blindfold in the palm of her hand. For roughly thirty excruciating, silent seconds we only stared at one another.

As I prepared to open my mouth ready to defend myself, her state of shock transformed into a hungry lust. She began slowly moving her hips, pressing herself into my hand as she pursed her lips. Without further hesitation, I explored her insides, pleasuring her center. Reaching out, she ran her fingers through my hair as I cautiously leaned closer toward her mouth.

"I was hoping it was you," she whispered against my lips.

I smiled against her words, placing a gentle kiss on her cheek before standing up. Removing my pants and boxer briefs, I watched her squirming on the bed, ready for me. Trailing my fingers up her legs, I hooked my fingertips under the top of her panties, sliding them off. I tossed them over my shoulder as I climbed back on top of her. Snaking my hand behind her, I held her closely to my body as I unclasped her bra in a single motion. I tossed it over my other shoulder before I lined my erection up with her entrance.

"Are you sure about this?" I teased with my signature evil grin.

11 EXPOSED

Valentino

My evil grin altered into pure desire as I slowly entered her. She writhed beneath me, moaning into my mouth as I wrapped my arms around her, holding her close. Passionately and deeply, I kissed her sensual lips while breaking through her innocent barrier.

She cried out, arching her back as our fervent kiss masked her sound. I stopped moving my body to give her time to adjust to my size. Her breathing began to slow as she broke our kiss, gazing at me with tears in her eyes.

Leaning on one of my elbows, I locked my fingers with hers.

"Are you okay, bella?"

She nodded, a slow smile spreading across her delicate face. "Don't hold back please," she pleaded while beginning to grind herself against my body. "I'm a virgin, not a fragile bird."

I leaned down, resting my lips against her ear. "Oh, but bella," I reprimanded, "you must learn to fly before you can soar with eagles."

She gasped as I plunged deeper into her sheath, causing her to let out an involuntary scream.

"Are...you...sure...this is...what you...want?" I quipped with a smirk between thrusts.

Her arms automatically flew around my neck, digging her fingernails harshly into the muscular flesh of my shoulder blades. She painfully dragged them across my back ever so slowly as she moaned, hummed, and cried out with each thrust into her tunnel. I felt the burn of the streaks she was creating behind me.

"Fucking hell," I growled, "you feel incredible," I professed.

Her eyes were sealed closed as she enjoyed every moment. Tears began to trickle from the corners of her cerulean eyes as she met my pace, causing deeper penetration. Tucking her bottom lip between her teeth, she smiled as she opened her eyes, peering down at my flexed chest. She watched herself tracing the outline of my muscles as she hungrily studied my body.

"Look at me."

"Oh my God!"

I slowed my movement to a stop, draping my fingers around her wrists. Holding them over her head with a strong grip, I wrapped my other palm around her breast, nibbling her nipple before pulling it into my mouth with a strong suction. It was taking all my strength not to be rough with her, but so far, I maintained a good balance.

"Do not move your hands," I sternly instructed as I glared into her eyes with authority. "Do you understand me?"

She nodded, biting her bottom lip, smiling.

Taking her breast in my mouth once again, I slowly ran my hand down her body, locating her little pink button lightly pinching it. She bowed her back, releasing a loud cry, while gripping my shoulder.

"I said not to move your hands," I repeated my order more aggressively, applying more pressure to her button as my thumb massaged it.

"Oh…wow…oh…Val…what are you doing to me?" she panted, squirming beneath my body.

"Do you like that, baby girl?" I smirked as I continued my assault on her clit with my thumb as I plunged in and out of her core again.

"Something is happening to me!" she yelled, almost pleading for mercy. "I think I'm going to pass out!"

I felt her already tight crevice begin to form a vice on my shaft. Leaning over, I sank my teeth into her nape, turning her moans into screams of passion.

"Fuck…oh my God…yesss…oh my God!"

Internally, I began to panic as I could not hold back my orgasm any longer. Panting, I questioned, "You've been taking the pills I gave you the night we met yes?"

"Yes, of course," she moaned.

"Good," I confirmed as I immediately let myself go inside of her.

After what seemed like an exceptionally long time, I collapsed my head on top of her chest as the last spurt deeply entered her core. Neither of us spoke yet, as we were both still riding the waves of our euphoric high.

I carefully rolled off her, pulling her into my side, holding her tightly against me. Looking into her eyes, I smiled as I placed a gentle kiss on her forehead. She calmly moaned as she pressed her head into my lips.

"I hope I lived up to your *sexpectations*," I joked.

Stroking my pectoral muscles with her fingertips, she hummed, "I think I fainted a few times."

"That wouldn't surprise me considering you couldn't even stay conscious in an interview with me," I winked, chuckling quietly.

She suddenly became serious as she peered into my eyes with a content expression.

"What?" I smirked, unable to read her.

She sighed, "I feel like it's a dream." Pressing herself closer into my side, she grinned broadly, "I just can't believe you're him, or he's you or--."

"It's me," I confirmed, pursing my lips as I twirled a strand of her hair around my index finger.

She suddenly playfully slapped my chest and sat up, proclaiming, "I want more!"

"You're going to be one of those girls, aren't you?"

"I don't know what you mean."

"There are women out there, that no matter how much they get, they want more," I explained with a furrowed brow.

"So basically, like all guys," she snickered as she moved so she was facing me, sitting with her legs folded.

"Yes," I simpered. "Just like all guys."

She laid back down in my arms, curling her body around mine. This was a very foreign feeling to me. I had never allowed this, until Isabelle. I knew this was a quite different situation, but she was unique. Had she been a random girl I bid on, then yes, she would not have been in my bedroom or on my bed. She would not even still be in my house. I knew that the reality of what we had just done would hit me very soon. For now, I was going to enjoy this; enjoy her.

"Would you like to shower with me?" I offered, kissing her forehead again.

She sighed, "Is that breaking the rules?"

I shrugged, stroking her hair, "So was taking your blindfold off but that didn't stop you."

"Maybe if you were better at hiding your identity," she teased, "I would not have done that."

"You still broke the rules," I noted.

Her bare chest started to rise and fall heavily. She stared intently into my eyes with lust. It was as if she could sense what was coming. I could see the wheels turning in her mind as she conjured her reply. Bravery overtook her as her lust filled gazed turned to a starving glare.

"What happens when I break the rules, Sir?"

Isabelle

As I lied next to him silently after I asked him that question, I awaited an answer. I felt a sense of bravery come over me since Valentino and Sir turned out to be the same person. He took a deep breath, placing his hand on my leg just above the knee. As he began to run his fingertips slowly and seductively up my leg, his phone rang.

He threw his body back, groaning, "I hate my life sometimes."

"Yeah your life seems to suck really bad," I snorted.

He blindly reached over, swiping his phone off the bedside table.

Yes? he grunted.

I'll be there in a moment, he sighed, rolling his eyes before hanging up.

"You have to go?"

He dropped his phone on the bedside table then turned me, nodding, "I do for a little while."

He sat up, sliding his body to the edge of the bed then buried his head in his hands. My eyes widened and I sat up. I noticed the art that I had aggressively created on his back with my nails. He did not seem in pain or bothered by it.

"Oh geez, I'm so sorry," I apologized as I traced my fingertips around the scratches.

He shivered, closing his eyes while rolling his bottom lip between his teeth. "It's more than okay, Isabelle."

He sauntered into his bathroom while I sat on the bed, unsure of what he wanted me to do. I did not know if I should go to my own room or lie back, enjoying the scent of sex and his cologne in the air. I inhaled deeply, becoming intoxicated in the moment.

Before I could make a decision, he entered the bedroom, interrupting my thought. He buttoned up a pair of dark blue, jeans as he strolled toward me with a light grey t-shirt over his shoulder. Grabbing the shirt, he pulled it over his head before leaning down, leaving a gentle lingering kiss on my lips.

"Feel free to use my shower if you want," he smiled. "I mean, I don't mind, you know," he continued. "Towels are in my bathroom closet and help yourself to anything you need. If you do not find it, it's probably in your bathroom."

I nodded, grinning as I listened intently to his instructions.

Taking the remote off his nightstand, he turned the television on. "It's pretty simple to work so you'll figure it out," he winked as he handed it to me.

Gently taking it from his hands, I laid it in front of me on the bed before turning my attention back to him.

"I shouldn't be too long but please do not come to my office," he requested but in a commanding tone. "If you need me, please text me."

"Okay."

I lied back down as he leaned over the bed, pressing his lips to mine once again. Prying my mouth open with his tongue, he aggressively began to assault my own tongue as he entangled one hand in my hair and reached down to my thighs with the other. Gently, he stroked my soft, warm skin before reluctantly pulling back from our kiss. I sat up once again, holding onto his arm.

"I don't want to go, trust me."

"Then stay," I whined, dragging out the Y.

"I'll be back before you know it," he smirked, before marching out of the room, closing the door behind him.

I threw myself back on the bed, covering my eyes with my palms, grinning from ear to ear. Oh my God! I just lost my virginity and it was the single, greatest moment of my entire existence. I wanted to squeal loudly. I wanted to dance.

I stood and that is when I realized that I was a little sore. I limped uncomfortably into the bathroom, feeling the remnants of our sex slowly running down my thighs. After grabbing a towel from the closet, I stepped into the shower to turn it on. There were buttons and faucet jets all over the walls. For a moment I was unsure if I was in a shower, or a spaceship.

"Ok shower," I contended confidently, "we're going to not spray me in the face, okay?"

I turned a nob, but nothing happened. Rolling my eyes, I tried another. Again, nothing happened. I finally pushed a blue button, resulting in me getting blasted in the face with a stream of ice cold water. I jumped back, giggling in humiliation, but happy no one was around to see my unfortunate accident. I pressed the red button, which made more sense. The water began to warm up. I found the regular, *non-alien* settings for the shower, noting what each one did as I tested them. I swiftly cleaned myself off then stepped out, drying off.

I realized I did not have any clothes in his room, so I debated crawling into his bed and remaining naked or running to my room in a towel, which was on another floor. I decided to get in bed instead, but I got sidetracked on the way by his closet door, so I entered.

Rotating in a slow circle, peering around the massive room, I felt completely swallowed up in the space. Unhurriedly, I roamed around, running my fingertips over his luxurious suits, taking mental pictures as I noted all his perfectly polished, pricey shoes, next to his designer sneakers.

I came to a stop in front of his shirts, glancing back over my shoulder, checking for any sign of life. He was still gone. I probably should not have, but I slipped one of his dress shirts off the hanger. Sliding my arms through it, I hugged it tightly around my body. I pranced over to the full-length mirror, admiring how it fit me compared to how it probably fit his tall, muscular body.

Suddenly, I realized how different I felt and looked. I felt...*free*. I could not explain it. It felt as if he took a piece of me, then gave me back a bigger one; a much bigger one in his case. I giggled to myself. Not that I had anything to compare his size to, but I had seen them before, of course. He was definitely larger than the ones I had seen.

Twisting my body to see my perky rump in the mirror, I winced at the soreness between my legs, being reminded that I had just been having an amazing time with a demigod. Biting my bottom lip, I tried not to smile so big even though no one could currently see me. My face instantly contorted to confusion when I realized why I had been brought here. The guns. The men. What was happening?

Valentino

After my wonderful night with Isabelle, I practically sprinted to my office. I wanted to be upstairs with her, but instead I just left her alone after I took her virginity, forcing her to deal with it on her own. What if she panicked? What if she regretted it then tried to make a run for it? I messed everything up, sleeping with the one person I was told specifically not to be with. She was now in danger, and it was my fault. Angrily, I threw the doors to my office open.

"This better be important," I announced furiously as I marched around my men and threw myself into my desk chair.

They stared at me, as if they were waiting for me to yell. Glaring at each of them, I formed a triangle with my fingertips as I leaned back in my chair. Still no one uttered a word. Joseph cleared his throat and William shifted his weight.

"What?!" I shouted, finally breaking the silence, hurling my hands in the air.

William took a small step forward, with his hands in his pockets. "We have a slight issue and you're not going to like it," he sighed, crossing his arms.

"Well then," I scoffed, gesturing toward him, "please fucking enlighten me, Liam!"

Averting his eyes to Blaine, he bowed his head. Stepping to the side of the room, he leaned on the wall, folding his arms over his chest, bracing himself for whatever was to follow. I had seen that look in his eyes many times. It was never a good outcome. Blaine gave him a worried glimpse. William lifted his hand signaling for him to proceed.

Blaine stepped forward with a file folder, dropping it on the center of my desk. He wrapped one of his arms around his stomach as he lifted his other hand to his mouth, wincing a bit.

"Why are you making that face?" I snapped. "What is that?" I suspiciously questioned, almost scared to touch the folder based on the appearance of Blaine's expression.

"You're going to want to see that," Joseph chimed in from the back of the room.

Glancing up at him, I rolled my eyes, huffing as I reached out. Before I could touch it, William appeared out of nowhere, slamming his hand down on it, pulling it away. He held it close to his body as Blaine took a giant step back, retreating to the other side of the room.

"Listen Valentino," William cleared his throat.

Normally William referred to me as Boss, or Val, depending on the situation so I knew that whatever was in that folder, I was not going to like. He turned his back to me.

"Would everyone please step out and leave Blaine and I alone with him?" he requested of my security team.

Joseph lifted his chin, awaiting my approval. Raising my hand, I waved them away. After the doors were closed, William turned his attention back to me, gripping the folder.

"I know I shouldn't preface anything like this," he warned, "but I need you to not freak out."

"Give me that fucking file," I snapped, snatching the folder out of his hand.

I opened the cover, thumbing through the pages. My eyes searched for answers I thought they already knew. William got ready to speak, but I lifted my hand in the air signaling for him to not dare open his mouth. It was in that moment that my eyes fell on the face of an extremely familiar man.

"The masquerade!" I exclaimed. "He's the asshole who kept bidding against me!"

William cleared his throat, tapping his finger on his mouth, mumbling, "We were able to find out who was behind the mask, and well, just turn the page."

"What did you say?" I growled, gritting my teeth as I glowered at William.

He lowered his eyes, taking a deep breath while shaking his head. Pinching the bridge of his nose, he opened his mouth to speak, but failed. I averted my eyes to the papers once again, turning the page. That moment, rage grew within me as I was face to face with a zoomed in photo of the one person in my life that I loathed.

"Uh no," I chuckled sarcastically, slamming the folder closed before tossing it onto my desk. "Nice one. Where's the real one?"

William shook his head, sliding his hands into his pockets as he stared directly into my eyes. Blaine shifted his weight from one foot to the other, seemingly more nervous at my reaction. I rolled my eyes as I placed my hands on my hips.

"You're joking!" I snapped. "Please tell me that you are fucking kidding me!"

I stomped to the wall, drew my fist back, and punched it as hard as my strength would allow without shattering my knuckles. Spinning around, I pointed at both of them, disapprovingly.

"Are you fucking kidding me?!" I roared.

I slowly opened the door to my bedroom seeing she was asleep. Trying to be as quiet as possible, I crept into the room, slowly clicking the door closed. Among my anger tonight, I still smiled to myself as I inched closer to her, carefully removing the pillow off her face before slipping my clothes off. As I slid into bed, she turned the opposite way. I pulled her body into mine, wrapping my arm around her, holding her.

She squirmed a bit, trying to settle herself once again. I began to grow against her backside. Slowly and gently, I ran my fingertips up her smooth skin, placing small kisses on the back of her neck. She woke up in a fright, peering back over her shoulder in fear.

"Shhh," I soothed, "it's just me."

"Everything okay?" she mumbled with a sleepy voice. "I heard yelling before I fell asleep."

"Si, bella," I rasped, running my fingers through her hair.

She instinctively rolled over to face me, wrapping her leg around my waist. I smirked coyly as I gazed into her eyes. Leaning forward, I gently kissed her soft lips.

"Nothing you need to be worried about." I lifted my chin, resting a lingering peck on her forehead.

Her sleepy eyes were struggling to stay open, but she sluggishly sat up, wiping them with her fingertips. I altered my weight, propping up on my elbow, wondering what she was doing. She began to stand, but I tugged her wrist, pulling back into the bed.

Turning to face me, she whispered, "I was just going to go to my room."

I tilted my head, smiling at her adorable face with messy strands of hair falling into her eyes. She puckered her lips before yawning. Caressing her arm, I watched her face began to contort in confusion.

"Why do you have to go?" I mused.

"I'm sure you want to sleep," she conceded, "and that is my room."

I chuckled, running my palm up her thigh, "Well I need you next to me tonight."

While that was the truth, tomorrow I would have to come clean about a few things. I was not looking forward to it at all. She deserved to at least know that Tanya was not wronging her. I am sure if anything, she could use a friend at the moment. I was getting ready to turn her entire world inside out. Correction, I was about to turn both of our worlds upside down.

That night, I fell asleep holding her in my arms, tightly against my body. It was something I had sworn off doing with anyone, but a line had been crossed. It was a line that I had been wanting to cross for a long time with her.

The black, lace veil would come out to play again soon, but it would not be because I did not want her to see me. Next time, it would be because I did not want her to see what was coming.

The next morning, I called down to the kitchen, ordering my executive chef to make us a nice filling breakfast with mimosas. Tenderly, I stroked her cheek as I kissed her sensual lips to wake her. She stirred, smiling as she woke to my gesture.

"What time is it?" she yawned, stretching.

"Time for you to get a watch," I joked.

"Ha-ha Valentino has old people jokes," she teased as she stood on the bed with a foot on each side of my body, peering down at me smirking beneath her. She smiled, "Are you always this cheerful in the morning?"

"I am now that I can see your eyes," I asserted with a cheeky grin.

Reaching out, I grabbed her ankle to pull her down, but she danced out of the way, dodging my hands as I continued to grab at her legs. I gave up, allowing her to have the win. She positioned herself in the same stance above my body, giggling as I rolled my eyes.

She playfully glared down at me taunting, "You gotta be faster than that, *Sir*." She purposely enunciated the former nickname that I had ordered her to call me.

I pulled my pillow from underneath my head, tossing it at her. It smacked her face, muffling whatever she said next. My mouth fell open as my eyes widened, unsure if she was hurt or not. I know it was just a pillow, but I did not expect it to hit her so hard.

"Oh my God," I laughed harshly, apologizing with half concern, "I'm so sorry!" I covered my mouth, trying to hide the amused expression.

She began to snicker as she hopped off the bed. "I'm going to shower and get dressed," she called as she entered my bathroom.

"We can just eat naked in here if you want," I shouted back to her, dreading getting out of bed.

She emerged from the bathroom wearing only my robe which was loose on her small frame. I stood, stretching as I approached her. Snaking my arms around her body, I pulled her tightly against me.

"I need to go to my room and pick out something to wear," she murmured.

I nodded, hanging on to her as I walked to the door. She smiled, peering up into my eyes. Opening the door, I sighed as I leaned in the threshold, still wearing nothing but the scent of her essence.

"I'm going to shower too," I noted, "then I'll be downstairs on the patio, so I'll meet you there."

She nodded, exiting my bedroom with a smile.

Isabelle

I wanted to stay casual this morning, so I chose a pair of dark jeans and a little black, off the shoulder t-shirt. I navigated my way to the patio for the first time with full sight. It was much easier this time since I could see where I was going. I took mental photos on the way downstairs, eyeing everything I was once blind to. His home was even more beautiful than I ever imagined.

As I stepped outside onto the patio, I spotted him. Basking in all his splendor while sipping hot coffee from a fancy little mug, he studied a file folder. Perhaps it was work related. Standing still, I admired that I could see him in full detail now. I could not take my eyes off of the way the sunlight kissed his tanned skin, his piercing blue eyes, and the way his tousled hair appeared as if he has just run his fingers through it in some form of frustration.

Why me? If this is the hand life dealt me then I was okay with it now, but there would be a lot of questions he would have to answer in the near future. Sipping his coffee, he intently fretted over whatever he was reading while a newspaper laid close by on the table. What was it with this man and newspapers?

He slowly glanced up from his reading. "Isabelle, are you going to just stand there, or are you going to join me for breakfast?"

It was then that I realized, I had been standing with my mouth hanging open as I gawked at him. He briefly smirked then lowered his eyes once again to whatever he was concentrating on. His face became solemn.

"Everything okay?"

"Hmm," he hummed. Reaching for the picture of Mimosas, he poured us both glasses as he narrowed his eyes on mine. "I just cannot figure something out."

"Like where your servants are?" I teased.

"I wanted privacy with you."

"So, what can't you figure out?" I mused. "Maybe I can help you."

"I doubt that, bella, but thank you," he chuckled, tossing the file on the table causing the corner of a photo to slip out.

"Who's in the pic?" I casually wondered aloud.

He took a sip of his mimosa, rolling his eyes. "My brother," he growled.

"Awe," I giggled, "can I see?"

He bowed his head in approval, pushing the folder closer to me. Reaching over, I slipped it out, flipping it right side up. Immediately, I gasped, dropping it on top of my plate.

Valentino's eyes widened as he quickly snapped, "What? What's happened?"

"Um," I choked and clarified, "This is your brother?"

He nodded, interrogating me in a calm tone, "What's going on?"

Tears formed in my eyes. I could not breathe as the world began to spin. He shot up out of his chair, stepping around the table to me. Kneeling down next to me, he placed my hair behind my ears. He cupped my face in his palms.

"Bella, what's wrong?!"

12 SECRET REVEALED

Valentino

She began to shake as if a sudden chill had come over her entire body. As she looked up toward the sky, a single tear rolled down her soft, flawless cheek. Why did she get upset so suddenly? I knew my brother made me angry, but I did not realize he had that effect on others as well. I wanted to question her, but I did not bother yet. She needed me to be silent and present for her at the moment.

"I need to leave," she sniffled.

Placing my hand on her knee, I decided to shamelessly plead with her. "Bella, please tell me what's wrong."

Taking a shaky breath, she lowered her eyes to the ground as if she were both ashamed and scared. Tears dripped into her lap as she fidgeted with her fingers. She squirmed in anxiety, unable to speak. Cupping both of my hands around hers, I noticed they were cold and slightly clammy. After another few agonizing moments, she returned her gaze to mine. I acknowledged her with a gentle smile to let her know she was safe, and it was okay.

"He's my ex-boyfriend," she managed to choke out a little louder than a whisper.

I am sure from her point of view, I turned pale. It was now my turn to panic. All the blood drained from my face as I rocked back, sitting on the ground next to her chair. Bending my knees, I propped my elbows on them as I buried my forehead against my palms. We were both silent for what seemed like an eternity, with only the sound of birds in the trees and her sniffles every so often.

"My brother is your ex-boyfriend?" I confirmed as if it has not quite settled in yet.

Trying to hide my confusion, I peered up into her eyes. I rocked up to a kneeling position next to her, placing my hand on her arm. Her eyes focused on mine as she nodded. I sighed.

"He is," she admitted.

"I--," I began, trying to find a sentence. Any sentence at this point would do, but I was in fact incredibly speechless at the moment. I tried again, "I just--."

She took a deep breath then began to cry again, shuddering, "It was not a good experience."

My thoughts started to shift to my brother. What did he do to her that warranted this reaction to only his photo? I stood, taking her hands in mine. I pulled her up from her chair into my body, immediately wrapping my arms around her. She was still shaking but leaned her head onto my chest.

I did not know what to say to her. For moments, I remained silent, only holding her. She sobbed into my chest before her head slowly rose. I reached for her face, wiping away any tears with my thumbs.

"I want to know what he did to you," I growled tensely, "but I want you to tell me when you are ready."

Her eyes widened as she started to back up from me as a look of terror spread over her face. She glared into my eyes, with a combination of anger and sadness. I knew exactly what she was doing. She was now scared of me.

"Isabelle," I defended, "I had no idea!"

She rolled her eyes, then spun, storming into my house in a state of panic. I decided to not race after her. I was new to all of this *caring about women* thing, but I knew running after her would have been the right choice. Against my better judgement, I decided to give her some space.

My eyes lowered, focusing on my brother's tear stained photo. I felt sick to my stomach. As selfish as it sounds, I was extremely glad they did not have sex. I picked up the picture, enraged as I frowned at his face in disgust. From the way she acted, I knew he hurt her badly for her to have that response toward me. The question was now, how?

After studying him for a few moments, I quickly sprinted inside, coming to the four story, open foyer. I stopped, turning a circle, wondering if she was still in the mansion. I peered up at the third floor, where her room was located, throwing my hands up.

"Isabelle!"

My butler popped his head out of the hallway, and pointed, "Sir, the last time I saw her, she was walking to her bedroom."

Nodding, I took off to the elevator, impatiently waiting as it descended to the ground floor. It never seemed to move so slow and I grew angry. I rushed to the stairs, galloping up them as quickly as my legs would carry me, skipping several at a time.

As I cleared the last step, I caught her storming down the hallway in the direction of her room. Grabbing her by the arm, I pulled her into my body in one swift and smooth motion. She struggled slightly, but I gently stroked her face, placing her hair behind her ears which caused her to calm down for a moment. I searched her eyes for the answers she was not verbally telling me.

"Can we sit?" I requested gently.

It was the first time I had ever requested anything of anyone, instead of commanding. She stood her ground, but I tugged her toward a small bench that sat against the wall of the wide corridor. She reluctantly sat with a sigh.

Suddenly, I had a flashback of the time my brother had a girlfriend. The only time I actually remember him having one, even if for a short moment. I remember my family was shocked because we never saw him with anyone. He was always so private when it came to his personal life. It was then I realized that Isabelle was that girl.

"It was you," I muttered, placing my hand on her cheek.

Terror swept over her face again as she recoiled at my touch. "I have to go, Sir...I mean Valentino."

She stood, then quickly sprinted away. I jumped off the bench, following her down the hallway into her bedroom. She threw herself onto the bed, laying on her stomach then grabbed a pillow, burying her face into it.

"Was this planned?" she mumbled into the pillow.

I crept up to the bed, slowly sitting next to her. Lying on my side facing her, I reached out, slowly stroking her arm. "Isabelle, look at me."

As she inhaled deeply, I tried with all my might to suppress the questions I had about my brother and her. Biting my bottom lip, I slowly rolled it between my teeth as I gave her a chance to compose herself. She sighed once again as she sniffled.

Before I could say another word, she slowly turned her head toward me as she sat up. She had a look of resentment on her face as she scowled at me, but all I saw was how alluring she appeared. I really wanted to grab her, nibbling her alluring bottom lip but I could tell by her expression that she would not have been agreeable.

"Your brother and I dated for roughly a week," she recounted, "so I didn't even really count him as a boyfriend, I guess."

She finally began to tell me what I was dying to know so I sat up attentively and nodded. She paused between sentences, still treading the topic lightly. I remained as patient as possible, but my insides were burning with desire to know every detail. I had to admit that the other part of me was jealous of him.

"From day one he kept pressuring me for sex," she sighed, fighting back tears. "He wanted to touch me, and I would tell him no." Swallowing hard, she closed her eyes, concluding with gritted teed, "Over the course of the week, he became more and more aggressive about what he wanted."

"I *dumped* him," she made air quotes with her fingers, "if you can even call it that."

I smirked at her cuteness.

"A couple of months later, I was at a party with some friends and he showed up," she explained, averting her eyes to the bed. "I wanted to leave immediately but my friends were having the time of their lives and didn't want to go."

Shifting on the bed, I placed my hand on her knee, attempting to comfort her.

I decided that I would walk around and look at the house," she resumed, her voice becoming shaky. "He had been stalking me and pushed me into a bedroom, where he --." Her words trailed off.

Sitting up, I grabbed her, pulling her forehead into my lips. "It's okay, bella," I comforted, "you can trust me."

"His hands were all over me," she mumbled as she buried her head into my chest. "I tried to scream but he put his hand up to my mouth with so much force that he busted my lip."

She paused again. I was still trying to hold in my anger. Her terror was genuine, and she was struggling to tell me this story.

"When I continued to fight him, he reached for an object," she choked. "I think it might have been a trophy of some sort. He hit me so many times with it that I ended up with a bad concussion and in the hospital for three weeks."

I stroked her hair, whispering, "It's okay, bella."

Wrapping her arms around me, she cried, "At first I didn't remember much but as the days and weeks passed, the memories came flooding back to me." The tears flowed down her cheeks as she sobbed in my arms. "I was terrified that he raped me when he knocked me out."

"Did, uh, he touch you at all?" I tried to pry a little more.

Shaking her head, she concluded, "No, I don't think so. I was told that some guy at the party heard the commotion on his way to the bathroom and came into the room to check on the noise." She shrugged, sighing, "That scared your brother off."

Gnawing the inside of my bottom lip, I nodded.

She sat back, half-smiling, "It's ironic ya know."

"How so?" I mused, tilting my head.

"He would tell me all the time that he would be my first even if he had to hurt someone else in the process," she snickered. "I don't know, maybe I laugh at bad times, but I find it funny that his brother was the one to get me into bed."

"Do you regret it?"

Shaking her head, she wrapped her arms around me tighter. "I know it's weird to say," she confided, "but I feel safe with you."

I leaned my face closer to her, leaving a small peck on her cheek.

"I think I feel better now that you know," she inhaled deeply as she peered into my eyes. "For so long that entire situation haunted me."

I circled the small of her back with my fingertips.

"I was so scared he was watching me and would find me," she groaned before burying her face in her palms. "I was scared he would end up stealing that from me."

"I understand," I muttered, unsure of what to say.

An evil grin grew on her face as she studied my stressful face.

"What?" I nervously asked.

"If you kill him, can I watch?" she sneered, folding her arms over her midsection.

Wow! She was bold! An involuntary snort escaped my nose. Crossing my arms, I matched her expression. She smirked, waiting for my reply.

"What makes you think I will kill my own brother?"

"I felt the way you tensed up when I spoke about it," she hinted as she began to draw little circles on the bed with her finger. "I know there is more to you than you let on."

I shrugged, "Maybe you will have to stick around and find out."

She giggled as she averted her shy gaze.

"He knows I'm with you, doesn't he?" she sighed. "That's why you have that file on him."

Cradling her face, I slowly trailed my thumb across her bottom lip. "Let me worry about him," I countered as I searched her eyes for approval.

Slowly, she blinked. "The guys in my apartment with the guns," she gulped, I mean, the reason I had to leave," she fumbled. "Was he a part of that?"

I nodded, believing it to be true at the time. There was no point in lying anymore. She would hate me when I told her the rest of the story anyway. That would be the day she probably ran away from me, for good. I watched as she articulated her next sentence carefully.

"Am I truly safe here?" she fretted.

"You are," I reassured, peering into her eyes with a smile, "here, there, everywhere."

A gentle smile stretched across her lips as she accepted my reassurance.

"I will not let anything happen to you," I continued, taking her palms in mine.

"How can you be so sure?" she mused.

Placing a little kiss on the back of each of her hands, I confidently smirked as I gazed into her eyes. "You have my word."

My phone rang and I rolled my eyes as our moment was interrupted. Sliding it out of my pocket, I silenced the ringer before returning it back in place. I laid down facing her. She fell sideways on the bed, propping her head on her elbow as she exhaled. A bewildered expression appeared on her face as I reached over to her leg, circling her goosebump covered skin. Her face quickly turned into a glimpse of lust as she watched my fingers dancing on her body.

"You don't...need to take...that call?" she stammered, reacting to my touch.

Trailing my fingertips slowly up her thigh, I smirked, "I have other needs right now."

It was weird being in this room with someone I cared about. Glancing around I sighed, not wanting to make any move on her in here. I felt like she deserved to be in the one place she would know she was cared about. Stretching my hand out toward her, I stood up. She instantly locked her fingers in mine, standing to her feet.

"Where are you taking me?"

I picked her up causing her to wrap her legs instinctively and tightly around my waist as I strode to the door and down the hall. Our lips crashed together, and I could not get enough of her. It felt impossible to ever be close enough to her to be satisfied.

I gently placed her onto the floor outside the elevator, pinning her arms above her head while pushing her into the wall. She pulled away arching a brow at me. Tilting my head, I stared into her eyes waiting for her to catch her breath.

"When I got here," she whispered, "you spanked my--."

She did not want to finish the sentence as she was unsure which word to use. Her face began to flush a crimson color as she shyly averted her gaze. Rolling her bottom lip between her teeth, she peeked up into my eyes.

"Pussy?" I smirked. "Yeah I have bad habits, I guess."

Her chest swelled as she took a deep breath at my response. I thought about the word, *bad*. It did not do me justice. My eyes glossed over with thirst as I stared into her eyes.

"Well not bad," I corrected, "just very naughty."

"I liked it," she grinned bashfully.

My hungry gaze lowered on her collarbone as my mouth lowered to her soft, enticing skin, nibbling her neck as I kissed it. Reaching over to the elevator, I pressed the button again, unsure if I had actually pressed it the first time. Isabelle threw her arms around my neck, pulling me as tightly against her as our bodies would allow.

"That was child's play compared to what I'm capable of, bella," I muttered against her neck before I bit her.

She moaned loudly, arching her back and tilted her neck to allow me easier access.

Grinding myself against her, I rested my lips next to her ear, growling, "You can't even imagine what I'm going to do to you."

"Show me," she panted as she gripped my shoulders harder.

The elevator doors finally opened. We stumbled inside, undressing one another as we left a pile of clothes on the floor. My phone continued to ring but I ignored it as my priority was getting her back into my bed that instant. By the time the doors opened, she was completely naked and wrapped around my body once again. I only wore unbuttoned pants.

Pushing the door to my bedroom open, I carried her in, slamming it closed by accident with my foot. I carried her to the bed, dropping her on her back. Her legs instinctively fell open on impact, but she closed them.

Isabelle

He stood over my body like a wild animal ready to attack his meal. I laid beneath his gaze with eagerness and anticipation for his next move. Jerking back the blankets on the bed, he pushed me under them before climbing in next to me. Positioning himself on top of me, he slowly started to leave a trail of kisses from my lips to my breasts, each one becoming more aggressive and slightly more painful than the previous.

He took my nipple in his mouth, sucking it with force while gripping it tightly between his teeth. His clothed member pressed and grinded into my nakedness. The friction of the bulge in his pants rubbed against my sensitive little button exactly right, causing a borderline unbearable throbbing sensation. I moaned loudly as he continued his assault on my other nipple, however this time it was much more aggressive. I arched my back, yelping through my euphoric cries. Suddenly, he stopped, raising up and peering into my eyes.

"Am I hurting you?" he smirked, before taking my nipple back into his mouth harshly.

"Yes."

He smiled, staring up at me with my nipple between his teeth. "Good," he growled.

My entire body was beginning to tremble as he reached down, cupping my mound. He roughly ran his fingers up and down my slit quickly before shoving two of his digits into me with an unexpected force. The power behind his touch was less friendly this time, but I did not mind it whatsoever. The aggression worked well. He was driving me insane.

"Oh my God!" I cried out, just as his bedroom door flew open.

He instantaneously stopped, turning his head around as someone marched in. His body was shielding me from whoever it was, causing me to not be able to see them either. He stiffened up as he rolled off me, helping me pull the blanket up to my neck.

"Well, now I fucking know why you haven't been answering your fucking phone!" the man irritatingly scoffed.

"Can't you see I'm busy?" Valentino barked back harshly, gesturing toward me.

"Yeah I can but guess what," he snapped, "you have a visitor who refuses to leave."

Valentino groaned with irritation in his voice as he rolled toward me, wrapping his arm around my body, and burying his face into my chest. I ran my fingers through his hair for a moment, tickling his scalp with my nails. The man's attention was now focused on his phone screen. Valentino peeked up at me, smirking before he slid out of bed.

I sat up inelegantly, inspecting the man standing in the bedroom while Valentino disappeared into his closet. The guy glanced up from his phone, jerking when he saw me staring directly toward him. His eyes widened as he froze, unsure of his next move.

"Um, Valentino?" he called out. "She removed the--."

"Yeah I know," Valentino interrupted as he walked back into the bedroom, pulling a shirt over his head. "Long story."

"Isabelle this is William," he sighed as if he were regretting the introduction. "He is my best friend," he noted, while buttoning his pants.

I shyly smiled as I pulled the blankets closer to my body self-consciously. I glanced away.

"It's a pleasure to finally meet you," he suddenly sounded cheerful, almost relieved.

I glanced up, murmuring softly, "You too."

Valentino turned to him, whispering something that I did not understand. William nodded, immediately exiting the room. Valentino took a few quick strides to me. He leaned over the bed close to my face, resting his palms on my thighs.

"You're not trapped in here," he smiled, "but please stay off the ground floor until I say so."

He gently kissed me on the lips, stroking his hands up my legs to my sweet spot. Placing both of his thumbs on the outside of my sensitive area, he began to massage me. My body trembled at his touch.

"Valentino," I moaned in a loud whisper against his lips.

His mouth curled into a smile as he pressed his lips to mine before he pulled away. "When I come back," he muttered, "you'll be saying that much louder, bella."

"Mmm," I moaned at his touch, rocking my hips forward as I pressed into his hand.

He winked, placing his lips against my ear while his index finger found my slit. "You make me crazy," he whispered seductively in a heavier Italian accent than usual.

I craved more of him. He was my drug and I was an addict. I longed for him to push me back, climbing on top of me and having his way with me once again. I pursed my lips as I attempted to control my breathing. He inserted his finger slowly, deep into my core. Arching my back, I moved my hips.

"God," he growled, "you're so fucking wet."

"I want you to take me right here," I cried out.

He removed his digit, placing it in his mouth. Wrapping his lips around it, he slowly dragged it out, sucking it clean, torturing me as he lustily gazed into my eyes. Leaning close to my mouth, he took my bottom lip between his teeth, biting it before kissing me. Suddenly, he forced himself to pull away, as if an electrical current shocked him. Sensing his tension, I stiffened my body, involuntarily mimicking him.

"Is everything going to be okay?"

He pressed his lips against my forehead, leaving a lingering kiss on my skin. "It will be fine," he reassured.

I slightly smiled, not quite buying his response. "Okay."

"Don't even think that I'm finished with you," he asserted as he winked.

He left the bedroom, leaving me to wallow alone in my arousal. Lying back in bed thinking about how wonderful this man was, I could no longer hide the smitten grin that spread across my face. He seemed to be so genuine and compassionate despite his very enigmatic nature.

I stared up at the ceiling, wondering if I would ever be able to return to the penthouse. Did I live here at the mansion with him now? What was going to be the permanent arrangement? Would I have to leave again? Would I even want to leave?

We were not exactly in a relationship. I was so unclear on what was even going on between us, other than a sexually charged connection. I tried not to read too much into it but, I am a woman. We definitely all overthink things sometimes.

"Whatever," I uttered under my breath to myself, shrugging.

I decided not to worry at the very moment. It was then that I began to reminisce about the crazy way we met, both times. The real version of him came to mind first. His smoldering eyes captivated me as he watched me work. The day we ran into each other after my run in the park, he smiled unforgettably, luring me further in. The coffee shop as he read the obituary section made me internally giggle. He did not think I saw that, but I did.

My brain shifted to the other version of him at the masquerade. The masks. The contract. The entire elaborate nonsense for what? I snickered, rolling my eyes. He kept his word by not forcing me into anything, which I appreciated. He could have easily been some masked murderer or rapist, but he was the opposite. I had yet to figure him out completely, but I was enjoying peeling back the many layers he had hidden underneath both personas.

He gave his identity away so many times. I began to think my mind was playing tricks on me every time he did something similar to the other version of him. I liked both of them and wanted them to be the same. However, looking back on it, I am shocked it took me so long to figure it out.

The smile quickly faded from my face as I sat up as if someone lit a fire under my back. My mouth fell agape. I thought back to William. *It's a pleasure to finally meet you for real*, is what he said to me at the gala.

It was then I realized that I had just officially met *the* William, sans the mask. He was Tanya's boyfriend! Everything was finally coming together. I sighed thinking about how I was ever going to approach this with my best friend.

Burying my face into my palms, I groaned, "Tanya is in so much trouble!"

13 CONFLICT

Valentino

I stepped into the hallway to see William waiting for me. He was leaning against the wall staring at his phone. Glancing up, he smirked then opened his mouth ready to speak about what he had just witnessed. Burying my face into my hand, I groaned before I flashed my palm toward him.

"Just don't," I scolded, attempting to stop whatever was about to exit his mouth.

He chuckled, shaking his head, "Well you might want to go change into something more appropriate."

I scowled in confusion, "And why is that?"

"Valentino, I'm literally standing here wearing a suit," he hinted. "You cannot wear that, I assure you."

My chest began to feel constricted. I knew that I was about to have to face a demon of some sort. The only time William cared about attire was when it was what we referred to as, official business.

Inhaling deeply, I muttered, "Hang on."

Pivoting toward my room once again, I stepped in. Softly closing the door behind me as not to disturb Isabelle, I quickly noticed she was nowhere to be found. I strode to my closet, finding her naked when I entered. She quizzically glanced up at me causing me to snicker. She smiled broadly as her gaze returned to a row of my shirts.

"Wear whatever you need, it's okay," I offered as I sauntered over to another section of other formal clothing.

"I just need to go to my room for a sec," she commented as she thumbed through my garments.

I began removing my clothes to change into a suit. She froze in place, turning her attention toward me. I smirked as I watched her studying my body, enjoying the view in front of her.

"Come back for more already?"

I glanced down chuckling slightly as I pulled my pants on. "I wish, bella, but I have a meeting."

"And you have to dress up?"

I nodded, "For this one I do, because it's apparently very important."

She grinned at me, stepping to my side. Trailing her fingertips over my arms, she lustfully gazed up toward my face as she continued over my shoulders. I dropped my gaze, meeting hers. Instantly, she stood on her toes, placing a small peck on my lips. Startled but turned on by her confidence, I rolled my bottom lip between my teeth then bit it to keep from smiling. This was a new side to her that I had not seen quite yet. However, I liked it…a lot.

"What are you doing?"

"I don't even know," she giggled, "but you have this effect on me."

Attempting to focus on my task, I reached forward, grabbing a white formal shirt from the hanger, and sliding my arms through it. As I began to button it up, she placed her hands on mine, keeping me from finishing. I gave in to her silent demand, pulling my shirt open for her enjoyment. She placed her fingernails on my chest and with a slight pressure, she slowly dragged them down to my lower abs causing me to flex every muscle in my body at the sensation.

She awakened the beast in me, and I harshly yanked her close, growling in her ear with approval. We glared into one another's eyes, playing a game of chicken. Who would give in to the other first? She was mistaken if she thought I would ever let her have control. I was a gentleman but definitely not a gentle man. Control was something I was never willing to give up.

Raking her fingertips to my back, she gripped tightly digging her nails into my flesh, causing me to arch my back. Leaning forward, I rested my forehead on hers, backing her into my hanging clothes. She continued to challenge me, watching my eyes with a ravishing hunger.

"Whatever has come over you," I growled, "I'm loving it."

Pursing her lips, she slowly leaned forward into my chest, pressing her lips to it before peering up into my eyes once again.

"What game are you playing, Isabelle?" I glowered.

"I really don't know how any woman can stand in the same room with you," she taunted, "and not pounce on you...*Sir*."

She was playing with fire, pushing my every button. I thought she was about to kiss my chest again, but she shocked me. She took my nipple between her teeth. Without further question or games, I grabbed her by the hair. Yanking her head back, I forced her to look into my authoritative stare. She rolled her tongue between her inviting lips.

    I reached around, connecting the palm of my hand to her bottom, lightly spanking her. Her eyes lit up as she smiled, temporarily breaking the facade of her attempt at dominating me. I bowed further, pressing my lips to her neck, biting down hard while sucking her skin. She arched her back, gripping my arms tightly while moaning. Pulling away, I placed my mouth next to her ear.

"Whatever game you're playing right now," I whispered, "will only result in you cumming hard for me."

Peeling myself away, I scowled down at her, my pupils dilated. Smirking at me, she slanted her head, challenging my words. Damnit! This woman was driving me crazy. I had business to attend to downstairs, but she was playing games on my level. I swallowed hard, then quickly glimpsed at my watch, checking the time.

    Without warning, I charged at her, forcefully pushing her backwards towards a large ottoman that lay in the middle of the closet floor. She fell onto her bottom when the back of her knees made contact with the edge. I vehemently pushed her legs open as I leaned over her flawless, enticing body.

    She propped on her elbows, stalking my body's every move as her glare traveled with unnerving thoroughness.

Running my hand softly up her thigh to her center, I plunged two of my fingers into her eager, pulsating core. Her hips bucked as her back bowed. She let out a loud moan as her body writhed beneath my touch.

"Fucking hell, bella," I smirked, "you're soaked."

She panted, trying to catch her breath. "I need to cum so bad," she begged.

"Cum," I commanded as I pummeled her harder, curling my fingers inside her, hitting her special place as I circled her button with my thumb.

She sat up, wrapping her arms around my neck while grinding herself harder on my hand. Our lips crashed together, before she began to moan loudly into my mouth. Her essence began to suffocate my digits as she lost every ounce of her self-control.

"Oh… my…God…Valentino!" she shrieked through her loud moans. "Don't…ever…stop!"

I smirked, watching her squirm and gasp. It made me crazy seeing her this way; not only under the control of my touch, but also satisfied. She eventually came down off her blissful high when I removed my fingers from her core. Gripping my shirt, she tugged me toward her, forcing her lips against mine.

Leaning away, I pushed my fingers into my mouth one at a time, sucking them clean before kissing her passionately, allowing her to taste herself on my tongue. She tasted like heaven. I was utterly addicted to both her scent and taste. I would have been satisfied having her flavor in my mouth all day, every day.

"I hate to go but--," I reluctantly pulled away from her.

"Go," she interrupted lying back on the ottoman.

I nodded, enjoying looking at the woman who pleased me in every way. Smiling, she rolled onto her side, still panting from her explosive orgasm. I leaned over her, leaving a kiss on her forehead then one on each of her exposed, rosy nipples.

I buttoned up my shirt then grabbed a tie. "I'll be back before you know it," I reassured as I perfected the knot in the mirror.

"Mm-hmm," she murmured, still draped over the ottoman.

I hurried out of the room, laughing to myself as I closed the door. As I entered the hallway, William now stood with his arms angrily folded across his chest, glowering in my direction. Rolling my eyes, I shrugged.

"Really?" he scolded with widened eyes.

"What?" I inquired indifferently.

"You realize that shit is about to get all fucked up downstairs and you just fucked her," he snapped as we strode down the hallway.

"For your information," I interjected as we stepped into the elevator, "I did no such thing."

He chuckled, sliding his phone out of his pocket, checking it. "Well whatever you did," he muttered, "I heard her."

"Good," I snapped sarcastically.

Rolling his eyes, he smirked, "Ha, remember that in a few minutes."

"Oh yeah?" I muttered, straightening my tie once again in the reflection of the elevator door. "Who's here?" I questioned.

William turned to me, silently staring, the smirk still plastered on his face. "Her father," he cautioned as his expression became serious, wiping away any leftover amusement.

Fuck!

Isabelle

I rested on the oversized black, leather ottoman in the middle of Valentino's closet, catching my breath as he left for a meeting. I was not sure what had come over me. But then I realized that I knew exactly what had come over me. It was him.

He was the most gallant and remarkable man I had ever laid eyes on. Just his presence alone, made me lose all sense of my reality and self-control. I felt so intoxicated around him, giving me little room to breathe. I was entranced in whatever spell he had placed on me. I stood, roaming toward his shirts. The closet smelled of jasmine, tobacco, and leather with a hint of sex. I almost had another orgasm as I took a deep breath, recalling the scent of a specific cologne on a nearby table.

I slipped on one of his formal, button-up shirts, before sprinting down the hall to the elevator. I waited impatiently tapping my foot. The minute the doors slid to the side, I wasted no time hopping in and taking it one floor up.

I ran down the hallway into my bedroom, swiftly closing the door behind me. Grabbing my bag, I pulled my phone out of the side pocket. I thumbed over Tanya's phone number, taking a deep breath. I wanted to call her. I needed her more than anything right now. I missed my best friend. I wanted to yell at her, but I also knew that there was more to this which led me to believe she might possibly have the answers I was searching for.

Trying to speak to her right now, would probably do more damage, so I was on the fence about my next move. I thought I might speak with Valentino first before I caused any possible drama. The internal battle continued as my need to call her became more prevalent. I was ready to hear what she had to say.

Valentino

I marched through the threshold into my office, coming face to face with a room full of people. Six of my staff and bodyguards stood at the entrance and back door, all darting their eyes toward me in annoyance the moment they saw me. Five strangers stood spread throughout the room but blocking my view of a single person who was standing near the front of my desk. As the crowd parted, he turned to me with a menacing smile inching across his face. A young man who remained next to him, glared at me as though he wanted to kill me.

"Felipe!" I greeted Isabelle's father by name as I shook his hand with a fake smile plastered on my face.

He bowed his head in acknowledgement, gripping my hand harder than the last time I saw him. I smirked at the fact the hand he just shook was all over his daughter a few minutes before. I had completely broken my agreement with him. Lurching around to the other side of my desk, I was about to sit down.

"Not here," he abruptly interjected before I could take a seat.

"Where would you like to go?"

"You and I are going to go for little a drive to talk," he grinned wryly, narrowing his eyes.

I wanted to roll my eyes, but I knew it would only start trouble. Felipe carried a dominant personality like myself, so I knew that this meeting would be anything but fun. Neither one of us were ever known to back down from a conflict. He was a drug lord, I was a businessman, with questionable underground practices.

Everyone in the room followed Felipe and I outside. The young guy who had been standing next to him followed us to the car, but Felipe held up his hand to stop just outside my front door.

"I got this, Xavier," he displayed a cluster of keys, jiggling them in the air.

Xavier nodded, taking a step back while crossing his arms over his chest. He frowned in my direction. William quickly marched over, opening the passenger door for me.

I pulled the seatbelt over my body as he leaned into the car next to my ear.

"I'll have you followed," he whispered.

I shook my head, mumbling, "I got this, so don't do anything stupid."

The truth is, I would have to take my chances. Felipe had people spying all over the place and if one came across my guys following us, it would result in death for me, or possibly a blood bath for everyone.

Felipe played the same games I did with his enemies, so he could see anything out of the ordinary coming at any point. I was not about to cross Isabelle's father right now with her upstairs in my bedroom, possibly still naked. I had my gun in my waistband. That would have to do for now.

"Are you hungry?" he cheerfully inquired as he slid into, the driver's side, starting the car.

This was not like him whatsoever, so I knew something was up. This had to be a trap of some sort. He was never one to ask anything. He usually only made demands which came with a price.

"I could eat, but I prefer to drink," I half joked.

He chuckled menacingly then drove in silence to a nearby restaurant. The moment we entered through the front door we were greeted by a younger looking blonde waitress. She sashayed through the establishment, swaying her hips, trying to get our attention as she escorted us to a private booth in the bar area.

As she laid our menus on the table in front of us, she took extra care to press her pert breasts together as she leaned over. Felipe took an immediate liking to her. He could not help himself from flirting.

"How are you, beautiful young lady?"

She giggled, twisting her hips back and forth with an ink pen in between her teeth. "I'm great," she grinned. "What can I get you handsome gentlemen?"

Felipe was the first to order. "Vodka Martini, wet," he winked, "up, with a twist."

She playfully giggled at the word, *wet*, before turning her attention to me. "And you, Mr. Greco?"

"How do you know who I am?"

Nodding her head up toward the television on the wall, my gaze followed. Rolling my eyes, I sighed.

"Everyone knows you are," she confirmed cheerfully. "Now, what can I get you?"

Pursing my lips, I gnawed the inside of my cheek as my gaze met hers. "Whiskey, neat."

She smiled, nodding as she flipped her ponytail around then pranced off to the bar. Felipe made himself comfortable as he cocked his head, watching her. Rolling my eyes, I cleared my throat, peeling his attention away from the barely legal waitress.

"Oh, sorry," he chuckled evilly, giving me his undivided attention. "Tell me Valentino, how is it going with my daughter?"

I thought about this question, unsure of how to reply. Snickering to myself, I rehearsed my sarcastic answer in my head. *Well I fucked the shit out of your daughter, and she screamed my name.*

He glowered almost as if he could read my mind. He pulled a cigar out of his pocket and lit it.

"She is safe and happy," I smiled, omitting the sexual details, but also not lying. "I'm keeping an eye on her as best as I can."

He nodded, puffing his cigar in my direction.

Fanning away the cloud, I affirmed, "So far, no harm has come to her and I will continue to do my job."

"Good," he grinned, pinning the cigar between his teeth.

The waitress returned with our drinks. She made eye contact with me and smirked as she flirtatiously smiled.

She glanced down at her chest, hoping my eyes would follow.

"Mmm," Felipe moaned, "you should come work for me."

She playfully smirked at him as he reached over, grabbing her backside before she paraded away. She gave us one last glimpse before she disappeared behind a wall. My eyes instantly lowered on my drink as I was not interested in her in the least. My only focus was at my house. Isabelle's beauty was unmatched, in my opinion.

"Well," Felipe sighed, "I wanted to talk to you today because I am going to void our agreement."

Did I hear him correctly? This was incredible! I could finally be with her without any issues. Of course, his words fell silent as he puffed on his cigar, waiting for me to understand he was not finished. A part of me thought maybe this was a test to see my reaction.

There was a catch. Of course, there was a catch. Felipe was as complicated as I was. None of his statements were ever that black and white. I lit a cigarette as I waited for his cloud of smoke to clear the air. Before I uttered a word, he continued.

"Tell me, Valentino," he requested alarmingly. It was never good when someone started a sentence this way. "Has my daughter given you any trouble at all?" he chuckled. "You can be honest. After all, look at me." He held his arms out with pride, as if he were expecting me to both admire and worship him.

"No," I murmured, taking a drag of my cigarette. "She's been no trouble whatsoever."

"Good," he paused then repeated. "Good."

"Can I ask why the meeting?"

"Has my daughter dated anyone since she has been in your care?" he wondered as he studied my every movement.

"She's not had time," I muttered, half truthful. I continued as I knew he was looking for a better answer, "I gave her a job at my company, and she will be starting this Monday."

He smiled, nodding as he seemed satisfied with the information before suspicion swept across his face. "Does she know who you are?"

I decided to dig my grave a little deeper. "She knows who I am," I smirked, "but she doesn't know that it is me who is watching her."

Quizzically, he tilted his head.

"I figured what better way to watch her, than to have her work for me without knowledge of our arrangement."

I smiled, "However I am now guessing that the arrangement is over, and she will live her life freely."

He threw his head back and guffawed, then froze, lowering his gaze to mine. The few other patrons in the restaurant darted their eyes in our direction trying to pinpoint the ruckus from his laugh that reverberated through the bar. I chugged the rest of my drink then took a long, slow drag of my cigarette.

"I am right, aren't I?" I muttered as the smoke drifted from my mouth.

He slowly lowered his eyes, peeking over the top of the sunglasses he never removed. "I have another plan," he confessed in a sinister tone.

I did not like the sound of that. In fact, I was starting to become extremely nervous. I fumed, assuming the worst at this point. He held his hand up to the waitress, signaling for another round of drinks. She nodded, smiling in her signature flirtatious manner as she acknowledged him then spun to make our refills.

"Care to share?" I requested, drawing his attention back to the table.

"Of course," he snickered, "You have done good for her, but now I'm turning her care over to my top guy."

"I'm sorry," I choked as I lit a new cigarette. "What?!"

He bobbed his head, sneering, "You didn't think I would expect you to watch her, forever did you?" His grin grew wider, "You are a busy, rich rich rich man, and I have no doubt that my daughter is probably a big cock block for you. Women would kill to have one night with you."

Your daughter is the reason my cock is happy, I thought to myself. "I can handle my own affairs, I assure you," I did not want to sound too desperate. "Isabelle is safe, and I know her routine. I know her inside and out." *Literally*, I chuckled to myself. "Why change it?"

"I have made an arrangement with Xavier," he informed, "the young man you saw back at your estate."

I took a gulp of my drink.

He grinned broadly, "They are to be wed in six months!"

I choked, spitting my liquid back into my glass. "What the hell Felipe?! Are you fucking serious?!"

He leaned forward, laughing loudly once again, "I know, right? He's perfect for my princess!" He inhaled deeply before continuing, "He brings in so much money for my business and that way, I can keep an eye on things. She will be able to travel with us."

Someone was about to die, and it was not me! I clenched my jaw as I squeezed my glass to the point of almost shattering it in my hand. His gaze met mine as he smiled. I furrowed my brow before forcing a fake grin. The other part of me was about two seconds from reaching in my waistband, pulling my gun, and killing this bastard. I chugged the rest of my second drink before placing my glass on the table.

"So, what happens now?" I snapped, showing a tinge of anger.

"She will stay with you through next week," he proclaimed, "and then she will be with him full time."

I inhaled my cigarette deeply as I focused my gaze on the table. I did not want to make any sudden movements or say the wrong thing yet. However, I was beginning to think he was enjoying every moment of this. Something told me he was suspicious about Isabelle and myself or he was testing me.

"I will send for her."

He pulled our contract out of his trench coat pocket, holding it in front of me. Picking my lighter up off the table, he placed it on the bottom of the paper by our signatures. The moment he lit it, fire began to spread rapidly. I watched in awe, hypnotized by the reflection of the flame in his sunglasses.

My thoughts drifted as I imagined him being burned alive before my eyes. I would enjoy every moment of watching his flesh completely melt as he screamed before his nerves were shut down. Morbid? Only when it came to people messing with someone I care about. I would go to any length to keep her to myself while also making sure she remained safe.

Yes, I considered myself quite possessive, but what her father was doing was wrong. He had just made an enemy. He was smart and powerful, but he did not have what I did, his daughter. She was mine and I was not about to give her up to some kid.

The fire dwindled to nearly nothing. He shook his hand as it had gotten a bit hot next to the flame. I rolled my eyes, hoping there would be no further conversation today. I yearned to get home to Isabelle, making sure she was okay and planning my next move.

"Are you ready to go?" he scowled as he handed me his keys. "You drive."

Nodding, I took the keys from him and we made our way to the car. I drove the entire way back to my estate in complete silence. I had to come up with a plan to get Isabelle away from everything, but I was unsure how I would be able to flawlessly execute it. I would need to meet with my guys the minute we got back after Felipe and his crew left the grounds.

The moment we returned home, we made our way back to my office. Xavier stood with a smug expression on his face in the corner. I glared directly at him. He frowned in return, matching my expression. Pursing my lips, I slightly exhaled as I perched on the edge of my desk, crossing my arms over my stomach.

"We must be on our way," Felipe reached out his hand to shake mine.

I reluctantly obliged as I glanced at William and Blaine. They were visibly bothered. The three of us shared an unspoken conversation with our eyes before I glanced at Joseph who was observing each person in the room with great purpose.

We escorted Felipe and his men to the foyer. He shook my hand again before we shared one last goodbye. The moment I closed the door behind them, I leaned on it, exhaling.

Isabelle

"Isabelle, get up!" Valentino harshly commanded as he marched into the room, slamming the door behind him with such a force, I jumped.

I sat up quickly and confused, watching as he gestured toward me to stand before disappearing into the closet. I sighed getting ready to obey but a knock at his bedroom further startled me.

Before I could exit the bed, I yanked the covers over my bare breasts as the door swung open. William and another man swiftly waltzed in. I pointed toward the closet as I assumed, they were looking for Valentino. William shook his head before he took large, angry strides to where Valentino was. The other man crossed his arms, staring at me as I mildly recoiled on the bed. I suddenly felt uncomfortable and overwhelmed.

Valentino stomped out of the closet holding two bags, while being followed closely by William. He dropped the bags in the middle of the bedroom floor before stopping and pivoting to me. Placing his hands on his hips, he studied my lack of emotion. I was still utterly confused as to what was happening.

"Isabelle," he snapped harshly, "go pack!"

"I'm naked under here!"

He rolled his eyes before disappearing into his closet again. He stepped out, tossing me a shirt. I caught it then twirled my finger in a circle, indicating for William and the other man to turn away. The moment they turned their backs, I pulled the long t-shirt over my head as quickly as possible before I stood, sprinting out of the bedroom and down the hall. I could hear William speak as I was on my way out the door.

"I wish you would reconsider," he pleaded.

"Just get my fucking jet ready and shut the fuck up!"

14 LONDON BOUND

Isabelle

We gathered in Valentino's driveway next to two limos, surrounded by six security guards and drivers. I peered around with wide eyes, wondering what was going on as the hushed murmurs spread through the air. Something intense was happening for Valentino to have snapped at me like he did earlier.

Joseph stood close to my side, bobbing his head as he listened to the chatter in his earpiece. Valentino stood alone, staring at the mansion while smoking a cigarette. William and two other men exited the house, approaching him. As they shared a private conversation, William glanced toward me before turning his attention back them.

Great. I knew they were discussing me which made me a bit nervous. I trusted Valentino, but it pained me to admit that I was very nosy when it came to people talking about me. They broke their conversation and William turned to me again, nodding his head at me to follow. Sluggishly and hesitantly, I trudged behind him wondering what was going on, but scared to ask. As I passed Valentino, he tapped my bottom with his fingertips.

"Walk a bit faster."

I spun my body around, narrowing my eyes at him. He grinned evilly while winking. I turned back around, skipping a little to catch up to William who came to a stop next to a gazebo.

Crossing his arms, he studied me. "There are bugs outside," he muttered in a low tone, barely above a whisper, "so we have to keep it down, okay?"

"What the hell kind of bugs are triggered by noise?" I hissed back, darting my eyes around in paranoia.

"Not insects," he groaned, rolling his eyes.

I giggled realizing how dumb I must have sounded when I understood he meant surveillance bugs and not actual six-legged creepy little creatures.

"You will be riding with me to the airport," he instructed in an all-business tone. "Valentino and security will be in front of us."

Confusion consumed my face as I tilted my head, waiting for a detailed explanation that William was not going to offer that to me at the time. I sighed, folding my arms defensively over my stomach. I caught a glimpse of Valentino in my peripheral vision then lifted my chin to meet his gaze. He nodded his head toward the car William would be driving, flashing a reassuring smile. Lowering my eyes, I trudged to the passenger door as William opened it for me.

Leaning forward, he whispered, "We can talk more in the car, Isabelle."

I nodded, sliding into the car. He closed the door for me then made his way around to the driver's door, getting in. I turned to get a final look at Valentino, but he was already in one of the limos that were pulling away.

We silently drove down the long, winding driveway out of the estate. I stared out the window, watching the trees pass us as I thought about the strange journey I had recently come to know. I began to pick at my fingernails as I bit my lip in deep thought, debating if I should speak my mind. With as many risks I had taken lately, I was feeling more inclined.

Deep breath, Isabelle. "How's Tanya?" I blurted without further hesitation, still staring out the window.

William cleared his throat, drawing my attention toward him. His hands curled tighter around the steering wheel. His knuckles turned white as his grip intensified. Glancing over at me from the corner of his, now narrowed eyes, he crushed the inside of his cheek as he chewed it.

"I'm guessing you're not allowed to discuss it?" I muttered. "I should have known."

"I think you should talk to Valentino about that."

He was trying to mask his irritation. I could sense it. I did not want to pry, but a part of me could not help it. I had burning questions. Suddenly, I found myself unable to control my mouth any longer. Tanya, despite what had happened, was my best friend. Maybe it was because I was trapped in the car with her boyfriend, but I was feeling bold and protective.

"Can I at least ask you something," I blurted, crossing my arms, hoping for a reply.

He sighed. "Do I have a choice in the matter?"

I shrugged, ignoring his remark. "Do you actually like her or were all of you in this together to--."

"Let me stop you there, Isabelle," he interjected signaling for me to stop.

I rolled my eyes, puffing my cheeks out as I slowly allowed air to escape my lips.

"Tanya and I are not together anymore, okay?" he lamented.

My eyes widened and my heart sank. "What happened?"

I slightly gasped, placing my index finger in between my teeth, lightly biting down on my fingernail.

"Well, she kind of went nuts on me when she lost your friendship," he grieved, "then stopped talking to me when it became too much for her, I guess. Truthfully, I don't know what happened anymore. She avoids me now."

"William, I'm sorry," I apologized with heartfelt sincerity.

"She misses you, you know," he resumed with pain in his tone. "She left my company." His tight grip found the steering wheel again. His knuckles turned whiter than before. "I took a lot of shit because of this, Isabelle."

"Dude, I don't even know what *this* is!" I blustered. "I didn't even ask for it, nor did I see it coming."

He ran his fingers through his hair with one hand as the other rested on the side of the steering wheel much more relaxed now. "I can't talk about it," he alluded, "I'm sorry."

Sighing, I fidgeted with my fingers in my lap nervously as the car grew silent. I opened my mouth to speak, but no words were spoken. Instead, I inhaled deeply then slowly exhaled, trying to keep from tearing up at the conversation. I was sad for him, but I was also missing my friend. I knew that she needed me right now as well.

"Your boyfriend can explain all of it to you," he smirked, trying to lighten the mood.

I blinked my eyes rapidly then matched his expression. "He's not my boyfriend," I snickered.

"No comment about that," he grinned menacingly.

"Do you want her back?"

He narrowed his eyes, scowling ahead at the road before darting his eyes briefly in my direction. "Not doing this with you, sorry."

"Okay, sorry." I mumbled, sinking into my seat, and sheepishly finding nothing interesting outside my window to focus on.

"To me," he coldly continued but winced at the same time, "you are still just a business transaction."

Pressing a button on the steering wheel, he turned the volume of the music up, blaring it from the speakers. It was so loud that I did not catch the rest of what he said afterward. The entire inside of the car was essentially a computer. I did not know how to turn the music down to ask him to please repeat himself. I sat silently, trying to mind my own business.

I knew he was upset about Tanya, but still, his words stung. It had been a while since I considered myself only a transaction. William's words brought back those memories, slightly hurting my feelings, but I kept my mouth closed, refusing to push him any further again.

Valentino

Isabelle and William arrived at the airport shortly after me. They both appeared distraught. Promptly, I strode to Isabelle's side, escorting her up the stairs of my private jet.

The moment she stepped inside the door, I spun to William, walking back down several steps closer to him. He had just lit a cigarette as he waited for me on the tarmac, peering up at the plane. Taking a long, slow drag, he watched me, waiting for me to speak as he squinted in the bright light.

"I'll call you when we get there," I shouted over the noise of a plane taking off.

"I'll be waiting," he called out.

He turned to walk away as I entered the plane. Isabelle stood in the aisle as if she were anxious to sit anywhere until I gave her permission. Nervously, she shifted her weight before I gestured for her to take a seat in a chair near the rear of the cabin. I sat in the chair across the aisle.

Reaching out, I took her hand in mine, slowly circling my thumb on her delicate skin. She appeared bothered. I had a feeling it was about whatever had transpired in the car ride with William on the way to the airport. Squeezing her hand tenderly but swiftly a few times, I grabbed her attention. Twisting her head toward me, her gaze met mine. She smiled shyly.

"Are you okay?" I whispered, as not to alarm any of my staff on the plane.

"This is so overwhelming to me," she confessed, lightly grimacing as the words left her mouth.

"I understand, bella."

She fought back a smile but failed. I curled my lips into a smirk before dropping her hand and slipping my laptop out of my bag. I set it on the table in front of me and opened it. Knowing that this was a lot for her process, I allowed her to get settled while I worked on a few things. I did not bother speaking to her again as I could tell she was deeply bothered. Trying to remain respectful, I did not press her for answers and focused on what was in front of me, trying to fix everything before it escalated anymore.

I found myself staring ahead but darting my eyes in her direction every so often. She paid me no attention as she nervously fidgeted with her nails and stared out the window. I did not exactly know what to say, rendering myself speechless.

Taking a deep breath, I exhaled as my flight attendant, Amanda, appeared next to our seats. Isabelle glanced up, acknowledging her presence beside her, but she rapidly returned her interest to the window again.

"Mr. Greco, what may I get for you and your guest?"

I reached my arm out and Amanda took a step back. Gently, I stroked Isabelle's arm, commanding her attention. She jumped, spinning to face me then exhaled before returning her gaze out the window.

"Would you like some wine?" I murmured.

She shook her head, never looking back.

"Water for me," I requested, "and would you bring her some as well?" I muttered, gritting my teeth in frustration.

She nodded before she spun, sashaying to the front of the plane.

Isabelle finally tore her gaze away, turning to me with a smirk. "You certainly don't listen do you, Sir?"

I grinned coyly, as I reached toward her, swiveling her chair to face me. Her mouth fell agape in shock and she nervously grabbed the armrests, stabilizing herself.

"Yeah they spin," I rumbled, narrowing my eyes. "Are you a nervous flier?"

Her eyes widened. "A bit yeah," she confessed self-consciously, "but I'm usually stuck in cramped coach on a commercial plane."

Cocking my head, I listened carefully to her. I did not always listen to women, but I hung on her every word. Between her facial expressions and tone, I was utterly captivated by her.

"I could dance in this plane," she joked.

I nodded, smirking, before narrowing my eyes on her. "Knock yourself out." I gestured to the aisle floor.

Her face flushed a bright shade of red as she scratched the back of her head. Her eyes darted around looking at everyone up front.

"I'm not going to dance on your plane," she hissed. "That's weird."

"But you said you could."

She shifted uncomfortably in her seat averting her gaze to her lap. "Could, not would."

Reaching for her hand, I grabbed her wrist, tugging her in my direction. "Come here," I demanded mischievously.

Wasting no time, she stood, stumbling over into my lap, but caught herself on my shoulder and the table with my laptop. Sitting sideways, she crossed her ankles then wrapped her arms around my neck, lacing her fingers together behind me. I pressed my lips to hers just as the flight attendant returned with our water.

"Amanda," I addressed her, lifting my eyes, "we changed our mind." I glanced at Isabelle, smiling, "We would like a bottle of champagne instead."

"Of course, Mr. Greco," she professionally replied with a warm grin before quickly spinning away.

Isabelle snorted, "You probably drive your employees so crazy."

"I try," I smirked.

"So where are we going Mr. Mysterious?" she whispered, placing a kiss next to my ear while running her fingers through my hair.

Amanda promptly returned with two glasses of champagne, setting them on the table. I nodded in acknowledgment. Isabelle had not taken her gaze off me.

"To my place in London," I smirked, reaching out and taking the glasses, handing one to her.

Puzzled, she took a small sip. "You're from Italy," she countered.

"Si," I confirmed with a nod, "but I have a place in London as well."

"Surprise, surprise," she joked sardonically then chugged the rest of her drink.

I took her empty glass from her, setting it on the table with my own. I lifted her off my lap, twisting her body so that she was straddling me. I wrapped my arms around her, gripping her bottom in my palms as I pulled her into my lips. Our tongues danced as I ran my fingertips slowly up her side under her shirt. She peeled herself away from our kiss, glancing back over her shoulder at Amanda and my security team.

"You realize we're not on here alone, right?" she sighed, turning back to me, her cheeks flushed with embarrassment.

I nodded, gazing into her eyes with lust and desire. "It's not like I'm fucking you in front of them, bella."

"But you would," she snickered, "wouldn't you?"

"Maybe," I muttered, yanking her into my mouth once more, planting a playful peck on her lips. "I just don't care what I do in the privacy of my own plane."

She glanced down at our laps, smiling shyly. I noticed that Isabelle had two sides to her. The first part of her was a shy little girl who blushed when someone put any focus on her. The other side was a caged animal ready to be released into the wild.

I loved both of these sides of her. It was what provoked me to purposely make her frequently blush. I found myself staring at her as she wrapped her arms around my neck again. Subtly, she began to rock back and forth on my lap with the guidance of my hands on her hips. She smirked when she began to get a reaction in my pants. Resting her lips so close to mine, I felt them graze my skin.

"It's so very tempting," she whispered.

Just as I was about to reply, Joseph asked to speak to me privately in the very rear of the plane. I nodded before asking Amanda to refill Isabelle's champagne for her. I then followed Joseph, leaving Isabelle to drink and relax in my chair.

Isabelle

Once alone, I sat completely awestruck that I was in a private jet on my way to London with the most beautiful man on the planet; and he wanted me, of all people. I knew something secretive was being discussed in the back of the plane.

I did feel safe with him, and oddly enough, I trusted him. Undeniably so, this entire situation was insane. Things like this did not happen to people in the real world. This seemed too good to be true.

When I paused to think about how I got here, I laughed at the thought that I was placing all my trust into a man who bought me. Most girls would have left a long time ago or called the cops. Here I was, enjoying almost every confusing moment of this insane journey that Valentino had me on.

The flight attendant glided over to me with the bottle, refilling my champagne as ordered while she hummed a tune, gazing into the glass thoughtfully. She was beautiful and her attire, while professional, was a little on the small side. Her breasts peeked out of her top while her skirt stopped mid-thigh.

Maybe that's how Valentino liked the women who worked for him. Based on what I had witnessed so far, it certainly seemed that way. I snickered at the fact that I was jealous of her, yet five minutes ago, I was straddling

Valentino's lap, making out with him in a plane full of his staff.

I swallowed my envy, beaming, "Thank you."

She nodded, matching my face, "You're welcome."

Shortly after she returned to the front of the plane, Valentino emerged. I stood, stepping into the aisle, allowing him enough room to squeeze by so he could return to his seat. He held his hand out, motioning for me to return to his lap. Settling on his lap sideways, I suddenly felt somewhat lightheaded.

He smirked, "Only glass number two, right?"

"Mm-hmm," I hummed taking another sip.

I offered it to him. He curled his lips around the rim, sipping from my glass before motioning for the flight attendant again. She waltzed over immediately, seemingly flirty this time.

"Yes, *Sir*?"

Her desperation now showed. As a result I involuntarily rolled my eyes, snickering as I buried my face into his neck, remembering the effect it has on him. He gently squeezed my thigh causing me to lift my head.

"Could you just leave the bottle at the table this time?"

She nodded, setting it on the table next to his laptop before disappearing once again.

He gently kissed my cheek. "You're the only one who calls me that," he growled in my ear, "and it results in me fucking you."

Valentino

I swiveled my chair around to face the table. She glanced at the computer screen as I pulled up several documents. I planned to attempt my work with her on my lap. It was not like she would understand what I was doing, so I felt it was safe for the time being.

"What are you working on today, boss?" she murmured, admiring the files open on the screen. "I mean, you are technically my boss, now right?"

I nodded, smirking, trying to hide the fact she was driving me crazy. She was stirring something in me that I had never allowed myself to experience. Slowly, but surely, she was breaking me. I wanted to show her the darker version of me.

Something was holding me back, but I did not know exactly what that was. I found myself wanting us to find out together. Truthfully, I was starting to feel real things for this woman. I was trying hard to stop fighting it. The reality was that our lives were complicated. Somehow that turned me on even more.

I clicked one final folder and the screen lit up, tabs cascaded down the display screen. I planned to tell her most of the details when we safely arrived at my house in London. For now, I kept my work to myself as I wanted to tell her in a more relaxed environment. I froze, realizing that I opened the wrong file; the one file I did not want her to see. I began to rapidly close the tabs on each window as she intently watched. Suddenly, she audibly gasped.

"Oh my God!" she exclaimed loudly, causing my staff to all turn and look at us. "Go back!" she demanded harshly.

"What?" I was closing windows so rapidly that I did not know she had seen anything yet.

"The photo!" she snapped.

I took a deep breath, realizing she had in fact seen what I was trying to hide. I was caught. I struggled to play it cool as I opened up a few of the previous tabs one by one. She studied each one, some of which contained photos of various buildings.

"No, that's not it," she insisted.

I was avoiding the obvious one, but I was out of pages to flip through. Taking another deep breath, I opened it, ready to accept my fate. Nothing would be more awkward than arguing in an enclosed space with four more hours to go. The page loaded the photos and information.

Her eyes widened as her mouth dropped open. Reaching out, she touched the screen of my laptop, swiping through a set of photos on the bottom right side of the screen. Each photo contained parts of my hidden secret. She began to shiver. I felt her lightly vibrating my legs.

"Bella, I can explain," I blurted.

"Shhh," she hissed as she continued to scroll through all the documentation I had.

"What the fuck is this Valentino?"

Her photos, her father's photos, information on both of them, information on my job, and finally, a copy of the contract I signed in Spain. It was all in front of her. I sat completely exposed and vulnerable.

In no version of this scenario could I win. I was stuck. It was finally time to come clean. No time like the present and she was not going to take, *let's talk later*, for an answer.

She crossed her arms over her stomach, glaring at me with narrowed eyes.

Rolling my eyes, I exhaled, "Bella--."

"Valentino," she growled, cutting me off, "what the actual hell is happening?"

A look of paranoia and terror slowly spread across her face. I sighed, wishing that I would wake from the nightmare I was now living. It was unenviable that after hearing what I had to say, she would never trust me or speak to me again.

"Your father asked that I not tell you anything bu--," I began to explain.

She interrupted with eyes full of betrayal, "What does my father have to do with this?"

"Bella," I sighed, "he asked me to watch you." I lowered my head in shame.

She jumped off my lap, blustering, "What the hell are you talking about?"

I attempted to explain, nodding toward the photos on the laptop, "Your father asked that I watch you but--."

"My father is dead!" she shouted.

The cabin fell so silent that you could hear a pin drop if it were not for the low hum of the engine. I lifted my hand, signaling for my staff to mind their business. Part of them returned to their positions but exchanged glances with one another.

Confused, I peered up at her, arching my eyebrows. "Bella, I met with him," I muttered as I pointed at the screen. "He is right there, and you see, he hired me to--."

She began to cry and shake so I stopped speaking. She fell back in her seat, recoiling as her eyes welled up with tears. Immediately, I stood, stepping across the aisle, kneeling in front of her. I placed my hands on her thighs, gazing up at her with the most non-threatening look I could muster in the moment.

"I wanted to tell you so many times, but I wasn't allowed," I explained quietly.

"No no no," she lamented.

"What do you mean, no?" I faltered.

"Valentino my father was killed years ago," she finally choked through her tears. "That is my evil uncle."

A waterfall of tears began to flow down her soft, rosy cheeks. It took a minute for me to process what she was talking about. I tried to press her for more information, but as delicately as possible.

Reaching my hand to her face, I swiped my thumb under her eyes, wiping away her tears. "What do you mean?" I inquired.

"He killed my father and raised me as his own," she sobbed, peering out the window. "He killed my dad in front of me then kidnapped me."

15 NEW REVELATION

Valentino

My mouth fell open and I stood, immediately running my fingers through my hair in a silent panic. Joseph hurried to us after overhearing what Isabelle had just blurted. She was now curled up in her seat with her knees to her chest. Her palms covered both of her eyes. I paced the aisle back and forth, taking multiple deep breaths to calm myself down.

I ran my fingers through my hair once again, unsure if she was crying at this point or just hiding in her personal bubble. What the fuck was going on? I was incredibly confused. Joseph was better with people than I was. He knelt down in front of her, trying to calm her in the midst of my own anxiety.

"Isabelle, it's okay," Joseph soothed.

"Amanda!" I barked harshly. "Water!"

She scurried to the mini kitchen area, then quickly sprinted to me with two bottles of water in her hands. I snatched them from her immediately, opening one for Isabelle.

"Here, drink it," I commanded as I lightly tapped the side of her upper arm with the full bottle. She peeked out from behind her hands to see what I was offering. Her soft, pink lips curled into a tiny, thankful smile, but she did not say a word as she took it.

Felipe was not her father. No. This could not be correct. I had to have more information. Just as I opened my mouth to speak, an announcement echoed throughout the cabin on the intercom:

Mr. Greco, we are going to be going through a bit of turbulence. It's going to get bumpy so please, for your safety, I need everyone to return to their seats and buckle your seat belts.

Nodding to Joseph, he patted Isabelle on the knee before he returned to the front of the plane. I harshly sat down in my seat, buckling my seat belt, and staring straight ahead with a clenched jaw. I did not know what to say or if I should say anything to her at the moment. She was probably waiting for answers while I was just sitting idle, consumed in confusion and anger.

"Isabelle, I--," I muttered but froze, losing all train of thought.

Nothing I could say or ask her would help right now. She peeked out from behind her palms with red, watery eyes, meeting my gaze. Her body was stiff and tense, her lips pursed as she choked back her tears, sniffling.

I took a deep breath, regrouping, then tried once more to speak. Leaning over the armrest of the chair, I opened my mouth. Before I could utter another word, Isabelle lifted her hand into the air, signaling for me not to say anything. I sighed, sinking back, angrily exhaling as I irritably gripped the arms of my chair, my knuckles becoming white.

I was not angry at her. I was pissed off at myself. Shaking my head, I thought back to my meeting with Felipe in Spain. His words and urgency for the protection of Isabelle seemed so genuine. It was not easy to fool me, but when I saw her photo, I knew that I would not be able to turn him down.

At the bar, he maintained a level of authority as he voided the contract. I was not sure what Xavier actually had to do with it now, but I was going to find out. Me protecting Isabelle was more than likely about to become a mission that could potentially become more dangerous, especially when Felipe discovered that I took off to another country with her. It would not be long before the hunter became the hunted.

For the next hour, my plane jolted and shook as we rode out the turbulence. Isabelle was now gripping her armrests tightly, appearing nervous. I reached my hand out to comfort her, but she ignored my kind gesture. *That's okay.* She was possibly just as confused as I was right now, if not more, considering what I had put her through lately. I would have to contact William the moment we landed.

William

After dropping Isabelle off at the airport, I clutched my steering wheel tightly, speeding back to Valentino's estate. I was craving to release some anger and frustration out on something...or someone. Valentino left me to attend to Isabelle's former boss, Jesse. I was ordered to press him for more information, killing him in the end.

However, after the meeting with Felipe, I was annoyed that Valentino had run off and taken Isabelle to another country. While I respected his choice to do so and understood his need to get her far away, I was angry that I could not go with them to help protect them. I knew this would not result in anything but further complications for all of us.

As I pulled up to the front gate of the estate, I noticed Tanya's car sat off to the right side of the entrance. She had been avoiding me lately and I was upset. Isabelle triggered the anger and hurt in me by bringing her name up earlier in the car. I knew she meant no harm to me, but I was caught off guard.

Tanya and I started off with casual sex shortly after she began to work for me, but truthfully, at some point during all the time we spent together, I fell in love with her. While I had other things that I needed to get done today before Valentino arrived in London, Tanya being here was more important to me. I was glad she had come by. One of the guards stood next to the gate, by the guardhouse. I lowered my window as he approached the car.

"Let her in behind me," I ordered.

"Yes, sir," he nodded in agreement.

Turning around, he gave a thumbs up to the other security guy through the window of the guard house. The large wrought iron bars slowly opened, and I drove through, hoping she instinctively knew to follow me, but I had not motioned for her to do so. Peeking up into my rear view mirror, I noticed she had.

Once in front of the house, I stepped out of my car, leaning against the driver's side door, waiting for her next move. I held my keys in my hand as I folded my arms over my chest. She slowly stepped out of her car, softly closing the door. It was then that I noticed her eyes were red and swollen as she carried a stack of papers in her hand. Defensively, I huffed to myself, resting my fingers on my hips. In my world, nothing good ever came from a stack of papers.

She trudged over, coming to a stop in front of me, never making eye contact. She sighed, seeming shy and distracted. I arched a brow, wondering why she was here and what the papers had to do with it.

"Hi Liam," she rasped.

I did not know how to respond but I gnawed the inside of my cheek for a moment before responding. "Would you like to come in?"

She nodded, following me to the porch. I unlocked the door, pushing it open and gesturing for her to enter ahead of me. I followed her through the threshold, closing the door behind us. Taking a deep breath, she stood on her tiptoes searching around for something before lifting her gaze to mine.

"Where are they?"

"Out," I blurted in a low growl, not wanting to put her in danger by giving her any more information.

Sighing, she nodded before lowering her head, nervously rolling her bottom lip between her teeth.

"Would you like a drink?" I muttered, hinting a half smile.

"No thanks," she murmured, shifting her weight back and forth.

It was at that moment, I knew this was a meeting and not a makeup sex session. Valentino's butler poked his head into the foyer, but I lifted my hand, letting him know his services would not be needed at the time. He promptly disappeared and I turned my attention back to Tanya.

"Follow me," I exhaled.

We navigated the hallways, coming to a stop in front of Valentino's office. She suddenly stopped dead in her tracks. She began to dart her eyes around timidly.

"Um," she gulped, "I was hoping we could speak in private."

I smirked, "I told you they're out."

"I thought you were just saying that," she sighed.

Shaking my head, I corrected, "They're out of the country right now."

"Both of them?"

I nodded, opening the office doors.

"Where and why?" she bleated, rubbing her arm uncomfortably as if she were worried.

Ignoring her question, I gestured for her to enter the room. She crept in and I followed closely behind her, shutting both doors immediately. She roamed to the middle of the room, taking in her surroundings as if it were the first time she had ever been in it.

I marched behind the desk. "Shall we begin?"

Her eyes settled on me. "Begin what?"

I lifted my hand to my chin, bowing my head toward the paperwork in her hand.

"Oh these," she smiled awkwardly, "yeah it's just something from my doctor."

"Are you okay?" I blustered, widening my eyes.

She shook her head before laying her handbag and papers on Valentino's desk. I strode back around to the front of the desk, coming to a stop in before her. Reaching out and stroking her arms with my fingertips, I noticed that her face of uncertainty had transformed into mild fear.

"What's wrong?" I soothed, dropping the *tough guy* act. "Tanya, whatever is going on, you can talk to me, baby."

"Can we just take a walk and not talk about anything right now, please?" she pleaded, avoiding the topic.

"Tanya, tell me what's going on." I repeated as I gazed into her eyes, hoping they would tell on her as they often did.

"Liam," she exhaled with tears in her eyes. "I know I have been avoiding you but with everything going on," she lamented, "I just need my best friend right now and she's not around."

I dropped my head, knowing this was something I could not fix for her. I was not Isabelle. I would never be Isabelle, but I wanted to try to be that person for her when she needed me. Isabelle would not always be around, and I would. At least I hoped I would.

When Tanya stopped talking to me, at first it drove me crazy because I wanted the power and control in the relationship. As the days went on, I realized that she meant more to me than I was ready to admit at the time. Now, I was concerned about whatever it was that she was bothered by. I just wanted her to be okay.

"Unless," she corrected, "you're lying and she's upstairs?"

Shaking my head, I lifted my gaze to hers, sighing, "She isn't here, Tanya, I swear."

She continued exhaling deeply, "I started distancing myself from you because I thought you would freak out and walk away from me."

Tilting my head, I placed my palms on her arms. "Baby, I would never walk away from you regardless."

"You say that now."

I pulled her into my body, wrapping my arms around her as I held her tightly against me. "At some point during all the sex, work, and spending time with you as friends, I fell in love with you."

She inhaled sharply, beginning to cry with unsteady breaths as she buried her head into my chest.

"What the hell would I even freak out abou--," I relented, but I fell silent when I realized why she was here.

I peeled myself away from her, my gaze locking on her. She slowly found mine through her tears. She sniffled several times.

"Y-yes," she stammered, confirming my thought.

Gripping her arms, my eyes widened as I gasped, "You're pregnant?!"

She nodded, inelegantly smiling, unsure how I would respond.

"You have been avoiding me because you're having my baby?" I scowled.

She nodded once more. "I know it's dumb," she sighed, "but I needed my best friend to be there for me first and it just--."

Placing my palms on her cheeks, I cut her off. "I don't even need an explanation," I consoled. "You need to know that I'm crazy about you and nothing will ever change that."

Throwing her arms around my neck, she pressed her body into mine. I leaned forward, placing a gentle kiss on her forehead. Her body relaxed in my embrace. I never knew if I wanted to be a father before today. I had never thought about it, but now with her, I wanted it more than anything in the world.

"I love you," I whispered.

Isabelle

We touched down in London, having spent the last few hours of the flight in silence. Why did he have all that information on my uncle? Why did he think Felipe was my father? Furthermore, why did he look both upset and confused about all of it?

Once again, I was riddled with so many questions. Part of me was terrified, but a part of me felt safe. I wanted to believe that Valentino would not allow any harm to come to me, but I wondered what he had to do with my uncle. My mind burned with confusion as we both stepped out of the plane under the, still dark sky.

Still in silence, Valentino placed himself in front of me, taking my hand in his without saying a word as we plodded down the stairs. A long, black rug stretched toward four black SUVs. He led me to the closest one.

"Good evening, Mr. Greco," the driver greeted us as he opened the back door for us.

"Buona sera," Valentino murmured.

He ushered me into the car then walked around to the other side, sliding in. The entire ride was awkward and quiet between Valentino and me. Even the driver and Joseph sat quietly in the front as we rode through the roads of London. Normally, I would have enjoyed looking out the window, trying to catch small glimpses of the scenery and buildings as we passed. Right now, I did not have it in me to care. More pressing matters dominated my mind.

I was not sure how much time had passed because I was in my own world. The next thing I knew, Joseph opened my car door. I stepped out onto the sidewalk in front of a tall building. Valentino suddenly appeared next to me before Joseph led us to a side entrance and into an elevator.

Valentino placed his right index fingertip on the sensor. The elevator started to speed upward. Still in silence, he crossed his arms over his chest. Waiting impatiently, he stared ahead never making eye contact with me.

The elevator eventually came to a stop and the doors opened, revealing a magnificently decorated, modern penthouse with ceiling to floor, windows. It was the kind of apartment I would be scared to touch anything in. Just like his other house, everything had a place. At least the other place felt a bit more like a home. This place felt like a museum.

I was completely in awe of the costly artifacts throughout the open floor plan. Valentino did not seem shallow whatsoever, but he did enjoy the finer things in life. Money was no object to him.

I roamed around, slowly making my way to a row of windows. Looking out across what I could see of London was surreal. It was beautifully lit up in what was left of the nighttime sky. The reflection of the lights in the rain made for a perfect photograph.

Suddenly, I felt a chill come over me and shivered. Shortly after, a hand lightly grazed my arm and the presence of his body was behind me. I did not turn around to face him but continued to peer out the window at the wet, London night.

Valentino

As I gently ran my fingertips up her arm, I sighed, "Can we talk?"

"Hmm," she hummed.

"I'm sure you have a lot of questions," I whispered. "I know I do."

I saw her reflection in the window as a single tear rolled down her cheek. I hated seeing her this way. I could not stand crying. In the past it was annoying, and I had no sympathy, but with her it was different. In fact, everything was different with her. I was a shell of the man until she came into my life.

She exhaled slowly before she turned to face me. I curled my lips in a slight smile as I wiped a tear from her cheek with my thumb. I wrapped my arms around her, hugging her tightly against my body.

"If you are not ready to talk," I surmised, "we can talk tomorrow, or something."

I was trying to let her control the conversation even though I was dying to know details. In reality, this was a dangerous situation. She held the key to the answers I needed. Soon, I would have to notify my team back home, letting them know to watch their backs extra closely. I could not quite grasp yet, how my decision to get Isabelle out of New York would come back to haunt us later on.

William was there living in the middle of it all. If anything happened to him as a result of this new discovery, I would never forgive myself. He did not want to do this anyway. He warned me something was not right with Felipe a long time ago, but I did not listen to him.

He never quite understood why a drug lord would ask a billionaire to watch his *daughter*. At the time, I thought maybe he saw my money as a bargaining chip, and he paid me in legitimate cash to watch her. He did seem dishonest in many ways, but it was in his nature. At the time, I told William and the others that it was just the default personality of a drug lord.

Isabelle took another deep breath, craning her neck while peering behind me. I pivoted to see my security team standing in the room listening intently. I held my hand up, dismissing them.

"I will notify you guys of any necessary information," I informed, "but please give us time alone right now."

Joseph nodded, ushering the rest out of the room, then disappeared behind them.

"Do you want to sit down?" I suggested.

She nodded, frowning, still fighting back tears as she got ready to sit on a nearby couch. I shook my head, holding my hand out for hers. She placed her palm in mine, smiling shyly.

"Come on," I lightly tugged on her, putting her in front of me.

Moving my hands to her bottom, I guided her to my bedroom, closing the door behind us, leaving us completely alone. She trudged to the bed, sighing. I crawled onto the bed, lying next to her on my side. Resting my hand on her hip, I carefully watched her, trying to read her emotions at the moment. She was no longer crying, but she was still visibly upset as she laid silently for a few moments then slowly sat up.

"I suppose I should tell you what happened," she sighed, leaning forward as she buried her face in her hands, "but I want to know how it got to this, first."

I nodded, getting ready to speak, but she continued.

"On the way to the airport," she interjected, "William told me that I was just a business transaction."

I gulped as anger began to rise within me. That was very unlike William to just blurt something out like that, but it was the truth in the beginning. I would still have to speak with him about his choice to say something to her without my permission. Isabelle folded her arms over her chest then turned to face me, glaring into my eyes.

"So yes, I need some answers now."

"Then, do you want to go first, or would you like me to?" I offered.

"Why don't you?" she snapped.

She stood, beginning to roam the room as I remained on the bed. I told her every detail I could recall about Spain and the meeting with the man I thought was her father. She glanced over at me a few times, but she continued pacing.

"So, when I saw your photo," I continued, "I really didn't have a problem watching you."

She paused, not making eye contact with me. Her eyes lowered to the floor as she whispered, "Why me though?"

"Are you kidding?" I smirked, "You are an absolute perfect piece of priceless art, Isabelle."

She darted her eyes toward me, blushing.

"Your former boss knows your fath...um, uncle as well." I cleared my throat, concluding, "Jesse works for a sex trafficking ring and I know he has ties to your uncle through that."

"Damnit, are you serious?!"

Nodding, I added, "Jesse planned to sell you and I think Felipe was--."

"I cannot ever go back to my uncle!" she shrieked, interrupting. "He is not a good man!"

She began to break down, shaking. Her knees began to give out as she started to have a colossal panic attack before me. I jumped off the bed, sprinting to her and cradling her before she hit the floor. That is when the realization hit me that it was deeper than I thought.

"Bella, I will never let you go back to him," I soothed. "Come here." I wrapped her in my arms tightly, holding her against me.

"You might not be able to stop him," she sniffled against my chest.

"I will need to know what happened, so I know how to approach it," I suggested. Turning my head, I leaned my cheek on the top of her head. "You don't have to tell me right now," I alluded, "but sooner than later, please."

She took a deep breath, shivering again, "I was eight." She paused, pulling away then looking up into my eyes. "Can we sit on the bed please?"

I nodded, guiding her back over to the bed. Averting her gaze to the floor for a moment, she appeared almost as if she were ashamed before she positioned herself to face me. Reaching out, I took her hands in mine.

"My uncle Felipe showed up to our house in Ohio," she recounted, "and got into an argument with my father, Carlo, about business gone wrong in the States. At the time, I did not know what I know today," she choked. "I was an innocent child." She began to sob, fighting back tears as she lost control of her emotions.

"It's okay if you need to do this later," I comforted.

"My uncle had always taken a strange liking to me to the point he seemed a bit obsessed," she continued through her cries. "He never was able to produce a daughter, so unfortunately when his meeting with my father went badly," she remembered, "he took me and forced me to be his daughter."

"Bella," I mumbled, "I'm so sorry."

She did not miss a beat as she continued, almost as if she had taken no breath. "He shot my father eight times in front of me and made me count them." She paused, trying once again to control her emotions. "O-one shot-for each year of m-my age," she stammered. "He didn't kill him with the first shot."

"Isabelle, I--," I began, but stopped, realizing nothing that I could say at that moment would have fixed it.

"He made sure to make him suffer," she wept.

She took another deep breath and pulled herself together, appearing stronger than when she started, shaking off whatever nerves she had gotten. I ran my fingertips up and down her arms, caressing her soft skin. She swallowed hard, which told me she was about to tell me the most difficult part of all of this.

"After probably the sixth shot, my father stopped breathing," she lamented, "and once Felipe was finished killing him, he made me kiss his dead body goodbye on the cheek."

"Oh my God, Isabelle," I blurted. "I cannot imagine the pain you felt." I was shocked.

"Then he took me, and we disappeared," she recalled through her sniffling. "He raised me as his daughter and groomed me to give my virginity up to one of his men."

I realized it sounded familiar to what I had encountered at the mansion, but I listened intently, hanging on to her every word.

"He wanted me untouched until he came for me, but he let me go with the intention of having me brought back to him when he was ready," she sighed. "He knew he could not keep me hidden from the public forever." Her eyes darted to the wall and she mumbled barely above a whisper, "When I started dating your brother, I thought things would finally turn around for me, but your brother was almost as bad."

I nodded, exhaling, and gently pulled her into my body, hugging her. "I know," I confirmed the statement about my brother. "There is a lot we need to talk about."

She pulled away. "Can we not talk tonight?" she pleaded.

She rested her head on my chest and wrapped her arm around me. Softly, I stroked her back with my fingertips, mentally taking in everything she had just spilled to me.

"Now, I just want to be in your arms forever," she insisted.

I smiled, "Why don't we go take a nice hot shower and crawl back into bed?"

She leaned her head back, lifting her gaze to mine, "Do you have Netflix here?"

I chuckled playfully, "Never heard of it."

She snickered and teasingly slapped my chest.

I raised my head, kissing the tip of her nose. "Yes, we have Netflix here," I smirked, rolling my eyes.

I slid off the bed, standing, then took her hands in mine. Pulling her into my body, I bent over, tossing her over my shoulder before I teasingly slapped her on the rear. She let out a yelp then giggled while she continued to sniffle the last few tears away.

I tenderly put her down on the floor then leisurely began to undress her as we stood next to the shower. She then undressed me, watching my chest as she unbuttoned my shirt. I turned the water on and while giving it time to heat, I yanked her into me. Picking her up, I set her on the bathroom counter, stepping between her legs.

Tilting forward, I pressed my lips to hers. As I kissed her zealously, I ran my fingers through her hair, pushing myself against her, trying to get as close as our bodies would allow. Without warning her, I vehemently clenched a handful of her hair, snatching her head back as I proceeded to bite her collarbone.

"Stop!" she gasped.

I immediately peeled myself away, resting my palms on the counter on either side of her. Looking deep into her eyes, I smirked as I watched her face begin to flush with nervousness and lust. She knew I was calling her bluff, so she averted her eyes to avoid my gaze.

"What is wrong?" I teased. "Am I turning you on?"

She giggled, "You're holding back with me, aren't you?" She then took me by surprise when she lifted her gaze to mine, glaring into my eyes.

I grinned evilly, placing a kiss on her lips. "And?" I muttered.

She glowered, biting her bottom lip. "Don't," she hissed.

"What?"

"I said, *don't*," she tilted her head, repeating with more emphasis as she reached up, running her fingers through my hair. She lightly dragged her fingernails across my scalp. "Don't hold back with me," she whined, "I am not breakable."

I snorted, pushing away from the counter, and turning my back to her, "I'm not sure you're ready for that side of me."

She reached out for me, yanking me between her legs. The moment I spun around to face her, she started to grind her hips on my already hard shaft. Wrapping her legs tightly around my waist she impishly smiled.

"Try me, *Sir*," she challenged.

16 CONFESSION

Isabelle

The moment I said that, a switch flipped in Valentino. He grabbed my bottom, yanking my body to the very edge of the counter, crashing his lips into mine. Rubbing his naked, hard member against my wet slit, he pushed the top of my body back so he could access my pink-tipped, sensitive nipples. Taking one in his mouth, he bit relentlessly, sending electric jolts directly down to my sensitive area.

"I need you inside me," I begged between my moans.

He slowly pulled his teeth off my nipple without loosening his grip, causing me to arch my back, crying out in both pain and pleasure. Tilting his head, he glared at me in an untamed approach with a mischievous grin on his mouth. I rolled my bottom lip between my teeth, never taking my lustful gaze off his.

"Not yet," he growled, "get in the shower."

I hopped off the counter, obeying. He slapped me on my bottom as I passed by him. I gasped. The moment I stepped into the shower, his body was pressed against the back of mine. He started to grind himself on me as the steaming, hot water cascaded down the front of my body. I yelped as he pulled himself away, slapping my backside again, this time with a bit more force. Moving my hair to the side so he could access my neck, he bit the back of my shoulder, pulling my skin into his mouth with a forceful suction.

"You're still holding back."

His body tensed up at my words, and he immediately backed away. I seductively bit my lip, spinning to face him. His head was cocked to the side, with his eyes locked on mine. They were full of lust and aggression as I innocently peered up at him. So far, I had never witnessed this look on him before, but I liked it. It was exceedingly arousing.

"Kneel," he commanded in a low rumble, clenching his teeth.

I nodded, kneeling down before him on both of my knees. I bit the inside of my lip to hide my smirk. Was he about to lose control and dominate me? I had only ever heard about this. Still, I liked wherever this was going.

Grabbing my hair, he pulled my head backwards into the water, allowing it to cover my entire body, then pulled me back toward him. He smirked, glaring down at my drenched body. His fingers tangled themselves further into my hair as he tightened his grip.

"Isabelle, do you really think you can handle my world?" he muttered in a seductive tone.

I nodded silently, wiping the lingering water out of my eyes. That was not the answer he was looking for. Thinking for a moment, I remembered back to the word that sent him into a frenzy every time I called him it.

"Yes, Sir," I smirked.

He nodded with approval, "Much better."

I smiled, proud that I had figured it out.

"I'm going to fuck you now," his lips curled up into a wicked smirk.

I began to stand but he harshly pushed me back to my knees. My body quivered in arousal whenever he spoke dirty to me. Every sense within me was heightened. Kneeling beneath his muscular, tanned body, I peered up into his hungry eyes, waiting for him to do what he wanted with my body.

"I didn't say I was going to fuck your pussy, Isabelle," he growled. Reaching down, he cupped my chin in his hand while pursing his lips, "I'm going to fuck your beautiful mouth."

I swallowed hard, realizing I had never done *that* before and I was about to. Time seemed to freeze as my brain started to wander. I had seen movies with blow jobs in them, but I had never tried. What if I was terrible and did it wrong? Would he laugh at me? Somehow, I would end up ruining our erotic moment in the shower.

I stared at it, erect, pointing directly at my lips. I became restless and intimidated even though I was turned on beyond words. I craved him. I yearned to please him and wanted to do it. I just did not know how. How was it even going to fit? I began to panic. He must have sensed it.

Valentino

I laughed to myself after I said what I did. She had never sucked a cock before. Even if she and I had never discussed it, the expression on her face at the moment told me all I needed to know. It was her fault. She told me not to hold back, so what was I supposed to do with her? She asked for this.

Was I supposed to show her mercy now because she was new to this? I do not think so. She said multiple times not to hold back with her. If I did, she would instinctively figure it out. Truthfully, I had shown her more than enough mercy at this point. I knew she was not like the other women I had been with, but I never once showed them any hint of mercy and they loved it.

Isabelle wanted to be a part of my dark, secretive world. There were some things she would have to be taught. Before she came along, I was never willing to teach a woman how to please me. I expected them to know. I did not have those same expectations with her. She was special to me. Teaching her would be different, but she would soon know exactly what I liked and how to do it.

Without further warning, she reached out, taking my throbbing member in her palm. She began to move her hand in a perfect rhythm up and down my hard shaft. Her touch was perfect, rendering it difficult for me to focus on anything other than how beautiful she looked right now. Her wet hair was wrapped around my hand. Her perfectly toned body knelt before me in full submission.

I kept having to remind myself that she was not even my girlfriend. She had a hold on me that no one ever had. She had me so messed up in the head and I was oddly okay with that. She was mine.

She rested her lips on the head of my cock, taking a deep breath as if she were preparing herself for what was to come next.

"It's okay," I reassured her, "I will help you if you need."

Her gaze met mine as she slowly took me in her mouth, then pulled me back out. She licked the head and all around the tip before she swallowed more, creating the perfect amount of suction. How was someone who had never done this before, so good at it already?

She read my mind and needs as she continued. She was instantly so in tune with me and it drove me crazy. I pushed her head further into me, ever so slowly pumping in and out of her mouth until she got used to it. She began to moan, caressing my balls as her lips worked magic on my shaft.

When I realized she was a natural at this, I picked up the pace. She watched me intently. Immediately taking control, I fucked mouth harder, entering her throat with each thrust. She gagged, but she never once tried to back away.

Just before I was about to completely lose myself in her, I pulled out then helped her to her feet. I shoved two fingers into her soaked core, using them to forcefully guide her backward, up against the wall. She let out a yelp and my mouth found hers.

Biting her bottom lip, I growled, "You are too fucking perfect at that for it to be your first."

"I need you inside me now," she choked in between her moans. "Now!"

I smirked against her lips, shaking my head, "I'm not finished driving you absolutely fucking crazy yet."

I nibbled, kissing from her lips, trailing down her body to her mound. She bucked her hips, grinding herself against my face. My fingers continued to explore her insides while my mouth assaulted her button.

"Cum," I commanded.

Her body instantly reacted to my demand and she immediately tightened around my fingers. She began to shake while sinking down the side of the wall, her knees slowly giving way beneath her. I pulled her on top of me as I rocked back, sitting on the floor of the shower. Straddling my body, she lowered herself onto the length of my ready shaft, wincing.

"I'm not sure I'll ever get used to your size," she moaned, sinking her teeth into my shoulder, biting down.

I chuckled malevolently, leaning into her ear, growling, "I can help with that."

I jerked my hips up while pulling hers down, completely impaling her on my rod. She cried out against my neck. Rocking her back and forth, I held her down, forcing her to ride me at a hard, quick pace. Her nails dug into the back of my shoulders as her head fell back. Squeezing her eyes closed, she continued to moan incoherently.

"Valentino!" she gasped, "It feels so good!"

Letting go of her hips, I grabbed her hair. Gently nibbling her neck, I trailed my tongue all the way up to her lips, tugging her head toward me. Taking her bottom lip between my teeth, I sucked it hard as I bit down.

"I'm....going....to...c-c...again-n," she mumbled.

Letting go of her lip, I interrupted her, "Look at me."

Our eyes locked as waves of pleasure crashed over our bodies like a tidal wave of ecstasy. She finally collapsed onto my body, resting her head on my shoulder, panting against my neck, placing small kisses all over. I smiled to myself as I caught my breath, gently massaging her back.

We were silent for what seemed like an eternity, basking in the aftermath of our sex. I closed my eyes, leaning my head against the wall, mesmerized by the feeling of the water cascading over our bodies. Isabelle's breathing began to settle as we both remained still.

"How do you feel about toys?" I smirked.

She sat straight up, leaning back, and staring at me with widened eyes. She did not speak.

"Sooo, I'm guessing that's a hard no?"

Her eyes slightly narrowed as she conjured up a clever reply. "I said don't hold back, didn't I?"

Arching a brow, I aggressively yanked her to my lips, kissing her fervently before we finished actually cleaning ourselves and got ready for bed.

The following morning, I rolled over, recalling that we were in London. Sitting on the edge of the bed, I ran my fingers through my hair as I peered outside. Another rainy day. London was beautiful even in the rain. I actually quite enjoyed the greyer weather.

As I watched the city through the window, I leaned my elbows on my knees, taking in the view beneath us. I stared down toward the Thames River, watching the boats float along the path, heading to their next destination. I wondered if those people ever had to deal with such complicated things.

Running my fingers through my hair once again, thoughts of my current situation began to take over my mind, as I knew there was more that I had to tell her. I also knew there was more she would want to tell me.

I suddenly felt sick to my stomach. Nothing that I could say would fix any of this or make it disappear. The last thing I wanted to do was hurt her. She was so special to me and I wanted her in my life. The thought of her in any sort of pain, killed me inside but I knew she needed to know the truth about it, all of it.

Isabelle

I slowly opened my sleepy eyes, observing him sitting on the edge of the bed staring out the window as he slouched over. Not alerting him that I was awake yet, I took a moment to appreciate the view I had of him against the London skyline. His chiseled body displayed a perfect sight for my eyes. Everything about this man was flawless, though he would argue that.

After watching him for a few moments, I sat up, stretching. He felt me shifting on the bed and turned to face me. Smiling, he held his arm out to the side. Sliding over, I wrapped my arms around his neck.

"Good morning." He pressed his lips to mine.

"Good morning to you," I smiled against our kiss.

He guided my body around his, sitting me on his lap so that I was straddling him. Grabbing my backside tightly, he leaned forward, placing another kiss on my lips, this time lingering as he massaged my bottom. I melted into him as he trailed his fingers up my sides, coming to a stop under my pert breast. Running his thumbs in circles over my bare, erect nipples, he smirked.

"How did you sleep?"

"Perfect," I blushed, whispering, "thanks to you."

"Good."

His phone rang and we both glanced over to the nightstand next to us.

"Will you hand me that please?"

I leaned sideways, then picked up his phone, checking the caller ID. It was William. Rolling my eyes, I handed it to him and though I was close, I only heard his side of the call. He spoke in Italian. I shyly sat as he watched me with a smile on his face, knowing exactly what that did to my body.

He reached down, running his finger teasingly up down my slit as he listened to William on the other end of the phone. My eyelids flickered as I enjoyed the way he caressed me. He knew exactly what I liked without me having to tell him.

Honestly, any way this man touched me, I loved. He constantly sent me to the edge, then pushed me over. Spreading his legs, he smirked as he caused mine to part by force. His index finger found its way inside my tunnel as he explored every part of my aroused core. Lifting his finger to his face, he wrapped his lips around it, slowly cleaning my juices off.

Mmhmm okay, he replied to William before he hung up the phone.

"You are delicious."

"After tasting you," I countered, "I can say the same about you."

Leaning forward, he pressed his lips against mine before he suddenly peeled himself away, meeting my gaze.

"What's wrong?"

"Uh, William and Tanya will be here tomorrow," he muttered, searching my eyes for a reaction.

I said nothing as I lowered my eyes to our laps.

He sighed, lifting my chin. "Darling, all this is my fault."

I nodded but not in agreement. It was just to acknowledge his news. Nothing could prepare me for their arrival. I wanted to see Tanya and I missed her, but I was still quite nervous. I had to trust him. I took a few deep breaths, trying not to overreact and maintain a sense of coolness about it.

Just then, there was a knock at the bedroom door. I crawled back into bed, hiding my naked body underneath the blankets. Valentino stood, sliding on a pair of pants then strode over to the door. He opened it and sauntered to the middle of the room, allowing Joseph and a man I had never seen before to enter.

"Did William call you?" Joseph inquired, crossing his arms over his chest.

Valentino nodded, pursing his lips then lifted his hand to his chin in thought, "He did."

Joseph turned his attention to me, teasing, "Will there be any running this morning, Miss Ayala?"

I giggled, challenging him. "Would you like to?"

"Yes Joseph," Valentino chimed in, "let's go running."

He nervously rubbed the back of his neck, mumbling, "If that's what you both want."

My eyes darted back and forth between them.

"I know you hate it so much," Valentino admitted.

"Oh God," I gasped, apologizing, "now I feel so bad!"

Valentino snorted at my response. "The day you made him run in the park," he recalled, "he was dying afterward even though he's in shape."

Joseph rolled his eyes, shrugging, "I just hate it."

"I'm so sorry."

Valentino smirked and Joseph winked, indicating it was okay.

"Boss," he addressed Valentino directly in a rather serious tone, "may I please speak to you in private after breakfast?"

Valentino nodded, becoming instantly serious.

Joseph and the other man, who never spoke, exited the room without another word.

Valentino

I turned to see Isabelle with her arms crossed over her chest clutching the blanket that had been hiding her naked body. Now was the time to discuss Tanya and William's role in my so-called game. The last person I wanted her upset with was her best friend. She was innocent and I needed Isabelle to know that. This, however, would make me look unbelievably bad. But she deserved the truth. She cared about Tanya and I knew she felt the same about Isabelle. They had an unbreakable bond. Sitting next to her on the bed, I sighed deeply.

"What's up?"

"I need to tell you more about Tanya." I took a deep breath. "After all, she is your best friend and played a role in this for me."

She dropped her arms, scowling at me knowingly. The blanket somewhat shifted, exposing her left breast. I smirked when my eyes found it immediately. She glanced down, rolling her eyes while slightly smiling, but still maintaining her frown.

"Yeah but I don't know what to think right now," she finally whispered.

"God baby," I dropped my head, taking her hands in mine as I turned my body completely toward her. "I--," I lowered my eyes to the floor, pausing before meeting her gaze once again

"Just say it," she sighed, seemingly staring directly into my soul.

"I was so desperate to protect you, that I staged your bid with her help," I bluntly confessed.

She tilted her head, raising her eyebrows, "What do you mean?"

I groaned, closing my eyes, knowing that I was about to possibly undo everything I had done so far. All the trust I had built with her was about to go out the window. I could not risk the lie any longer and I wanted her to know everything, every single dirty detail.

"Valentino?" she whispered.

"I paid Tanya to lure you to the masquerade ball," I blurted.

Her eyes widened and she balled her mouth up.

"Please let me finish," I pleaded, placing my hand on my forehead.

She huffed, fixing the blanket to cover her once again as she crossed her arms, glaring at me.

I rested my hand on her thigh over the blanket, continuing, "She was dating Liam. I knew you were her best friend."

"Hmm," she hummed, wondering where I was going with this.

"I knew I could protect you better if you were with me," I sighed.

"But, I'm so confused."

"I held the ball and auction as means to keep a closer eye on you," I confessed. "At least this one anyway."

"So, you staged the auction?" she confirmed, narrowing her eyes. "Those girls are safe?"

I swallowed hard, "Uh, they signed up for that and--."

"You purposely humiliated me in front of hundreds of people!" she shouted then stood.

She started to pace the floor in front of me. I could not help but take notice of her picture-perfect naked body, but I was trying my best to focus on the seriousness of the discussion. She spun to look at me, catching me staring.

She rolled her eyes, marching to her bag, pulling out a little black dress and lace thong. Her anger once again showed as she pivoted toward me, focusing on my eyes.

"Continue!" she snapped, throwing her arms up, gesturing before she crossed them impatiently.

"You have to know," I declared as I stood, facing my palms toward her, "Tanya did not want to do it and she argued it, but Liam demanded she do it for me. We all knew the masquerade was the only way."

Isabelle tilted her head, glowering.

This was beginning to sound worse and I was not sure how to make it sound at all appealing. I was not always good with words. While I had no problem getting women, talking to them was another story. It was hard for me to articulate my words with them. However, I continued as I looked Isabelle in the eyes.

"She did not even want the money," I admitted, "but I made her take it. I knew you would listen to her."

She inhaled deeply, averting her gaze.

"I had to do what I needed to protect you," I pleaded, which I was not used to doing.

"You did not answer my question, Valentino!" she protested loudly.

"The women know why they are there," I explained, understanding exactly what she wanted to know. "They are auctioned off for a night with a wealthy man and most of the time they turn into, what you would call, a *Sugar Baby*."

A look of disgust replaced her look of anger. She took a step backwards, then froze, "Wait!" she retorted as a tear rolled down her cheek. "What the hell do you mean, *most of the time*?"

I sighed, "I--." I tried to speak but fell silent.

Taking a step closer to me, she clenched her fists, growling, "Are you telling me that wasn't the first time?"

I hung my head in complete shame, unable to find the words to defend myself.

"Valentino," she hissed, "how many women have you paid for sex?" Crossing her arms, she waited impatiently for me to reply.

I took a deep breath, slowly meeting her scowling glare, "Six."

She shook her head as she let out a disbelieving huff. Biting her bottom lip, she rolled her eyes. I thought she was going to snap. The expression on her face was extremely disapproving and made me feel utterly ashamed of my past.

"Why? You're so sexy!" she contested. "Why do you need to pay for sex? Look at you!"

"I didn't want to give my heart to just anyone," I muttered, carefully approaching her. "I held the auction as a way for me to have fun without having to commit to someone who wasn't special to me."

She sighed as her expression softened just a bit, but her eyes were still locked on mine.

"I know it is shitty when you think about it," I confirmed. "I frowned at the floor realizing how messed up I sounded.

"Personally, I don't really want to think about it."

I sighed, "Fair enough."

"So, what happened to these women?" she questioned. "Where are they now?" She rested her hands on her hips, quizzing me on their well-being.

I bit my lip, thinking carefully about what was about to come out of my mouth. "I really don't know," I confessed. "I never saw them, and they never saw me."

"A veil?" she snorted, rolling her eyes at me once again.

"Blindfold," I corrected, "not a lace veil."

She turned the other way, meandering toward the mirror on the dresser.

I continued with sincerity, "I never wanted them to see so much as a silhouette of me."

She pivoted her body toward me but only for a moment before turning back toward the mirror. "And what made me different?" she mused.

I ambled to her, standing behind her while admiring her reflection in the mirror. She cocked her head, making eye contact with me as we gazed at one another's reflections. I smiled gently, snaking my arms around her.

"They were not you, Isabelle," I murmured. "I knew you long before you knew me."

She lowered her eyes, blushing.

"You became special to me," I recalled. "You were a different situation. I wanted to protect you and yes, your fucked up, crazy uncle hired me."

I ran my fingertips up her arms, triggering her body to react with goosebumps. She shivered as I wrapped my arms tightly around her, pressing myself into her backside.

"Did I fuck up by lying to you?" I asked rhetorically. "Of course, I did, but please don't be mad at your best friend."

She tensed up, pursing her lips as she gnawed the inside of her cheek.

"She was so angry with me," I smirked, "and I honestly thought she was going to slap me."

"No comment," she snorted.

I chuckled, "Bella, all I'm saying is watching you gave me insight into who you are without you having to be on your best behavior the first few months of dating you."

"Like what?" she placed her hands on her hips, biting her lip.

I softly touched her lips with my thumb, "You bite your lips when you have something on your mind." I placed my hands on her rear, "You poke your ass out and check it out in store windows."

She narrowed her eyes at my reflection.

"You look at the floor and pick your fingernails when you get nervous," I smiled, resting my chin on her shoulder.

She folded her arms over her chest, playfully glaring at the mirror, "Creepy much?"

"No, just hired to watch you and somewhere along the way, began to notice how much I wanted you in my life so decided I would do anything to protect you," I blurted all at once.

She exhaled slowly, trying to hide her smile.

Standing straight, I intertwined her fingers with mine. "So many times," I continued in a low growl, "I wanted to tell you how much I wanted you."

She spun to face me, peering up into my eyes, questioning, "And now what?"

I placed a soothing peck on her forehead as I eased her closer to me. "I'm fucking crazy about you, Isabelle."

17 SHEDDING LIGHT

Isabelle

The minute that sentence left his mouth, I began to blush, but this time it was not the way he had made me blush before. I could not contain my emotions any longer. I know I had cried several times during all of this, but this was different. I completely broke down, crumbling to the floor. Everything seemed to have built up over time and came crashing down on me. I do not know what triggered it. The entire situation was so puzzling to me.

Valentino was genuinely nice, caring, charming, and protective. The problem I had now, was that though he was such a seemingly great guy, what we had between us was all built on lies and deceit. I felt betrayed in so many ways. Why the heck would a very wealthy man choose to take money to watch me? Why did he need someone's money at all?

He lived in a castle, owned a penthouse with a secret access door, a helicopter pad, and possibly more. In my world, that stuff only existed in films. He was very well-known. Again, why me? I was no one compared to him. As I began to replay all this and more in my head, he knelt next to me, placing his hand on the back of my shoulder.

"Isabelle," he sighed.

"Don't," I squeaked through my flowing tears.

"I just--."

"Not right now," I sobbed, "I need some time alone."

I managed to finish my thought before I stood, trudging into the bathroom. I closed and locked the door behind me. Leaning my back against the door, I slowly sank down, coming to a halt on the cold, tile floor. I lifted my knees to my chest, burying my face in my hands.

I wish Tanya had just come clean and told me what she had done. My life had drastically changed because of her and Valentino; not to mention that fact that she and William had broken up and it felt like it was my fault. William blamed me. I felt so bad. I caused trouble and did not even know anything about it.

Valentino

She had just slammed the bathroom door and I heard the lock click. I placed my arm on the door frame above my head, leaning my forehead against the door. The sound of her muffled sobs broke my heart. I did not want her hurting. The truth, was the only thing I felt would fix this. Now, she was questioning my character. Everything I had done was for her. I never meant her any harm whatsoever.

"Bella, please," I pleaded.

There was no reply, still only crying. I felt frustrated, but I was not angry at anyone except myself. I should have been honest from the beginning, but I could not take that choice back now. The only reason I never told her, was to protect her.

I knew everything was finally hitting her. I could not blame her one bit for this. Tanya showing up would hopefully help and not damage matters more. At this point, it could go either way. All I knew was that I needed to make this right before it got worse. I stood still for a few moments until I heard the bath water turn on. Deciding to give her some time to decompress and relax, I went to find my security team.

I strode to the kitchen to pour myself a drink then found everyone crowded around the living room, eagerly awaiting details. I leaned on the wall next to the fireplace, crossing one foot over the other. Taking a sip of my whiskey, I searched the room for any sign that one of them would start the conversation. Joseph, not too shy to cut the thick atmosphere, spoke up.

"For your safety," he began before pausing, pinching the bridge of his nose, "for everyone's safety," he crossed his arms, "I need specifics."

I sighed, nodding.

"Every detail you know about this situation," he alluded. "We cannot hide or stay in London forever."

I sluggishly sipped my drink, rolling my eyes as he continued to lecture me. I knew he was right, but I did not like being addressed this way. Still, Joseph only meant well and was my head of security.

I stared out the large windows, starting to wonder if Isabelle was okay. Seeing her cry in front of me was one thing but listening to her whimper behind a closed door was somehow more haunting to me. I wanted to go back and check on her.

Joseph brought me back to the conversation when he interrupted my thoughts. "Isabelle could die!"

It felt as if an electric current flowed through my body as I jolted back to life, almost losing my grip on my glass as I glowered at him.

"Welcome back!"

I shook my head, rolling my eyes once again while taking the final gulp of my liquid. Placing my glass on the mantle next to me, I crossed my arms over my chest. I peered around the room, studying the faces of each man, thinking. Everyone in this room could be dead soon and it would be my fault.

Sighing, I focused all my attention on Joseph, "So what do we do?"

He lifted his hand to his chin and began to slowly pace the living room in deep thought. All our eyes followed him as he chewed on his bottom lip, staring at nothing. He stopped on the other side of the room, turning to us.

"If you are here," he explained, gesturing to the penthouse, "you will bring the danger here."

I nodded in agreement.

"Once Felipe finds out you took her," he continued, "he's going to be pissed at you. He will come after her."

"Let him try!"

"Oh, he will," Joseph affirmed indignantly.

I clenched my fists. "I will fucking murder him if he so much as looks at her again!"

It was then that I noticed everyone's eyes were on the staircase. I quickly turned my head, my gaze meeting Isabelle. She was uneasily shifting her weight back and forth on the bottom step, wearing a robe with her wet hair falling over her beautiful face. She timidly glanced around the room, then her eyes found mine.

"Um," she mumbled, "can I talk to you for a moment please?"

"Of course," I smiled, attempting to pretend nothing had happened upstairs.

She turned away, climbing the steps back toward the bedroom.

I spun to Joseph. "We will continue this. For now, please contact William and tell him to handle Jesse immediately before he comes here." I spoke in Italian so Isabelle would not understand what I was saying.

Joseph nodded.

I ascended the stairs, skipping steps along the way. So much for being honest, but I wanted to make sure from this point on, she knew everything from me first. I sauntered with wide strides down the hallway, stepping into my bedroom. Quietly, I closed the door behind me.

Isabelle stood in front of the wide windows, facing the city with her arms folded over her stomach defensively. She held her robe tightly against her body even though it was tied. I did not take another step toward her. Instead, I exhaled deeply, lowering my eyes to the floor. Preparing a statement, I rehearsed in my head what I wanted to say.

"Isabel--," I sighed.

"Who are you?" she questioned sharply without turning around to face me.

I slid my hands into my pockets, lurching to the middle of the room, remaining within her view. I knew she was studying my reflection and every move in the window. I wanted to play dumb, but I also knew at this point there was no use. In any other circumstance, I would have hidden my world from them. She had been exposed and there was no turning back now. I chose my response carefully.

"How much did you hear?" I mentally braced myself.

She spun to confront me, quietly murmuring, "All of it." Taking a shallow breath, she snapped, "I don't give a crap about my boss!"

My eyes widened, "You speak Italian?!"

She shook her head, rolling her eyes, "I heard his name, so I figured you were speaking about him, however, I do know Spanish and sometimes can understand certain words."

A sigh evaded my mouth, forgetting that she knew Spanish, but relieved she did not fully understand Italian.

"My only regret is that I cannot watch him die," she continued, narrowing her eyes.

I bit my bottom lip, struggling to hide a slight smile. She had suddenly turned aggressive. I had to admit that I was amused and wickedly turned on by her confrontational demeanor.

She threw her hands in the air, gesturing to me. "But, what the hell, Valentino?! I'm in danger okay cool, but you are too!"

I cocked my head, wondering where she was going with her statement.

She pointed at the door, snapping, "What about them?"

"I am only worried about you, Isabelle."

She sarcastically snorted. "Um, well you need to worry about more than just me!"

I cautiously approached her, placing my hands on her arms. Slowly, I ran my fingers up her arms. She relaxed mildly as I placed her arms around my waist. Leaning her head against my chest, she gave in to my touch as she exhaled a sigh of relief. Holding her tightly, I pulled her harder against my body. We were both silent for a moment before she finally spoke again.

"This is nice," she admitted, "but it does not answer my question." She tilted her head back, looking up at me.

My gaze lowered to hers. "Who am I?"

She nodded.

"Bella," I took a deep breath, "I am not a bad guy," I paused, smirking, "well sometimes, but I do have some dark secrets."

She peeled herself away, taking my hands in hers. Something was stirring in her mind. I had a feeling I knew what it was, but I did not think she would have the guts to ask such a thing. She opened her mouth to speak but closed it just as fast. Her face then became full of seriousness and concern.

"Are you in the Mafia?" she blurted suddenly.

There it was. She asked. I could not help but to smile at her question. Even though I expected that, I began to laugh. Yanking her hands away, she huffed, crossing her arms, waiting for an answer. I tried to match my facial expression to hers, but it was not possible. I was too amused.

"You think because I am Italian that I am in the Mafia?" I smirked, still trying not to make her feel like a fool. "Do you know that is the first question I am asked by everyone?"

She shrugged, tilting her head, "I mean, no I don't think that and I'm sorry people ask that, but you do also hurt people."

"People who deserve it, yes," I rolled my eyes. "But that doesn't make me a gangster." I reached over, taking her hands in mine as I tried to keep my smirk to a minimum. "No Isabelle, I am not in the Mafia, I promise."

"It's not like you would tell me even if you were," she countered with adorable sarcasm.

She had a point, however I was telling her the truth. I shook my head as she arched a brow, studying my face for lies. Snaking my arms around her body again, I pulled her against me.

"True," I agreed, "but I'm just a man who will go to whatever magnitude I have to when it comes to the people I care about." I leaned forward, whispering against her pouty, soft lips, "And I care very much about you." I pressed my mouth to hers with a lingering kiss.

Isabelle

The moment those words left his mouth, I felt weak. The man had a habit of making me feel incredibly vulnerable and desired. I did not know exactly how to respond to him. I was rendered speechless.

Unfortunately, I was terrified for my future. The truth was that my uncle would probably kill me soon. He was the only person on the planet that I truly feared. He had instilled fear and anxiety into me as a child. I had spent a great part of my life dealing with it as I tried not to let him get to me so much that he ruined me as a person.

When I started working, Jesse's advances seemed benign compared to what I dealt with within the walls of my uncle's house. Although, Jesse was still irritating and inappropriate, I tried to ignore him. Money would help me flee my uncle sooner or later. I was deep in thought about my past when Valentino suddenly broke the silence.

"I want to show you who I am," he whispered, placing a gentle kiss on my neck.

I backed away, gripping my hands on my hips. "I want to know who you are besides all th--," I waved my hand back and forth at him, "sexy man that you are."

I plodded across the room as his body gave off a level of sexual tension. I was not willing to reciprocate right now, but since he made me weak, it might have happened. I had to be strong. I turned around to see him covering his mouth, as he leaned on the wall next to the window.

I continued my rant, "I want to know Valentino and *Sir*!" I crossed my arms, thinking I was making a legitimate request.

The humor washed off his face. He marched to me, standing before me within seconds. Backing me against the wall, he cocked his head as he searched my eyes for any sign of vulnerability. I swallowed hard as I met his lustful gaze, trying to hide my desire.

He smirked, slowly resting his lips against mine, "Be very careful what you wish for." He licked his lips, but they were so close to mine that his tongue grazed mine as well, "Bella, how much of me do you actually want?"

"All," I gulped, knowing what I was getting myself in to.

He chuckled derisively, "You did say that you didn't want me to hold back, didn't you?"

"And I meant it," I glared directly into his eyes.

Suddenly, there was a knock at the door. We both sighed.

"Come in," he shouted as he twisted to face the door.

Joseph entered the room with papers in his hand, holding them out for Valentino. He stepped over, snatching them, beginning to look through each one with a very intense expression. I observed as Valentino's body language matched Joseph's. They were both extremely tense but poised.

Joseph glanced over in my direction, giving me a half-smile. That was when I knew that whatever was on those papers was about me. Valentino turned to me, a nervous expression appeared on his face.

"Joseph, please leave us alone," he requested with his eyes still on me.

Joseph crept out of the room as quietly as possible, pulling the door closed as he exited. Valentino remained next to me, handing me the papers. He ran his fingers through his hair anxiously when I took them.

"You wanted me to be honest with you about things so here is your first test."

Before I browsed through them, I furrowed my brow, "What do you mean *test*?"

Gesturing toward the papers, he scowled, "This will explain everything."

I thumbed through the papers as I stood before him. He watched me intently as I scanned each one carefully. Without raising my head, I glided over to the bed, taking a seat while still reading over each sentence. My mouth began to open a little wider in shock as I read the details of each one. My eyes fell on the portion of the paperwork with details of my future engagement with Xavier.

I shook my head in a panic, shrieking, "I am not marrying anyone!"

He strode over, sitting next to me and pulled my body in to his embrace. "I am not going to let that happen," he soothed, "don't worry."

Valentino

I felt Isabelle tense up before she jumped off the bed, twisting her body around to face me. She tossed the papers on the mattress. Pacing back and forth several times at a rapid speed, she played with her lips in thought. She suddenly froze, spinning to me.

"You have to kill him now!" she demanded harshly.

I sharply inhaled, running my fingers through my hair. "You realize what you're saying." I began to gather the papers up, organizing and holding them in my lap.

She nodded as she started to roam around the room, "I do. You have to kill him!" She commanded once more. "I don't want him to hurt me," she paused, still pacing, "or any of you for that matter."

"I know," I sighed, "I don't want anyone to get hurt, especially you."

She stopped walking, lowering her gaze. I saw a tear form then run down her nose, dripping onto the wooden floor. I marched to her, yanking her body against mine.

She giggled through her tears, "Believe it or not, I'm not a cry baby but since you came into my life, I feel it's all I do."

My body became tense instantly. Taking a step away from her, I dropped my arms to my side. I felt completely defeated. The worst part about all this was, she was right. I should have stayed silent, watched her then handled all this on my own. She sheepishly watched me, sensing the hurt that her statement caused me.

"Listen Valenti--."

"Isabelle," I cut her off in a low growl, "feel free to roam the apartment."

"What do you mean?"

"I am going out for a while," I snapped harshly as I marched toward the door. I turned to her once more. "Security will remain here with you and keep an eye on you."

She took a step toward me, pausing, calling after me, "Where are you going?"

Without replying, I closed the door as I stepped into the hall. Joseph had been waiting for me, leaning against the wall, on his phone. I shoved the papers in his arms as I passed him, without speaking.

"Boss!" he called after me.

I did not acknowledge him as I marched at a quick pace for the elevator. I pressed the button, closing the doors before any of my security could get to me.

Isabelle

I was frozen in the moment, standing in the middle of the room like a statue scared to move a muscle. Valentino had just stormed out. I did not know whether to run after him to find him or stay put. There were times he decided to go after me, so I concluded that it was time that I return the favor.

I did not want him hurting over something that came out of my mouth the wrong way. Truly, I enjoyed his company even if things were very intense right now. He was the one thing keeping me somewhat sane.

I left the bedroom, jogging to the living room, but there was no sign of him anywhere. Joseph was speaking in Italian to someone on the phone but hung up the minute I approached him. He crossed his arms, glaring at me but it did not seem as if he were upset with me, only the situation.

"Where's Valentino?" I tried to ask as nicely as possible.

Joseph sighed, "He went out for a while."

I nodded but knew he was not telling me everything. I searched the room, noticing everyone else was gone as well. I returned my gaze to Joseph, who was busy on his phone texting as quickly as his thumbs would allow.

"They're out with him," I confirmed, "and you had orders to stay with me?"

Joseph placed his phone in his jacket pocket then absorbed my facial expression before he calmly spoke. "My job is to strictly watch after you. I stayed behind to make sure you are safe. Mr. Greco will be fine."

I lowered my eyes, muttering, "I feel like you've got some secrets."

He chuckled amusingly, "About what?"

"Me." I smirked. I was going to get this man to open up if it took years.

"Listen," he murmured, sauntering to the kitchen while I followed him. He continued on the way, "I know you want info and I will tell you what I'm allowed to share with you."

He poured us both a glass of water then slid one across the counter to me.

"Why are you so nice to me?"

He placed his glass on the kitchen island, smiling, "I think you're good for him."

"For Valentino?"

He nodded as he took another sip of water.

"He seems more stressed with me around."

He crossed his arms, snickering, "No more stressed than normal."

I rolled my eyes.

"Okay okay, maybe a little more stressed," he admitted, "but that's because he cares about you."

I could not hold back my grin, then I thought about him storming out of the bedroom and I became serious once again. Joseph read my mind, sighing.

"None of us will allow Felipe to hurt you. You are safe here."

I nodded, awkwardly sipping my water, suddenly becoming shy.

He continued explaining, "I know this whole plan was a bit off the wall and extreme," he smiled, "but he is usually right about things."

I took a long, slow, deep breath. Just as I opened my mouth to reply, Joseph's phone rang.

He held his index finger up, whispering, "Hold that thought."

Yes?

Okay.

Yes.

She's right here.

Let me know when you find him.

My eyes became the size of saucers as I waited impatiently for him to hang up the phone so I could question him. His eyes met mine and he guiltily blushed.

I have to go. Just keep me posted.

I crossed my arms suspiciously as he hung up.

"Wait," I snapped, "he actually left without *any* security?!"

He shook his head then buried his forehead in his fingers, "We will find him, don't worry." He was trying to be comforting but I could tell that he was exceedingly nervous.

I snapped, "Don't lie to me!"

I left the kitchen, marching toward the living room with Joseph following behind me. Now, I was extremely worried for his safety, especially knowing that my uncle was somewhere out there possibly hunting us down. Joseph grabbed my arm then placed his hands on my shoulders slightly squeezing, but not enough to hurt me.

"Isabelle!" he snapped, trying to get my attention by using my name. "Listen to me!"

He frowned as he watched, demanding my full attention. I crossed my arms defensively, glaring back at him, challenging him. He dropped his hands and folded his arms, mimicking me.

"We will find him," he assured, "just please try to relax. I assure you that he will be okay. This is not the first time he has ditched us and left security hanging." He took a step back, facing his palms toward me, "Never over a woman, anyway."

I nodded, not that it bothered me, I just wanted to make sure that he was okay. Sleepiness began to overcome me as I realized just how jet lagged, I was. I was starting to feel the exhaustion hitting me, so I curled up in a nearby chair.

Joseph left the room returning with a large, fluffy, white blanket. "Here, Miss, have this," he whispered softly and covered me.

"So, it's back to *Miss* now, huh?"

He did not find me amusing. He rolled his eyes before he turned away and walked out onto the balcony. I watched as he furiously texted on his phone for a moment then placed it to his ear. He was having a very intense conversation with whoever was on the other end. He was making all sorts of gestures with his hands which amused me since they could not see him.

I closed my eyes, resting for a moment, silently praying that Valentino would soon return safely.

The next thing I remember was waking up, but I was no longer in the living room and it was not daytime. I was back in bed, completely naked. I sat up immediately in a panic. A shadow slightly moved from across the room, catching my attention. The silhouette of a man stood against the glass, peering out at the London skyline. Squinting my eyes, I tried to study the outline, wondering who it was.

"Good evening, Isabelle."

18 NO SAFE WORD

Isabelle

I swallowed hard then sucked in a shallow, sharp breath as I watched the silhouette slowly glide across the room. He came to a stop over me, sitting on the bed next to my naked, defenseless body. At first, I was not sure if I was dreaming or not.

Folding my arms over my chest, I pulled the fluffy blanket tightly against my body. A tear rolled down my cheek, but I quickly wiped it away. The blanket began to sink without my grip, exposing my right breast. Neither of us spoke for a moment. I saw his chest slowly rising and falling as he took long, calming breaths.

"Where were you?" I whispered.

He slowly turned his body toward me, caressing my cheek. His deep blue eyes now sparkled in the dark room against the twinkling city lights through the window. Without speaking, he rested his hand over my own, his eyes never leaving mine.

Without a word, he gently wrapped his fingers around my hand as he stood, guiding me off the bed. Slowly, he ran his fingertips up my arms, so lightly that they caused my skin to react with goosebumps. He slid one of his hands into mine as he turned his back, meandering toward the terrace off the master suite.

"I'm naked," I hissed as we stepped out onto the platform high above London.

He spun my body to face him and I realized he had grabbed a blanket off the chair next to the door on the way outside. He wrapped it around my back, pulling me into his embrace as I smiled against his muscular chest. He held me tightly, resting his chin on the top of my head, sighing.

The smell of his cologne mixed with cigarettes and whiskey filled the atmosphere surrounding us while the sounds of the city's night rippled through the night air. A chilled breeze swirled around our bodies, causing me to shiver as it caught a small opening in the blanket.

"Are you going to speak?" I asked concerned, peering up at his troubled eyes.

He stepped back a little, gripping the blanket as he tugged my forehead to his lips. His gaze finally met mine and he took a deep breath. I was not sure if he were about to give me bad news or bend me over and have his way with me.

"Isabelle," he whispered.

My entire body quivered, quaking from just him uttering my name. He did not say anything else at that point. He did not need to. I understood his tone and him saying my name the way he did was enough to tell me everything was okay with us.

He cupped my face, pulling my lips into his. His tongue danced with mine as he slid his hand through my hair, gripping, while his other hand slowly moved down my arm then snaked around my waist. He peeled away but his lips remained close to mine with his eyes barely opened.

"Isabelle," he muttered again, placing a small peck on my lips, "I don't want you to leave me."

My eyes popped open and I moved my head back a bit as I peered into his eyes, "Valentino, I'm not going to leave you."

"You say that now."

I stood on my tiptoes, trying to make myself as eye level with him as possible, but his height made that almost impossible. I smiled, "Why would I ever leave you?"

He sighed, "I'm not perfect."

I giggled, "Then you don't see yourself as I do."

"I'm not good at relationships," he admitted, "but I also know I want to be with you, so I will do whatever it takes." He stared off into the distance. "Just tell me what I have to do to keep you and I will."

I reached up, caressing his jaw, and guiding his gaze back to mine. "You already have me," I reassured.

"I swear I am going to fix this," he groaned.

"I know," I sighed, "and I trust you."

He let go of me, backing away then pacing the terrace. "I fucked up so bad."

"How?" I winced. "Were you with someone else?"

He began to massage his temples, "Isabelle, no for fuck's sake."

I did not speak and allowed him to process whatever it was that he was about to tell me.

"While I was out roaming around," he explained, "I received a call from the estate back in New York."

I gulped. This did not sound good. I took a seat in one of the lounge chairs, pulling my knees to my chest. I watched him continue to walk back and forth in front of me.

"The guy you are supposed to have the fucked up arranged marriage with is actually Jesse's cousin, so Jesse and Felipe have to be working together," he revealed.

My eyes widened as I gulped, "What?"

He nodded, continuing, "William was going to be taking care of Jesse before he and Tanya fly here but somehow Jesse escaped from my holding area."

"You're kidding!"

He nodded, confessing, "I just found out a few hours ago. I already told my security team. Joseph is looking into it."

"My former boss is roaming around somewhere in New York?" I panicked.

"Well, that would be preferable actually." he shrugged.

"What do you mean?"

He lit a cigarette, taking a long drag. "I had him chained underneath my house in one of the hidden rooms."

The smoke slowly drifted out of his mouth and he blew the rest out as he finished his sentence. He roamed to the edge of the terrace, leaning on the railing as he looked out across London, puffing on his cigarette. Observing him, I understood that he was putting all the blame for this on himself.

While I grasped his reason, I knew that he had no idea that it would come to this. He was looking out for me. If anything, this was all my fault. I stood, creeping toward him.

"Okay so have them comb your entire castle…or yard…or land whatever it is that surrounds your palace thing."

I playfully nudged him in the arm trying to help him calm down. Maybe it was the wrong timing, and as upset as I was, he was carrying so much of the burden himself. He turned his head toward me as I rested my head on his arm.

He took another drag, smirking, "Why the fuck do you have to be so adorable?"

I blushed, "I can't help it." I fluttered my eyelashes and playfully smiled, still forcing a lighter mood.

Rolling his lip between his teeth, he thought for a moment. "For starters, it's not a castle," he corrected. "It's a--."

"Palace? Chalet? Hotel? Chateau? Manor? Big ole' fortress?" I teased.

He prodded my side with his finger, making me jump.

Smirking, he shrugged, "Mansion maybe? I don't know." He glanced away then back toward me. "Why can't it just be a house? Why are you making this weird?"

For the first time in a while we shared a genuine laugh. He snuffed his cigarette out on the railing then tossed it in a nearby ashtray on a table. I began to get a little cold, so I sashayed toward the balcony door, looking back over my shoulder.

"Living in a big house like that alone, is what's weird, Sir," I winked.

Spinning, he reached out, grabbing the blanket before I could walk inside. It fell to the floor and his eyes trailed hungrily up and down my body. Heat began to instantly form between my legs as he clutched my hand then jerked me into his body.

"You know what that word does to me," he growled as he placed his lips next to my ear. "I've warned you many times before."

Smirking, a sense of bravery rose within me. "And yet you have on way more clothes than you should." I scraped my fingernails down his shirt with enough pressure to cause a sensation on his skin.

He leaned me backward just a bit, nibbling my neck, growling, "You want me naked?"

"If I had my way, you'd always be naked," I hissed as his stubble tickled my nape.

Valentino

I stood Isabelle straight. She immediately ran her fingertips under my shirt, teasing me as she stroked inside the hem of my slacks. Her touch felt unreal causing me to involuntarily shiver. She gazed into my eyes as she pulled my black t-shirt over my head. Dropping it to the floor, she bit her bottom lip, never taking her eyes off my tight, rippled abs.

I peered out at the skyline and buildings, wondering if anyone could see us from here. I did not want anyone looking at her, but it made this moment much more spontaneous and interesting. Knowing people could be spying on us, was a bit erotic.

I was completely into this new venture. Here we were, out on the penthouse terrace, about to do unholy things in front of whoever would be able to see us; anyone from other tall buildings or low flying planes, arriving at both Heathrow and Gatwick airports.

Suddenly, she took me by surprise when she bent over, kissing my abdomen then slowly trailed her tongue over each muscle as she unbuckled my belt. I felt it snapping through each of the belt loops, as she slid it off my pants. Raising up with a devilish grin on her face, she rolled my belt around her hand then handed it to me. She craned her neck, placing her lips next to my ear.

"I believe you know how to use this, Sir."

"Fuck!" I growled, yanking her to my mouth. I bit her bottom lip, before harshly facing her away from me. "Yes, and this time we're going to play a different game." I brushed her hair off her shoulder, sprinkling her neck with small kisses. "You might want a safe word."

She tried to turn and face me, but I held her in place.

"Isabelle," I muttered, "pick a safe word."

She shook her head, rasping, "I won't need one with you." Leaning her head back against my chest, she peered up at me, smiling, "Safe words are limitations and wimps." She moved her hips in a figure eight against my already erect bulge. "I don't want you to hold back."

I spun her around quickly to face me, wrapping my fingers around her throat, but only gently applying pressure. "Pick a safe word Isabelle!"

She grinned hungrily with a mischievous gaze in her lust filled eyes. "No, Sir," she swallowed hard, "no safe word. Do with me as you desire, Valentino."

"As you wish, Darling."

Pulling my hand away, I spun her body facing away from me, seeing her reflection in the glass doors. She smirked while I secured her hands behind her body tightly, wrapping my belt around her wrists. I drew my hand back, swiping it across her bare round bottom. She jumped, yelping at the unsuspected contact on her flesh. I pushed her chest over to the railing of the balcony, bending her over the edge.

Leaning forward I whispered, "You are going to wish you had one."

I spanked her five more times and each time she yelped, more of her wetness, slowly trickled down her thighs. I smirked proudly at my accomplishment as she attempted to grind her rear on my erection.

Isabelle

I shivered every time this man spoke to me whether it was in my ear or not. His tone, combined with his accent, kept me weak in the knees. His touch crashed blissful waves of ecstasy over my body every time he pleasured me. I bowed forward against the terrace railing, eagerly anticipating his next move, quivering as he preyed on my yearning body.

His hand slowly slid up the center of my back with a mildly scratchy object intertwined with his fingers as he trailed my spine. Placing the object in front of my face, he held it out for me to see. Immediately, I recognized it.

I could still somewhat see through little holes as he pulled it against my eyes. Shivering, I remembered the recent past of having to wear this in his home. While this did feel remarkably familiar to me, it brought a whole new sensation to me this time as I knew who was on the other side. I sucked in a sharp breath as the knot on the back of my head got tighter.

"Too tight?"

"No," I squeaked as I felt more increasing warmth and wetness between my legs.

"What a shame."

A devilish grin spread across my face as I started to experience the darker side of him. He formed a ponytail with my hair, holding it in his hand as he reached down between my legs with the other. He quickly tapped the bottom of my backside.

"Spread."

I obeyed, separating my legs shoulder length apart. I moaned, feeling his hand trailing up my thigh, pinching my pearl, then repeating on the other leg. Forcefully pressing his hand on my slit, he circled my opening causing me to tremble. That sensation was quickly replaced by him slamming two fingers into me hard and deep. I let out an involuntary gasp while crying out in pleasure at the same time.

"You're always so wet for me," he growled, leaning toward my ear. "Tell me you are mine."

He began to pump his fingers in and out of my core at a faster pace, as deep as my body would allow. I felt his knuckles crashing hard into my opening. I was barely able to speak as he took away my breath with every movement.

"I'm…yours," I moaned through the painful pleasure of his thrashing fingers.

Just as I was getting used to the feeling, he ripped his fingers out of me. A groan of frustration escaped my mouth as I longed for his touch once again. Just as I was about to protest, he taunted me.

"Are you sure you don't want me to hold back with you?" I heard him licking my juices off one of his fingers before he pressed the other into my mouth. "Suck."

I obeyed, wrapping my lips around his finger as he slowly pulled it out. He then harshly turned me to face him, grabbing the back of my head, yanking my mouth into his. His tongue fought with mine over dominance and he was not backing down. I loved this game. I managed to pull away long enough to breathlessly speak.

"Yes, Sir," I squeaked as he pressed his fingers into me once again, "I'm sure."

Without warning, he picked me up, backing me into the edge of the balcony railing. "Hold on tight," he grinned as he managed to pull his pants down enough to free himself.

I wrapped my legs tighter around him as my arms were still behind me, restrained by his belt. He slid my body down to the tip of his arousal, pushing his hips up as he slightly loosened his grip, impaling my insides on his shaft.

I screamed random incomprehensible phrases as he pinned my body against the side of the half wall, thrusting himself into my core faster than I had ever experienced. I thought my cervix was being pushed deep into my stomach.

"All of London can hear you."

"Let...them!" I cried out.

Resting his forehead against mine, he gazed through the black lacy veil with a starving scowl as he picked up the pace. I continued to moan loudly, trying my best to communicate with him but I could not form a full sentence.

"They...should...all...know...I...love...you," I finally managed to proclaim loudly.

He immediately froze, ripping my veil off over my head, pulling a few strands of my hair out of my head along with it. His eyes never left mine, but he also did not move away. The glazed over lustful appearance left his eyes. I was now staring into an empty, icy blue abyss that I was not familiar with.

He pulled me off him, gently standing me on the floor then pulled up his pants and buttoned them. Turning me around quickly, he unfastened the belt from my wrists, gripping it tightly as his knuckles began to turn white. He leaned over the blanket and picked it up, handing it to me without looking at me.

"Put this on."

"That was not my safe word!" I called out irritably, but he disappeared inside without another word or glimpse of me.

THE VEIL

I was frozen in my sadness as I replayed that awful life altering moment in my head, over and over again. I could not believe I said that to him. I mean it yes, I could but why the heck did I have to say it to him? You never ever tell someone you love them during sex unless you know the feeling is mutual. It should definitely never be said for the first time during a heated moment such as that. I felt so stupid and small. Collapsing in a lounge chair, I promised myself that I would not cry.

Staring up at the sky, I leaned back, trying to identify constellations to get my mind off the moment that probably changed everything forever. The twinkling lights of the city cancelled out most of the stars in the sky, but I counted a few bright ones as I tried to take deep breaths.

Surely this would blow over. I wanted to go inside to defend myself, but I did not dare move. I had no defense. If I told him I did not mean it, then it would be a lie. However, I would also dig my hole much deeper trying to explain, only to make him feel more awkward than I am assuming he felt now. He would come to me when he was ready to talk about it.

Valentino

I left Isabelle standing naked on the balcony as I found myself mindlessly plodding back into the bedroom. It was as if I were a robot, having no control over my movements. Something switched in my body the moment she said that, and I froze.

Everything suddenly became so real to me because of her words. How could she love someone like me? I lied to her. I betrayed her. I scared her. I went to shower and did not even look outside as I passed the windows. I am sure I left her with sadness and pain on her face and I could not stand to see it.

After quickly scrubbing myself, I turned the water off, stepping out of the shower and wrapped myself in a towel. I headed back toward the bed noticing her wrapped tightly in a blanket, lying on a lounger, staring at the sky. I prayed that tears were not running down her flawless, beautiful face. Hurting was the last thing I wanted her to do, but I did not have it in me to face her right now.

I dropped the towel on the floor next to the bed then crawled in, leaving myself uncovered. I hoped she would come in and get into bed with me. However, I felt she might end up wanting more time alone.

I believed me not saying it back to her, hurt her. Why did I keep screwing things up with her? I did not understand why everything could not be simple with us. They were never that way.

Since day one, I had been lying to her, and I still was. There was one secret left that I had not told her yet. It was one that I kept so close to myself that I was not sure I could ever tell her. The truth is, I was scared she would walk away the moment she knew.

I sighed loudly, pulling the blanket over my exposed body. I closed my eyes and my thoughts began to run wild about how I would handle all of the drama with her uncle, then handling what she told me he did to her.

※

I rolled over to check my phone, realizing it was a few hours later than it was before. I must have dozed off. Placing my arm behind me on her side of the bed, I discovered that she was still not there as there was only emptiness. A panic rushed over my body as I shot up out of bed.

I sped over to the terrace door. She was still lying in the chair asleep. I exhaled deeply, both relieved she did not leave but heartbroken she did not come to bed. I observed her face for a moment then opened the door, stepping outside.

Placing my arms under her back and knees, I carried her with the large blanket inside placing her on the bed in her spot. She was still wrapped tightly in it and I did not want to bother her, so I knelt over her, adjusting a pillow under her head to make sure she was comfortable.

I would sleep on the sofa in the room to give her space. As I began to back away, her eyes fluttered open. She glanced up at my face and I reached over, running my fingers through her hair. Her heavy eyelids fell closed again and I slowly backed off the bed.

I stood, admiring her for a few moments before I turned to walk away, but I was not able to move. My eyes fell on her once more and I was enthralled in her inner and outward beauty. She was simply amazing.

Fuck it.

Carefully and as quietly as I could, I inched into bed, kneeling over her body once more. Bending down, I placed a gentle kiss on her forehead then moved my lips to her ear. I needed her to know how I felt.

"I love you too, Isabelle."

19 VISITORS

Isabelle

I opened my eyes as the morning light shone into the bedroom. Gently warming my face, I rubbed my eyes. Suddenly, I realized that I was in the bed and not still outside on the terrace. He must have carried me to bed at some point during the night.

Smiling, I rolled over, excited to see he was okay, but my heart instantly sank when I discovered that he was not next to me. I ran my fingers up and down the cool sheets where he would normally have been. Sighing, I turned back over, picking up my phone off the nightstand, checking the time. I could not believe it was almost noon!

Jumping out of bed, I sprinted to my suitcase, slipping on a cute, white, off-shoulder floral romper. Then, I gave myself a quick glimpse in the mirror. I paused, thinking about last night and that I had ruined the moment by telling him I loved him. I groaned in disgust with myself as I reached over to the dresser, grabbed a hair tie, and pulled my strands up into a stylish messy bun.

As I trudged down the hallway, I heard familiar voices in the living room, but they stopped the moment I came to the top of the stairs. Tanya and William stood in front of Valentino. All their eyes met mine the minute they noticed me.

Valentino slid his hands into his pockets, smiling up at me then nodded his head, indicating he wanted me to join them. William chewed on his bottom lip studying me. Tanya took off jogging up the stairs, meeting me halfway. She threw her body into mine, gripping me tightly in a hug.

"I freaking missed you!" she wept on my shoulder.

I began to tear up as well, "I missed you too."

We pulled away from one another and she held my hands in hers, looking into my eyes, "Listen I'm so sorr--."

I shook my head, smiling, "Valentino explained everything, it's okay."

None of that mattered any longer. I just missed my best friend. She wiped away her tears as I glanced over to the guys who were watching our exchange. She hugged me once more before we made our way over to where they were standing. Valentino held his arm, pulling me into his side the minute I approached. Tanya raised her eyebrows at me, smirking before leaning into William for a side hug.

"I need a moment alone with Isabelle," he announced, "so why don't you guys go get settled in and we'll meet back in here in a bit."

They nodded in unison.

"Isabelle--," William cleared his throat, but paused, trying to figure out what to say next.

My gaze met his. "It's okay, you don't have to say anything."

He nodded as we both understood that he was trying to apologize. I was happy to see them reunited and her with us. Tanya stepped forward, giving me another hug.

"We have so much to talk about!"

I giggled, pulling away and rolling my eyes, "Later."

"Come on," Valentino ordered as he placed his hands on my hips, guiding me up the staircase. He turned to William and Tanya. "You girls can talk in a bit."

He ushered me back to the bedroom, closing the door behind him. Instantly, his gaze became predatory as he backed me against the wall, pinning my arms above my head by my wrists. His lips immediately found my neck. His warm breath sent shivers down my spine as he brushed his lips across my soft, sensitive skin.

Aggressively, he covered my flesh in kisses, trailing to my lips before harshly probing his tongue into my mouth. My body was beginning to betray me as I weakened. He snickered, supporting my body so I would not crumble to the floor. Pulling away, he kept his gaze locked on mine as he ran his fingers through my hair.

"In case you didn't hear me last night," he sighed, "I want to tell you again."

Quizzically, I tilted my head, confused.

Cupping my cheeks in his hands, he smirked, "Isabelle, I love you. I fell in love with you a long time ago, but I had to fight it."

I smiled, beaming with happiness.

Placing his lips next to my ear, he continued, "I was scared. I know I shouldn't be, but this entire situation is fucking madness."

Snaking his arms around me, he picked me up, carrying me over to the bed. He set me down, then crawled on top of me, forcing me to recline. He hovered over my helpless body, propping up on his hands.

"I realized that because I love you," he reassured, "I will fight for you, I will fight for us, and I will end this shit that is hurting us."

I was speechless for moment as I realized that he was pressing himself into me, slowly moving his hips. He rolled off me, lying on his side. I reached down, unbuttoning then unzipping his jeans. Placing my hand in his boxer briefs, I began to stroke his semi-erect shaft, feeling it grow in my hand.

Sitting up, I tugged his pants off, before kneeling between his legs. Taking his hard arousal in my hand, I stroked him slowly up and down before I bent over, pressing a light kiss on the tip, causing him to twitch. I slowly began to take him in mouth, tucking my teeth behind my lips while massaging his balls.

"This was not the plan," he moaned. "I don't want to give up my control."

I gently pulled him out of my mouth, peering up into his eyes. "I love you too," I teased.

Taunting him with my tongue, I licked the precum as it was slowly running down his throbbing shaft. He arched his back, grabbing a fist-full of my hair while pushing my head down as he bucked his hips up. Taking him all the way into my throat, he held my head down until I began to choke.

He suddenly sat up, pushing me off him. I unleashed his animal side and he was about to ravish me. He harshly pointed to the floor. I instinctively knelt next to the bed. He walked across the room, grabbing his belt and my black lace veil off the chair the stood before me. I got excited, clutching his hard, pulsing member out of pure lust.

"Um no," he smirked, slapping my hand away from his body. "I'm in control now, Isabelle."

I smiled, averting my gaze to the floor while biting my lip. Unhurriedly, he circled my body while dragging the tip of the belt across my exposed skin, making me tremble. He came to a stop behind me, stretching around my head with the veil then pulled it tightly. He did not bother to ask me if it was too tight this time. He did not care. I was in his territory now.

He strode around to the front of me, pulling me up to my feet. Smiling evilly, he completely undressed me as he caressed each part of my body with his touch and gentle kisses. I now understood how Valentino's naughty mind worked, so I knew this would be the calm before the devilish storm. Just as I began to get used to his soothing touch, I heard the tip of the belt snap as it grazed my mound. He knew that drove me crazy. My body, however, involuntarily jumped.

Stepping to my ear, he growled, "If you move, you will be punished harder."

"But I like your punishments," I playfully challenged.

Valentino

A defiant grin spread across my lips. She was unbelievably terrific at giving me exactly what I wanted. Slowly, I pulled my belt back before I flicked my wrist, causing it to connect to her most sensitive area.

Stepping behind her, I yanked her body against me, grabbing her flesh ruthlessly as I massaged her perfectly toned thighs. Running my hands up to her hips, I pushed into her exposed body as she pushed back onto me.

Picking her up in one motion, I reclined her back on the bed, burying my face between her thighs, licking while plunging a finger deep into her eager, wet core. She let out a loud moan before crying out in sheer ecstasy. I grinned against her mound, stopping momentarily.

"Shhhh, bella," I scolded, "everyone will hear you." I wrapped my lips around her little swollen button, creating another sense of pleasure for her.

"I don't care!" she screamed, writhing beneath me. "Don't stop!"

Smirking, I immediately stopped.

Propping up on her elbows, she huffed, "Where are you going? I said don't stop!"

I dragged a suitcase out from underneath the bed, and opened it, revealing many rolls of lace fabric. I pulled out a black spool, laying it next to her naked body. Grabbing her by the feet, I flipped her over onto her stomach and began to rip strips of lace off, tying each of her ankles to rings I had installed on the bed. I then stretched each of her arms upward, spreading them, repeating the same pattern with the strips of fabric.

Her back was rising and falling slowly as she attempted to control her breathing, anticipating my next move. I picked my belt up, folding it into a loop.

SNAP!

I cracked it against her backside.

She squirmed, raising her bottom in the air as she squealed, "Ow!"

Leaning over, I rubbed the area that I had just spanked. She cooed at my touch, enjoying the soothing of her skin. Suddenly, I drew my hand back, pausing to see if she would say anything. She tensed up but smiled.

SNAP!

I swiped it across her rear once again. "Do not ever defy me in the bedroom," I commanded, "You take orders from me in here, am I clear?"

She nodded without saying a word.

I spanked her once more. "I said am I clear?!"

"Y-yes, Sir!"

"That's better," I muttered under my breath, smirking as I placed myself between her legs. I put my hand between her thighs, massaging her mound. "I love how you please me."

"I love how hard you fuck me," she whined, attempting to press herself into my touch.

I placed my throbbing shaft at her entrance, sinking into her core, bottoming out in one thrust. She let out a scream, gasping. I froze for a moment, being nice enough to allow her walls to adapt to my size again. I wanted her to feel pain, but I did not want to truly hurt her.

"I know I'll never get used to your size, oh my God," she whimpered.

"Well good thing you have plenty of time."

Pumping in and out of her hard but slow, she moaned while mumbling incoherently. I bowed over her back, placing kisses and small bites all over her body. She thrashed and struggled beneath me, trying to take control but it was no use.

"Your skin is like silk," I whispered.

I wanted to feel her against me, so I pulled a knife out of the nightstand drawer, cutting each of the lace restraints. Rolling her over, she smiled as I pulled her body against mine while guiding myself back inside her essence. Kissing her passionately, I yanked the veil off her head as I looked deep into her eyes, making love to her.

"I love you so much, Isabelle."

"I love you too, Valentino."

"Cum for me."

Instantly, her walls tightened and we both released together as I kissed her deeply. Panting and smiling, we relaxed as I collapsed onto her chest. I kissed the side of her bare breasts, kneading them while she ran her soft fingertips gently through my hair.

I raised up, pressing my lips to hers before I stood, pulling her to the edge of the bed. I cut the lace from her wrists and ankles then helped her to her feet.

"Shower?"

I nodded, picking her up over my shoulder, carrying her into the bathroom.

Isabelle

I emerged from the bedroom, sore and basking in the hour Valentino and I spent having fun. I made my way to the kitchen, noticing William and Tanya in deep conversation, so I cleared my throat to indicate I was in the room giving them a warning in case they were trying to have a private conversation. They suddenly stopped chatting, looking in my direction. Tanya took long wide strides to me.

"Can we go talk now, please?" she requested, biting her bottom lip, scared of my reply.

"Of course," I grinned, "come on."

She followed me toward the master bedroom. We passed Valentino in the hallway on the way. He grabbed me by my wrist, pulling me close to his body, not caring that Tanya was present. Leaning forward, he pressed his lips to mine quickly before letting me go. Smirking, he winked at me then smiled at Tanya before he continued to go wherever he was headed, which I assumed was to William.

We went out onto the terrace. The moment I closed the door, she froze then turned to stare at me, smirking as she crossed her arms over her chest, waiting for answers. I knew what was on her mind.

"Sooo?" she hinted, arching her eyebrows at me.

I giggled, nodding, "Yep, we are officially a thing now."

She threw her arms around me, hugging me as a tear fell down her cheek, "I'm so happy for you and I'm so so so sorry about--."

"Tanya," I sighed, tearing up as I did when we first saw one another, "it's fine, I swear we are okay."

She hugged me even tighter. My eyes widened as I awkward held on to her, unsure why my best friend was having an emotional breakdown. She reluctantly let go.

"Why are you crying?" I sighed, "I know something more is going on."

"Stupid hormones," she snickered, wiping her eyes with her sleeve.

"Tanya--," I gasped, unable to finish my sentence, grabbing her wrists.

She giggled, sniffling.

"Oh my God!" I screamed. "You're having a baby!"

She nodded, rubbing her stomach in a circle, "I am but it's still kind of new."

"We have to celebrate!"

Grabbing her hand, I pulled her into the house and back down into the living room. Valentino and William were standing next to each other with Joseph furiously speaking to them in Italian. We came to a halt and I leaned on a pillar. Tanya hooked her arm in mine, leaning her head on my shoulder.

"What do you think they're saying?" she whispered.

"I don't know," I shrugged, "but I know that look well."

"What do you mean?" she hissed.

"Something big is happening."

Just then, Valentino glanced over at us. He held his arm out to me while he was still listening to whatever Joseph was saying. I immediately wrapped my arm around his waist, and he pulled me close into his body. Tanya followed, planting herself on the other side of William.

After a moment, I felt Valentino tense up when Joseph asked a certain question that William replied to.

Valentino nodded, looking down at my face, "Bella."

I glanced up at him but did not speak.

"We are going to dinner tonight," he smiled.

I nervously smiled back but nodded, being agreeable. Tanya and I exchanged uneasy glances as we both wondered what was going on. It was clear we both put a lot of trust in these men, who were clearly dangerous.

I had grown to accept that I was in love with someone who did bad things to terrible people. Though I would never handle anything the way he did, I was thankful for his courage. Whatever was going on, I knew was probably just him trying to keep me safe. That seemed to be his only focus. How could I not love someone like that?

Valentino

For the rest of the day, I thought hard about everything Joseph told me. It would be a very risky move, but it would be one that would have the outcome I wanted; the outcome that we all wanted. I knew that I would have to make all this right before much longer or we would never be safe. I wanted us to be able to live in peace, and I would do whatever it took to see to it that we were.

I was on the patio speaking to William when I glanced at my watch, realizing it was 6:15 p.m. I excused myself to go check on Isabelle, who was already getting dressed for dinner. I opened the door, leaned against the door frame, and watched her in silence for a moment as she took my breath away.

She was zipping her floor length black dress as she gazed at me. I strode over to her, turning her body toward the mirror while I finished assisting her. She tilted her head to the side as I ran my fingertips around her neckline. We watched one another's reflections in the mirror as I placed my lips next to her ear.

"You look so stunning, my love."

Spinning to face me, she threw her arms around my shoulders, locking her fingers behind my neck as she stretched up for a kiss. I pressed my lips to hers then sighed. She smirked, leaning back, peering up into my eyes with need.

"You shouldn't do that to me right now."

I ran my fingers down the front of her clothed body, circling her mound through her dress, teasing her. She moaned, laying her head against my chest. I pressed my fingers harder against her causing her to inhale a sharp breath.

"I'm tempted to just stay in," I growled, "and fuck you all night long."

Taking a step away from me, she glanced over her shoulder, teasing me as she played with her bottom lip.

"Fucking tease," I mumbled as I adjusted the erection she had just given me.

"Yet, you love me," she countered as she put on her earrings.

Rolling my eyes, I grinned at the effect this woman had on me. I was not used to having a girlfriend. Something in me changed when I was watching her. I felt a connection with her before she knew there was one.

I thought back to every moment I ducked behind something because she glanced my way, then her living with me as I pretended to be two people. I was lucky she had even given me a chance after that. I realize that I might have presented myself as serial killer material with that whole facade. Suddenly my thoughts were interrupted by hands slipping around my waist from behind.

"*Sir*," she playfully whined, "are you ready to go?"

I pivoted my body around rapidly, glaring into her eyes before I smiled and nodded.

The ride to the restaurant was interesting to say the least. The girls wanted to sit together in the back so all I could hear was them talking about Tanya and William's baby on the way. They were both equally excited. William and I spoke in Italian in the front about Felipe and the new plan. It would be a game-changer if we could pull it off. Our conversation tapered off when we pulled up in front of the building.

As we stepped out, the valet drove off with my car, leaving us standing with security who had followed us. Joseph nodded and walked ahead of us, leading the way into the restaurant. Isabelle glanced up at the sign before entering the building.

"Of course." she smirked.

I took her hand in mine as we made our way through the front door.

"Greco's?" she questioned under her breath.

I nodded as the hostess approached us with a smile, interrupting any further conversation between us.

"Mr. Greco," she greeted cheerfully, "we are so happy to have you and your guests dining with us this evening."

We navigated our way through the dining room as she led us to my favorite table in the back; a nice, big, round table with a great view of the other diners and foyer area. I slid my chair closer to Isabelle. She smiled, resting her hand on my thigh under the table.

Isabelle

I searched around the room noticing that this place was extremely intimidating. It came as no surprise to me that he owned it. I giggled to myself as he got my attention by placing his hand on my thigh, squeezing rapidly several times. I turned my focus to him.

"Love, would you like something other than wine and water?"

"No thank you," I declined politely. "That's more than okay with me."

THE VEIL

Tanya glanced up from her menu with only her eyes, watching us intently. I caught a glimpse of her. She smirked, winking at me. I knew she was so enthralled with the idea of Valentino and me. She was obvious as she watched us like she was proud that she had a part in us being happily together.

The server approached, taking our drink orders. Valentino ordered several bottles of wine, but I could not have pronounced the names if I tried. I knew they were a variation of both red and white. The server smiled and nodded at Valentino then disappeared.

William leaned forward, whispering across the table, "Val, why do you always have to be so fancy?"

I laughed and a snort escaped my nose. Gasping and blushing, I suddenly stopped, but the three of them snapped their heads toward me, catching my moment. Tanya covered her mouth, trying not to laugh, but failed as she snickered a bit.

Valentino leaned into my ear, murmuring, "I am going to fuck your brains out when we get home."

My face suddenly became serious as I tucked my lips into my mouth, averting my gaze to my lap.

He turned his attention back to William, smiling, "Because I *can* be fancy."

William nodded, smirking, "Always."

The server returned with the wine. After Valentino did a fancy wine tasting and approved it for the table, we were served. She waltzed away to give us time to look over the menu. I studied it carefully as every entree description made me want to try that dish. It would be impossible to choose.

I felt Valentino squeeze my thigh again but this time extremely hard. He did not loosen his grip. I almost yelped in pain, but I remained silent. Instead I glared at him, realizing that he was glowering straight ahead, his eyes slightly narrowed toward the entrance.

I followed the trail of his vision across the restaurant. It was not until I peered around William that I noticed a remarkably familiar looking person. I froze.

Oh no! No! Not him! I began to repeat in my mind as I silently panicked.

William and Tanya both glanced up simultaneously, seeing Valentino and I both staring at the lobby of the restaurant. They both paused, wondering what was happening. Tanya waved her hand, trying to get our attention, but neither of us budged.

William turned his body as he spoke. "What are you looki--," he began but froze. "Oh fuck."

20 TAKEN

Valentino

I loosened my grip on Isabelle's thigh, apologizing under my breath. She grabbed the top of my hand under the table, squeezing it hard. Tanya remained confused trying to ask Isabelle what was wrong.

In the lobby, he rested his hand on the back of a woman who stood next to him wearing a floor length, navy-blue dress. Her platinum blonde hair stopped just past her shoulders. I did not recognize her. Just then, he glanced up and we made eye contact. A sinister grin slowly crept onto his face as he stared at us.

Turning to the restaurant hostess, he whispered something in her ear, as he gestured in our direction. They began to walk our way, his eyes never leaving mine. The moment they were at our table, he pulled a chair out for his guest before sitting next to her, situating himself in an arrogant manner.

The server approached immediately to take their drink orders. My brother, Marco, turned his attention to Isabelle as he ordered, but it was evident that his thirst for her was greater. His date sat clueless next to him with a beaming smile plastered on her face.

"Hi!" She greeted everyone cheerfully. "I'm Amy."

Tanya, also clueless, turned to her and introduced herself. "I'm Tanya and I'm so bad with names, so I'm likely to forget yours."

"It's A-M-Y, like the name, Amy," she clarified unhurriedly and louder than necessary as if she thought Tanya was hard of hearing.

Ignoring them, I continued to stare at my brother. "What are you doing in London?"

He narrowed his glare on Isabelle. "Just doing a little sightseeing," he smirked, "and I think I'm enjoying the view."

Isabelle jerked her head up, mildly distressed. My security and William awaited my signal. Isabelle started to shiver, and I knew I needed to get her away from him. I raised my hand and Joseph appeared next to me within seconds.

"Take the girls back to the--."

"Oh, you don't have to do that," Marco interrupted coyly. "I'm just spending time with my favorite people so Joseph you can be gone."

Joseph gritted his teeth. "I do not take orders fr--."

"Take them now."

He nodded as Marco snorted, rolling his eyes as he gawked at another woman walking past our table. Amy sat clueless, looking around at everyone with hopeful eyes while I gave silent signals to William and Joseph.

Isabelle and Tanya stood, immediately following an incredibly enraged Joseph. He did not want to follow my orders at the moment, but he did without further question. I could tell he would have instead, rather put a bullet in Marco in front of everyone.

As the girls left, Isabelle glanced back toward me in dread.

I gave her a comforting look. *It's okay*, I mouthed before she turned away to leave.

Once they were out of sight, I focused my attention on Marco's date.

"I need you to leave immediately, uh--."

"It's Amy," she whined as she dragged out the Y.

"Okay, please excuse us." I tried to be polite to her as I plastered a fake, smile on my face. "I need to speak with my brother."

Marco picked up a knife, slowly twirling the sharp tip on the tablecloth as she got up. Clueless she paraded toward the bathroom as she shook her bottom. He never took his eyes off me as he sneered, challenging me to make a move. Shifting in my seat, I glowered as the three of us dared one another to speak first. I had bigger issues to worry about right now, and I did not want to be here.

"Marco," I sighed impatiently, "as much as I am enjoining…whatever this is, I cannot play this game right now." I spoke as calmly as I could, propping my arm on the back of the chair Isabelle had been sitting in. "I have to deal with Felipe right now."

He abruptly stopped spinning the knife, letting it fall to the table. He leaned forward, "Ayala?"

I nodded as William exhaled, rolling his eyes.

"Well, why didn't you say so, brother?" Marco wickedly laughed. "I'm in London to kill him, myself."

"Oh no," I shook my head, lifting my hand. "I do not want your help."

He held his arms out to the side, shrugging, "And I didn't ask your opinion or permission."

He pulled out his wallet, sliding out a card and tossed it onto the table. William picked it up before I could reach for it. Studying it, his face twisted in confusion.

"Is this a fucking joke?" William asked Marco as he flipped the business card to me, covering his mouth as he propped his elbow on the table.

"What?" Marco smirked.

William watched me, waiting for my reaction. I started to laugh, throwing my head back. I suddenly narrowed my eyes, glaring at Marco. I leaned forward, resting my elbows on the table.

"You're a fucking hitman now?" I rolled my eyes, shaking my head in disbelief.

"With business cards apparently!" William amusingly chimed in as he guzzled his glass of wine.

"Who paid you to kill Felipe?" I stroked my chin, wondering if he would answer the question.

"Who cares," he shrugged, smiling. "The point is, we have a common enemy now, don't we?"

"*We* had one," William snapped. "It was you!"

Isabelle

The ride back to the apartment was unbearable as Tanya and I sat in the back of the security's SUV, silently staring out our own windows. Joseph sat in the passenger seat as another man drove. I had not seen the driver before, but I trusted Joseph, so I knew we were safe with him.

He texted furiously on his phone before he received an incoming call. He spoke a language I had never heard before but sounded rather middle eastern, maybe. I arched my brows as I shifted in my seat, trying to eavesdrop. Who was I kidding? I did not understand anything other than English and Spanish.

Tanya glanced over to me, acknowledging to the front with her eyes. I smirked, shrugging. It was as if we were nervously having a silent conversation.

Before long, we arrived back to the penthouse, trudging out of the elevator and into the living room. I threw myself back onto the couch, still hungry. My stomach churned with stress, so eating was not an option at the moment.

Tanya sat on the couch across from me, leaning forward tapping her lips with her fingers. We both watched intently as Joseph paced the room, running his fingers through his hair. He was visibly distressed as his eyes darted back and forth at the two of us.

"Joseph are you okay?"

Seeing Marco was absolutely terrifying for me. Shaking, the reality finally set in that he was in London and I wondered why. I was not clear on the business he had with Valentino or why he was here. Was he working with Felipe? Surely not! I found myself becoming suspicious of everyone.

Joseph began to loosen his tie as he yanked his earpiece from his ear, glaring at me, "May I speak to you in private, Miss Ayala?"

Slowly rising to my feet, I made eye contact with Tanya, who widened her eyes. I shrugged, following him out onto the terrace. He plodded over to the railing, squeezing it so tightly that his knuckles turned white.

He sighed loudly, muttering, "Fuck fuck fuck," under his breath.

Exhaling, I reluctantly crept to his side. Defensively, I folded my arms over my mid-section, holding it tightly. He slowly turned to me, taking another deep breath. He shifted his weight as he lifted a hand to his chin, resting his elbow on his other arm as it was also defensively curled around his stomach.

"What?" I choked, "Is everything okay?"

"I don't know how to say this, but I will just say it," he buried his face in his palm. "Felipe has been spotted in London. He knows you guys are here."

My mouth fell open and I began to tear up, frozen in place.

"Please don't do that," he insisted. "Your friend will wonder what's going on and I don't need you both going mad."

He pulled a tissue from his pocket, hanging it to me. I wrinkled my nose as I studied it, searching for any sign of disgust.

He rolled his eyes, "It's clean."

I dabbed the corner of my eyes, hissing, "Shouldn't you tell Valentino this?"

"I wanted to but he was busy with his brother, and my job right now is to protect you," he paced back and forth a few times in between his explanation. "I have to get you guys to a--."

Just then his face dropped, and his eyes widened as he glared into the house. Just as my eyes followed what he was looking toward, he grabbed me, harshly yanking me to the terrace floor.

"Get down, Isabelle!" he hissed.

Ow! I crumbled to the floor. I managed to peek between two chairs, seeing at least six men had barged into the penthouse. One was pulling Tanya by her hair and throwing her around. She thrashed as she attempted to fight him. He was shouting at her, but I could not hear what he was saying. She never looked our way, but she was also screaming and kicking while swinging her arms, in what seemed like a fight for her life.

I began to cry, panicking, wanting to help my friend. Crouching, I got ready to run, but Joseph jerked my arm back down as he read my mind.

"Don't fucking move!"

"What the hell is going on, Joseph?"

"Do you have your phone," he ignored my question as he continued to watch inside. "I need to use another phone."

I nodded as he glanced toward me for a quick second.

"Give it to me," he commanded, holding his hand out.

I pulled it out of my bra, then laid it in his palm.

"Unlock it," he huffed, as he watched the inside of the penthouse intently.

I did as he said and passed it to him once again. He swiped the screen then tapped on it before placing it to his ear. Watching inside, I began to lose control of my emotions as I sobbed, watching her struggle getting weaker. Once again, I tried to run for her, but Joseph caught me, pulling me to the floor and pinning me against his body.

"Joseph they're taking her away," I cried, staring inside through my tears. "Oh God, Joseph, help!"

"Shhh," he covered my mouth.

Wiggling out of his grip, I slowly rose up peering through the chairs again to get a slightly better view. Tanya was no longer visible, but I saw the back of a tall man with lengthy, dark hair wearing a long, black coat. He was puffing on a cigar. I knew that stance anywhere. It was my uncle Felipe.

As he stood in the middle of the living room, he looked all around while his men searched every room. I began to panic as I realized Joseph was speaking Italian now. He hung up the phone then gripped my elbow tightly, causing my body to jump.

"I need to go after her," he declared, visibly bothered. "I need you to stay right here. Do not move and stay hidden!"

I started to shake my head quickly, frightened. He placed his hand on my knee. I rocked up, crouching as I darted my eyes back and forth between him and Felipe.

"Please don't leave me!" I quietly wept.

"Miss," he sighed, "I mean Isabelle, please take a deep breath."

I tried obeying him, taking unsteady, shallow breaths as I wiped tears on my arms.

"I need to save your friend," he whispered. "You know how your uncle is."

I nodded, knowing that if he did not go help Tanya, she would be dead soon.

"Please for your friend's sake, let me do this," he pleaded, trying his best to comfort me.

I had been squatting for so long that my knees started to shake, giving way. Collapsing onto the hard surface of the terrace floor, I caused a thud when I bumped a chair. Felipe speedily veered to the door, marching our way. Joseph mumbled something under his breath, but I did not hear him.

"What?" I murmured.

"Crawl behind the shrub box now!"

I quickly made my body as small as possible as I ducked behind the box holding a large bush of some sort, just as I heard the door slide open and my uncle's voice. Joseph stood with his palms facing Felipe, stepping sideways into his view.

"Where is she?!" my uncle shouted at Joseph.

"She's not here," Joseph snapped. "It's only me."

"Why are you out here alone?" Felipe interrogated.

Joseph, swift to react, contended, "I came out to secure the penthouse and wanted to smoke."

"Well you're coming with me now, asshole!" Felipe interjected.

"I don't think so!" Joseph gritted his teeth.

I buried my mouth into my hands as I listened to a scuffle. After a few minutes, I heard glass shatter. Peeking out from behind the shrub, I made myself as tiny as possible. Joseph and Felipe were rolling around on the floor inside the living room while I crouched down outside, helpless.

I could not disobey and run in to help him free himself of Felipe. He was trained for this. I was not. I realized I did not have my phone so I could not call for help. Glancing over near the broken window, I spotted it, laying on the floor, in the middle of the glass. The only way I could get to it would be to crawl through the shards on my hands and knees because I could not risk being seen.

As I saw Joseph and Felipe continue to fight inside, I quietly snuck over to the glass. Taking a deep breath, I slowly crawled over it as I made my way to my phone, trying to remain undetected.

Each time my knees crunched the glass, it broke more under my weight, causing excruciating pain as the little sharp fragments entered my flesh. My hands were getting pierced repeatedly by shards of glass. They burned as blood began to drip from my fingers every time I raised them up.

I was almost to my phone when Felipe turned, looking toward me. I dropped my body to the floor hiding behind a chair. Lying flat, a sharp, stinging sensation began to spread through my head as the glass lacerated my tender face.

"Who's out there?!" Felipe shouted.

He began to stomp toward me, but I peeked under the chair to see Joseph got a hold of his gun. I heard gunshots then suddenly the world became silent. I began to panic, craning my neck to see what was going on. There was no sign of Joseph or Felipe.

I slithered to my phone in the pile of glass, picking it up, dialing Valentino. I continued to look for them as the phone rang. I called out to Joseph while waiting for him to answer, but no one replied so I stood.

I felt the wetness of the blood trickling down my body. My phone slipped from my hands onto the floor landing in a broken windowsill next to the completely shattered door. Bending over to pick it up, I heard a crackling noise above me.

"Oh no!" I yelped, diving out of the way into the living room.

That was awfully close. I stood, faltering to the elevator but managed to trip on the rug that had become wrinkled during the struggle. Falling to the floor, I banged my head on the way down.

Sighing, I stood once again, grabbing the top of my head, attempting to apply pressure to the sharp, radiating pain spreading throughout. It gradually progressed through my entire body. The room began to spin. My vision tunneled and my surroundings soon became black.

Joseph

When Felipe saw my gun, he took off for the elevator. I sprinted after him through the fire escape, exiting the twentieth floor. I jumped on the other elevator, pacing angrily while I rode it down to the ground. The minute the doors opened, I dashed outside but he was gone. There was no sign of Tanya either. It was as if nothing happened as the world continued to function normally.

I noticed my earpiece was hanging off my shoulder, so I shoved it into my ear as I sunk down behind a car, leaning against the tire. Pressing the microphone button, I sighed when I noticed it was not working. I yanked it from my ear inspecting it then pushed it back into place. I crouched down a bit more, remaining out of sight.

"Sir, I need help," I demanded in the mic of my watch instead. "Come to the penthouse as soon as you get this. I already called for backup."

I stood, searching around the car trying to see if there was a trail, any sign, anything that was left behind. I needed a clue that would help me locate Felipe. Tanya was in danger. I knew they would hold her, using her for bargaining trying to get to Isabelle. That is how he worked.

I was familiar with people like him. They all wanted the same things in life. Unfortunately, if we did not act fast, Tanya would be killed and there would be no option of saving her. I sat back against the car and began to scan the ground.

Just then, I spotted a bloody cocktail napkin near the back side of the tire where I sat. I picked it up and read it.

Captain's Club was the name of the business. I knew that it was a gentlemen's club near the West End.

Glancing up at the top of the apartment building, I muttered, "Isabelle please be okay."

Sighing, I decided to make a run for the SUV. I fidgeted impatiently as I sped to the club, still praying Isabelle was okay upstairs. I knew I needed to go back to her, but I also knew that if anything did happen to Tanya, I would be in just as much trouble. Isabelle was safe. She was hiding right where I left her, or so I hoped.

Valentino

We made our way back to the penthouse in a hurry and irate after receiving Joseph's message. The doors to the elevator slowly opened and we gasped at the sight before us.

"Holy shit!"

We marched in, shouting for Isabelle, Tanya, and Joseph. Nothing. There was blood everywhere and bullet holes in the walls. I ran upstairs to the master bedroom continuing to yell for Isabelle. No reply. I checked the bathroom, closet, and other rooms upstairs. Still nothing.

"Valentino!" I heard William bellowing from downstairs.

"No no no no no," I repeated under my breath as I ran to him as quickly as my legs would carry me.

That is when I saw her, looking as if she had bathed in blood with it pooling beneath her body. Various sizes of glass stuck up from her torso and legs. William was squatting over her, applying pressure to her head. It appeared as if she had possibly hit it on the coffee table after falling. I began to ball my fists.

Dropping to my knees, I took over William's position, applying pressure to a large gash. William stood, calling an ambulance without me having to ask. He rambled to the emergency service, trying to tell them the information we knew as he gave our exact location.

"Isabelle!"

She was limp. I placed my head by her mouth, listening for any sign of life as I reached for her wrist, checking for a pulse. I felt a sign of life.

"She's alive!"

"Baby, wake up!" I tapped her lightly on her only uninjured cheek. "Please be okay!" I pleaded with her. "Don't leave me! I need you to be okay!"

William hung up his phone, getting ready to assist me.

"William, we don't have time to wait," I announced. "She will die!"

That is when I did the one thing you are not supposed to do when unsure of the extent of a person's physical injuries, but I was panicking. I was no medical professional but judging by her blood loss and pulse, I knew that if we did not get her to a hospital soon, she might not make it much longer.

Glancing back at Marco, I noticed he was frozen, looking down at Isabelle. His eyes were widened, full of shock. His mouth was balled tightly as if he were actually mad that she was hurt.

"Marco you have to drive!" I demanded as I lifted her off the floor, cradling her in my arms.

For once I was thankful my brother was next to me. Without saying a word, he nodded, taking my keys from my pocket. William followed us into the elevator and the doors closed. It seemed to descend slower than normal. William stared ahead without saying a word.

"We'll find Tanya, I promise."

He did not respond but only focused on the numbers counting down as we got closer to the bottom of the building. The doors opened and we hurried out of the elevator as quickly as possible. The doorman saw us and before we could tell him Marco was driving us, he opened the building doors, flagging down a cab.

The three of us got in the back seat, holding her across our laps. I held on to her as tightly as I could without doing more damage. The cab driver sped through the streets of downtown London as fast as he could.

We arrived at the hospital emergency department in record time. Barging into the waiting area, the staff quickly met us, taking her from me. I tried to follow but they assured me they would take care of her. I shook my head, running with them. Hospital security approached me.

"Sir, you have to wait out there," one of them informed me, holding his hand out toward me with his palm facing me, motioning for me to stop. "Let the doctors do their jobs."

My brain was unable to process his words at the time, but my body instinctively backed away as a tear rolled down my cheek. A nurse followed me out to the middle of the waiting room speaking, but I did not hear a word she said. I was watching Isabelle be carried into a room at the end of the hallway as the doors slowly closed before my face.

"Excuse me," the nurse murmured, placing her hand on my arm to get my attention.

I slowly met her eyes with a lost, but angry stare.

"What happened to her?" she questioned. "Were you in an accident?"

My eyes lowered to the floor as I took a shallow, unsteady breath. Another tear rolled off my cheek, landing on the floor. My entire world was beyond those doors, and I could not see her. Nothing mattered to me right now except her. I needed her to be okay.

21 EMERGENCY

Valentino

I stuttered, "I...I don't know."

The nurse rested her hand on my shoulder. "Well, in order to help her--."

"Don't fucking touch me!"

She quickly withdrew her hand. "Sir, I ju--," she sighed, carefully choosing her words, "any information you give me will help her."

My brother stepped over, anchoring himself between the nurse and me. He crossed his arms over his chest, doing his best to intimidate her. I was a bit shocked at his sudden need to protect me.

"He said he doesn't know!"

I nudged him to the side, stepping in front of him. "I actually really don't know." Inhaling deeply, I continued to explain, "We were all out to dinner and she left early with her friend." I averted my gaze, trying to swallow my pain before making eye contact with her once again. "When we got back to my apartment, she was unconscious in the living room, covered in glass and blood."

Just then, I glanced over to the security guard who was now on his phone as he glowered my way. He whispered into the mouthpiece as if he wanted me to know he was talking about me.

Right now, I just wanted to know Isabelle was okay. The nurse assured me they would do whatever they could, and I could see her as soon as it was okay. She excused herself, disappearing behind the double doors. I trudged over to Marco and William, falling back in a chair, and burying my head in the palm of my hands.

William paced the floor before he suddenly squatted in front of me, muttering, "Where the fuck is Tanya?"

I slowly lifted my head, glaring at him. Understanding that was his main concern, I tried to be as calm as possible.

I sighed, my eyes burning and swollen. I could barely see or think straight.

"I have no idea Liam," I sighed. "I wish I had that answer."

He stood, massaging his temples with his fingertips, "I have to go find her right now."

Marco took a step closer, whispering, "Call Joseph first. Clearly they're together."

I flew out of my seat, leaning close to his face. "I swear to God, Marco," I poked his chest, "if I find out you had anything to do with this--."

"I swear I didn't."

I fell back in my chair again, leaning forward, propping my elbows on my knees. I glanced up at the security guard who was now glaring at all of us with his arms crossed, but he was off the phone. Rolling my eyes, I turned my attention back to William and Marco.

William took a few steps away with his phone, trying to get in touch with both Joseph and Tanya. Marco quietly paced in front of me as he stared into a void. I lowered my eyes to the floor, repeating prayers in my head.

Suddenly, the large doors opened and a woman in scrubs appeared. She hurried toward us, and I stood, placing myself in front of her, eager for any information she had. My heart sank the closer she got. I wanted to grab her and shake any information out of her.

"Hi, I'm Doctor Samantha Harrison," she held her hand out to shake mine.

I did not reciprocate. I was covered in Isabelle's blood. Furthermore, I did not care about the formalities right now. She awkwardly withdrew her hand, bowing her head.

"We are preparing the patient for--."

"Her name is Isabelle!"

"I apologize," she took a sharp breath. "We were not told her name and I am in a hurry to return to her."

My eyes lowered to the floor as I took a deep breath to calm myself down. Just as she was about to continue, I felt the breeze and presence of a body run past me. My head snapped up just in time to see William bolting out of the emergency department exit. My eyes darted toward my brother who shrugged with widened eyes before taking off after him.

"Mr.--."

I snapped my head back toward her, my gaze meeting hers, "Greco."

She nodded, smiling gently, "I know who you are."

I rolled my eyes, crossing my arms and focusing my attention on her.

"Isabelle needs a CAT scan," she continued, "I want to check her head for--."

"Is she going to be okay?" I interrupted, immediately overcome with sadness.

She placed her hand on my forearm. I choked back tears, exhaling. Glaring down at her hand, I ignored her touch, knowing she was only doing her job. I was not making it easy on her, but I was too upset to communicate at that moment. I should have been at home in bed with Isabelle. Instead, I was hoping she would live through the night.

"I am going to do everything I can to make sure she is," she sincerely met my gaze.

I nodded silently.

She disappeared through the doors. I took a deep breath, glancing around the room, suddenly remembering that Marco and William had both run out of the hospital. I did not have it in me to worry about them right now.

After settling back in my chair, I finally got up the nerve to peek around at the empty waiting room, trying to calm myself down. A muted flat screen television on a nearby wall caught my eye as I noticed an interview with my friend, Giovanni Rovati. We did not see each other often as he was busy with his own family in Scarsdale, but we kept in touch when we could, occasionally meeting up for lunch in the city.

I continued scanning the room. For the first time, I realized that I was not alone. A mother sat across the room, cradling an infant with a small child sitting next to her. The girl stared at me with wide eyes. When I made eye contact with her, she looked away, burying her face in her mother's side.

I pulled out my phone, noticing my reflection in the black screen. I did not realize how much blood was on me until now. My face was covered. I am sure I looked horrifying to a child.

I stood, searching for a bathroom. I wanted to try to clean up as much as possible. Spotting a sign, I held my head down, hurrying toward it. I did not want to touch the door, so I carefully leaned on it to open it.

The minute I entered, the door automatically closed, and I pressed my back against it, sliding to the floor. I buried my head in my hands, feeling tears welling up in my eyes. I loved Isabelle more than anything. If something were to happen to her because of me then I would never be able to forgive myself.

For the first time in my entire life, I felt so helpless and ashamed. All of this was because of me. Her uncle was the most sinister person I had ever met. He had me fooled. It was not easy to deceive me. I was distracted by her beauty. I thought Isabelle made me stronger but she in fact rendered me powerless.

I slowly stood, gathering my emotions while stepping over to the sink which had a large mirror hanging over it. I rested my palms on the edge of the counter, staring at my bloody reflection. I let out a sigh as I began to wash my face and hands. As I was grabbing a couple of paper towels out of the dispenser, the door opened. Glancing up in the mirror, I saw the reflection of Giacomo, one of my bodyguards, who was with us at the restaurant.

"Sir, you were not supposed to disappear like that."

I turned to face him as I threw the paper towels away. "I didn't have a choice."

I continued to clean myself as much as possible. Grabbing more paper towels as I needed, I wiped myself until my skin was somewhat clean. I sighed as I looked at my bloodstained suit. I was drenched in the blood of an innocent person. I wanted to vomit, but I had to remain focused on bigger things right now.

Giacomo opened the bathroom door for me. We stepped back out into the hallway that led to the waiting area. Leaning on the wall just outside the door, I ran my fingers through my hair. He paused, folding his arms.

"While you and the guys were busy securing the building, Isabelle needed help."

"And where is everyone?" he asked, taking out his phone. "Where is Joseph? He has not answered."

I shrugged, "I have no idea where they are."

He sighed, scrolling through his screen, before sliding it back in his pocket.

"Marco and William took off too and I'm the only one here," I muttered. "Giacomo, I need to see her."

He nodded as his phone started to vibrate loudly in his pocket. He pulled it out, placing it to his ear.

Yes?

Ok.

Yes, he is here, and Miss Ayala is being examined.

I won't.

Thank you. He hung up promptly, returning his phone to his pocket.

"You won't what?" I narrowed my eyes on his.

He took a deep breath, "Felipe has Tanya."

I grabbed my head, shouting, "Are you fucking seri--?"

"Shhhh."

"Are you fucking serious?" I repeated, barely above a whisper.

He nodded, "Joseph went after her and I am guessing that's where Marco and William ran off to."

Anger rose within me as I felt my blood begin to boil. I marched to the waiting area where I began pacing back and forth. Giacomo remained close by, occasionally texting on his phone while keeping an eye on me.

***

About one hour and forty-five minutes later, the doors opened again. The same doctor appeared. I did not take my eyes off her as she approached us. I was still anxiously awaiting news that my girlfriend was doing ok.

"Mr. Greco," she smiled warmly. "she's asking for you."

I gasped, "She's awake?"

"Yes," she nodded. "She didn't particularly like my male nurse touching her, but she is physically okay."

"I'm ready to see her."

She peered around me. "Your friend will have to wait out here, though."

I looked back to Giacomo then to the doctor. "He is my bodyguard," I conveyed, "and will stand outside the door in the hall but he's coming with me."

She bowed her head, not putting up a fight. "Very well, this way."

We followed her through the doors and long hallway. There were whispers at the nurse's station as we passed. I did not glance in their direction as my focus was on Isabelle, but it was obvious they were talking about me.

Isabelle

I laid in a strange, cold place, with a stabbing and burning discomfort radiating throughout my entire body. Blinking my eyes a few times, blurry images formed before me. I tried to make sense of the hospital room I was in.

Attempting to lift my arm to my face, I felt cords attached to my finger and the back of both my hands.

Suddenly my vision caught movement in the doorway as a blur came toward me in what seemed to be slow motion. I blinked twice more, and the fuzziness started to take shape. Valentino! He had come for me! I became excited, unsure if my expression showed it.

He pulled up a chair, sitting quickly. Gently, he took my hand kissing it then held it against his lips. I smiled, at least I think I smiled, so happy to see him. I winced as my face hurt with movement. He turned my hand over and frowned at my palm.

"Bella," he sighed, tearing up, "I am so very sorry."

I tried to shake my head but was not sure if it was moving. "It's ok," I whispered.

He looked up at my doctor, inquiring, "Is she really going to be okay?"

My eyes slowly found her, focusing.

"Yes, but she has a lot of glass in her that we need to get out." She glanced at me and slightly smiled. "She needs to let my nurse touch her for this."

Valentino smirked as his eyes fell on mine, "Well, I will sit here with her while he does his job, if that's okay with her?"

I nodded as best as I could.

He faced the doctor, explaining, "She's been through a lot as you can see."

I tugged on his hand.

He immediately met my gaze with concern, "What is it, bella?"

"Fe...Fel..," I could not get the name out.

He nodded, "I know, darling."

"Is Tanya okay?"

"You rest and we will talk in a bit, my love," he avoided the topic, but I was assuming it was because of the doctor.

I gasped, "Joseph!"

"Isabelle," he soothed, placing his hand gently on my cheek. "Rest."

My eyes fell closed as I felt a presence on the other side of me.

He spoke to Valentino directly. "I'm going to give her some antibiotics and pain medication in her IV. We cannot fully sedate her to remove the glass. I will get out what I can, but the glass will continue to push itself out of her over time."

He continued to speak to Valentino as I felt the pain medication kick in. I started to slip into a light sleep as they conversed.

Valentino

The doctor filled me in on Isabelle's injuries while she checked her eyes. She informed me that she would be okay to sleep since her eyes were reacting to light and she was able to speak. She had hit her head on a blunt object which meant she did not get stabbed in the head with glass, thankfully. She got knocked out and did not pass out from blood loss as I thought. Head injuries were prone to bleed more, and always looked worse than they were.

The doctor left us alone after we chatted for a few more moments about her care. I buried myself in my phone after I saw Isabelle had fully fallen asleep. The nurse continued to extract small pieces of glass out of her body.

Now that I knew Isabelle was okay, I wanted to hear news from anyone about what was going on elsewhere. I texted William, Marco, Joseph, and Tanya. I exhaled, as I waited for a reply.

Isabelle stirred. I scooted my chair closer to her, resting my head next to hers on the pillow. I was scared to touch her, but I placed my hand on her stomach and closed my eyes.

Joseph

I managed to track down Felipe and Tanya to an old abandoned warehouse near the club. Watching carefully, I crept to an opening I saw on the side of the building. Slipping between the broken and jagged bricks, I made my way into a dark hallway.

My vision was limited due to the lack of light. I heard a female voice screaming for help, so I followed it. I knew it was Tanya. As I got closer to the sound, I felt the presence of someone behind me just as they touched my shoulder. I grabbed their wrist, twisting myself around.

"Fuck!" William hissed. "It's me!"

I darted my eyes back and forth between him and Marco. "You brought him?!"

"I fucking hate Felipe," Marco grumbled, "and I want him dead!"

I rolled my eyes, nodding as I refused to fight with Marco at the moment. Spinning around, we continue down the narrow corridor. Just then, a loud wail echoed through the building and William pushed past me, sprinting toward the sound.

I threw my hands in the air and called out in a loud whisper, "Wait, William, wait!"

He did not stop so Marco and I took off after him.

"You fucking bitch!" Felipe bellowed, "Where is Isabelle?!"

"Leave her the fuck alone!" William shouted as he entered the large, open room where Felipe stood over Tanya.

I appeared behind William but checked over my shoulder to see Marco was nowhere to be found. I cannot say that I was shocked. I was fairly sure this was a set up and he was a part of this. I did not trust him one bit.

William reached back, drawing his gun at the same time Felipe slid over behind Tanya and knelt next to her, holding a knife to her neck. Tanya yelped and wept, begging for him to stop.

"I wouldn't do that if I were you!" Felipe challenged William.

"Let her go!" William shouted.

Felipe taunted him, "Oh, is this your little slut?"

"Liam!" Tanya cried out. "Please just kill him!"

Felipe let out a menacing laugh but suddenly became serious, pressing the knife to her neck. A small drop of blood appeared on her skin, running down into her dress. I quietly but rapidly began assessing my next move.

"I will fucking kill her if you don't shoot her yourself or slide your gun to me so I can!"

Felipe could not see my gun as I was behind William. I caught movement in my peripheral vision above Felipe. I noticed Marco peeking through a large hole in a brick pillar from the second floor platform. William must have seen him too because at that moment he held his gun in the air and showed Felipe that he was surrendering.

"Okay, okay," William announced, "I'm laying it down, just don't hurt her anymore."

He kicked the gun over to Felipe who picked it up immediately, guffawing. William took a step back and glanced at Tanya who was cowered over crying. A few pebbles fell from the bricks above, causing Felipe to jerk his head up. He aimed, firing up at Marco. William took wide, quick strides over, yanking Tanya her out of his reach.

"You fucking idiot!" Felipe pointed the gun at Tanya, but William pushed her to the ground just as Felipe fired toward them.

I drew my gun, firing three shots toward Felipe as that was all I had left. He took off racing out of a side door, but I know at least two of the bullets hit him.

"No no no!" Tanya sat up, shaking William, screaming, "Oh my God!"

I heard six more gun shots in the distance, outside the building. I lunged over to William and dropped to my knees.

Tanya held his head, sobbing as she screamed, "Please don't die!" She rested her forehead on his chest, shrieking into his lifeless body, "Liam! No! Get up!"

"Move!" I harshly nudged her out of the way and bent over, gripping him as hard as I could. I picked him up, throwing him over my shoulder and glanced at Tanya. "Can you walk?"

She nodded through her sniffles.

"I need you to be strong and walk, Tanya, can you do that for me?"

She nodded, taking several steps, and stumbled. Marco appeared in the room seeing that she was struggling and caught her, scooping her up. We promptly moved as fast as we could to the car.

It was a long, painful walk for everyone, but we made it. Tanya sat in the back seat with William's head in her lap. Marco sat in the passenger seat as I sped back to the hospital where Isabelle was.

I heard Tanya's weeping in the back seat as she pleaded for William's life under her breath. I glanced at Marco and nodded. He reached back, taking William's wrist, pausing for a few moments as he stared at his watch. Turning back to me, he blinked his eyes but said nothing. Fortunately, it was so late by this point that there was minimal traffic on the road so I raced as swiftly as I could.

We pulled in front of the hospital. Marco and I rushed in, carrying them. The receptionist called to the back and hospital staff ran out to immediately get them. I stepped over to the desk and the security guard's eyes lit up the moment he saw me.

"Joseph!" he gasped.

I nodded, "Would you please show us to Isabelle Ayala's room please?"

"Of course!" he quickly agreed, escorting Marco and I down the long hallway to her room.

THE VEIL

I turned to him when we reached the open door. "Thank you."

"Anything for an old mate," he smiled before he returned to the waiting room.

I made eye contact with Giacomo and he sighed, glaring at us but did not speak. He knew better as I was his boss. A man in scrubs was wrapping medical supplies in a towel and exiting the room.

I stuck my head in the doorway, "Sir--."

He looked up from the bed with defeat in his eyes, pleading for answers, "Joseph, what the fuck happened tonight?"

22 FORGIVENESS

Valentino

Joseph sighed, entering the room, followed closely by Marco. My eyes narrowed as I saw no sign of William or Tanya. The appearance on Joseph's face gave me an entire story itself.

Marco kept his eyes lowered to the floor and did not dare speak. He stood motionless as he wrapped his arms around his stomach in a cautious posture, slowly blinking as if something were burning on his mind. I had never seen my brother this way. He was normally obnoxiously boisterous. Silence was not his strength.

"Can I see you in the hall please?" Joseph finally mumbled.

I nodded, turning to my brother, "Marco, you cannot be in here while I'm not."

He rolled his eyes before focusing on mine, "I won't hu--."

"No," I shook my head, "if she wakes up and sees you, she will go insane."

Marco rolled his eyes once again but quickly nodded, realizing that I was right. I noticed him wincing as he scuffed slowly out of the room, holding his side. Joseph and I followed closely behind him.

I leaned on the wall in the corridor listening as Joseph told me what happened when they found Tanya. My eyes widened as I took a deep breath, running my fingers through my hair. The sadness and frustration built up inside me, rippling through my body like an angry river. I felt myself starting to shake as I was witnessing my entire life coming to a head.

I reached my arm out toward the middle of the hall, stopping a passing nurse. She gave me a friendly smile. I wanted to punch a hole in the wall, but I remained as nice and one could in this situation.

"Would you please get my girlfriend's doctor?"

I am sure she sensed my anger because she immediately spun around, walking speedily back down the hallway in the direction that she came from.

I peeked into the room, seeing Isabelle was still sleeping. She looked so beautiful and peaceful even though she was in pain. She was stronger than I originally gave her credit for; a woman who had been through so much as a child and still turned out to be so incredible.

The effect she had on me at first and the hold she has on me now meant I would do anything for her. Lost in my thoughts, I had not realized the doctor had approached us. She was speaking to Joseph and it forced me to become alert once again.

"We should take a look at your injuries," she was lecturing Joseph.

I turned to examine him closer, as I had not bothered to take notice until she said something. Dried blood encrusted the side of his face that smeared into his hair, a large gash on his eyebrow that still bled and a bloody lip. What the hell happened?

"I'm fine but thank you," Joseph confirmed, before turning his attention back to me and nodded as he patted my arm. He stepped into Isabelle's room and spun back to the hallway, "I will watch her for a bit."

I slid my hands into my pockets, facing the nurse. "I need to check on my friends."

She glanced at her tablet, reading for a moment before meeting my concerned gaze. "I'm guessing the male and female who were brought in?"

I nodded, "William and Tanya."

She scrolled through her screen. "William is in surgery and Tanya is in room 107."

"Thank you," I tried my best to smile as she gave me a single nod before sauntering away.

Marco groaned behind me and I spun to face him.

"Did you get hurt?" I hissed, lifting my fingers to my chin, and stroking my scruff as I studied him.

He lowered his gaze to the floor, grumbling, "I'm fine, Val."

I gnawed the inside of my cheek as I crossed my arms over my chest, analyzing his face. He was lying. I knew that expression anywhere. As if his body reacted on cue to his lie and my realization, he began to slowly bob his head as his body shivered.

"Marco?"

He started to sway, ignoring me as he stared at the wall. I grabbed his black jacket, finding a hole. I felt a wet sensation on my hand. Yanking it back, I turned my palm face up. Blood! Yanking his jacket open, I realized his abdomen covered in a significant amount of blood seeping through his white shirt.

"Merda!" I cursed. "Someone help!"

His body crumbled to the floor, but he grabbed my biceps on the way down, pulling me to the floor with him as his eyes rolled sideways. I hovered over him on my knees, ripping his red stained, buttoned shirt apart. A gunshot wound on the left side of his abdomen was visible. Without hesitation, I applied as much pressure as possible.

I was shortly pulled out of the way by hospital staff as they took over his care. Placing him on a gurney, they wheeled him away as quickly as possible. I remained on the floor, covered in blood that was not my own, leaning my head back on the wall behind me. I stared robotically at the ceiling tiles, with my arms draped over my bent knees.

I was now realizing the entire night was turning into an even bigger nightmare. Vaguely, I overheard Giacomo on a phone call with Blaine. I buried my face into my blood soaked hands, taking shallow, shaky breaths.

A nurse squatted next to me, resting her hand on my shoulder. "What is his name?"

"Marco Greco." I sighed, mumbling. "He's my brother, please save him."

The entire world moved in slow motion and I watched her sprint down the corridor toward Marco. The hallway spun as I gradually came to my feet, taking a deep, agonizing breath. I glanced at the room numbers, taking note of where we were, trying to maintain my focus. Swiping my sleeve across my face, I wiped some blood off and smeared the rest.

Someone stepped over to the blood on the floor, cleaning it as I ran my fingers through my messy, black hair. I took another deep breath and carefully trudged to Tanya's room. I passed many rooms on the way and for some reason, I found myself glancing in all the open doors. Normally I did not pay much attention to other people when I was upset, but I extensively studied everything around me.

I passed a room with the mother and kids I saw in the waiting area. She stood over the bed holding both of her children as she wept over the body of a man who was hooked up to many machines. The little girl I made eye contact with before, glanced at me. A tear rolled down her cheek and she rapidly looked away, burying her face into her mother's shoulder. My eyes lowered to the floor as I continued walking. I passed four more rooms before I came to Tanya's.

Poking my head in, I knocked at the same time. She was reclined in bed alone, hooked up to an IV. She was staring silently out the window at the nighttime city lights as they flickered outside.

She did not turn to face me as I made my way over to the bed, perching on the edge. I placed my hand on her knee. She instantly covered her face, beginning to weep.

"Liam--," is all she could choke out before her emotions completely overcame her.

I slid closer to her, wrapping my arms around her body. "He'll be okay," I mumbled into the top of her head.

"You don't know that."

"I do," I tried not to show my sadness and remained strong. "He has to be."

"Where's Isabelle?" she sobbed.

"She's resting and will be fine."

She sighed unsteadily, stuttering, "Y-you should g-go back to h-her."

"How is the baby?" I slid away a few inches, resting a hand on her knee once again.

She gazed down at her stomach, rubbing her small baby bump, "Tough as beef jerky."

I chuckled, "Good."

Just then, her doctor entered the room. "Oh hello," he stated, seeming somewhat shocked.

I stood, stepping to the side out of the way, but observing closely as he examined her progress in front of me.

"Your wife will be okay."

"Oh no," I smirked, "she's--."

"He's my brother."

I rolled my eyes at her small lie.

The doctor turned to me, "Great, well your sister is free to go." He focused his attention to her. "You need to rest. Your baby is fine, but you need about a week to be lazy."

"I will make sure she doesn't move," I sarcastically glared around him into her eyes.

She rolled her eyes, but suddenly they welled up with tears once again. Taking a deep, unsteady breath, she choked back as much as she could, but they began to drip onto the blanket.

I cleared my throat, "Can I speak to you in the hall please, Doctor umm--?"

"I'm Doctor Enfield."

Tanya gasped, trying to stop her tears. "You're going to discuss Liam!"

I sighed, not bothering to make any form of eye contact with her.

"I want to know everything!"

I massaged my temples, sighing, "William is her fiancé and is in surgery."

He quickly glanced at his tablet. "They should be finished shortly," he nodded, "but I will have someone come speak with you soon."

"I am going to take her to my girlfriend's room," I announced without asking. "Please have them come to Isabelle Ayala's room to update us."

Doctor Enfield nodded as a nurse rolled a wheelchair in the room before she stepped over to remove Tanya's IV. Tanya winced as she stood. She stepped off the bed, stumbling a bit. I reached over grabbing her arm, helping her sit in the wheelchair. The nurse handed her the discharge paperwork and after a quick few signatures from Tanya, we were off to Isabelle's room.

Just as we arrived at Isabelle's doorway, I saw a surgeon approaching us. Oh no. I took a short and shallow breath, bracing myself for the worst possible news since our night was full of negative surprises. Tanya shot up out of the wheelchair, standing anxiously. I rested my hand on her arm to stabilize her but in a way, I think I was subconsciously stabilizing myself.

"Mr. Greco," I knew that tone.

"I was your brother's surgeon."

I felt Tanya's grip loosen a bit as this was not the news she was hoping to hear. I swallowed hard, crossing arms tightly in front of me. My vision turned to a blur as the sounds of beeps and medical chatter filled the hallway. I felt tunnel vision overcoming me. I slowly blinked my eyes as I read the surgeon's lips form the words.

"I'm sorry but your brother's brain is no longer functioning, and he is being kept alive by a ventilator."

The words pierced my chest, rendering me speechless. I lowered my head, fighting back emotions. Though Marco and I had a troubled past, he was still my family. In the end, our common enemy brought us together for what would be the last day of his life. Nothing would change the past, but I finally felt we made some progress.

He and I both came to an agreement at the restaurant after the girls left with Joseph. We agreed to start over and put the past behind us if he helped without turning on us. He even wanted to apologize to Isabelle, but that was no longer an option. I planned to encourage her to forgive him in her own time. None of that mattered now.

The surgeon continued, "Does he have a wife who can make the decis--?"

THE VEIL

"No," I interrupted. "No wife. I will make have to make the decision and I can produce necessary paperwork if need be."

I turned, nodding to Joseph who confirmed that it would not be a problem. He rested his hand on my shoulder as Giacomo stood close by. Tanya hooked her hand on my arm, leaning her head on me.

Just as I felt myself slipping into a dark tunnel, my head snapped up at the sound of a woman crying in the hallway, tugging on the lab coat of a doctor. It was the woman from the waiting room who was standing next to her husband's bed sobbing with her two children. She held her baby while her small daughter stood behind her.

"Please!" she pleaded loudly, "my husband cannot die!"

"I'm sorry miss, but without--."

"Find him a heart, please!"

I tilted my head, lifting my gaze to the surgeon. "If my brother is a match, I want her husband to have his heart." I sighed, steadying my breath, "Is that still an option?"

He nodded, "Are you sure that is what you want?"

I nodded, "But, I want to go say goodbye to him, first. I know he is a donor so give her husband his heart if you can and then do what you need with the rest as long as he saves lives." I took a deep breath, "I want to remain anonymous as the press would have a fun day with this in America."

He nodded, "Of course, Sir." Gesturing to the hallway he murmured, "I will take you to see him now."

Isabelle

It had been three weeks since that horrible night in London, and two weeks since Marco's funeral. I opened my eyes to a room I thought I would never see again. The sun shone through the blinds and created a perfect morning glow in the bedroom I now called *ours*.

Reaching over, I felt the empty space that belonged to Valentino. I knew he was possibly busy as always, working in his office downstairs. Placing my sore feet on the floor, I limped into the closet, slipping on a pair of sweatpants and one of his t-shirts.

I faltered to the elevator, taking it to the ground floor. Making my way through the familiar halls, the smell of bacon filled the air. I grinned as I veered to the kitchen before his office. As I stepped in the doorway, my eyes widened as I saw Valentino standing in front of the stove, cooking. Tanya sat at the large distressed wood table nearby reading, while William sat at the kitchen island, sipping on a cup of coffee.

"Good to see you smiling again," I grinned, nudging William as I passed.

"Easy," he winced, smirking, "I'm still sore."

"Sorry," I snickered, slightly limping to Valentino.

He held his arm out and pulled me in for a side hug as he flipped a pancake. I wrapped my arms around his waist, peering up at his handsome face.

"You're cooking?"

He placed a gentle kiss on the top of my head as he filled a plate with an abundance of food and set it next to William at the island. I glanced at both Tanya and William who had almost finished their breakfast. Valentino, turned around to face me, sipping his own coffee.

"Sit and eat."

"I see you are back to your bossy self, *Sir*."

"Oh, for fuck's sake," William rolled his eyes, "get a room."

"I have a room," Valentino shrugged, "In fact, I have a whole fucking house and you are in it."

Tanya chimed in from the table, "Guys, language!"

Valentino focused his attention on her, sarcastically mocking her, "Fucking." He made sure to over enunciate and drag out every syllable.

I watched, snickering as I ate a pancake.

Tanya angrily crossed her arms, "My baby will not be ruined by your foul mouths."

"Relax babe," William defended. "If anything, they'll take after you and be a perfect angel."

I snorted again as I tried to hold back the laughter. Tanya smiled sweetly, before it dawned on her that William was being sarcastic. Valentino turned around with a plate of food that he had prepared for himself. He bit off a piece of bacon, smirking at her.

"A real devil if you ask me."

"Fuck you!" she snapped before gasping then rapidly cupping her mouth.

Valentino and William laughed loudly at her slip.

"Ouch," William winced as he held his abdomen.

After breakfast, Valentino and William went to into the office. Tanya asked me if I wanted to take a walk. I shrugged because we were both still recovering but I knew I needed to get out and walk around at this point. Thankfully, no glass had gotten in the bottom of my feet but they were still painful.

We stepped out on the patio and took the wide, stone staircase down to the path. I turned around to see Joseph lurking behind us, trying to remain unnoticed. I rolled my eyes, folding my arms.

"Joseph," I sighed, "you don't have to watch me on the property."

He pointed to his earpiece, "Well I have orders from the boss to watch you regardless." He brought his hand to his chin, tapping, "Miss, until we find your uncle, I will always be around you."

Tanya giggled, amused.

I rolled my eyes again once again, smiling, "Joseph, you desperately need a girlfriend."

"We have a friend back in the city a--," Tanya cheerfully began.

"If I distract myself with a woman," he interrupted, "she might end up dead and I don't need that on my watch." He pointed at me.

"That got dark fast," I smirked, "but I'm finding you a girlfriend anyway."

His eyes lowered to the ground before lifting his gaze back to us. "Please continue your walk and I will step back a bit more." He took several steps backwards, trying to give us a bit more space.

We giggled and Tanya hooked her arm in mine as we strolled through the grounds, chatting about her upcoming wedding and the baby on the way. I was ecstatic that William and Tanya had gotten engaged. Planning her wedding and a baby shower was such a wonderful distraction during this time. We did not dare speak about the recent events as we both needed to avoid that topic for now.

Valentino

William and Tanya left earlier, and Isabelle had been resting in our bedroom. I continued to work but could not concentrate. I stood by my office window, leaning on the windowsill. Peering out at the rainy night, I took a deep breath and was taken back to the afternoon we buried Marco.

Watching my parents, sister, and other brother, in tears over it broke my heart. I could not tell them everything. My other brother had his suspicions, but my parents and sister remained clueless. It needed to stay that way. They would never understand.

Isabelle did not attend the funeral as she was still recovering. She made her peace with the situation as far as I knew, supporting me through my pain over his death.

My phone vibrated in my pocket and I pulled it out to see a text from her.

Are you coming to bed soon?

I glanced at the time and my mouth fell agape.

Be right there.

Another alert popped up on my phone and I ignored it, sauntering to the stairs. Joseph met me at the bottom, sighing. I spun to him, my eyes widening when I saw his furrowed brow.

"What now, Joseph?"

He sighed, "Your brother is outside the front gate."

I took a drawn out, deep breath, loudly exhaling, "Let him in." I stepped on the bottom stair, "I will be back down in a few."

I hurried up the stairs and into the bedroom. Isabelle was lying in the middle of the bed on her side in a black nightie. I smirked, quietly closing the door behind me. Leaning on the wall, I slid my hands into my pockets, knowing if I took another step, my brother would be waiting until morning to speak to me.

I rolled my eyes, "Alessandro is waiting for me downstairs."

She slowly moved to her knees. "I don't care," she arched a brow as she trailed her fingertips over her breasts. "Are you really going to turn me down?"

I tucked my bottom lip between my teeth, shaking my head as I hungrily glared at her.

She ran her tongue over her bottom lip, taunting me, "Come play with me."

"Cazzo."

She bit her bottom lip, dipping her fingers into her panties as she arched her back, moaning every so slightly.

I chewed the inside of my cheek hiding my smile, but my eyes gave it away.

"That's what I thought."

I rolled my eyes, shaking my head as I chuckled darkly. Slowly approaching the bed, I made her nervously giggle in anticipation. She began to move her hips, eagerly awaiting pleasure.

"Let me make two things clear." I growled, holding up two fingers. I stood over her as she knelt before me on the bed, nodding.

"Yes, Sir?"

I sighed, holding up only my index finger, "Number one, this will have to be very quick as I cannot leave him waiting too long."

She nodded again, running her fingertips over her nipples seductively, "And number two?"

I held up two fingers, leaning over her, forcing her to recline. Trailing the outside of her mound with my fingers, I gradually increased pressure. She moaned loudly, arching her back.

"Number two," I growled, pressing my lips to her ear, "never fucking tell me what to do."

23 DEFIANCE & LUST

Isabelle

I shivered as he spoke into my ear, immediately becoming weak at his touch. He had not caressed me this way in too long. He was scared that I would break. I had been in a lot of pain until recently when I finally started to feel somewhat normal again. This was exactly what I needed right now. I craved him.

I moaned as he pressed harder on my overly sensitive sheath. He evilly grinned as he crawled on top of me, never breaking the contact his hand had on me. Leaning down, he pressed his lips gently against mine, circling them, lightly grazing my mouth. I parted my lips, begging to be kissed. He would not give in and it was driving me crazy. He loved pushing me to the edge, teasing me, making me beg for his sex.

"Valentinooo, fuck meee."

Smiling against my skin, he sat back onto his knees, grabbing my waist. He rolled over onto his back, pulling me on top of him as he guided my face close to his.

"I told you not to tell me what to do."

He spanked my bottom before reaching down, pressing his thumb to my little button, massing in a loop. I moved my hips on his erection, demanding with a glare.

"Am I driving you crazy yet, bella?"

I nodded, leaning my head back as I was close to exploding. I brought my body forward, staring into his eyes. I was on edge, about to let myself erupt. An evil grin crept across his face as he yanked his hand away. Panting, I shivered against him.

"Next time you will remember that I take orders from no one in the bedroom," he smirked, sitting up.

He leaned forward, passionately kissing me before making me move off his lap. My mouth fell agape in disappointment and shock as he stood. He adjusted his pants then smoothed out his shirt. I sat still with a throbbing sensation rushing through my panties. Resting his palms on the bed on either side of me, he bowed toward my flushed face.

"If you touch yourself while I am gone," he scowled, "you will regret it."

I exhaled, nodding.

He closed his eyes, running his tongue slowly across my bottom lip as he reached between my legs. Gently, he moved my panties to the side, stroking my slit with his finger. Pulling his hand away, he stuck his finger in his mouth as he smirked before spinning away to exit the room.

Once he was in the hall and the door closed, I threw my body back on the bed. "Damnit!"

Valentino

I stepped into the hallway and sighed. That had taken a lot of restraint. I did not want to break her in half, not yet anyway. I wanted to toy with her, driving her crazy first. She hated that she loved when I did it.

She would end up touching herself and I would pretend to be mad. Then, we would have the kind of sex her body was craving right now. It would be worth it. I did not feel like waiting for the elevator, so I hurried down the steps to the foyer. Joseph met me at the bottom.

He followed me into the closest sitting room where my youngest brother, Alessandro, was pacing back and forth in a dapper, navy-blue suit.

Alessandro stood the same height as me and was the only one of us who was born with brown eyes, like our father. The rest of us inherited our mother's blue eyes. He was the youngest person to open a casino and hotel in Atlantic City, New Jersey at the age of twenty-five. Now, at twenty-seven, he was remarkably successful.

As I entered the room, he stopped pacing, turning to face me. "Took you long enough," he smirked, sliding his hands into his pockets.

I rolled my eyes, crossing my arms over my chest.

"She must be…fun," he observed with a devilish grin, pointing to his collar.

"Watch it," I warned under my breath as I checked my collar, noticing a small lipstick print.

He bit his lip, holding in his laughter. He loved to push my buttons whenever he had the chance. It was not so much that he was mean to me, but he was just arrogant and loved to give people a hard time whenever possible, especially family.

"What brings you all the way out here from A.C.?"

He began to pace once again as he explained his reason for coming. "I'm not stupid, Val. The more I thought about this shit, the more it bothered me."

"Hmm," I hummed, listening.

"Our brother is dead," he continued, coming to a stop. "Granted he was a dick," he shrugged, "but none of what you told mom, dad, and Laura made any sense to me."

Glaring at me, he waited for me to spill every detail. Folding his arms, he bit the inside of his cheek. Exhaling, this was not a conversation that I wanted to have but Alessandro was exceptionally intelligent. Hiding anything from him was impossible.

"What do you want me to say?"

"How about the fucking truth!"

I shook my head, averting my gaze, remembering the traumatic moment Marco collapsed in front of me, and it being the last time I saw him.

"I'm protecting you by not telling you," I sighed, plodding to the doorway before I paused, not glancing back his way. "Follow me."

We made our way down the hall to the kitchen. I pulled out a bottle of whiskey and two glasses, pouring us both a drink. He instantly gulped his down then grabbed the bottle, refilling it all the way to the brim this time.

I took a sip of mine, rolling my eyes. "If you think you're staying here tonight--."

He interrupted me with a chuckle, "No, I have to get back to Jersey."

Just as he was finishing his sentence, my eyes caught a small motion in the doorway. Isabelle stood, leaning in the archway, with her arms folded against her. Alessandro's eyes followed mine. He propped on his elbow, smiling at her as his eyes hungrily trailed every inch of her body. I began to feel anger rise within me.

"Well hello there," he greeted her with a shit eating grin that charmed absolutely everyone he met.

She stepped into the kitchen, holding up her hand in a small, shy wave, "Hi."

Quickly making her way to me as smoothly as she could, she wrapped her arms around me, and I held her against my body. Her gaze lifted, meeting mine.

"I couldn't sleep but I did finish up a project I wanted to work on," she winked, knowing she had defied my orders.

"We will have to discuss that in a little while then," I poked her side, smirking.

"You must be Isabelle?" Alessandro introduced.

"I am," she grinned sheepishly.

"Il tuo corpo e' perfetto," he winked at her.

Isabelle tilted her head toward me with confusion on her face, "What did he say?"

I glared into his eyes, "He wants me to punch him."

Alessandro raised his palms, snickering, "I am just joking."

"You're Alessandro, right?"

He flickered his eyes back to Isabelle, nodding, "You can call me Alessio."

Isabelle smiled, approvingly.

He continued, "So, you are the infamous girlfriend my brother refuses to introduce to the family."

"I have been recovering."

"Right, right," he nodded.

I sighed, "I haven't exactly had time lately." I rested my glass on my lips. "I have been a little busy with the recent situation." I took a drink.

Before I could stop him, he addressed Isabelle, inquiring, "And, what do you think about all this, Isabelle?"

She opened her mouth to speak, but I cut her off, gently squeezing her hand. "Darling, would you please give me some time with my brother?" I placed a kiss on her forehead.

She nodded before turning to him. "It was nice meeting you."

He smiled, "I hope he doesn't keep hiding you from us any longer."

She smiled politely at him but spun to give me a look of sadness before she left the kitchen. I knew what he said to her impacted her because it also impacted me. We loved each other and I was trying to protect what we had. I wanted them to know her, but I had never taken anyone to meet them before. My brother spoke, interrupting my thoughts.

"You love her."

I nodded, finishing off my whiskey.

"Are you bringing her home for Christmas?" he leaned back on the stool, sipping his drink slower this time.

I leaned my palms on the granite countertop of the island, sighing, "I hadn't thought about it because no woman has ever been worthy of that."

"I'll have my new girlfriend there," he shrugged, "but she's already met the fam."

I arched a brow. "You have a girlfriend and she's met the family? Our family?"

He nodded, grinning warmly, "She's pretty fucking amazing."

I chuckled, "You said that about the last seven."

"This one is different," he smirked, chugging the rest of his liquid. "She's got a job that doesn't involve getting naked."

We shared a laugh, before he suddenly became serious again. "But you should definitely bring her home for Christmas." He crossed his arms, "And I hope you know I was just joking when I was flirty."

I nodded, "But I still hate when you do that shit."

He gestured toward his glass and I poured him another.

"Sorry," he apologized sincerely. "I'm having to get used to not being single any longer and definitely having to get used to you having a girlfriend."

"Fine, forgiven, this time."

THE VEIL

Isabelle

As I left the kitchen, I overheard Valentino saying that he never felt any woman was worthy of taking home to meet his family for Christmas. I was fine with the fact no one from his past was worthy of meeting them, but I would hope he would feel I was different. He did not seem interested in taking me to meet them and never brought it up to me, not even around the time of the funeral.

As I slightly hobbled to the elevator, a tear rolled down my cheek, but I fought it off. I felt foolish but I was a bit hurt. Silly me for thinking that I was different from them when it came to being serious.

Once in the bedroom, I crawled into bed, rolling over to face away from the door. I stared at the wall, fighting back feelings of sadness. Unfortunately, the events of everything we had been through began to fight back, reminding me of the angst this had caused. I decided that I should just go sit in a hot bath, ignoring my emotions. In case he came up, I did not want him to know I was in the middle of having an internal meltdown. A long soak in the tub would help relax me.

I stepped into the bathroom, turning on the water as hot as my skin could stand it. While I waited for it to fill, I removed my clothes and lit all the scented candles I had put in our bathroom. I glanced at myself in the mirror, beginning to lose myself in thoughts about how our relationship got to this point.

I knew that I was more in love with this man than I thought possible. After seeing the tub was full, I turned off the bathroom lights then stepped in. Immediately I reclined back and relaxed in the hot water as the candles flickered all over the room. I closed my eyes, overthinking what I heard him tell his brother and let out a small cry.

"What's wrong?" I suddenly heard his deep voice.

Startled, I jumped, quickly opening my eyes. Valentino was leaning in the doorway of the bathroom with his hands in his pockets. His eyes sparkled in the twinkling reflection of the candles. I did not want him to see me crying so I turned my head to face the other direction. I saw him in my peripheral vision slowly creeping toward the tub.

"I asked you a question."

I remained silent.

"Bella, why are you ignoring me?"

I did not move a muscle and in fact I began to weep, burying my face in my palms.

"Okay fine," he shrugged.

I turned my face toward him, "What are you doing?"

He pulled off his shirt then stepped out of his shoes but left his pants on. One foot entered the tub, followed by the other.

"Valentino, what are you doing?" I snickered as the water splashed me.

Kneeling between my legs, he rested his palms on either side of my head on the edge of the tub behind me. I could not help but allow a large smile to cover my face. Leaning forward, he pressed his lips into mine. Our kiss became aggressive as he grabbed my face, pulling my lips tighter against his mouth.

"You're crazy," I giggled, "You still have your pants on!"

Ignoring my statement, he cocked his head to the side, pursing his lips. "Let's discuss this project you finished without me."

I bit my lip giving him wide, sad eyes, "Sorryyy."

Valentino

"Those eyes won't work on me."

Reaching down between her legs, I shoved a finger deep into her core. She arched her back, moaning loudly. Leaning down, I bit down on her shoulder before pressing my lips to her ear.

"What did I tell you before I went downstairs?" I narrowed my eyes, playfully.

"Mmmm."

I pressed my thumb to her button, massaging it in circles. "I asked you a question, Isabelle."

She panted, grabbing my wrist under the water. "You said if I touched myself, oh God," she moaned loudly.

"Look into my eyes when you speak to me and finish your sentence," I commanded as I curled my finger inside her, stroking her.

"Ahhh, um, God, uh, mmm, I would, mmm oh, regret it," she grabbed my shoulders, digging her fingernails into my flesh.

I pulled my finger out of her as I felt the walls of her tunnel start to tighten. I was not ready to allow that just yet. She let out a loud groan in protest. Pushing her hands off my shoulders, I stood, removing my pants, freeing my arousal.

She immediately rocked up on her knees, stroking me slowly. I placed my hand on the back of her head, entwining my fingers in her hair, grasping a handful. She sighed as she pressed her lips around my shaft, slowly taking my entire length into her throat without gagging.

I titled my head back, closing my eyes as I realized she was winning the game I intended to play with her, and I could not do a thing about it. She had me right where she wanted me, as she was in control right now. I was never one to surrender.

I gripped her hair tighter and slid in and out her throat at a faster pace. When she started to finally gag, I pulled her face away from my body. She tried to grab it with her mouth again and I yanked her head further away.

"No," I barked.

She rocked back, resting on her knees, helplessly peering up at me.

"I don't recall even telling you to kneel," I leaned down, growling in her ear.

"What would you like me to do, Sir?"

"Stand up, Isabelle."

I helped her to her feet, and I sat on the bathtub floor. She moved to the side, allowing me to slide to the back.

"Come here, baby."

She straddled my body as she stood above me. I reached out, tugging her hand, silently commanding her to walk a little further. Her sex hovered over my lips. I reached around, spanking her on the bottom.

She positioned herself on my face just as I wanted. I held her in place, stabilizing her body as I ran my tongue up and down her slit. I circled her button in a figure eight then slid my tongue into her sheath. She began to grind her hips and her juices flooded my face. I pulled her back and turned her facing away from me.

Gripping her hands, I yanked her down. She squatted over my lap, slowly allowing my hard shaft to enter her from behind. I pulled her back into my body.

"Don't move," I whispered.

She raised her arms up behind her, running her fingers through my hair. "I need to cum, baby." She leaned her head back on my shoulder, kissing my cheek.

I turned my head, pressing my lips to hers. "You will cum when I tell you to, Isabelle."

I began to knead her breasts with one hand while sliding the other down to her button. I pinched, tugging it up and down. She instantly placed her hands on top of mine, moving with me as she cried out in pleasure.

"Valentino, I love you." she panted.

"I love you too, Isabelle." I placed my lips against her neck, gently kissing her soft skin.

She rolled her head toward me. I immediately kissed her zealously. I was falling deeper in love with this woman every day. She was everything I craved and needed in someone. There was no one who even came close to comparing to her.

I pulled away only long enough to command her to ride me. She swiveled her body, facing me. We both moved in a rhythm together, our breathing was becoming shallower as we both moaned in each other's mouths between kisses. I leaned away, pressing my lips to her ear, kissing, sucking, and licking her everywhere my lips and tongue would reach.

"Cum," I growled as I filled her.

She erupted on cue, screaming out in pleasure as we both exploded with focused intensity.

The next morning, I left Isabelle a note telling her I needed to run out for a while. My brother did end up spending the night at my house and I called both Blaine and William, demanding a meeting with them immediately.

Alessandro and I arrived at a small coffee shop close to my house. They were quite busy, but I called ahead to make sure they would reserve a table for us on the patio. When we arrived with Giacomo by our side, he stood nearby as we made our way through the morning crowd.

Blaine and William were already seated at a round table for four, waiting. They glanced up from their menus with wide eyes as we approached. William stood, patting us both on the back as he greeted us. I took a seat on his other side.

"Alessio Greco in the flesh," Blaine joked as he stood, shaking his hand, pulling him into a quick hug.

"Blaze," Alessandro joked as he stepped around him, taking a seat.

We picked up our menus, silently studying options even though I always ordered the same coffee and pastry every time I came to this particular café. A young, brunette waitress approached our table, smiling.

"Good morning, gentlemen."

We quickly placed our orders and she disappeared in a hurry. I noticed William had not taken his eyes off me since we got here. He was waiting for it. He knew something big was coming. Tilting his head, he propped his elbow on the arms of his chair, his fingertips stroking his chin.

"Spit it out, man," Blaine blurted suddenly.

He was on to me as well. I never called morning meetings at cafes. Meeting in private was important to me and we usually had breakfast on my back patio when business was involved. However, this morning I wanted a change. I felt like a new person in many ways.

William nodded, "Your brother is here so I can only assume this is about Felipe, but it's too public."

Alessandro's eyes darted toward me. I took a deep breath, shaking my head. His eyes narrowed and I knew that he would not forget what he just heard. Alessandro did not miss anything.

"Well what the fuck is it?!" Blaine blurted.

Before I could reply, the server returned with our order, arranging everything neatly on the table in front of us. After thanking her, she sashayed away, checking on other tables around us. I sat silently for a moment, staring at my cup before lifting it to my lips, taking a sip as the three of them stared at me, waiting for me to speak.

"I am going to ask Isabelle to marry me," I smirked before taking another sip of my cappuccino.

24 MAMMA

Valentino

Three weeks had passed since I told my brother and two best friends of my plans to propose to Isabelle. They were all happy for me and even offered to help me come up with the perfect setting. As nice as that was, I needed to do this myself. It had to be perfect.

The media began to get wind that a woman was living with me. The paparazzi camped out in front of my home on the other side of the wall. Twenty-four hours a day, seven days a week, they tried to get any glimpse of her. Magazines were offering us money to do exclusive interviews and I continuously declined.

Trying to come and go from the estate in private was hard enough but once they were focused on my love life it

THE VEIL

was a damn circus. It was unheard of for me to be in a relationship and I went from being New York's most eligible bachelor to untouchable overnight.

We started using a private back entrance to come and go from the estate, hoping that they would not catch on. Thankfully, so far no one had. It was much easier to use a decoy for the front.

Isabelle spent a lot of time on the grounds of the property, away from the streets. She was still a bit nervous to venture out with Felipe missing and the media frenzy, so she worked from home. She insisted that she needed to work, so I let her.

I sat at my desk in my office building, waiting for my first meeting of the morning. Since Isabelle now handled my schedule, I told her I needed time to myself to catch up on things I had missed in the office. She did not to book any meetings for me until after 1:30 p.m, so it gave me some time. One of my employees, Asha, knocked on my office door.

"It's open!"

She stuck her head in the doorway, announcing, "A Mr. Silas is here to see you, but Miss Ayala sent me your list of meetings and I don't see--."

"It's okay." I stood to my feet, waving her off, "Please send him in."

She nodded, pushing the door open all the way, allowing him to enter as I stepped around to the front of my desk.

He approached me, shook my hand, teasing, "You've already broken many hearts, Mr. Greco."

I smirked, "Yeah, well there is only one heart I care about."

He grinned, "Shall we?"

I nodded, gesturing toward a large, round table in the middle of my office. He gently laid his briefcase down, popping it open with both of his thumbs. LED lights illuminated the beautiful diamond rings that lined almost every ounce of space inside. I became overwhelmed, my eyes widened as I studied them all ever so delicately.

"It's overwhelming I know," he chuckled, shrugging, as if he read my mind, "but you said spare no expense, so I brought as many as I could fit."

He picked one out, presenting it in his palm. "Keep in mind that we can always combine multiple designs if you want something custom made."

I nodded, glancing, "Yes, I definitely don't want anyone to have the same ring as her."

"Well, have a look and I will help you design the perfect one for--," his voice trailed off.

"Isabelle," I commented as I leaned over, closely analyzing each ring slowly and carefully.

"Well, I wish you the best Mr. Greco and I am sure she is lovely," he alluded in a friendly tone.

Glimpsing at him out of the corner of my eye, I corrected, "She's more than that."

After going over every tiny detail of every ring, I showed him five to combine into one. I took small details from each one, creating the most exquisite engagement ring for the most incredible woman. A lot of people did not know, but I was somewhat of an artist, so I was able to draw a sketch of my design well enough for him to make something out of it back at his shop.

He closed his briefcase, patting the top of it as he smiled, "Right, so I will get started on this and keep you posted on its completion status."

I held my palm up as I strode around to the other side of my desk, writing a number on the back of a business card. I held it out for him. He stepped over, taking it between his index and middle finger. He peered down puzzled.

"That is William's number," I explained. "Please send any updates to his phone as I don't want Isabelle to see anything."

He nodded, "Good thinking."

I escorted him to the door, but before he left, I had Asha make him sign a non-disclosure agreement, forbidding him from speaking about my engagement or relationship to anyone. He was a trustworthy business associate, but when it came to my relationship with Isabelle, I spared no room for mishaps, especially with Felipe still on the loose. Any wrong move could lead him directly to her.

The moment Silas was out the door, Alessandro came barreling into my office, slamming the door closed behind him, almost as if he were in a panic.

"I thought you were going back to A.C.?"

"What the fuck is going on?" he hissed, ignoring me.

I arched my eyebrows, "He is the jeweler that is--."

"No, not that!" He rolled his eyes.

I sauntered to my desk, sat down, and propped my elbows on the arm rests as I formed a triangle over my mouth with my fingertips. I knew this moment would come. He hated Felipe for other reasons.

Marching frustratingly over to me, he leaned on his palms on the other side of my desk. "What business do you have with Felipe Ayala right now?"

I gnawed the inside of my cheek, avoiding responding.

He exhaled loudly, shaking his head with a disbelieving smile as he pushed off my desk. Crossing his arms, he glared down at me. "Val, for fuck's sake what did you get yourself in to?"

I rocked back in my seat, entwining my fingers behind my head, nodding toward the chair in front of me. "Sit."

He backed up, sitting as he crossed his leg over his other knee. Pulling out a cigarette, he lit it. I also lit one before sliding an ashtray to his side of the desk. He sat silently smoking for a moment as I processed my thoughts. Alessandro's temper was a force to be reckoned with.

"If I tell you," I sighed, "it will put you in danger."

Dropping his foot to the floor, he leaned forward, placing his elbows on his knees, "I don't fucking care!" He sat back, taking a long drag of his cigarette. "You're my brother and I got your back so talk because I am about to fuck his world up."

"Okay, this is why I didn't tell you."

I took a deep breath before I began to explain the series of events that took place over the course of the last year. His eyes widened and he chain-smoked while I talked, paying attention to every small detail that came out of my mouth. When I told him about London and the incident there, my ill-tempered, short fused, brother stood. He started to pace back and forth in front of my desk as he continued to take forceful drags of his cigarette.

"What you're saying is," he chuckled menacingly, "you're dating the niece of a fucking drug lord and our brother is dead because of this?" He stopped in front of my desk, pointing his cigarette at me. "Tell me please, how I am not supposed to go off on you about this?"

I quickly stood, slamming palms on my desk, snapping, "Because I will beat your fucking ass if you do!"

He took a step back as his eyes expanded, "As much as I hated Marco at times, he still didn't deserve that shit." He suddenly changed his attitude, becoming solemn.

I dropped my head, "I know." Taking a deep breath, I slowly roamed over to my office window, peering out at the city. "He chose to save Tanya, William, and Joseph's lives though." I placed my hand above my head, leaning on the glass, "No one made that choice for him and he even helped get both William and Tanya to the hospital before he collapsed on me in the hall."

"Funny," he snorted sarcastically.

I spun to face him, confused. "What?"

"His last moments were spent being selfless," he sighed. "It's just poetic I guess." He slid his hands in his pocket after snuffing out his smoke. "His daughter will never really know him though, and that's a bit sad."

I hastily marched to my desk, sliding my hands into my pockets. "What are you talking about, *daughter*?"

He nodded, smirking, "He never told you, did he?"

I threw my hands out, shrugging, "Clearly not!"

He massaged his temples with his fingertips, muttering, "Marco was a father."

I gasped, "The little girl at the funeral with the brunette woman standing with us?"

He bowed his head, "That was her and the mother, yes."

"Shit!" I placed my hands on my hips and brought my hand to my forehead as my eyes averted to the floor, "Now I feel even worse."

He shrugged, "I mean there's nothing you could have done better, right?" He folded his arms. "He made the choice to help."

"Yes," I sighed, "but it's no excuse." I lifted my gaze. "I want to meet the mother and our niece."

"I actually keep in touch with them," he murmured, "so I will see what I can do for you, but I make no promises."

"Bring them to me."

He rolled his eyes, snorting, "God, why are you so demanding?"

I shook my head as I sat down. "Get out, I have work to do." I waved my hand at him, shooing him toward the door while finishing up writing some business notes on paper.

He snickered, "Alright, I have to get back to Jersey anyway."

Before he left, he turned to me and froze, waiting for me to speak.

"Yes Alessandro?" I asked sarcastically as I set my pen down then leaned back in my chair.

"Just thought you might want to know our mother is in town," he smirked, instantly exiting the room before I could reply.

I rolled my eyes, leaning my head back, staring at the ceiling. "Figlio di puttana," I muttered under my breath.

Isabelle

I sat at Valentino's desk in his home office, working on replying to many emails that were not handled while we were away in London. Everything seemed to be getting back to normal, whatever *normal* was. I suddenly found myself growing very sleepy and decided to go upstairs and take a nap. I texted Valentino to let him know in case he needed me for anything.

Hey, I'll be napping for a bit if that's okay.

Moments later, he replied, *Sure, get some rest and I will see you in a couple of hours. I love you!* XO

I love you too : xoxo*

I smiled as I closed my laptop, meandering to the elevator. As I entered the foyer, Joseph was standing with an older woman. She was dressed in what I can only describe as the classic *rich lady* attire, but it was hard to tell much about her from where I was standing.

Joseph glanced toward me and his eyes enlarged as he gave me a tight-lipped smile. Her demeanor changed as she tilted her head toward me. For the first time, I got a good look at her appearance. She appeared young for her age, but I could tell she was an older woman. Wearing a black dress with black shiny jewelry, she draped a small, black bag over her wrist while her frost dyed hair made her blue eyes much more piercing than I expected.

"You must be the woman my son is hiding from me."

She greeted me abrasively in a prominent Italian accent as she waltzed toward me, placing a kiss on each of my cheeks. Joseph smiled at me, slightly rolling his eyes behind her back. My gaze widened in shock as I stared back at him. He appeared silently apologetic while he watched helplessly as she held on to me tightly. I smiled courteously as we parted, her hands still holding onto my wrists.

"You are Valentino's mother?"

She nodded, smiling "I am, and I would love to take you to lunch so I can get to know the woman who has stolen my son's heart."

I blushed, glancing toward Joseph for help.

He slightly shrugged, smirking, "I will prepare the car and call the restaurant."

"Actually--," I blurted louder than I should have.

Joseph turned toward me, and Valentino's mother dropped my arms.

"Joseph would you please help me with something before we go?"

He cocked his head to the side curiously, as Mrs. Greco was staring down at her phone.

I pursed my lips, jerking my head in the opposite direction.

"Excuse me Mrs. Greco," he informed her as he followed me, "we will return shortly and then we can leave."

"Take your time, Joseph." She nodded without looking up, "I will see myself into the living room."

I marched down the two corridors, returning to Valentino's office. Joseph closed the doors quietly. I turned to see him leaning against them, smirking.

"Why is she here?" I hissed. "Does Valentino know she's here?" I began to pace in front of him.

"She just showed up and it's not like I can deny her access."

I took a deep breath, as I stopped. "Joseph, look at me!" I gestured toward my outfit. "I cannot go out with Mrs. *Country Club* looking like--."

"You look fine but if you want to change," he interrupted, "I respect that." He rolled his eyes then glanced at his watch, "I would, however, hurry because while she is very nice, she does not like to be kept waiting."

"Oh, even better!" I sarcastically remarked, jogging out of the room, and taking a back staircase to our bedroom.

I sprinted into the closet, wincing slightly as I had not recovered in full just yet. Sometimes glass would work its way out of my skin, causing small abrasions. I frantically filed through dresses, but nothing seemed good enough.

Finally, I came across a dress that would match her style, or so I hoped. I slipped it on before scurrying into the bathroom, touching up my hair and makeup then returned downstairs. She was standing in the middle of the foyer once again, appearing slightly impatient but she smiled anyway.

"Are you ready?"

I glanced toward Joseph and he nodded, faintly winking, approving of my outfit. Relieved, I sighed, smiling at him before turning to her.

"Yes ma'am."

Joseph escorted us to the car and slid in the front seat next to the driver after opening our doors.

"I notified Mr. Greco," he announced, "and he will be meeting you at the restaurant. I also have had it closed for your privacy."

"Valentino is coming too?"

He nodded, chuckling lightly as he read my mind. I pulled out my phone, sending Joseph a text.

Thank you! I owe you!

He replied within seconds, *No worries. Now, be yourself. She will love you!*

Mrs. Greco turned toward me, lowering her sunglasses, "Tell me, how does it feel to date a billionaire?" She pursed her lips awaiting a reply.

"Ah, um," I fumbled, completely and utterly caught off guard, "well I don't really think about that to be honest." I sighed, "There is so much more to him than money."

Internally, I flinched. If she only knew how we met. I began to feel less than worthy of Valentino. She meant no harm and was just being a typical mother who cared for her son's well-being. However, if she ever knew the truth about us, she might instantly dislike me, thinking I was after his money or status.

She smiled, nodding approvingly, "I agree with that."

"Mrs. Greco."

"Oh, please just call me Giulia," she placed her hand on my knee.

"Okay sorry, Giulia." I continued, even though it felt strange to call his mother by her first name. "Valentino is the most amazing man I've ever met, and I never once cared about his financial situation." I took a shallow, anxious breath, "I just know he's good to me and I'm good to him. He's incredible."

She shifted in her seat, pursing her lips. "Well, let's hope you can deal with the secrets he keeps."

I bit my bottom lip, holding in my thoughts as I picked my nails nervously.

I saw Joseph turn his head toward the back seat and sigh. He knew that statement piqued my curiosity. He then turned his attention back to the front.

"We are here."

The driver and Joseph got out of the car, opening our doors for us. Joseph escorted us inside to a large square table in the middle of the restaurant. I turned to him with a panic stricken face, silently seeking his help. Smirking, he took a step closer to me, leaning near my ear.

"She loves tennis and sailing," he muttered under his breath, before stepping away from the table and taking a position near the entrance.

Two male servers approached, pulling our chairs out for us. Before I could sit, I felt a hand on my lower back. I glanced up to see Valentino.

"I got it," he commented to the server nearest me. "Thank you."

He ambled to his mother first, placing a kiss on each cheek as he greeted her, "Mamma." He pulled her chair out for her.

She sat with a relaxed smile, almost as if he brought her instant peace. I could relate to that feeling. He turned to me, winking , placing a small kiss but sweet peck on my lips.

"Darling." He smiled, pulling my chair out for me.

I sat, folding my hands in my lap as the server laid cloth napkins in our laps. Valentino took off his jacket, handing it to an employee before sitting next to me. He propped his arm up on the back of my chair, pulling my body toward him. His mother watched closely as he displayed public affection with me.

"Come stai?" she murmured, placing her freshly poured glass of wine to her lips, taking a sip.

"I am fine, Mamma, thank you," he sighed, circling my shoulder with his thumb. "But, please speak English. Isabelle does not speak Italian." Leaning toward me, he pressed his lips to my cheek.

She rolled her eyes. "My apologies, Isabelle." She spoke quietly, smiling.

I did not feel as if she were trying to purposely be rude. She seemed like she was just maybe not a very trusting woman. Afterall, she had just questioned me about finances on the way. I would have been the same way if I were a mother in her shoes.

Valentino

"I am glad to see you Mamma," I assured her, "but why are you in New York?"

I was very curious and suspicious as to why my mother was here. She and my father were overseas on business for a while, so when Alessandro told me she was in town, I instantly had red flags popping up. She stared intently at her wine glass before she raised her head, smiling as she craned her neck to someone behind me.

My brother appeared out of nowhere, sitting across from me in the only available chair. I guess he did not return to New Jersey after all. He was all smiles as he patted me on the shoulder and gave a small wave and wink to Isabelle. I rolled my eyes, laying my hand below the table on her thigh.

"Ciao Mamma," Alessandro greeted her directly.

Isabelle appeared to be a bit more nervous. I trailed my fingertips up to her hand, giving her a few reassuring squeezes, before resting it on her thigh once again. I stroked her soft skin in small circles with my thumb.

"Since your brother died, I have missed you boys more than normal," my mother continued, answering my question. "I want to make sure we are all together for Christmas." She turned to Isabelle, reaching across the table. "And I hope you will join us if my son will not keep you from us." She withdrew her hand, moving it back to her wine glass. "We will be spending Christmas at our home in Austria this year."

"That's great," Isabelle blurted excitedly, "I would love to play tennis with you!"

My mother froze and her eyes widened. Alessandro snorted, subtly covering his mouth. My eyes suddenly focused on Joseph whose eyes were diverted to the floor as if he refused to make eye contact with anyone.

"We will be in the mountains and there will be several feet of snow on the ground," my mother noted.

"Oh," Isabelle blushed, relaxing her posture in defeat.

"But definitely bring a skimpy bikini because there is a jacuzzi and indoor pool at the house," Alessandro exclaimed, winking at Isabelle.

Annoyed, I shot him a warning stare, "Shut it."

Before any of us could further speak, Isabelle excused herself to the bathroom. I took a deep breath the moment she was gone. I knew she had disappeared to hide her embarrassment. Before I could say anything to my mother, Alessandro glanced at me. I shook my head.

"Ma, he is going to propose to Isabelle."

"Is she pregnant?"

"What?!" I snapped. "No!" I sighed, "I genuinely love her, and I want to spend my life with her."

"Well, that is wonderfu--."

Before she could finish her sentence, my phone vibrated and I slid it out of my pocket, interrupting my mother. "Sorry, one second," I apologized, scrolling to a text Isabelle had sent.

Can you come here please? I need to speak to you.

I cleared my throat, placing my phone back in my pocket, "Excuse me for a moment."

I made my way to the Ladies' Room, opening the door, calling out, "Isabelle?"

She grabbed my hand, pulling me through the doorway, wrapping her arms around me. She then pulled my head down to meet her lips.

I pulled away, chuckling, "What the hell are you doing?"

"I need you to calm my nerves immediately," She gave me puppy dog eyes. "She's so intimidating!"

I nodded, smirking. We both glanced toward the door, spotting a lock. I reached over, turning it, trapping us in the privacy of the luxury bathroom. I picked her up and she wrapped her legs around my waist, hooking her ankles together.

"Tell me what you want me to do to you, bella."

She ran her tongue over her bottom lip. I pressed my already erect member against her, carrying her over to the counter and set her down. She began to move her hips, grinding herself against me.

"I want you inside me now."

"And how do you ask?" I bit her neck, before slowly running my tongue up to her ear.

"Please," she gasped.

Unhurriedly and firmly, I stroked her mound outside her panties, growling into her ear, "Please what?"

"Please fuck me, Sir," she breathlessly cried out.

25 AUSTRIAN CHRISTMAS

Isabelle

He placed his forehead on mine, impatiently staring into my eyes like a ravenous animal. "That's all I needed to hear."

Placing his fingers on the elastic strings of my thong, I lifted my bottom, assisting him as he slid them delicately down my legs.

"I don't know why you bother wearing panties anymore," he muttered.

They got stuck on the heel of my shoes. He rolled his eyes, chuckling evilly as he clutched them tightly, jerking them apart in one motion. I heard my panties rip and he stood up with them dangling between his fingertips.

"They broke," he smirked as he shoved them into his pocket.

I giggled but it was cut short when he grabbed the back of my head, yanking my lips to his for a hungry, fervent kiss. Our tongues swirled in each other's mouths, dancing to a perfect pattern.

Valentino made me absolutely crazy and I was a different person with him around. I was now a sex crazed vixen, thanks to him, and I was proud of it. I unbuckled his belt, getting ready to pull it through the belt loops, but he grabbed my wrist to stop me.

"We don't have time for that," he whispered through our kiss.

Pulling away from his face, I gave him a sultry, devilish grin, "Then make time, Sir."

His eyes rolled back, and he sighed, "You're in so much trouble." Smirking, he pulled his belt off his pants, securing it around my wrists as tightly as he could.

He grabbed the tip of the leather that was dangling down between my hands, jerking me off the counter. I almost fell but he caught me, tugging me over beside the sink. Using his body to push me against the wall, pinning my arms above my head by gripping the belt.

"Don't move," he commanded as he unfastened his pants, pulling his erection out, then placed it at my throbbing entrance.

I panted with anticipation.

"Don't scream," he kissed and sucked my neck before grazing my skin with his lips all the way up to my ear.

I moaned, pleading for more of him.

"And most importantly," he growled, "don't ever tell me how to fuck you unless I ask."

"Yes, S--."

He impaled my core and bottomed out before I could fully agree. My eyes watered. I opened my mouth trying to scream.

"Don't you dare, Isabelle," he whispered, cupping his hand over my mouth, muffling my noises.

"Fuck fuck fuck, Valentino," I moaned in a low whisper through his palm.

I was pinned tightly between his body and the hard, cold bathroom wall of the restaurant. He removed his hand from my face as he pulled my arms over his head, hooking my bound wrists around his neck. He lifted me off the floor, holding my waist with one hand and reaching down to my button with his other. He began to pinch, rolling my sensitive, pink pearl between his thumb and index finger.

"Oh God!"

"God can't help you now," he growled as he violently pounded my tunnel repeatedly.

I trembled as the sensation became too much to handle causing me to breathlessly moan, "I can't be quiet."

He removed his hand from my mound, cupping it over my mouth. I bit the flesh of his palm hard as we both erupted together. He rested his forehead against mine. We panted in unison as we came down off our blissful moment. A bead of sweat dripped down his brow as he ardently kissed me.

He carried me over to the counter, sitting me down. Unhooking my arms from his body, he smirked, noticing that I was still feeling the results of my earth-shattering orgasm as I crossed my legs.

He raised his eyebrows, winking, "You better pull yourself together, my love."

"T-trying," I stammered, still panting.

"We still have to sit with my mother and brother for lunch," he smirked as he handed me a small pile of wet paper towels.

"I'm not sure I can handle that," I admitted, groaning as I attempted to clean myself.

"Don't tempt me to fuck with you under the table," he grinned evilly as he adjusted himself then checked his clothes in the mirror. "Then you will know what it means to not be able to handle something."

He straightened his tie, winking as I watched his reflection. We both gave each other one last glance of approval before he took my hand. He unlocked the door and we exited into the empty hallway. My eyes widened and I froze, crossing my legs awkwardly, silently begging him for help.

"What's wrong?" He peered down at me, cocking his head.

I immediately panicked. "Oh no," I hissed, "Valentino, it's running down my thigh."

He snorted, placing his lips on mine, whispering, "You'll be okay."

"I need my panties!" I insisted under my breath.

"They'll do you no good now," he smirked, grabbing my hand, pulling me back to the table where we finished lunch with his mother and brother. The entire time I kept my legs tightly crossed, praying that when I stood, I would be able to make it to the car without incident.

Valentino

"Do we have everything?" I snorted, sarcastically commenting as I glanced at Joseph who was surrounded by a large pile of luggage.

"I certainly hope so, boss."

"Isabelle!" I called out in the large open foyer.

Her head popped over the railing as she peered down. "Just a second," she called out, "I have to do one more thing."

I checked my watch then glanced back at her, but she had already disappeared. "Hurry!" I yelled hoping she would hear me.

It had been almost four weeks since the last time we saw anyone in my family, and it was time to fly to Austria for the holidays. The front door opened, and William and Tanya came stumbling in mid-kiss. I glared toward them, clearing my throat. They reluctantly peeled apart as he removed Tanya's coat, exposing her small baby bump. She quickly adjusted her sweater.

"Nooo nooo," I pointed at them. "Put her coat back on," I snapped. "We are running behind, and I will not reschedule our departure."

Helen, our housekeeper, emerged from the elevator with Isabelle, giving her a hug. Isabelle turned to her, thanking her, and then spun to me. She awkwardly smiled.

"I'm ready," she beamed.

I rolled my eyes, taking her hand in mine. We stepped outside on the front porch and Joseph froze, staring ahead. We all stopped, our eyes all locking on a pile of suitcases and bags in the driveway.

"What...is...all...that?" Joseph scowled, gesturing to the luggage.

William and Tanya made their way past him hand in hand as Tanya cheerfully turned back, "That's our luggage!" She shrugged and smiled as they disappeared into the back of the limo.

Joseph sighed, pivoting to face me. "Sir, are you guys *moving* to Austria?"

I chuckled, "I'll make sure we do not over pack the plane."

Isabelle stepped in front of me, standing on her toes and threw her arms around Joseph's neck, hugging him tightly. "Have a great Christmas," she sniffled.

"You too Miss Isabelle," he reluctantly hugged her in return.

She backed away, pulling something out of her pocket. "This is for you from us," she smiled, placing a medium sized rectangle box in his hand. It was wrapped with green metallic paper and had a white and red bow on top.

He grinned as he held it close to his body. "Thank you both."

"You're welcome."

He sighed, "I really think it's a good idea if I accompany you because with Fel--."

I held my palm up to stop him. "We will be okay, Joseph." I rolled my eyes, "My parents have security covered."

Isabelle chimed in, "You deserve to spend Christmas with your family too."

Before we could say another word, the luggage was fully loaded into another car by staff and we made our way to the limo. I helped Isabelle in and followed closely behind her.

"Merry Christmas," Joseph peeked in the back door.

We all waved, wishing him the same as we pulled away. The ride to the airport was loud and full of chatter among the girls as they talked about the upcoming wedding and baby.

William and I had a silent conversation as we watched them with amusement. Their conversation finally died down after a while and Isabelle sat back in the seat, leaning into my side. I placed my hand on her knee.

"I'm glad you guys are coming too!" she gestured toward them with a big grin on her face.

William nodded and smiled, "I have spent many Christmases with them, and it would be weird if I didn't."

She did not dare ask him about his family and I am glad. William had not had an easy life before our friendship and my family practically adopted him. He was more like a brother to me than my own. The car came to a halt on the tarmac and we boarded the plane.

Isabelle passed out shortly after taking off and Tanya soon followed. William and I took advantage of their nap, spending the time discussing Felipe and what the next plan was when we returned to the states after the new year.

"I just think it would be better to hire people to do it this time," he sighed.

Amanda, my flight attendant, brought us both a whiskey before retreating to the front of the plane. I swirled the liquid around in my glass while processing what he had just suggested. He sipped on his drink, waiting for my approval.

I slowly nodded, "I agree but he's already hurt people close to me." I pointed toward him with my glass. "Look at your scar."

He narrowed his eyes at me, "Exactly and you won't have to worry about the others like you did about us." He leaned forward, whispering. "They're expendable." He scratched his chin, sitting back again in his seat, taking a large swig of his liquid.

I began to bob my head, weighing the words he just said, as I took a small sip of my drink. "I haven't given orders like that in a long time, Liam."

He smirked, "Maybe it's time." He held his glass up, arching a brow.

I pursed my lips, nodding sluggishly.

Isabelle

After a short layover, ten hours more in a plane, and an hour and a half drive, we were here. We rounded the corner of a large snowbank and my mouth fell open.

"Oh my God!" Shocked, I turned to Valentino, "This is breathtaking!"

Tanya and I peered out the window of the limo like little, wide eyed children as we came to a stop in front of the largest chalet I had ever seen. It was so magnificent that I almost cried. Luxurious, with panoramic views of the surrounding mountains, each eave held its own perfectly rounded accumulation of snow. The warm interior lighting reflected off the bluish-white evening snow outside, creating a glow.

We stepped out of the car into the crisp, dry, winter air. The walkway had been cleared so we ambled our way up to the front door. Hired staff unloaded the luggage from the car. Valentino opened the door and Tanya and I stepped through first, followed closely by William and him. Immediately a young woman came marching up with a smile, throwing her arms around Valentino and then William.

"So good to see you guys, ahhh!" she excitedly exclaimed.

She pulled away, smiling at Tanya then quickly hugged her as she gripped a glass of wine in her hand. "I'm Laura."

She let go once again and stepped in front of me. Valentino rested his hand on my lower back and smiled as she took my hands in hers. Her piercing blue eyes and smile looked remarkably familiar.

"You're the woman who's stolen my stubborn, big brother's heart."

My cheeks warmed and I smiled, "I hope so."

Valentino smirked, gazing down at me, "Yes she--."

Before he could finish his sentence, his mother and father appeared in the foyer, greeting all of us. His father stood around his height, with grey hair and his build was fit for his age. I could definitely see where Valentino got his looks and charm from. I saw so many similarities between them. His father was very polite and welcoming. His mother seemed more relaxed as she hugged me, telling me how wonderful it was to see me again. Introductions were quick.

William and Tanya followed Laura off to another part of the house while Valentino took my hand as he led me up the stairs. He stopped halfway to turn to his mother.

"We will be back down in a moment," he squeezed my hand a few times, "I am going to give Isabelle a tour."

She smiled, "I will have Luisa make you something to eat and brew coffee on the stove."

He turned to me for approval and I nodded. His mother disappeared. He placed me in front of him, cupping my bottom with both hands as he guided me up the stairs. I giggled when we got to the top and he pinned me against the wall, kissing me passionately.

We entered the large bedroom and he closed the door behind us. I paced around nervously as I ran my fingertips over the furniture, studying every small detail in the room. It was decorated in different shades of stained wood with luxurious décor, fit for royalty.

I roamed over to the window but only saw darkness and the reflection of us in the window. He stepped over to me, wrapping his arms around my waist, resting his chin on my shoulder. I exhaled watching his hands explore my body in the reflection.

"In the morning," he murmured, "you will look out to see a beautiful surprise."

I rested my hands on his arms, lightly massaging. He pulled my body against his. I felt his erection growing in his jeans and I turned to face him, giving him an evil grin.

He chuckled, "Not yet, my little nymphomaniac."

I sighed, whining playfully, "Why not?"

He ran his fingertips up my arms as he gazed into my eyes, "What are you doing to me?"

I smiled innocently, "Trying to satisfy you."

He spun me around, switching places with me, backing me toward the bed as he hungrily glared into my eyes with sheer thirst. The back of my thighs bumped into the side of the mattress and he turned my body to face away from him. He reached around and unfastened my jeans then pulled them down with my thong in one movement. Pushing my hair to the side, he aggressively kissed my neck as I heard him freeing his arousal from his own jeans.

"Bend over," he commanded, as he pushed my body forward toward the bed.

I obeyed, bracing myself, "Do your worst, Sir."

He leaned over me, pressing his body into mine, "Wait until you see the surprise, I have for you back home."

Just as I was about to ask, he plunged deep into my core in one hard stroke, causing me to let out a loud moan. I instantly buried my face into the bed to muffle the sounds that I could not control.

Wrapping my hair around his hand, he pulled my head back as he pumped in and out of me hard and fast. I was scared that my noises would carry throughout the house, but I could not form any sentences or words to warn him. I squeezed my eyes shut, trying to focus on keeping myself quiet, but he played a dangerous game of trying to see how loud he could make me.

I suddenly felt my orgasm building and let myself go, crying out. I felt him begin to pulsate inside me. Without warning, he ripped our bodies apart and pulled me off the bed, turning me to face him.

"Kneel," he commanded, pointing to the floor with his eyes.

I immediately fell to my knees, opening my mouth knowing what he wanted. He slid down my throat, releasing himself as his body trembled. Moments later, he bent down, deeply kissing me as he pulled me back to a standing position.

Valentino

Once downstairs, we entered the sitting room and my family was gathered around talking. A strange woman and a child were sitting on the floor by the fireplace. I paused, analyzing them. The woman stood, grinning sheepishly in our direction. I cautiously approached them.

"You are the mother of my niece," I stated the obvious, but did not exactly know how to speak to her just yet.

"I'm Eliza," she nodded, smiling shyly, "Marco loved her."

I peered down at the little girl who held her mother's hand tightly, burying her face in her arm.

Kneeling down, I greeted her with a soft voice and warm smile, trying not to scare her, "Hello. I'm your uncle, Valentino."

The first thing that I noticed as I looked into her eyes was that she was the spitting image of Marco. Quickly, my mind flashed back to that fateful night where he collapsed in my arms. I knew that I could not have changed the outcome. Unfortunately, I could not help but blame myself just a bit, for my niece losing her father.

"Hi," she smiled, twisting her body back and forth.

Taking her small hand in mine, I studied her face, wanting to hug her and tell her that I was sorry, but she would not have understood what I meant. The only peace I had was knowing that my brother's heart was indeed able to save another father as he ended up being a match.

"And how old are you? Ten?" I teased her.

Withdrawing her hand from mine, she cupped her mouth, giggling as she peered up at her mother.

"Tell him how old you are," her mother encouraged with a wide grin.

She held up four fingers, proudly inspecting them with a smile. "I'm four."

"Whoaaa four!" My eyes widened as I acted impressed to please her, "What is your name?"

She bounced a little then twirled in a circle, jumping, "Carissa."

"That's a beautiful name," I chuckled as I stood.

She skipped off to go sit in my mother's lap and I held out my arm to Isabelle. She made her way over, wrapping her arm around my waist. I introduced her, but she had put the pieces together by this point. She appeared a bit shocked, but she seemed happy about it.

"So," I sighed, "You were not together when--."

Eliza shook her head, "Oh no, but he took care of both of us."

I nodded, thankful that my brother had not completely abandoned them while he traveled the world with the dense blonde.

We spent the next hour visiting with my family and catching up. They also got to know Isabelle and Tanya more. I was delighted they all approved of them both which was particularly important to me. Contrary to what people assumed of me, I was awfully close to my family and I could not wait to make Isabelle one of us soon.

"Oh my God!" Isabelle shouted.

I opened my eyes, blinking a few times as my eyes adjusted to the light in the bedroom.

She bounced out of bed, sprinting for the window, "Valentino, oh my God, is that real?!"

I sat up, sluggishly getting out of bed, and making my way over to her, chuckling, "Yes baby, it's real."

"It's so beautiful!" She gushed over the white, snowy mountains outside the window.

THE VEIL

Our home sat on a mountain, but larger snowy mountains surrounded our property and it was a perfectly clear day. She was in awe as she took it all in. She opened the sliding glass door that led to a deck, but immediately closed it, turning around and shivering.

"Nope!" she exclaimed with chattering teeth. "It's freaking cold out there!"

I laughed loudly, "That's how snow works, bella."

She rolled her eyes, smiling, "Thanks, smarty pants."

I grabbed a blanket off the sofa, wrapping it around her, pulling her close to me as I scowled. "That's Mr. Smarty Pants to you, young lady." I gently kissed her cheek. "Come on, we have to get ready."

"Where are we going?"

"I thought I would show you around the village."

She glanced out the window then back at me, "What village?"

I chuckled, "We are on a mountain but at the bottom, there is a small village and I want to show you how beautifully it's decorated for Christmas before we meet up with the family for dinner."

She glanced at the clock on the bedside table, gasping. "Oh my God, we slept almost all day."

I nodded, "It was a tiring flight."

She happily skipped to the bathroom to get ready. I followed, getting ready as well, having to refrain from touching her for now but I was tempted. She was the definition of perfection.

When we got to the village, she and Tanya were gawking excitedly in all the shop windows. We went into a couple of them, buying small souvenirs here and there. Before we knew it, two hours had passed, and it was time to head to the restaurant my parents had closed for the night so we could enjoy a peaceful family dinner. This was a tradition of ours.

We strolled under the Christmas lights strung up, zigzagging from building to building. The girls could not stop complimenting every small thing they laid their eyes on as a light snow fell from the sky. The restaurant was located next to the Christmas Market, so we had a stunning view of all the Christmas lights and vendors that illuminated the outside square.

As we entered, we greeted my family then all took a seat around a long rectangular table. I had requested that the center of the table have two empty seats, one for Isabelle and one for me. I wanted to be able to converse with my family equally for the night.

There was a set menu, so after we got settled and beverages were passed around, the servers began to bring our first course. As we dined and chatted with my family through four courses of food, I began to get a bit nervous, which was an exceedingly rare occurrence for me.

I laid my hand on Isabelle's thigh, leaning over to her ear, whispering. "I love you so much and I'm happy you're here with me."

She smiled, her eyes tearing up, "I'm happy too and I love you the most." She leaned toward me and gave me a small kiss. "This is a perfect Christmas."

It was tradition for my father to make a toast at the end of the meal every year, so with his signal, the staff walked around the table, filling everyone's glasses with champagne and Tanya giggled. She picked up her water glass instead.

My sister, Laura, happily reached over, grabbing her champagne flute, "I'll gladly take that!"

THE VEIL

My father got ready to make a toast, but I raised my hand, interjecting, "Can I say something before you do that?"

He nodded, "Ok, my son."

I stood, taking a deep breath. "As many of you know, I hid Isabelle from you, but it wasn't because I was ashamed." I glanced at Tanya who covered her mouth to hide her smile. I turned my attention back to Isabelle, "When you love someone, you want to protect them and since the first moment I laid eyes on you, I have protected you with everything in me."

William chuckled, muttering, "And you did protect her, almost to death."

Alessandro snorted.

I shot them both a glare before resuming, focusing on Isabelle once again. "For the first time in my life, I cannot imagine myself without someone to truly love and worship."

Laura covered her mouth, gasping under her breath, "Oh my God."

Ignoring the sounds around us, I smiled, "But not just any someone, only you for the rest of our lives."

A huge smile was plastered on her face, as she was frozen in both excitement and shock.

"You showed me what love truly was," I proclaimed, "and took all my fear of commitment away, turning it into pure unconditional love. Thankfully, you now exist in my life and I no longer feel any emptiness."

She began to tear up again. She attempted to fight them back, but she failed.

I held back my emotions, murmuring, "Isabelle--."

I placed my glass on the table and reached into my jacket pocket. She covered her mouth with both hands, gasping as I pulled out a navy-blue, velvet ring box. I slid my chair back, kneeling on my left knee in front of her. Slowly, I opened the box and a bright LED light, lit up the beautiful custom designed ring. Tears were now streaming down her cheeks as she rapidly fanned her face.

I gazed up into her eyes, grinning, "Will you marry me?"

ABOUT THE AUTHOR

V.B. Emanuele is an author who began writing professionally for a visual story app, under the username VioletBlue. She quickly found herself wanting to expand her art, and wrote her first online novel, The Veil in 2019. After the rapid success of the book, she released several more online novels. Just Business was the first book to launch the Club Euphoria Novels and Violet's publishing debut.

She has lived in both Europe and the United States and obtained a fine arts degree. She is also a playwright, artist, musician, photographer, special effects makeup artist, chef, and former ice hockey player. In her spare time, she can be found doing something outdoors, spending time with her family and pets, or gaming.

Visit **vbemanuele.com** for exclusive access to special content, playlists to her writing world, videos, photos, contests, social media links, and more.